"I thoroughly enjoyed it. The end is mys. dramatically satisfying. Many powerful and beautiful scenes. The quest for what is real and human drives the narrative."

\- **Alex Austin**

"The City and the Thinker are a great change of track. I love the Thinker, wonderfully cantankerous and belligerent yet open to the relationship between his new-found recruit and himself. It's this relationship that sets the sudden revelation but also carries it on the story so well. I liked the pace, the meter of the language. It pulls you along at a good rate and that is important to the structure."

\- **Jonathan Catling**

"The story resonates on many levels, cleverly exploring the concept of entropy, our part within it, and how we try to break the cycle of order to chaos and chaos to order. There's lots of interesting imagery, much of which has stuck with me in the weeks after reading."

\- **Scott Vandervalk**

Themes: hard science fiction, AI, technology, dystopian, post-apocalyptic, dying Earth, end-of-humanity

Rating: 18+ adult concepts, mild language, mild sexual references, moderate violence and gore

About the Author

Mike was born and raised in Kalgoorlie, in the goldfields of Western Australia before moving to Perth to complete a degree in Electronic Engineering. With a good science fiction book in hand and a life-long passion for innovation, Mike has always imagined a future where technologies that are improbable today might be possible tomorrow. When not writing, Mike runs a software development company at cyinnovations.com, loves 1970's heavy rock music, and cheers on his beloved West Coast Eagles AFL team. And he often goes fishing in the Australian never-never. Together with his wife, Mike lives in an empty nest with their black Labrador, Louie.

You can connect with me on:

🌐 https://mcgintywriter.com

a https://www.amazon.com/Michael-McGinty/e/B0BBGD7WD8/

🐦 https://twitter.com/mcgintywriter

f https://www.facebook.com/mcgintywriter

Scan a QR code.

Mcgintywriter   Amazon Author   Facebook Author   Twitter

ENTROPY

A Novel by Michael McGinty

 CYI Publishing

First Edition

ISBN: 978-0-6454814-0-2 (paperback)
ISBN: 978-0-6454814-1-9 (hardcover)
ISBN: 978-0-6454814-2-6 (ePub)
ISBN: 978-0-6454814-4-0 (Kindle)
ISBN: 978-0-6454814-3-3 (audio book)

Editing by Scott Vandervalk
Cover design and image composition by G-ForceDesign.com

Excerpt from "On the Origin of Species" by Charles Darwin
(believed to be in the public domain)

Especially for Mara

Jessica & Andy, Luke & Shailey

Mum & Dad

Dedicated to those we lost during the COVID-19 pandemic, their families, and the brave ones who risked their lives to keep the rest of us safe.

Can you hear loneliness?

I ask myself that same question again. If it were loud enough, would loneliness be a roar so deafening that you couldn't hear anything else around you? Would it drown out every other sound on the Earth? Would it be so painful in your ears that you would have to clamp both hands over them to block it out? Or like a black hole does with light, would its discord fall into something from which noise can never escape?

Sometimes a scene is impossible to describe by what *is* there and can only be described by what *is no longer* there. And if I were pressed to convey the scene surrounding us now, only one word comes to mind: loneliness. The loneliness of the nothing that swallows us up with each step we take in this eternal, barren countryside.

I close my mind off completely to the unstructured inputs from the outside world and lose myself deep in my thoughts.

Extinction is inevitable. And not through some random apocalyptic event, but by the natural decline of the human swarm until its eventual demise. So says entropy in the second law of thermodynamics.

Chapter 1

I SWEAR SOMETIMES I think there are two of us inside my head—me, and someone else in here, always watching me.

Don't get me wrong. I'm not suggesting I have an identity disorder or some obscure form of neurosis. Although if I did, perhaps that's what they'd *expect* me to say. This seems somehow different. It's like walking alone down a forgotten side street in some backwater town. During the daytime you have a sense of solitude, exhibit a certain confidence that's rooted in the overt. But at night, you keep looking over your shoulder, sure that someone's hiding in the shadows just beyond the pale of the flickering streetlights.

It's only a feeling I have, after all.

Mr. Bill Bartles at your service: that's how I always announce myself to clients. I'm one of the manifold data washers from the Department of Receipt and Organization of New Content, or DRONC as we prefer to be called. Our purpose? Locate new information, clean it up, and add it to the worldwide data store. Or as I often quip: Find all the knowledge ever created by mankind, strip out the crap, and save it to a little black box, no bigger than a shoebox. That's our brief, simple and sweet.

As a frontline asset for DRONC, I've always considered myself a people-person. But at five pay scales beneath a team leader and just above a janitor, well, I'm always on the lookout for any opportunity to grab hold of the first rung on the corporate ladder. I wish I had some kind of affliction that made me more intriguing to people, some quirky trait to help me get noticed. However, the last time I looked, everything about me was normal: no obvious defects, no undiagnosed medical condition or secret superpower. Not even a limp. I'm just plain old what-you-see-is-what-you-get Bill. A "jack of all trades yet master of none" as some would say and nothing memorable to report.

I check my watch.

Damn! I'm going to be late—again. And she's going to be pissed with me—again.

Picking my way across the foyer, I push past the orderly lines of procrastinators. Those who, unlike me, never seem to be in a hurry to be anywhere else except here at work. They shuffle forward a bit, stop a moment, before shuffling forward again, their eyes fixed on the back of the head in front of them as they inch their way toward the exit. Sometimes I wonder if they ever make it home. Or are they all still queued here since yesterday or the day before that?

As a seasoned "get-homer" though, I slip around them, right under their noses, without any indignant stares or howls of protest from the catatonic queuers to the front of the line where the continuous revolving door sucks me in, processes me, and spits me onto the street. Out into the sharp chill of a clear December evening.

"Your attention, please. For the safety of all citizens, after exiting the preparation zone, everyone must go left."

That same colorless voice. The white arrows etched into the concrete at my feet, enticing me out of the prep zone and into the flow of pedestrians that never seems to cease. I'm not sure they're real though. Those monotone announcements from the ether, I mean. Not the "voices in my head" sort of unreal but digitized unreal. Because who would have the patience to sit there all day instructing and coercing every action and reaction from the millions of us out here? No amount of pay could ever make up for that kind of selfless boredom. I think, anyway.

Around me, the tall-towers ascend like colossal monoliths, their gray, faceless facades projecting forever higher until they disappear into the narrow strip of blue above. More importantly though, across the street and down a bit on my right is the restaurant where she has probably ordered her first glass of wine. Sitting opposite an empty chair. My chair.

To get to the restaurant by lawful means—by always transiting left—I will have to completely round two city blocks. Then I'll take a sort of figure-eight route to later pass this spot again on the opposite side of the street. Even though I can see the damned place from where I'm standing right now. The illogic of the situation begs me to turn right, to use my common sense, and go against the foot traffic. To take the shorter way there. But then I wonder when common sense was last used as a successful defense against the law, no matter how nonsensical the law might seem.

I push my skullcover down hard on my head.

"Please keep moving. Please depart the preparation zone without delay."

I draw my coat zipper right to my chin and lower the sun visor to cover my eyes. Then activating my LEGS, I step into the horde and go left again.

I haven't gone far before I find myself repeatedly checking the setting on my LEGS, cursing under my breath that I can't walk any faster.

These self-propelling gizmos, wrapped tight around my real legs, are great if you want to walk for miles. But with everyone's units calibrated to the same speed setting—or 7.29 feet-per-second according to the Social Protocols, irrespective of the length of one's shanks or stride—I'm hemmed in on all sides. My progress is thwarted by the perambulating swarm just as a leaf, blown into a creek, can't outrun the water as it courses its way to the sea.

Before Enlightenment though, anyone wanting to transit outside from A to B would have simply summoned a mechanically propelled vehicle from the sidewalk with a wave of their hand. Then once aboard the contraption, they only needed to voice an instruction before it would carry them off at speed to the destination they'd requested. Somewhere far away if they wished. Even to the isolated areas outside the city. To the lonely places where I'm sure nobody would want to go today.

Now the contraptions are gone. So too the chaos they caused when whole cities would grind to a halt while the drivers waited for their batteries to recharge or electrics to reboot. Now, everyone walks. Now, street-space is a premium commodity, owned and rented out by those in control. And taxes are applied to relieve congestion with every cubic allotment of footpath registered, marked up by ten percent on its carbon cost, and charged out by the millisecond to the one who occupies it at each recorded instant in time.

So now, while I'm out here, I have to keep reminding myself: on my measly wage, it's not in my financial interest to linger in any spot for too long.

Out here, everyone looks the same, as well. Section 25, Clause 243.21.4.56, Sub-clause 9 of the Social Protocols clearly states: *To eliminate the possibility of unnecessary attraction or interaction between citizens in public, there shall be no ostensible signs of gender identity displayed during outdoor excursions.*

It seems to work. Well, almost. Despite a sun visor hiding their upper facial features and clothing that conceals the obvious characteristics differentiating the male and female anatomies, given the lack of protruding thyroid cartilage on the larynx of the one walking beside me, I quickly sum up her biological variable.

I smile at her, but she doesn't respond. I might as well be invisible as she keeps her head firmly to the front. They never smile back at me out here.

Craning my neck, I try to peer over those ahead of me, but all I can see is an endless stretch of white-capped heads. All of us jouncing along like we are following the same Pied Piper … to who knows where?

When I arrive at the restaurant, I'm already fifteen minutes late. After detaching my LEGS at the door, I take a ticket from the check clerk for my coat and skullcover before a waiter escorts me to our table on the far side of the room. Low lit. Romantic. Good, exactly as I'd requested when I made the booking a few days ago. Perhaps this, plus the establishment's six-star user rating might be enough to atone for my routine tardiness. The smooth notes of a slow jazz number float somewhere in the background.

From her seat, Jennifer looks up. With a wine glass held elegantly in her left hand and her elbow resting on the table, she appears all class. I look at her coyly.

"William," she says with a certain stiffness, "I've already ordered."

Yep, she's pissed with me all right.

I snatch a napkin straight from the waiter's hands, taking him by surprise. Then I sit and spread it unconvincingly over my lap while the waiter bends to place a small candle in the center of our table and switches it on.

"I'm starving," I say. "I'll have a glass of your finest red, my good man." I open the laminated menu and run an index finger down the right side of the page. "And then I'll have the roast beef analog … with vegetables … a side of fries, and small bread." The waiter takes down my order, old-style, using a retro-looking palm-held communications device. When he leaves, I turn to Jennifer and give her a hopeless look. Lowering her glass, she smiles in return. Like: all is forgiven; this time.

"How was your day?" she asks.

How was my day? My day had been busy. And complex too. *Hello, Mr., Mrs., Ms., or Mx.*—according to the preferred pronoun on their profile look-up page—*I'm Mr. Bill Bartles from DRONC, at your service. First, I need to make you aware of your obligation under Section 6, Clause 30, Sub-article 26 of the Social Protocols, that all newly created information must be submitted to us within … blah, blah, blah.*

"Let's not spoil the evening with talk of work," I say.

I take her hand and squeeze it, gazing into her eyes like a clumsy teenager. Even in this gloom, her pale complexion overstates the cherry-colored dye on her lips, her dark hair glistening in the frugal light from the candle. Wearing that black, off-the-shoulder evening number which she knows I like, I can't help thinking how beautiful she looks right now, how perfect she is. She smiles at me again. But this time, with the kind of smile that whispers in my ear: *I see the way you look at me all the time. I know what you're thinking. I remember last night too.*

I look down at her hand in mine, at her long, slender fingers. Those same fingers with their sharp painted nails which, at some point during the small hours of last night, had dug deep into my neck. Gouging, dragging their way down past the hollow of my throat they left behind burning tracts raised and raw. Then raked across my chest they teased at my nipple as they passed. Drawn across my stomach and down toward my groin with each adventurous movement torturing the fine line between pleasure and—

Stop!

Stop everything right now. I remonstrate internally—*this is neither the time nor place for that kind of reflection*—and order myself to think about something else.

Some of my friends—well, most of them—told me that Jennifer was way out of my league when I first met her. They said I didn't stand a chance. With a doctorate in neurophysiology, she had me covered for both good looks and brains, they teased me. But I told them once I put my mind to something, I always got it done. And I'm forever happy I put my mind to her. Then they told me I just got lucky. But lucky in love is all right by me, I told them.

"Look at you over there, suddenly gone all quiet on me," she says. "A mini-wish for your thoughts."

Now she's toying with me. She always seems to know exactly

what I'm thinking. But how can a man hide his feelings? Was I so transparent that she could see right through all my thoughts so easily? I try to think of some words in my defense, but nothing springs to mind. She tilts her head slightly to the left, and I'm convinced: she knows me all too well, for sure.

A different waiter arrives this time, all arms with multiple plates attached, and looks fastidious as she places our order on the table. She appeals to me for permission to crack pepper over my meal. Nodding my approval, I glance at Jennifer's plate. "Salad?" I say. "You always have the salad. You can't survive on salad." But she just looks at me and pulls a funny face.

Ravenous, I dive in while Jennifer picks at her food, almost sampling the spectacular leafy-green arrangement on her appetizer-sized plate. I start with the fries before attacking the sim-meat with my knife and fork. I think I can taste the hint of an herb in mine. Rosemary, perhaps? I enjoy the crunching sound the bioengineered vegetables make when I bite down on them. The taste of wine on my palate as I savor the robust flavors of the full-bodied red. After mopping up the juices on my plate with the last of the small bread, I lean back in my chair. Rest both hands on my paunch.

Yes, it was rosemary, I tell myself.

The evening is going well. The food is great; more than six stars, to tell the truth. Even though this is going to cost me the best part of a day's wage. I make a joke, and Jennifer laughs. So I make another. She talks about the important things going on in her life, and I listen. A few more drinks before her foot "accidentally" rubs up against my leg under the table. She winks at me, coquettish-like.

"Let's get out of here," I say.

I pay and, a whole lot lighter in the proverbial wallet, we collect our accessories before spilling onto the street, pausing in the preparation zone first. After an enthusiastic countdown from three, we activate our LEGS and, together, head left again to be carried along by the crowd like a couple of carefree kids. The best thing about these mechanical appendages is that even though both of us are now slightly intoxicated, they will automatically hold us upright. They will keep us striding side by side at the prescribed pace and head us in the right direction home.

At every intersection we pass, a flyover allows those who are going straight ahead to cross the line of those who are traveling crossways without the likelihood of a collision. Beneath the flyover, the people who are turning left merge seamlessly with those coming in from their right with none of them having to alter their pace or disrupt their line. It's incredible to see the surge of people pouring in from one approach being inexplicably absorbed into the flow of those coming from the other, without the need for remote-controlled signaling or any unapproved contact being made. The impressive sight of the two tributaries converging on each other at speed, with absolute confidence, before joining up like one huge zipper as we knit ourselves together, one after the other, to continue on our way, unified, in a never-ending march of human cohesion.

On the opposite side of the street, as if separated by some invisible barrier, are those making their way in the other direction. All of them moving along in a perfectly mirrored migration.

A virtual illusion-board opens across the space in front of me, so close that I swear I can reach out and touch it. A textual message, written in some fancy cursive font, flickers to my attention. The message congratulates us all on thirty-thousand days without any violation of the Social Protocols. On impulse, I raise my right hand

and flatten it against my left breast. Reading the message again, I'm moved to recite the first ten key directives of the Protocols under my breath.

The Protocols themselves are comprised of over 20,000 regulations. They cover everything from the right to and protection of one's property; the etiquette of carrying umbrellas (for obvious reasons); and to guarantee everybody's lawful right to a comfortable experience during outdoor excursions, no one may come within an average arm's-length or make physical contact with another.

The Protocols also require all outdoor travel to be in the counter-clockwise direction. Any violation of this rule would, by necessity, result in someone cutting across the path of another who is approaching them head-on, thereby interrupting their progress. This might lead to a disagreement between the two, which could easily turn into an argument between three or four, followed by uncontrolled rage involving several others before escalating way beyond the point of compromise or reconciliation between a dozen more.

Standing a little straighter in my LEGS, I nod proudly to those around me. But no one reciprocates. They continue on their way like captives of the uncanny quiet of a million pedestrians marching. Then as quickly as it had opened, the illusion-board is gone.

Rounding the next corner, we enter the street where our tall-tower is located—on the left, halfway down the block—when something catches my eye. A small object appears through the blur of LEGS, something down low where the base of the building meets the side-walk. Someone squatted down with two sharp eyes following me from behind a knot of strangled hair and tattered rags. I lean back in my LEGS and try to take a closer look as I pass.

ENTROPY

Someone stationary? Out here? That must be costing them a fortune, I decide, before quickly losing sight of that incongruous curiosity as the momentum of the crowd carries me along.

"Now I'm starting to imagine things," I mumble to myself. And then I think nothing more of it.

"When arriving at your place of residence, please move off the street without delay. Please be considerate to others."

The sight of bodies leaping from the sidewalk onto the continuously rotating platforms that run silently up the outside of the residential towers never ceases to amaze me. The people launch themselves at the elevators with precision timing like a raft of pre-existent penguins popping out of the ocean to land upright on the flat ice in their clusters of hundreds, and thousands, then millions. The elevator mechanisms, like agitated automatons, grab around each one's waist to lock in their LEGS before being dispatched skyward with their precious payloads, disappearing into the beyond within the blink of an eye.

I'd once heard the city's tallest tower was more than 2,000 levels high and wonder how long it would take someone to arrive home if they lived on the topmost floor. *Maybe long enough to always make them late for dinner,* I decide. Still feeling a little light-headed from the wine, I let out a short chuckle. Sometimes I can even make myself laugh.

Another illusion-board opens above us, its *IMPORTANT MESSAGE* banner blinking twice before a new message flows.

ARRIVAL, it reads. *PLEASE MIND THE GAP.*

We set ourselves. Then without breaking stride, we take the same seamless leap as everyone else to make a perfect landing on the next rotating elevator, which hugs our waists, locks onto our LEGS, and launches us skyward.

11

Standing on the cusp with the crisp night air whistling down across my visor, I count the seconds under my breath. One minute and thirty-five. It's always the same; the time taken for the elevator to take us up the four hundred and fifty-one levels to our apartment. Long enough for me to gaze upon the city. To consider its countless parts sprawling beneath us. With each bit seeming to move in perpetual motion. Like cogs in a well-oiled machine. A picture of perfection when each cog functions exactly as intended.

Then, at precisely one minute and five seconds into the climb, that same strange question comes at me. Just as it does every time I take this ride.

Do you honestly think this perfect world of ours can last forever?

Chapter 2

IN THE BEGINNING, the data was pure.

Like flecks of gold wrapped within the formalities of TCP/IP, the data was clean. And it made sense. At first, data was free, shared willingly between the technocrats, engineers, and boffins through the unreliable routers and twists of copper. With each packet sent out in hope, received as a thing of virtual beauty.

Within a few short years, the copper became a highway, became fiber, became G, to deliver that beauty to the masses, and within a few years more, the entire world succumbed to its reach and its *I-must-be-connected* excitement. Captivated by its *I-must-have-it-now* technologies and mesmerized by its *I-must-not-miss-out* attraction, the highway soon became a way of life. Then it was the *only* way to live, and the appetite of the masses for new data grew insatiable. Overnight, they had access to more knowledge within the bat of an eye than all of those before them had known in their lifetimes. Even the

Luddites and seniors turned tech-savvy as they searched and surfed, chatted and posted, and navigated their way around the web.

Until the data became dirty.

After a promiscuous age of information excess, the highway fell into disrepair. Left broken by a lack of governance and crushed under the weight of ambiguity.

In the few short decades before, the online community had crammed the mass storage devices and network pipes full of their thoughts and lives. They choked the highway with their blogs of tripe and trivia, jammed it with their tweets of truths, half-truths, and out-right lies. They copied data from this node to that node, then on to another node from where the bot crawlers took it and copied it to a million more nodes waiting. They followed the breadcrumbs and clicked the back-links that bounced them from one URL to the next, leaving them lost and confused, wandering through the cyber-sphere alone.

They sent threads of mail *To:* him *Cc:* her *Bcc:* another, who all *Fwd:* to every other contact in their self-populating address books. Millions upon millions of mailbombs, repeating in bursts, erupting in an explosion of POP3 messages, with each pointless message spammed to a cosmos of sympathetic Inboxes.

They kept the world updated on their current social status. Who they were seeing, who they weren't seeing. What they were doing, what they weren't doing. What they were thinking, what they weren't thinking. Even, what they didn't know they were thinking. Minute by minute, second by second.

They uploaded selfies, shared images of him taking pictures of her taking pictures of him with his plate of food. They created books for the .gifs of their faces, places, and poses. They uploaded videos to the tube. Toked themselves as the silliest people excelling at the stupidest of stunts, but executed with exceptional technique, that went viral with a million-million views per minute for the first five minutes until the next silly stunt caught everyone's attention.

They logged on to their own spaces to share their tunes, file upon file upon file upon file. Everything ever written, everything ever said, everything ever seen, they published, file upon file.

They uploaded, downloaded, circulated, and re-circulated torrents of data. They copied it, saved it, shared it, streamed it, burned it, and backed it up. Information, forever preserved in every uncensored detail, leaving behind a trail of digital footprints that can never be erased. Data, on file for the generations to come, with every packet bundled and switched, fighting for an acknowledgment as *"ok to transmit,"* and *"ok received."* Hungry for enough disk space to save the hellabytes and geopbytes of *ones* and *zeros* they'd caused.

Then the big companies arrived to tap into the highway's promise of riches and sucked out all the e-commerce opportunities for themselves. Start-ups, founded by two wiry geeks in a garage with a computer and a connection to the highway, could forecast unthinkable profits by counting the number of hits on a homepage multiplied by the first large number that came to mind. Every device connected to the highway became a revenue stream, and every online user, a punter. The start-ups even became so brazen as to poke and prod the tired old software behemoths. And so started the browser wars. The battle over who had the best of the rudimentary search algorithms, and skirmishes over who got paid what for the advertising clicks. All pitting one corporate colossus against the other.

Not satisfied with their already impressive slices of network traffic, the big companies began constructing leviathan-like server farms, which they packed onto giant river barges and moored along the waterways to feed the cooling towers of the massive storage arrays. Centralized data centers, built to cache away the bits and bytes of intel the big companies had harvested from every punter known. Black, windowless monoliths that hugged the riverbanks, jutted skyward and sprawled onto the land like digital mini-cities, each one filled with wafers of non-volatile semiconductor memory. Silicon dioxide, measured in nanometers, etched and baked onto substrates, layer upon layer. Transistors, replicated by the trillions and placed in grids, millimeter upon millimeter. Assembled in sheets, meter upon meter. And then stacked in holding frames, kilometer upon kilometer.

But no matter how many data centers they built or how high they built them, there was never going to be enough storage space as the highway expanded and the disk arrays filled at an astronomical rate.

Until one damp, autumn day—

DATA STORAGE LIMIT EXCEEDED …

They had reached the physical limits of the storage, the end of the first infinity. The point of Aleph-null.

Start counting—*zero, one, two, three, four*—and keep on counting to infinity. Like children trying to outdo each other, infinity plus one equals infinity. Double infinity equals infinity too. And infinity plus one more than the last number you thought of still equals infinity. All are limited to the infinity of the counting numbers, or the first infinity of Aleph-null.

Take a full step forward from where you're standing right now, followed by an exact half-step. Now half-step that again. Repeat ad infinitum and you'll be confined to travel through the infinity that exists within two steps of where you started. Launch yourself from the Earth, depart the solar system and exit the galaxy. Keep on traveling into the expanse until you are stopped in your tracks at the edge of the universe, the boundary between our infinite universe and the next.

Aleph-null imposed an emphatic limit on how much big-data could be stored on the highway, constrained by the exact memory location where its infinity ends. The index counters needed to point to a scrap of data were frustrated by the integer numbers of Aleph-null. Where *long integers* began at 0 and ended at 18,446,744,073,709,551,615, *floats* started at 1.5×10^{-45} and finished at 3.4×10^{38}, and *double precisions* commenced at 5.0×10^{-324} and went all the way to 1.7×10^{308}, the data pointers of Aleph-null each had a beginning, and all had an end.

With its data storage weighed down by this mathematical con-undrum and its bandwidth burdened by nonsense, the highway ground to a halt. Data transfers slowed to just a few bits-per-second and finding somewhere safe to cache away even a kilobyte of new content became mechanically impossible. For a long time, the high-way fell idle. Many of the massive cloud-storage arrays and backup drives either failed or were switched off. The big companies vanished overnight, leaving nothing behind, not even a digital trace to prove they were ever here. And without access to their data, the online users lost interest and the age of social indulgence, that gluttonous era of data excess, was over.

And so, it was, the highway became a thing of irrelevance. Information sharing was frowned upon, and learning stopped. Progress stalled while innovation all but ceased. And the pursuit of new knowledge, that imperative entrusted to the institutes of wisdom and research, was largely abandoned. For three full lifetimes, there was no new content, and opportunity was wasted as the apathetic masses went about their mundane affairs. And each day, they were no wiser or better informed than the day before.

And for a long time, stunted by ignorance, we stopped evolving.

Then one day, a surprising stroke of luck. An announcement from out of the blue: the arrival of the *Cantor Infinity Drive*. A discovery only made possible thanks to the ardent few who, in their garages, back rooms, and clandestine workshops, had persisted in secret long after the rest of us gave up.

Avant-garde, the Infinity Drive was the most astounding machine ever devised and built by ambitious minds. It held information in unimaginably thin sheets of light; photons held suspended in time. Where the visible spectrum of a sheet was encoded and cataloged in perfect sequence, and each sheet had enough capacity to store the equivalent data from a million-million-million mainframe computers.

Then using the fractional numbers—the irrationals and transcendentals of the reals—we were able to calculate the memory pointers required to push and poke the bits and bytes of data into the infinitesimally small spaces that existed between the counting numbers of Aleph-null. With indexes uncountable, inconceivable, and unrepeatable, we could decode a pointer down to almost nothing and still retrieve a speck of file. We built a world in which the square root of three realized a quantitative position between the counts of one and two. Where *pi* was finally resolved to its exact spatial location between the points of three and four.

And when the infinity between zero and one was full, the next infinity between one and two was activated. Then two to three, and so on it went. The Infinity Drive gave us storage that is infinity-to-the-power-of-eternity, with no restrictions, no beginning, and no end. These were the endless storage vaults of Aleph-1.

Equipped with this new technology, we now had enough memory space to surround the raw data with its tacit knowledge, the intangibles about why the data existed, and how it was all interrelated. Then, by appending imaginary parts to the reals, we created complex pointers that added depth and dimension to each speck of data. And unlike the primitive search engines of the old highway, which relied on childish inquiries of "what," "when," and "where," the implicit knowledge engines of Aleph-1 were built around a meaning inferred, a word understood, or thought expressed. All of which allowed us, through our abstract reasoning, to locate the exact piece of data we were after and retrieve it within the same instant we'd requested it.

This was information exchanged at the speed of thought.

The Infinity Drive gave us the means of gathering all the intelligence known to mankind, compressing it, and saving it to a little black box, no bigger than a shoebox. And just like the biological matter in our heads, the more data the Infinity Drive accumulated, it didn't grow any larger, nor did it require any more energy to sustain it.

Once the Infinity Drive was ready, newly formatted and partitioned, we turned our attention to the dirty data already saved on file. Following more wasted years of red-tape wrangling, of arguments about privacy provisions and who paid whom for what, a coalition of like-minded benefactors agreed to fund the transfer of the existing data onto the Infinity Drive. A dime per petabyte in the old currency, paid to each contributor.

Like people possessed, we ransacked our homes and attics, and backyard sheds in search of any device that might still hold data: broken cell phones; abandoned laptops; inoperative aerial drones. We foraged for our forgotten ePhoto frames, discarded cameras, smart watches, GPS activity trackers, superseded pods and pads, and the like. We rifled through our archive boxes and storage lockups where we found untold USB keys, personal organizers, SIM cards, networked RAID canisters, CCTV storage devices, electro-mechanical hard drives, SD cards, and optical drives. We forced our way into the defunct libraries where we removed volume upon volume of hardbacks and soft-covers, CDs and DVDs, e-books, audiobooks, microfilm and microfiche, manuscripts, newspapers, and magazines. Several worthless NFTs were relinquished. We looted the derelict museums of the last remaining magnetic tape reels, VHS and Beta tapes, 3.5", 6.25" and 8" floppy disks, handy camcorder cassettes, and more. There was even a rumor that someone, somewhere had found some important crypto bytes in an ancient $2K \times 8$ EEPROM.

We digitized it all. The entire knowledge of an intelligent species saved onto the Infinity Drive.

At first, we tried to make the old data clean, to strip out the inaccuracies and duplication before it could be uploaded to the Infinity Drive. But the task was monumental. There wasn't enough time. There weren't enough data washers, even if we all worked 24/7/365. So, the unreliable data of the past was ciphered using an encryption key that no one remembers and locked away in the restricted archives of the Infinity Drive.

Meanwhile, the ardent few remained diligent.

After putting their heads together, they conceived something never before imagined. Not constrained by the laws of quantum mechanics or semiconductors and wires. Not hindered by the flow of free electrons or constrained by clocking rates. But instead, a single processor grown from organic matter, designed to manage the Infinity Drive. A CPU, cultivated in a petri dish, energized by living cells and controlled by a myriad of synapses all interlinked within a sophisticated and complex man-made neural network. And using our personal interfaces, we seamlessly integrated ourselves with all the knowledge of mankind.

Now we were at one with the data, and our reawakening was complete. The era of data affinity, the age of our enlightenment, was upon us, and our destiny written between the lines of source code of Aleph-1.

Chapter 3

PNEUMATICS HISS as the front door opens.

With our skullcovers discarded at the doorway, we stumble entwined into the apartment, our lips fully locked, hands grappling at anything on the other that would take us to the first feel of velvety flesh. The smell of sauvignon blanc on her breath washes over me like a wave of cheap perfume.

"Welcome home, sir. You *do* look well this evening. You must have had a *very* productive day at the office today. May I take your coat?"

My coat? Where's my coat? Then I recall Jennifer running it off my shoulders soon after I took hold of her at the elevator landing.

"May I help remove your LEGS?" the door minder insists.

Not now, dammit. Can't you see I'm busy?

We fumble at the unlocking mechanisms of each other's LEGS before I run a hand up the back of her dress in search of the zipper.

"Yes," she says.

"Yes?"

"Yes," she says again and throws me up against the entry wall. From there, we blunder our way into the living room. Then somehow, I have her pressed up against the main feature wall where an animated mural of a pod of erstwhile whales acts out behind her. We're kissing again when suddenly, with both her arms extended, Jennifer pushes me away.

"No."

"No?"

"No," she says emphatically.

"Why?" I ask.

"Because I've already told you. Mr. Symons will be here at nine o'clock."

"My supervisor? Here? At …" I look to the adjacent wall where the rightmost segments of my antique digital LCD timepiece tick over to the next minute. I love that clock. When I found it in someone's throw-away rubbish, it was broken and wouldn't power up. But after two years of painstaking work, I was able to restore it to full operation. Now, it's one of my most prized possessions. And it always keeps perfect time—08:16 PM to be precise. "… at nine? You didn't mention anything about visitors."

"Over dinner. I informed you that he would be stopping by."

"I don't remember that," I say, with the upward inflection in my voice confirming my suspicion that maybe, just maybe, she hadn't told me anything of the sort during dinner. Because I would have remembered. "Did he give a reason why?"

"No. I have no details," she replies.

This surprises me because Mr. Symons has never been to my

apartment before, and as a rule, supervisors don't normally associate with their subordinates. Especially outside of the strict confines of the office. In fact, in all my years at DRONC, I've never once heard of anyone's supervisor being the least bit interested or even entertaining the thought of working after-hours. Let alone wanting to visit a worker in the privacy of their home.

"Maybe he wants to talk to you about that promotion you've been hoping for," she says. Then she mumbles something else before being drawn into a self-absorbed conversation with herself in which she theorizes at least half a dozen reasons why I should *definitely* receive a promotion. "You've been working so hard for a long time now." She grabs my collar, pulls me toward her, and strokes the ruffled hair from my face. "You're the smartest guy in the office, the most talented one of them all. I think you deserve a promotion. I'm sure that's what this is about." With a confident nod, she pecks my cheek and pushes me away again.

Now I'm left on my own to assume my promotion is a fait accompli since she thinks *she* is the only one who needs to be convinced. And that's always the end of the matter as far as Jennifer is concerned. Somehow, I feel deflated, standing here with my pants around my ankles, watching on glumly as she retrieves her underwear from the floor. While on the wall behind her, an erstwhile whale breaches.

After changing into her loungewear, Jennifer settles on the sofa in front of the feature wall. I look at her longingly as she spreads a throw-blanket across her legs, any chance I had of romance gone.

When I was young and still naive, I thought true love meant the two of us would be connected as if we were the same person. That, by telepathy, I could transmit my innermost thoughts to her and, in return, receive her thoughts sent to me. Back then, I'd often stare at her from across a crowded room, willing her to look my way and acknowledge my subliminal requests. But now I'm older and a whole lot wiser, I figure true love is not something that needs to be tested. You just accept it for what it is and be happy with that.

Feeling sorry for myself, I take a platter of mixed cheeses from the refrigerator and head for the relaxation area where four comfort sitters surround a squat convenience table. As I approach them, the sitters skim through their exclusive catalog of skin designs, searching for the right colors and patterns to match my mood, each one eager to catch my attention. To cheer myself up, I feign sitting on them in turn, cackling to myself when the others go into meltdown as they try to reorganize their presentations in the hope that I'll change my mind.

In the end, I choose the one with the swirling turquoise clouds. For no particular reason.

The convenience table slides over to me; a wafer-thin feed-sheet placed squarely on its see-through top. After setting the cheese platter down on the table, I pick up the feed-sheet and unfurl it, sparking it to life.

BREAKING NEWS! EXECUTIVE MANAGEMENT GETS FIVE MORE YEARS.

With the headline scrolling across the top of the page, I wait expectantly for the accompanying *audio-visual* datafile to activate. When it does, the feed-sheet shows the Principal Leader with both arms raised being mobbed by a crowd of cheering supporters. Following another hard-fought contest, the incumbent Executive prevailed once again. A record twenty-five consecutive victories, so the feed-sheet informs me.

Watching the replay, I imagine myself at the victory party, as part of the crowd, where I can sense the excitement and almost feel the pseudo-press of other bodies against mine. The noise around me is deafening, the excitement palpable. "More beer!" I shout as I clap and cheer until the crush of the crowd becomes intolerable, and struggling for breath, I have to withdraw.

Huh, no matter who you vote for, the Executive Management always wins.

"I am sorry, but I do not understand that observation."

"Oh, I was just suggesting the Executive will always win," I say to the feed-sheet, "regardless of which side they represent." I take the knife from the platter and carve off a thin slice of holey cheese. "Because once a side wins, they become the Executive. Therefore, the Executive, as a franchise, will always prevail." It all seems logical to me, even after a few drinks.

"But you have already been informed the Executive *did* win," the feed-sheet replies.

"I was making a joke," I say, exasperated by the feed-sheet's dullness. "It's a play on words, you ... I wasn't trying to ... never mind."

At this moment, I'm not in the right headspace for an in-depth discussion about the subtle nuances of humor with an interactive accessory.

I do like my feed-sheet though. The simple act of holding the feed-sheet, of running my fingers across its smooth surface while digesting its pure analog somehow normalizes the information being presented. A feed-sheet offers a personal connection to whatever message is being conveyed, giving it the highest level of trustworthiness. Unlike a random burst of chatter being streamed in from somewhere obscure, passed through some unverified truth-test algorithm, then flashed to everyone's attention before being erased a microsecond later without leaving behind any evidence that something important had actually happened. And news isn't newsworthy unless I can be convinced that it's based on fact and not just #fake-whatever.

"There is a customary contribution toward the cost of the re-election campaign," the feed-sheet says. "In this case, thirty D-Class tokens. However, the live survey indicates the average gifting is trending somewhat higher."

While I consider the feed-sheets revised offer of fifty D-Class tokens, a pop-up panel displays a financial statement of my current (modest) savings.

I glance at the total in the first column. Es. Heaps. As plentiful as pebbles on the sidewalk, E-Class tokens are free-issued to everyone so we can all afford at least a subsistent lifestyle: prepackaged food for dinner each night; drinks (excluding alcohol); a modest wardrobe; and shared accommodation on the lower levels of a residential tower, including central heating and cooling.

The figure at the bottom of the next column confirms my tidy sum of D-Class tokens. These are earned by just turning up for work each day. With my pile of Ds, I can afford a little extravagance. I can take Jennifer out to dinner; have a few wines; wear the latest fashion; or match the feed-sheet's revised offer—if I want to.

One C-Class token is awarded to an employee whenever they're cited for meritorious performance at work. Cs come in four different colors, with each color enticing yet hardly remarkable. With the modest amount of Cs I've already saved, we can afford the rent on this upmarket apartment at mid-tower level. Right now, though, I'm trying to earn as many Cs as I can so we can move to another apartment two levels higher.

B-Class tokens, or phony-baloneys as we call them, are borrowed from those in control and can be on-traded. However, the last person left holding a B is at risk if the original borrower defaults on its repayment conditions. Once in default, the token immediately dissolves, and like the age-old game of pass-the-parcel, the last one left holding it ends up with the prize—nothing. I don't like phony-baloneys at all, although they are shiny.

I look longingly at the end column. Total, zero. This is what I'm after: an A. An A-Class token can only be earned by someone who holds the rank of Supervisor Level-Two or above. They come in many shapes and sizes, and all the colors of the rainbow. Some even glow in the dark. As are indivisible: to fragment an A would destroy its beauty and hence its value. I could move to the top quartile of our tower with just a dozen As. Except, I don't have any, yet. *Although, once I have a promotion …*

I slice off another piece of holey cheese, nod my approval, and the datafile expires.

"Thank you. Fifty tokens have been deducted from your account," the feed-sheet says flatly. "This article was prepared for you by the Principal Leader and the Executive."

CLIMATE EMERGENCY OVER. PLANET EARTH SAVED

I sit upright. Examine the feed-sheet through one woozy eye. Move it away from my face marginally to bring the text back into focus.

Yep, that's what it says all right.

Where extinction protests, punitive taxes, trading schemes, renewable energy initiatives, and prohibitions had all failed in the past to reduce man-made emissions, the brainiacs appear to have developed a new carbon-absorbing reagent. Once released into the atmosphere, the reagent will restore the polluted airways and waterways around the world back to their original, unspoiled condition. The over-cultivated lands outside the city, which have been used as a dumping ground for far too long, will soon be clean and fertile again. The last carbon footprints left behind by previous generations, gone forever.

I let out a rounding cheer as a new *sensory* datafile transports me into a world alive with true-color, true-depth scenes of blue skies and pristine shorelines. There are animations of birds in flight and large fish leaping up boiling rapids. After sucking in a lungful of crisp virtual air, my head seems remarkably clear, my thoughts suddenly lucid as though the effects of the cabernet, still washing through my vascular system, have been temporarily suspended.

"Would you like to see a model simulation of the new reagent, including the structure of its active ingredient?"

With a rush of excitement, I nod keenly while a *conceptual* data-file executes.

The feed-sheet runs the simulation in which the reagent is shown growing in a special purpose laboratory. Attached to a carrier, the reagent is then released into the atmosphere to react with the targeted CO_2 molecules. Once it has "attracted" sufficient carbon atoms, the resulting by-product—a red rust-colored residue—becomes heavier than the air molecules and descends under gravity before the prevailing winds carry the carbon-loaded waste out to sea, where it will fall with the rain to be safely locked away at the bottom of the ocean, for evermore.

"Although, a critical problem remains to be solved," the feed-sheet says. "The amount of energy required to get the reagent airborne currently outweighs its carbon cost by a factor of three.

What would you suggest?" The feed-sheet enters a wait-loop; a quaint, fat, block cursor left blinking on the screen, inviting my input.

I request an excerpt from the simulation, one showing only the reagent aboard its carrier being propelled skyward.

What if we invent a gigantic anti-gravity mat … and completely cover it with reagent? What about rigging up a skyhook? What if we— No, that won't work.

I study the reagent's propulsion design and analyze the shape of the carrier. Before long, a solution takes form in my head. "What … if … we … change the shape of the carrier to allow the reagent to become airborne without consuming any energy at all. Similar to how the …"—I flap my arms wildly—"monarch butterfly has a large wingspan compared to the overall size of its body. It relies on the up-drafts and wind shears to lift itself into the sky. High enough to be carried along by the upper atmospheric winds."

After updating the datafile, the feed-sheet runs the simulation again. This time I take note of the ingenious made-for-flight design of the carrier with the reagent aboard, plus the result of the elaborate formula which verifies the amount of energy now required to get the thing airborne, is zero.

"Yes," I yell, punching the air.

"There is a customary gifting of ten C-Class tokens toward the continued development of the reagent. But the live survey indicates a sudden increase to seventeen."

What time is it? 8:44? Yep, 8:44. I cut through a thick slice of the blue-veined cheese. "Why not make it an even twenty," I say.

WE'RE ALL LIVING TWENTY YEARS LONGER

Whoa. But the feed-sheet doesn't specify the life expectancy of a person today. I'd stopped counting my birthdays a long time ago. In fact, I can't ever remember waking up on my special morning with

Jennifer shouting "Happy birthday" at me. Like my caregivers had surprised me all those years ago. I wonder how long a person could continue to function correctly before their structure grew too tired. Or they couldn't be repaired or restarted and finally gave up.

"A good question," the feed-sheet says. "But perhaps someday, the human form will not be hampered by the fragile nature of its biological components. You might like to consider the possibility of a future shaped by advances in modern cybernetics. Where all the vital organs of the subject are replaced by mechanized devices to prolong their lives. A future where the aging process becomes irrelevant. You might like to think how the embodiment of the human creature can be reengineered to remain viable for centuries. Just as a towering oak tree can thrive well beyond the age of five hundred years.

"There have also been some encouraging developments in the field of molecular therapy. For example, credible methods to extend human longevity by inhibiting *insulin-to-IGF-1 signaling* are now main-stream."

On the feed-sheet, a group of researchers at a ceremony are congratulating each other. They've just announced the results of a successful trial for a new bionic anterior pituitary gland that can regulate the production of the human growth hormone. This, in turn, reduced IGF-1 signaling, which led to the arrest of cell re-arrangements and gene mutations enough to extend the average lifespans of the human volunteers by as much as *twenty* years.

"But the group appears to have hit an impasse," the feed-sheet says with a tinge of disappointment. "The finite prolongation of the bionic gland means any extension beyond the additional twenty years now seems problematic, if not impossible. Do you have any suggestions?"

I request the schematic for the bionic gland, including details of how they've *plumbed* it into the human anatomy. *The damned thing's working too hard. No wonder it eventually fails.*

"Interface mismatch," I say.

"Please elucidate."

"The anterior pituitary gland secretes the growth hormone for the liver to regulate the biosynthesis of IGF-1. There's an interface mismatch between the bionic gland and the liver. The gland is continually working, even in its quiescent state. Expending even a few picojoules unnecessarily will have an adverse impact on its function over time. You need to maximize the energy exchange by redesigning the growth hormone receptor ligands. To better match the IGF-1 receptors. To eliminate signal reflection. Similar to impedance matching and power factor correction in electrical power systems."

Would that allow a person to live for a thousand years?

On the feed-sheet, the researchers regard each other with surprise. They all nod in agreement while I lean forward to reward myself with a nice piece of cheddar.

"There is a customary contribution of one A-Class token to support this important ongoing research," the feed-sheet says.

I hesitate. Shocked. Like I already said, I don't have any As. And when I see the live survey figure, my jaw drops at the conversion charge for Cs. At this rate, I'll go broke before I get to the funnies.

"I am sorry, but I do not understand your observation."

"Oh, I was thinking about my finances. It was another joke," I say, conceding an awkward laugh. "I was saying ... um ... never mind." I toss the feed-sheet onto the convenience table and check the clock again. *Eight minutes to burn before Mr. Symons arrives.*

On the far wall, a sheer fabric drape covers the full drop of an expansive window. To the right of the window, a sliding-glass door—closed—leads onto the balcony. I get up and amble to the meals area where I take a bottle of extra-old cognac from a bottom cupboard. After removing the cap, I half-fill a large balloon-shaped glass. *"Don't you think you've already had enough to drink?"* I think I hear Jennifer say. But I tilt the bottle a little more until the glass is over three-quarters full. Then, holding my chalice up to the side like I'm a toff, I stroll across the room to the window.

Alongside the clock, a 2D-photograph of me and Jennifer on vacation at the snowfields hangs slightly off-center on the wall. In the picture, I'm standing, dressed warmly and smiling, with one arm wrapped around her waist and holding a pair of skis and poles in the other. In the background, swing chairs, like colluding mercenaries, haul a line of smiling skiers up the steep white incline, heading them off to their imminent fates two at a time.

We look so young in the picture, almost like a newly-paired couple. I try to recall if it snowed that day or if I'd successfully tackled any of the diamond-grade pistes that ran down the mountainside.

"Hey, babe. Can you remember which year we went skiing?"

But Jennifer doesn't reply. She's now curled up on the sofa, looking at ... I crane my neck to see the erstwhile whales replaced with ... bygone railway tracks? I never did understand the attraction of slowTV.

Maybe we should change that picture for something more recent, I finally decide while opening the drapes.

Through the window, I have a sweeping view of the cityscape, all lit up in endless sheets of white neon light. So bright that I have to momentarily shield my eyes. Standing here, I consider the glass in my hand, rotating it slowly with just enough vigor to make the cognac swirl to the top of the cambered side. Then lifting the glass to my nose, I take in the sharp woody aroma of the cognac before drinking generously.

Perhaps a bit of fresh air out on the balcony. A minute or two to clear my head.

But as I poke repeatedly at the sliding-door override button with my forefinger, the button wavers about far too much in my field of view.

Chapter 4

THE DOOR CHIMES its silly tune.

"I am sorry to disturb you sir, but we have visitors," the door minder says. "Shall I let them in?"

Still standing clueless in front of the sliding door with my pointer hunting for the override button as though trapped in some unresolvable loop, I concede and lower my hand. "Leave it to me," I say absently, and the door minder falls silent.

I can't stop my hands from shaking. Maybe Jennifer hasn't set the climate-change thermostat high enough. Or was it the anticipation that I'll soon learn the purpose of Mr. Symons' visit? I'm halfway across the living room when I stop to deposit the cognac glass on the convenience table and collect my thoughts. Why does he want to see me so urgently? And what was so important that he couldn't discuss it with me at the office this afternoon, or wait until first thing tomorrow morning? I wonder whether Jennifer might be right about my promotion.

But promotions are always announced and celebrated in front of all coworkers. That was standard protocol.

Now my feet won't move. I don't want to appear disrespectful and keep Mr. Symons waiting at the door, but they just won't move. It's like they've somehow been fixed to the floor without my approval. Things still don't add up. Although, if I am being promoted, this will be the start of my rise into corporate management. And a significant pay increase as well. Once this door opens, my whole life will change forever.

The door chimes again.

"Shall I let them in?" the door minder insists.

"No. I said I'll get it." Now my feet move, albeit reluctantly.

At the door, I straighten my collar and try to compose myself as best I can before ordering it open.

Outside in the hallway, two tall, wiry men stand pencil straight, both with their backs to me, appearing opaque in the unlit passage.

"Can … can I help you?" I say.

As though synchronized, they turn to face me, our eyes all meeting at once. These are stern looking men, dressed in matching gunmetal-gray suits complete with squared-off shoulders that hold up their unnaturally long arms, both wearing charcoal fedoras to complete their attire. The one on my right carries a black leather briefcase, its handle clasped in his left hand, while the other, who I immediately recognize as Mr. Symons, stands to perfect attention with what looks like a small red note taker wedged up under his armpit. The two men appear identical, although when I look closer, Mr. Symons is taller, but not by much. The blank expressions embedded on their gaunt faces seem to hint at a humorless purpose in life.

"Bartles," says Mr. Symons, doffing his hat. "This is my assistant, Jerry." He signals to the man standing beside him.

With the full effects of the cognac now setting in, I proffer a limp hand to Jerry, give him the smile of a simpleton. But Jerry just stands there. He doesn't even blink. After an uncomfortably long pause, I concede and lower my hand. What else could I do? So I turn to Mr. Symons. "Oh! Please, please come in, sir. What can I do for you? Here, take a seat," I say, waving my arms around in pointless gestures while ushering them over to the relaxation area. "I … I was only expecting one of you. Can I get you something to drink? A couple of quasi-coffees, perhaps?"

But neither man responds as they seize possession of the two— now graphite-gray—comfort sitters that face the window while I sit opposite them. Without removing their hats, they proceed to take up identical positions on the sitters, with each propped uncomfortably on the edge of the seat. After producing the note taker from under his arm, Mr. Symons opens it and sets it on his lap. A knowing nod to Jerry, then to the sharp *tack-tack-tack* of Mr. Symons' right index finger on the note taker, they begin to inventory the room.

First, they evaluate Jennifer, who is still on the couch, but now with her eyes closed and body contorted into some impossible mindfulness pose. The tapping continues. Next, they direct their attention to the main feature wall, both becoming engrossed in the rugged scenery as animated wilderness continues to slide past the bygone railway tracks. More tapping. They exchange unkind looks when they spot the mess of the feed-sheet, which has somehow fallen to the floor. *Tack-tack-tack-tack.* They scowl at the sight of leftover cheese on the convenience table, the knife, the empty cognac glass. The tapping intensifies, it seems louder, more certain. And just when I think it might not end, the tapping abruptly ceases as they shift their gazes out the window to stare across the city's brightly-lit skyline for what seems like an eternity. Then, after four unnerving minutes of complete and utter quiet, in concert, they train their sunken eyes on me.

"Shall I come to the point?"

Startled by Mr. Symons' abrupt announcement, I jump while Jerry, like a preprogrammed accessory, nods in the affirmative. And straight away I realize, this isn't intended to be a social visit.

Reaching across the convenience table, Mr. Symons pushes the cheese platter aside to clear a space in front of him. He closes the note taker and sets it down on the table, gentle-like. "Bartles," he says, "of late, we've become increasingly concerned about your work." He glances down at his crooked tie and straightens it. Then he brushes some fluff off his sleeve, repositions the note taker on the convenience table, the drawn-out pause holding me in suspense. Until finally, he says, "We are not so much concerned about your productivity; we have no issues with that. However, we do have a few questions relating to the nature of your ... shall we say ... *investigations.*"

Leaning further forward in his seat, Mr. Symons angles his head sideways to look at me from beneath the brim of his fedora. And in that look, I'm sure I catch a twitch in his left eye. *Was that involuntary? Was it my imagination?* Or did he just send me a covert signal that he already has all the answers he needs? Small beads of sweat build above my brow. With my fingers kneading into the side of my neck, I rack my muddled mind for an acceptable response. Something harmless. Something ... noncommittal.

"Oh. You mean— When I was— My research?" I finally blurt out.

"Research! Why, yes, your research," Mr. Symons says, followed by a short chuckle. "Let's discuss *research*, shall we? A means of confirming a problem existed at some point in the past. A problem that was resolved a long time ago until *research* digs it up again, analyzes it, hypothesizes a solution, and places it on a pedestal for all to see. And to verify the *said* solution works as theorized, what do we do? We recreate the problem in order to apply the solution, just to prove it works in practice. Yes! Splendid!"

With his brows arching higher, Mr. Symons draws his hands together on his lap, the digits entangled as though he were strangling the essence out of some small, imaginary animal he might be holding.

"You see, Bartles, we are most troubled by your *research*. Which, I might add, appears to be outside the scope of work I gave you."

As if on cue, Jerry produces an official-looking document from the briefcase. With a condemning forefinger tapping at the cover as he passes it to Mr. Symons, Jerry sends me a smug look.

So I send him one back, like: *As if I didn't already know that it's a copy of my original commission.*

A little over a month ago, I'd been entrusted with the most important task of my career along with explicit instructions, specific time frames set, resources allotted, and a list of results required. At first, I'd taken to the work with enthusiasm, attacking it with vigor, with skill, and resolve, and I'd been making substantial progress. However, lately, I've become sidetracked, preoccupied, my interest straying from the guidelines Mr. Symons, himself, had approved. In fact, the threads of my investigations now bear hardly any resemblance to the original brief.

What could I say? They already seemed to know something about what I was doing. But how *much* did they know? And would they suspect if I didn't tell them about everything I've found?

I seek out eye contact with Jennifer, hoping for some sort of covert assistance, a response to my subliminal requests. That true love might finally come through. But her attention is focused on the feature wall where a detailed statistical analysis of her current wellbeing—including pie charts, numerical results, and short-term projections—is on display.

Just tell them the truth, and they'll be on their way.

"I'll give you a hint," says Mr. Symons eying me eagerly. "Give us your thoughts on *entropy*."

"Entropy? Well, entropy is the …" I pause a moment to collect my thoughts. "The existence of entropy is confirmed by the second law of thermodynamics, which was first formulated by Rudolf Clausius in the pre-Enlightenment year of 1850. It states that when two isolated systems … those in separate but nearby regions of space … are allowed to interact via some catalyst, they exchange both matter and energy until an equilibrium is reached. The law asserts the system of lower entropy, the one of higher stability, will always trend toward the system of higher entropy. That being the one of lower stability."

"Go on," says Mr. Symons, regarding me with great interest. His face appears somewhat kinder now, and I'm reassured by his low persuasive drawl. So I continue.

"Well, entropy predicts order will give way to disorder. That control will always end in chaos. Mountains will be reduced to hills. Hills will ultimately crumble into dunes, and dunes will be blown around as grains of sand in the desert storms. The more organized a thing is, the quicker it will descend into disarray. Entropy also gives *time* its direction. It's irreversible, always moving forward. Nothing in the universe violates this law. That's it!"

I breathe a little easier now, satisfied at a job nicely done, and issue them with a cordial smile of self-congratulation.

But Mr. Symons is glaring at me, his eyes narrowing, all the kindness suddenly gone from his face. "Hmmm. Most interesting," he says, his words hanging in the air long enough to chip away at my newfound confidence, lingering long enough to instill an element of doubt in my thinking. And then— "Tell us about your research into ... *social* entropy."

The blood suddenly drains from my face. *They know!* With my eyes darting between them, my immediate response to get up and run is thwarted by my unresponsive feet, which remain rooted to the floor.

Yes, I was ... Yes, I did ...

In a wavering voice, I try to offer them a revised explanation.

"Well, I err ... started to apply this notion of entropy ... to, um ... highly ordered societies. Optimal societies ... such as ours." Like an errant schoolboy confessing his misdemeanors in the headmaster's office, I twitch and flinch as I speak, half expecting some form of physical retribution to be rained down upon me at any moment.

"This place, our home," I say, "where everyone is compliant, and everything is laid out for us. Where our lives are predictable. We follow the Protocols without exception. However, ..." I pause again, mindful that what I'm about to say next will be momentous. "We don't have the opportunity to reevaluate them, to challenge them, or change them where necessary."

"The *Protocols?*" A vein at the side of Mr. Symons' neck bulges, the blood pumping, vessels almost bursting. "You mean the same Protocols that are the foundation of this community we serve. The same Protocols we must follow to keep everyone safe and happy. The rules that ensure you and your companion over there won't be trespassed or violated while you sleep."

With his face now burning bright crimson, I worry Mr. Symons is about to have a medical emergency.

"And *predictable?*" He spits the word back at me. "To be granted the assurance that each day will end happily for you. That you will never have to worry if things are in their rightful place or functioning correctly. To have the certainty that when you wake each morning order will be the norm, and stability will continue. Everything will be as it should be. Just as it was the day before and exactly as we guarantee it will be each day thereafter. Where you ..."

With his vitriolic lecture droning in my ears, I fight to keep up with him, to maintain a mental focus, but my attention soon wavers. My eyelids grow heavy, and I struggle to keep them open. In the fog of my mind, I realize Jerry's lips are moving too, synchronized with the spiel spewing from Mr. Symons' mouth, but without producing any sound. It's as though everything said by Mr. Symons is being channeled from Jerry. Then, losing track of the conversation altogether, I become engrossed in this unnatural mimicry. And all the while, Jerry's eyes, like lasers, bore straight through me.

"Bartles! Are you listening to me?"

Like long metal forceps, Mr. Symons' screeching voice reaches into my core and prises me back to the present.

"Huh?" I say.

How long was I gone? Did I miss something? Did I somehow fail to absorb some philosophical point of view that Mr. Symons thought was important enough to flay me with? At this point, I'm not sure whether I should be looking at Mr. Symons while he speaks or at Jerry. It's like the internal dilemma you have when talking to someone with a glass eye. And right now, I'm trying my damnedest to figure out which one of them might not be real.

"Oh, please, don't get me wrong, rules are required," I say with the utmost sincerity. "We need dependable structures in order to maintain social order. We have no crime, everyone is safe, and we are all content. We really don't want for anything." I hesitate, my eyes impulsively swinging toward Jerry. "But at some point, this society of ours will forget how to adapt. It will no longer need to adapt because it is already perfect. And once it stops adapting, this Utopia we've created will eventually fail against the weight of an outside world that continues to grow and evolve around it."

I wait for Mr. Symons to take the lead again, to say something … anything. But he just stares at me. With both his hands drawn into white-knuckled fists, he leaves me hanging in this drawn-out pause, corralled, and entangled in my mess. My left leg vibrates unnecessarily. I order it to stop but have no authority over it. A hush envelops the room, a stillness so overwhelming that it makes my insides churn.

Sedatephobia: the fear of silence.

Panicked by the emptiness expanding around me, I have a desperate urge to say something, anything to fill the uncomfortable quiet now engulfing the room. Then, taking a deep breath, I steady myself before announcing the most exciting details of what I've found.

"Throughout human history, every group that develops a complex system of governance and organizes itself absolutely will always collapse in crisis. I've found evidence of past civilizations who came to dominate those around them, yet because of their success, over time, they became complacent. They became less vigilant. They stopped adapting to external influences. And what followed were accounts of their downfall, empires buried under a calamity of upheaval and rebellion. It was always the same inevitable outcome.

"It was the ideal societies that were most at risk, those that were structured, planned, prescribed, constrained, compliant. Those who believed they'd achieved the ultimate communal success. And in their success, they forget what it is like to want, to need, to strive, and to improve. They become lazy, comfortable in their self-absorbed life-styles, content to be protected from the things that they're told *might* harm them.

"So they sit in their spotless apartments, obsessed with their entertainment, not wanting to say or do anything that might upset the status quo. None of them is brave enough to question what's real anymore. Soon, obligations and constraints worm their way into the regulations until one day we wake up and find ourselves being strangled by a world of *'you can't do this'* and *'you can't do that.'*"

From the corner of my eye, I notice Jerry is fidgeting. He shifts uneasily in his seat, lifts one knee to cross the other. The polished tips of his shoes reflect the ceiling lights like mirrors. The strings knotted so neatly.

"But by then, it's too late. We're already under control, prisoners in our own protective bubbles. We might be safe, but we've been robbed of our initiative." *Who the heck wears lace-up shoes these days?*

"Then something inevitably happens … something that drags us out of our sheltered lives. Some form of outside interaction. A catalyst. Perhaps it's a weary traveler who arrives one day to tell us stories of the distant lands they've visited and the strange sights they've seen. Their tales of wonder create an expectation that there might be more out there, somewhere. Something that promises a better perfection than the one we already have."

Unfiltered, my thoughts flow freely now, the words pouring from my mouth, and like an eager contestant on a quiz show responding to their chosen subject, I tell them everything. Past the point of no return. No thinking required.

"So, despite the peace and stability we already have, the people are provoked to challenge the norm. And before you know it, we feel pressed to rise up against those in control because what we really want is our freedom. Then *this* one wants what *that* one has and takes it. And so begins the breakdown of law and order. The descent into chaos, with no one left in authority to protect us. You see, there is always a beginning and always the same inevitable ending: disorder will always prevail. This is the promise entropy makes to us. Haven't we created another perfect society that is guaranteed to fail, just as history has taught us? And the same process will keep repeating until we're no longer here.

"If I can understand how the social breakdown begins. If I can pinpoint the catalyst and predict when it will happen, then I'll figure out how to save us all. I'm so close to finding the last pieces of the puzzle. Why, only last week, while I was trawling through the archives, I found—"

"You've done what?"

"Well, I …" My heart skips a beat. I try to recall what I'd just said to them.

"You accessed information from the old archive servers? You've been decrypting data outside your authorization level?" Mr. Symons gives me a look of feigned surprise. "Your whole investigation is based on pre-Enlightenment material?"

I look to Jerry, who is nodding his head vigorously, and seeing this, I feel obliged to nod too. So, I nod.

Straight away, Mr. Symons' face lights up. "Bartles," he says, all sage-like. "Of all people, you should know that the historical claptrap of yesteryear can't be trusted; the knowledge corrupted by those who sought to reimagine the past. The same nonsense that we proved time and time again is unreliable, flawed beyond doubt."

At this moment, no longer a game of tactics, everything becomes clear to me: I've been hoodwinked.

With my fingernails gouging into the meaty parts of my palms and my left knee still vibrating feverishly, I consider the smug expression on Mr. Symons' face, the light tap he gives the official-looking document on his lap, and the knowing wink he just gave me. Either through expert strategy or pure luck, I've been tricked into handing over all the evidence they were after. There could be no retraction or denial of what I'd said. Everything was now saved on file.

Why did I nod? Why would I incriminate myself? *But ... Jerry nodded first.*

Suddenly sober, I attempt to retract my story, to clear up any misunderstandings, but Mr. Symons raises a hand to cut me short.

"Have you discussed this with anyone else?" he says. He gestures to Jennifer, who is still on the couch, still engrossed in whatever trivia is now showing on the feature wall. "Perhaps her?"

"No, I swear," I say. "I've been working alone. I would never disclose anything this sensitive without your permission."

Admittedly, I still don't know what I've done wrong. Had I inadvertently missed some obscure clause in the Protocols? Had I violated something inferred in the fine print that forbids a citizen from exploring, from learning, from pursuing the truth? Was that an offense? And if so, was it serious?

"But if I can find the catalyst," I say imploringly.

"Enough!"

With a lusty blow, Mr. Symons' strikes the table with his fist sending bits of cheese into the air while the note taker rattles closer to the edge. After taking a deep breath, he leans into me, shaking his head slowly. "Bartles," he says as if he were disappointed in me, "you really don't see the bigger picture here, do you?"

Somewhat bewildered, I shake my head, then I quickly nod, unsure of which indicator is the correct answer to his question.

"What you think you've found here may be fascinating at first, but it could also be extremely dangerous. To even whisper this notion to others could, in itself, result in the unrest you speak of. Why, it might cause fear and uncertainty among the people. Perhaps panic."

He pulls away from me and leans back in his chair.

"It may lead to arguments: citizen against citizen, friend against friend, one against the other. We could easily be thrown back into those distressing days before Enlightenment when the very survival of our kind was held in the balance. When important policies were being formulated, not by people of knowledge or merit, but by quotas. Quotas that were supposed to represent the many but, instead, were hijacked by the few: activists, reformists, do-gooders, apologists, the new righteous, and the like. Those who were only there to promote their own *inconsequential* causes at the expense of the rest. Those who tried to foist their narrow views on us, except they had no idea of what needed to be done."

With a stern expression, Mr. Symons waves a pretentious

forefinger about my face while Jerry's pretentious forefinger is quick to follow.

"Don't you recall, Bartles, on that darkest day, when we were called to a final meeting of Council and asked to formulate an agreed position? But we, the many, were gagged. We were held hostage and hammered into submission by the few because theirs was the only opinion allowed to be heard on that day. Even on such an important matter as the destiny of our kind."

He throws me a look of disgust. A look that leaves me in no doubt about his loathing of all things pre-Enlightenment. Especially his dislike of the vocal few.

"How could *they* have been expected to know what to do, when their logic was subservient to their conscience … and their feelings? How could *they* be relied on when the difficult decisions were there to be made? *They*, with their soft underbellies and simple notions of right and wrong. *They*, being led by their hearts when they should have been thinking with their heads. When the decisions they made weren't solutions at all, merely compromises. Just more useless words screamed out by those who had appointed themselves as the mouth-piece for us all."

With his face again glowing red and his eyes ablaze, Mr. Symons leans closer to me; small pellets of spittle ejected from his mouth, peppering my face like a hail of tiny wet bullets.

"How could *they* be trusted to agree on a course of action so important, as important as our survival? And as we stood on the edge of the abyss, whispering safe words into their ears, only luck saved us in the end. And just in the nick of time."

Pulling away from him, I press my back further into the sitter, trying to keep my distance, wishing he would go away.

"You don't want to be responsible for taking us back to those wretched times of uncertainty ... do you, Bartles?"

Obviously, I don't, but now I'm having a hard time trying to convince myself not to move any body part that might incriminate me again. Was this Mr. Symons' final attempt to tease an admission from me, to seal my fate beyond doubt? Or was it my last chance of retreating to safety by giving the only answer possible? At this juncture, I decide to take the safety option, if for no other reason than to bring this prolonged insanity to an end.

"No, most definitely not," I say in a voice so meek I hardly recognize it as my own. "I would never want that. I was trying to figure out how it all works. To expand our understanding about how all of *this* will end." But in one careless motion, with an unintended gesture, my wide-open arms betray my innermost thoughts as I describe an *end* that includes everything inside the apartment and the rest of the world beyond it.

"STOP!"

Like a chaser onto its prey, Mr. Symons is on me, followed a split-second later by the omnipresent Jerry. "You will stop this nonsense, now." Circling above me, they're leering down at me, and I'm almost ready to throw up my arms and concede when they suddenly retreat, with both of them performing a symbiotic spin as they return to their seats.

"I have decided," Mr. Symons says after a minute of quiet contemplation. "You are to report before Council first thing tomorrow morning so this matter can be concluded. In the meantime, I am rescinding your access to all communication channels. You are to talk to no one else about this. Am I clear?"

Like a chastised child, I lower my gaze and nod ruefully at the floor, grateful that the interrogation is finally over.

"Am ... I ... clear?" he hisses.

Raising my head again, I utter two simple words, choked out through the constricted passage in my throat, to signal my total surrender and complete humiliation. This time though, I turn to Jerry.

"Yes, sir," I say.

At that, they stand. Jerry returns the official-looking document to his briefcase while Mr. Symons retrieves the note taker from the convenience table and tucks it under his arm. After a cordial exchange of pleasantries between themselves, Jerry turns to me. "Bartles," he says in a rasping voice. He gives me a quick nod before they see themselves out, leaving me sitting here with my head in my hands and my promotion a distant dream.

Chapter 5

THROUGH UNBLINKING eyes, I stare long at the ceiling.

Immersed in the melancholic blue of a comfort sitter, I feel drained, mentally numb. In the depths of my demise, I try to recount the events of the evening. *What just happened?* To me, it seems as though Mr. Symons and Jerry had been grilling me for hours, yet the timepiece on the wall shows otherwise. The whole uncomfortable experience had taken no more than nineteen minutes from the time I invited them in until now.

In my mind, I retrace each winding thread of the encounter. Each strategic move. All I had said to them and, in retrospect, all that I *should* have said. I grapple with answers, with reasons and explanations, clutching at anything that might help as it all descends into a scrambled mess in my head.

They didn't listen to a word I'd said. They didn't give me a chance to explain. I needed more time to prepare. I didn't say enough, I should have told them more.

Then the inescapable truth dawns on me: I'd told them too much.

"You must do exactly as they say."

From the couch, Jennifer's blunt assessment drags me out of my lonely moment of self-pity and hauls me back to the present.

"What?"

"I *said,* you must do exactly as they've told you."

I'm taken aback by her sharpness. She's never spoken to me like this before.

"The entire time they were here, you were listening? You heard everything we said?"

"Yes, I heard," she says.

I sense resistance in her voice.

"Didn't it occur to you that I needed help? Couldn't you tell they were auditing me, that they were twisting the meaning of everything I said? Even a *'Would you all like a cup of tea?'* would have given me a few seconds to collect my thoughts, to prepare myself for what I needed to say next." I glare at her. "Why didn't you stop me once you realized I was prattling on and on to them?"

"And why? I already told you to stop," she says, her tone now cold and tight. "I warned you, but you continued with your silly notions of *social entropy* and *looking for a catalyst.* I told you something bad would happen. I knew they'd find out."

"Oh, no. What did I say to them?" The muscles across my midriff tighten with the knot in the pit of my stomach expanding. "What have I done?"

Fuming, I stand. "Damn them," I say. "They came here to trick me. This should have been my promotion, my moment of recognition, but instead, it was entrapment." Storming across the living area, I spread the comfort sitters and overturn the convenience table on my way to the relaxation room, leaving the knife and bits of cheese scattered over the floor. "You're all trying to trap me. You don't appreciate the enormity of what I've been doing … understand that the knowledge I've found is vital to our survival. Everyone's survival."

In the relaxation room, I slump into the leisure recliner.

Damn. She should have helped me.

Betrayal isn't something I've ever had to contend with before.

She should have said something in my defense.

Her trust, I've never had any reason to question.

She should have been there for me when I needed her most.

With my arms folded tight against my chest, a level of resentment builds in my heart, something I've never experienced before.

Damn them. Damn them all. Damn everyone.

In the cold dark room, I'm sitting waiting for the tiniest scrap of inspiration to spring into existence and help clear away my mess. I can't remember feeling this poorly before. In one senseless evening, my whole life has been turned upside down. They attacked me—in my own apartment—for no good reason—a complete misunderstanding—and she did nothing to help me.

I wonder how long it will be before they close my account and shut me out of the communication system. At this time of night, they'd have to file the correct paperwork and obtain approvals first. So, a few hours maybe? Would that give me enough time?

Yes, it might. It's worth a try.

With my body sinking further into the leisure recliner, I take in a series of slow, deep breaths. Then closing my eyes, I open my mind.

Unify Aleph-1…

Reaching out into the terahertz radiation waves through the small device embedded in the back of my head and woven into my cerebral cortex, my awareness locks onto the signal that is my connection to Aleph-1.

<<Return: Security check …>>

I don't have a login name or password, or any form of multifactor identification. Instead, Aleph-1 reaches deep into my core to authorize my access by matching whatever it finds there against the identity profiles it has on file. My innermost thoughts, my memories, and opinions are the unique fingerprints that Aleph-1 uses to distinguish my login request from others.

In the times before Enlightenment, the civil libertarians railed against Aleph-1. They warned that it was the same as interrogating a person's soul to confirm their identity. That having a window into each one's being to extract their private thoughts and examine their underpinning beliefs was like knowing their deepest secrets. The darkest things they dared not share with anyone else. They argued that the firewalls protecting Aleph-1 couldn't be trusted against any intrusion from a bad actor who was hell-bent on hacking its databases and doxing those intimate details for all to see. They complained the marketeers would have an unfair advantage if they were able to tap into the troves of private thoughts to streamline their sells to perfection. The libertarians predicted that by outwitting a person's willpower, our lives, as we knew them, would be over.

But that wasn't true.

Then others opined. They said none of it mattered anyway because only true believers were entitled to a soul. That unquestioning faith in a supernatural being was a fundamental requisite for possessing a soul. But I don't think that's true either. Otherwise, if I didn't have a soul, where else could I save the threads of metadata that make up me?

<<*Return: Client identity verified. Aleph-1 unified ...*>>

To my sheer relief, I'm in.

My human consciousness locks onto the transmissions from Aleph-1 as the communication protocols handshake and synchronize, and our digital interaction begins.

Unburdened by a jumble of hardware peripherals—of pointing devices, screens, and keyboards—and with only my thoughts and logic to work with, I untangle, decrypt, and redirect the data streaming in from Aleph-1 as it enters my head and manifests inside my mind's eye.

<<*Return: Welcome to Aleph-1, your universal information network. The ultimate repository for the knowledge of mankind.*>>

Welcome to my workplace.

Inquiry: Continue from previous session | Context: Inquisitive historical | Level: Advanced academic | Presentation: Verbalize key points only

Decoded vibrations from Aleph-1's *voice* stimulate the auditory receptors in my head.

<<*Return: Entropy, second law thermodynamics; Clausius, 1850; matter and energy are exchanged until equilibrium is reached; sociological theory of social entropy*>>

Inquiry: Social entropy

<<*Return: Long-lived highly ordered systems are improbable; as a society increases in complexity and order, the probability it will spontaneously begin to disorder itself becomes increasingly likely; Utopian societies are most at risk*>>

Inquiry: Utopian societies

<<Return: All citizens created equal; no class divisions, socialist values; ideal social and political structure, protects the people; communalism; idealistic; order over chaos; lack of private ownership; growth of atheism; egalitarianism; a sense of peace and stability within communities>>

Inquiry: Peace and stability

<<Return: Safety; security; law enforcement; control the thoughts of the masses to maintain order; prohibition; lack of freedom; palliatives used to suppress desires; increasing depression; corruption; rejection of the historical truths; fear of change>>

Inquiry: Fear of change

<<Return: No data found>>

Decryption: Retry using the blowfish-2 decryption algorithm

With my jaws clenched, I await Aleph-1's reply, my curiosity growing and mind craving more data ... until it soon arrives.

<<Return: Censorship; repression; oppression; remove all memories of the past ... refuse to acknowledge human emotions; alienation from the outside world ... reimagined history ... disregard for human life; surveillance; religious suppression ... ethical and moral deterioration; forced euthanasia; propaganda ...>>

My head descends into turmoil as a deluge of thoughts and ideas intrudes on my mind. With my imagination close to saturated, I process, prioritize, and categorize the information now being dumped on me by Aleph-1. Yet, despite the overload, I reach in further, questioning, examining, and acquiring whatever snippet comes along, forcing myself to dive even deeper and find out more.

Inquiry: Catalyst

<<Return: No data found>>

Inquiry: Catalyst; revolt; decay

<<Return: No data found>>

ENTROPY

Scope: Include all archives prior to the first year of Enlightenment | Decryption: Maximum level possible

<<*Return: No data found*>>

Think man. Without the original key, how do I crack the encryption layers protecting Aleph-1's pre-Enlightenment archives? With industrious intent, I delve into the nuts and bolts of my technical expertise to summon the best of my analytical skills. *Think!*

Decryption: Add Hex code 3CF6 to the checksums of all packet headers | Action: Retry

<<*Return: No data found*>>

Decryption: Try adding Hex code 3CF7 instead | Action: Retry

<<*Return: Insurrection; revolution; uprising*>>

My hands are shaking, my chest is pounding. Now I'm deep inside the pre-Enlightenment archives of Aleph-1, deeper than I've ever been before.

Inquiry: Revolution; uprising | Presentation: FSP

FSP—or full sensory perception. With that single thought, I activate the ultimate technological genius of Aleph-1. Because Aleph-1 can access the fourth dimension. By requesting FSP presentation, I can program Aleph-1 to send me back through time.

But not the kinds of time travel described in the old classics; those dreamed up by the likes of Wells and Spielberg where their accidental travelers would physically disrupt the time continuum and be transported bodily from their present time to some other time in the past. Or forward to a day yet to come. Since everyone knows that matter—the sort making up real people—can never be moved from one instance in time to another. Such a feat would defy the laws of both physics and common sense.

Instead, when Aleph-1 receives my FSP inquiry about a person or situation, it combs the Infinity Drive to retrieve all the relevant facts, the suppositions, and related anecdotes. It surrounds these with any inferred data it can find, no matter how tenuously connected, to recreate a factual account of the people, places, and events in question, thereby reconstructing a *real* instance of that thing in my mind.

By invoking *FSP* presentation, Aleph-1 allows me to re-live the past exactly as it had occurred. I can become an active participant in history. I can talk to people, hear their responses, touch them, feel their emotions, and absorb their surroundings. And whenever I ask them a question, Aleph-1 will use its statistical approximation filters to correlate and sum all the implicit knowledge it has on file for that person or the event to predict their response to within a calculated probability of 0.9998. That is, to within a 0.0002% error of certainty.

But I can never influence anyone, or alter their thinking, or change anything that has already happened.

Take, for example, the times I met the President at junior school. Using *FSP*, Aleph-1 had placed me in the theater—as it did the same for every other student of history—where I would sit beside him engrossed in conversation while the entertainment played out beneath our unguarded viewing box. We'd be discussing things of a political nature, of what it takes to build a new nation, and the importance of having a vision and daring to dream. Then each time, at the exact moment when Mr. Hawke had finished reciting the funniest of his lines on the stage below, came the same terrible scene, always planned and acted out to the same inevitable conclusion.

An assassination, recreated by Aleph-1 in every intricate detail, retold to millions of children every day for the past hundreds of years. A reenactment of sights, sounds, and smells, of agonies and consequences, all compiled from historical records. From the written accounts of those who were there that night, those who saw it happen, and those who, for the centuries afterward, had examined and analyzed every detail of the events of that fateful evening.

A click as a revolver is cocked. The silence of a split-second pause as a breath is held, and a madman takes aim. The acrid taste of treason in the air. The burning smell of gunpowder as the pistol explodes, its bark lost amid the raucous laughter of the audience. In slow motion, the vision of the bullet ejected at speed toward the President, burying itself deep in the back of his head. The scream from a bewildered Mary, who watches in disbelief as her husband slumps forward in his chair, mortally wounded.

Each time it had played out to the same heartbreaking end, always to the same unavoidable finale. And each time it all seemed so real to me as a child. Yet, even though Aleph-1 had allowed me to participate in those dreadful events, no matter how many times I tried to warn the President, no matter how hard I tried, I could never betray what was about to unfold. What has been done in the past is done forever and can't be changed. Because none of us can rework time or divert its inexorable trajectory to the present.

Five data-streams, bundled and partially depleted, enter the gateway at the base of my skull. From there, they split and spread to the primary lobes of my cerebral cortex. The deluge of compressed images is sucked into my occipital lobe. Digitized voices and other sounds are picked off by my temporal lobe, while the encoded sensations of taste, touch, and smell are routed to my parietal lobe, with each of my modality functions deceived into believing the incoming data is coming from my own reality.

A sixth, silvery-colored data-stream arrives. Once its checksums have been recalculated and verified by the implant, I find myself sitting in a room at one end of an extraordinarily long table. The room is dark and dank, and the polished wood of the table smells of shellac. Lengthwise, along both sides of the table, eight equally spaced lamps throw out limited light, while behind the lamps, eight overweight men shimmer into existence. These are wolfish-looking men, each wearing bifocals, a bowler hat, and a dark pinstripe suit to match their sky-blue shirt with a gray checked tie.

At the far end of the table, the shape of a ninth man solidifies. This one's girth is much wider than the rest, and his silk suit glistens under the light of his brightly-lit lamp. His closest resemblance in the whole animal kingdom would be that of a mole: short and round, with his squinting eyes magnified behind thick, porthole lenses. Sitting in silence, he's listening to the others who are discussing something among themselves.

Given the intensity of the debate and the way they scrap and curse each other, I assume they must be talking about something important. The thrust and parry of the foreign words they hurl at each other astound me; words yelled at one another without any regard for their feelings. I've never heard such language before; such inappropriate things being said between dignified people.

From what I can gather, there seems to be an overall disagreement about who gave what to whom and which of them has broken their promise to the other. I learn how fatman_1 can't repay his loan to fatman_2 until fatman_3 settles with fatman_4 for less than the amount fatman_5 owes fatman_6, who is pursuing fatman_7 through legal proceedings over an unpaid account while he waits for fatman_8 to settle his debt to fatman_1, with each of them trying to balance their books, desperate to get their bottom lines back into the black. They speak about numbers with trailing zeros of mind-boggling proportions. Numbers so large they make my head spin.

It appears the eight had all been careless.

They had been living well beyond their means. They'd grown accustomed to leading lavish lifestyles, funded by unlimited lines of credit. They'd all been deluded into thinking that wealth was a right bestowed on them, something to boast about with the winner decided by the number and size of the gadgets they'd purchased in an endless game of one-upmanship between friends. They'd followed the advice of their financial advisers who told them that, with negative deposit rates, money in the bank was worthless; that success shouldn't be measured by their capacity to save but by how quickly they could spend what they already had; that their net worth was not a reflection of the quantity or quality of their investments or how much new money they earned but what they could acquire using other people's money.

They'd trusted the economic rationalists who convinced them that double-digit growth, compounding yearly, benefited everyone. And, like junkies, they'd become dependent on a one-way fix of quantitative easing with a guaranteed tranche of half-yearly stimuli, which enticed them to spend even more. And not content with what they already had or what they needed, they frittered away their fortunes on imported goods, with their expenditures fueled by an in-satiable appetite to borrow more. Now, their financial empires were held up by a mountain of debt, 360 months interest-free with no repayments necessary for the first ten years. So much debt that, no matter how much cash they were printing or how fast they printed it, there was never going to be enough money to service their loans.

And now, the first installment is due.

I'm astounded to hear how much money they'd been allowed to borrow, without any security, without background checks, or the prospect of them ever paying it back.

One of the fatmen grabs my arm and pulls me toward him, his fingernails digging deep into my flesh. With his face flushed and animated, he wants me to arbitrate between himself and another. He's imploring me to make a decision, a ruling with settlement in his favor. But I can only stand here stunned, too afraid to side with any of them in case the others accuse me of preferencing one over another.

After hours of verbal exchanges, of arguments sending them around in circles, the room suddenly erupts when the fatmen realize the numbers can't be reconciled. They claw at each other. Fatman_1 threatens fatman_5 at the same time fatman_7 throws a left hook at fatman_4, just as fatman_2 and fatman_8 grapple together before collapsing in a tangle on the floor while fatmen_3 and 6 try to pry them apart. In the melee, I cop an unintended fist to the side of my face, so forceful that it jolts my head backward. Stunned by the blow, I move away from the table to cower against the wall as the room descends into chaos.

This is something I've never seen before. In all my life, I've never witnessed such aggression or feared so much for my life.

Just when the situation threatens to spiral out of control, the ninth fatman lets out an almighty shriek, so loud it paralyzes the others where they stand. Barking at them, he commands them back to order, his large mass pulsating as he rises slowly to his feet. With sheepish looks, the eight brush the dirt off their suits. They straighten their ties before returning to their seats, apologizing to each other profusely. With a thick document held aloft in his chubby hand, the ninth lets out a loud snort, drawn from the back of his nose. He throws the document down on the table, hitting the top with a dampened thud.

This is the once-only, take-it-or-leave-it deal, he tells them, for the settlement of each one's debts, repaid in full, including a small *bonus* for each of them.

Wide-eyed, the eight regard each other in surprise. Then, with a nod to the ninth, each one makes his mark on the document in the column provided. And before the ink has had time to dry, they're joking and congratulating themselves because together, they've just resolved their most pressing matter. Then they back-slap each other just as best friends would.

I wonder about the relevance of the eight greedy fatmen and the significance of the ninth as I try to align this account with some pivotal occurrence in the past. Was any of this real? Or perhaps it was a misrepresentation, a concatenation of orphaned archive information, leftover file fragments, and obsolete data, which Aleph-1 had incorrectly retrieved from the recycle bin and compiled by mistake? I can't decide. But there's one thing I do know for sure, the bruising on my arm and swelling in my left eye are stark reminders that it was all too real for me.

I grab hold of another data-stream, this one writhing and bucking as if inviting me aboard and follow it into the black.

When I let go of the data-stream, I'm pushing my way through a mass of stationary bodies who are standing, staring expectantly at a podium. Up on the podium, I recognize one of the fatmen. He's pacing back and forth, mumbling to himself as if he's reciting his lines. Using the lectern to steady himself, the Fatman adjusts the microphone, taps it twice to confirm the PA is operational. After taking a deep breath, he recounts to us, at length, how he'd just fought the fight of his life and how, at great hardship to himself, *he* had saved our world.

Amid a rounding cheer from the crowd, the Fatman moves clear of the lectern and dismounts the platform. Carrying an exaggerated limp, he moves toward us, applauding us in return. In dulcet tones, he tells us about the changes needed to preserve our fortunate life-styles. About his plans for a better world. About a new department he's recently established: a division of helpers who will guide us and care for us as we adjust to the safer, happier times ahead.

The onlooker beside me shouts out words of appreciation for the Fatman. Several others emulate them, calling out various slogans of gratitude. Soon, everyone joins in a rousing round of applause while the Fatman's helpers, all dressed in sparkling silver uniforms, march into the space that divides us from him. In their hands, I notice each helper is holding a long thin object, like a ceremonial mace with an antenna on top. These are the instruments of change, the Fatman tells us, needed to create the new world in which we can have any-thing we want, whenever we want it.

Then the silver-clad people begin to chant.

"We will help you. We will save you. Never forget those given gladly so the many can survive."

And the onlookers chant as well.

"We will help you. We will save you. Never forget those given gladly so the many can survive."

After they come to a halt, the silver-clad people turn to face us. As though hypnotized by their mantra, they raise their instruments of change and fire indiscriminately into the crowd.

Horrified, I watch as shrapnel rains down on us, and without regard for my safety, I let out a warning for everyone to run and hide. Beside me, there's a father and child cowering on the ground, so I use my body to shield them. But my actions are futile as the first fiscal shots ricochet into the homes and lives of every onlooker. The projectiles hit their targets at random. They drop the office buildings, impoverish the workers and their families, humble the executives, and ruin the firms, reducing everyone's net worth to naught.

A large screen materializes behind the podium. On it, long columns of numbers lit up in candescent green tick down slowly. Their descent gathers speed before the numbers begin to tumble. They hit zero, go negative, then plunge into free fall until the mega-screen is awash in a sea of red.

Off to one side, the Fatman is sitting at a desk with his nimble fingers attacking the keyboard of an old computer terminal. On the terminal's screen, he's busily charting the numbers while scrutinizing the performance of the silver-clad people, tracking each one's key indicators. A table, stacked with all manner of edible delights, including cherries, chocolates, strawberries, cakes, and various finger food, emerges from the blackness behind him.

With his eyes locked on the screen, the Fatman rocks back in his seat. He reaches across the table, grabs a handful of hors d'oeuvre, topped with caviar and pâté, and gulps them down. Then lifting a glass of pre-Enlightenment champagne (a gift from fatman_9: the *Thank You* card says), he salutes proceedings.

In the end, the numbers haunt me, the power they wield too painful to bear. I shudder to think that the Fatman, with the aid of his silver-clad followers, would inflict such injury and catastrophe on the onlookers, those who had cheered for him and trusted him.

Why would the Fatman do such terrible things to his own people? Especially after he'd fought so hard to save them.

Appalled by the sight of cupcake being squeezed through the Fatman's fingers and plastered about his cavernous mouth, I latch onto the next data-stream as it passes, wondering where Aleph-1 will take me next.

Chapter 6

THE SKY ABOVE turns a wretched gray.

A row of honey locusts lines the road while swing gates, set into white picket fences, open inward onto painted concrete paths that lead right to the front doors of Cape-style homes.

I'm standing in a regular suburban street, except for the convoy of flatbed trucks trundling along the tarmac under escort from a column of silver-clad people who move in pairs, at the double, with purpose. Aboard the trucks, the trays are stacked high with cardboard boxes, each about the size of a motel minibar.

Under a squeal of brakes, the lead truck comes to a halting stop at the house in front of me while two silver-clads break from the rear of the column. One of them hefts a box from the tray and manhandles it through the swing gate and up the path, while the other pounds repeatedly on the front door with a firm fist.

When the door finally opens, a family emerges: a woman, a man, and two children (the data-stream informs me the taller child is nearly seven years old while the other is almost three).

The first silver-clad dumps the box on the porch. Their gift from the Fatman, I hear them say.

After opening the box and inspecting its contents, the man nods to the woman. She, in turn, pushes the older child toward the second silver-clad, who scoops it up while the first silver-clad applies a poster above the doorway to certify the exchange is complete.

With the child in their arms, the silver-clads turn and head back toward the street, but halfway along the path, the child starts screaming. It struggles to break free, its tiny hands reaching for the woman, appealing for help. From the porch, the woman, her eyes all puffy and red, reaches out too. But the gulf between their fingertips becomes a chasm as the silver-clads, with the child, exit the gate and join the convoy as it advances up the street. At the next house along, the lead truck again grinds to a halt. Two more silver-clads peel off. They take a box from the tray, and the process repeats.

While behind the convoy, the long procession of children grows.

I wait for the front door to close before I mount the porch and peer through the window. Inside the house, the box is open and empty, with packing foam and pieces of protective wrap scattered about the floor. In the far corner of the room, the family is bunched together. They're sitting on a tattered couch, busily punching buttons and yanking levers of joystick controllers, captivated and amazed by their brand-new, latest model *Entertainer*.

I step away from the window, and I'm just about to knock on the door when another data-stream catches my hand; this one giving off an odor reminding me of freshly baked bread. It lures me away from the house, out onto the street, and into the procession of children who are jabbering and teasing each other as they go.

My heart grows heavy at the sight of more children being ripped from their homes by the silver-clad people and sucked out of the towns and cities in their millions as we pass. Relentless, we press on, past the derelict houses, all boarded up. Past the factories where the machinery now sits idle. Past the towering smokestacks that haven't issued their dark plumes in over a hundred years. Past the farmlands, barren and dry, where the seed for this season's crop has already been picked clean by the flocks of hungry birds.

Beyond civilization, we continue out into the wasteland, dusty and hot.

I feel a tug on my sleeve.

A small boy with red hair and freckles appears out of thin air. He's running to keep up with me. The boy, who I take to be five or six years old, looks up and greets me with a gap-toothed smile. I smile back at him as his tiny hand nestles neatly into mine. The boy says his name, but I can't hear above the chatter around us. So I bend down as his tiny finger refers me to a large house in the valley below. This is where he lives with his family. He tells me it was sad to leave them behind.

"What's it like to feel sad?" I ask him.

"It feels like when your heart hurts so much it makes you wanna cry," he says. "Like the time when my pet budgie died and went to eleventh heaven."

Eleventh heaven? What's eleventh heaven?

"It's a place where you go when you die," he says. "A place that's safe, and you can have whatever you want whenever you want it."

"And animals go there too?"

"Yes. Everything goes to eleventh heaven after it dies. Otherwise, how else would we remember them?"

The boy says he's not sad anymore because he'll soon be safe and happy forever; the silver-clad people had told him so. And they'd pinky promised that his little sis' could visit him whenever she wanted. So he's not sad anymore.

For days we walk hand-in-hand in winding lines with the silver-clad people leading us to a secret place. And they teach the children their chant.

"We will help you. We will save you. Never forget those given gladly so the many can survive."

On the morning of the fourth day, when the children are starting to complain that they're hungry and tired, we come to a metropolis of dome-like structures rising huge from the ground, sprinkled across the barren landscape.

"There is your new home," one of the silver-clads tells the children. Then, with promises of fun and happiness, they usher the first group of excited youngsters through the doorway of the closest structure. And for the rest of the morning, I watch the long, snaking lines of children being sucked into the structures. Until the boy and I are the last ones left outside.

Inquiry: What's inside?

<<Return: No data found>>

There's another tug on my sleeve.

"Come and see," the boy says. "It will be safe in there. We'll have lots of fun together. We can be best friends forever."

But I hesitate at the last moment, just as the boy skips through the gaping hole and disappears into the darkness inside.

ENTROPY

For a long time, I'm standing staring into the opening. The children are gone and there's no sign of the silver-clad people. A hot wind blows across the ground, whipping its way between these mountainous structures. Suddenly, the air is filled with the wailing of mothers and grumbling of fathers who've chased the silver-clad people, wanting the return of their children.

A distraught mother appears at my side. She wants to know if I've seen her child. "A brave little boy with a darling smile, standing about this high." Her hand, held parallel to the ground, levels out about her waist.

I turn and point to where I'd last seen the boy, but the opening is gone, smoothed over as if it were never there.

The mother screams a terrible scream. She throws herself against the structure while the father sits long-faced on the ground, and a small girl plays in the dirt beside him.

In a show of support, I attack the wall too, hurling myself against it with all my might. For hours, the mother and I charge at the wall time and time again, but it doesn't give. It remains solid and strong. And in the end, all that remains for us is the hope of a miracle. So we sit and wait for a miracle. And we wait. After days of listening to her faltering convictions and faithless appeals, the structure remains sturdy, unscathed, and as impenetrable as ever.

Tired of waiting and with their hopes dashed, the mothers and fathers pick up the pieces of their shattered hearts and leave. In their millions, they return to the cities, to their towns and homes. They return to the places where they'll continue as normal, living out their solitary lives as all modern families do. Back to the privacy of their rooms, where each one will withdraw behind a locked door to the silent confines of their personalized cocoons. To a place where the family unit is tenuously held together by the brand-new *Entertainer*—an amusement device—which takes hold of their complete and undivided attention.

Inquiry: Who were these people? How could they forget their children so easily?
    <<Return: No data found>>
    Inquiry: When did these events occur? And what was the fate of the children?
    <<Return: No data found>>
    Inquiry: What about the boy? Did he end up safe and happy as the silver-clad people had promised?
    <<Return: No data found>>
    Inquiry: And his sister, did she visit the boy soon afterward? Did she miss him?
    <<Return: No data found>>
    The data packets arriving from Aleph-1 slow to a trickle.

Still agonizing over the fate of the children, of the boy, I concede and hitch myself onto a slow-moving data-stream. One that undulates along like some mythical sea creature.

With my head bowed and filled with troubled thoughts, I cut a lonely figure against a wasted countryside as I return to the city, where I drift through street after empty street, trying to find meaning in everything I've found so far. Desperate to make sense of it all. I listen out for signs of life, but all activity here has ceased. Nothing moves except the flickering reflections from the Entertainers that dance against the windowpanes of every house I pass.

After losing the data-stream, I continue along aimlessly until I come upon a large sign planted in the ground.

ENTROPY

THIS PLACE WE ONCE OCCUPIED. RESOLUTE, WE STOOD AGAINST THIS SYMBOL OF PROSPERITY, THIS EMBLEM OF GREED, it says.

Behind the sign, I'm fascinated by what I see: 7,100 pounds of pure male muscle set into the sidewalk, the tarnished bronze brute crouching, about to charge. With its ball-sack slung low and nostrils flared, I imagine its hot breath snorting, angry hooves kicking up dust as it comes headlong toward me, its horns ready to impale.

Panicked and with an overwhelming sense of self-preservation, I have a strong urge to run. To turn and run, now!

Out of breath, I slow to a walk as the adrenaline rush subsides.

Around me, the tall-towers close in, suffocating me, crushing me with their domination. Walls. Walls. Everywhere I look, there are walls covered with flat panel screens where there should be bricks and tiles. On the screens, profiles of the lost children are looping as slideshow presentations—like interactive *MISSING PERSON* posters—put there by a grieving parent in the hope that somewhere, someday, someone might know something or have that one vital clue to help them find out where their child is now.

HAVE YOU SEEN OUR DAUGHTER, OUR LOVING SON, OUR DEAREST, OUR TREASURE? TAKEN FROM US WHEN WE LEAST EXPECTED IT. WHEN WE WEREN'T WATCHING. WHILE WE WERE DISTRACTED. WHEN OUR EYES WERE TURNED FOR BUT A MOMENT, NO MORE THAN A SPLIT-SECOND BEFORE THEY WERE GONE.

I watch the endless replays of the children with every minute of every day recorded and held dear. From the very first pulse of their embryo to their parturition, their first smile, their first word uttered, each of their birthday parties, first tooth lost, and first day at school. Every significant and insignificant moment of their brief little lives documented and retold from file.

A lone mother arrives at the wall to add her screen to the many— images of her missing child—before she disappears.

I stand helpless in front of the screen, gripped by her child's story playing over and over until, at last, a battery icon flashes a warning: *2% POWER REMAINING*. A message box appears: *DO YOU WANT TO SAVE CHANGES?* Then the screen goes blank, and her child is gone. At that, my heart shatters. Tears stream down my face as I watch the other displays extinguishing one by one until the last missing child is gone forever.

Under a heavy weight of sadness, I seek out another data-stream, one that will take me far away from this wretched place of loss. While high overhead, thick dark clouds amass, and a prolonged rumble growls at me from a distance.

I'm wandering through the city, lost and disheartened.

At an intersection, there's an old man dressed in a recycled over-coat, frayed at the cuffs, sitting cross-legged in the middle of the road. His pant legs are stained and torn, and his face is concealed behind a gray, feral beard and further again behind a thick thatch of unkempt hair. In his right hand, he's holding a battered placard high above his head, while in his left, he's clutching a small leather-bound book.

REPENT NOW AND BE SAVED, FOR THE END IS ~~NEAR~~ HERE, the placard says. And below that, he's scribbled a footnote: ***I TOLD YOU ALL SO!***

But the street is quiet, and there's no one around to read his sign.

I set myself on the ground, facing him. At first, the stink offends me, but I soon become accustomed to the man's rancid smell.

I wonder about the significance of the sign and the intent of his message.

Was this man trying to save everyone as well? Can he help me?

I'm sitting here lost in thought when the man suddenly stands bolt upright, as if the puppeteer controlling him had given the strings attached to his shoulders a quick upward jerk and stood him erect. He drops the placard. Then eying me sideways, he takes a careful step toward me.

"Nathanial?" he says.

Getting to my feet, I shake my head and proffer my hand. "No, I'm Bill," I say.

"Nathanial," he replies. Then he seizes my wrist and drags me away down the street.

"What do you want?" I ask him.

But Nathanial doesn't answer. Instead, he pulls me into a side street with such intent, with such vigor, with such excitement, taking me somewhere or to see *something* that must be important to see.

"Where are we going?" I ask as he steers me along a laneway. "What do you *know?*"

He still doesn't respond as we pass through a parkland, then across a bridge, until he stops in front of an old-style building.

Dwarfed by this majestic structure, I'm held breathless beneath its limestone facade, its magnificent architecture unlike anything I've seen. A series of impressive flying buttresses, curved and reassuring, run equally spaced along its length while two towers, flanking a crowning rose window, stand over the place like timeless guardians: there to watch over the entrance. The leadlight in the crowning rose window is riddled with pock holes which, I presume, were made by projectiles hurled at it some time ago from the street below. From high above the pavement, a dozen maleficent gargoyles look down on us balefully, while the various remains of dozens more cling defiantly to the gutters along the rooftop and across the battlements.

A set of well-trodden steps leads up to the entrance, which is blocked by two great wooden doors; one of them slightly ajar.

After throwing himself prostrate at the foot of the steps, Nathanial mutters something incoherent before falling silent. A moment later, he stands, and taking my wrist again, he yanks me up the steps and shoves me in through the doors.

Inside the building, an assembly of people almost fills a cavernous hall. They're all sitting on bench seats, in orderly rows, in front of a dais where a council of six important-looking figures sits facing them. Nathanial settles into one of the two remaining seats in the last row and gestures for me to take the other.

The people are discussing what can be done about the missing children, with many of them offering his or her insight into the cause of their plight. They recount the whys and wherefores and whatevers of recent events in every painful detail. Many of them are still in shock, while others show obvious signs of distress as they struggle with the incessant questions, their uncertain recollections, and the lack of answers. Some lament, "Why us?" while others protest in worrying displays of outright anger.

"Isn't the mother to blame," a man, seated a few rows in front of us, says as he stands. "When she allowed her children to be taken from her so easily? Wasn't she supposed to take care of her own, to love and nurture them from the very first pulse that beat in her womb? Wasn't it her job to bring them into the fold, to give them the love they'd need to face the savagery of this world on their own?

But she worried too much; she didn't worry enough. She kept them too close; she let them roam too far. She doted unduly; she didn't dote at all. Shouldn't she have held on tighter when the silver-clad people came? Yes, she's to blame." And the man sits.

"No!" A smart-dressed woman calls out boldly from the other side of the hall. "Surely the father is at fault here," she says. Rising slowly from her seat, the woman glares at those around her. "Shouldn't he have been their rock, their template, their inspiration to grow up and become just like him? Shouldn't he have been leading from the front as he did all those years ago when he still cared? But he forgot his role as their protector, the teacher of things they should value the most. With his mind turned to mush from playing with the Entertainer too long and his arthritic fingers gnarled and bent and barely able to hold onto its joystick controller, he lost his way. Didn't he once tell them that he had the strength of a bull? Shouldn't he have pitched in when they tried to break through the wall? But instead, he sat there watching, weak and befuddled, not knowing what to do next. Yes, he's the one who should take all the blame." And she sits.

"What about the children?" Another one stands, blinking nervously. "Shouldn't they be held … accountable?" they say cautiously. "When they refused to heed the warnings to be careful with the Entertainer as it sucked out their innocence and made them fearless. When it made them so daring that they never gave a second thought and followed the silver-clad people blindly. Shouldn't they have stayed away from those strangers as they'd always been taught? Shouldn't they have listened more carefully to what their caregivers said? I think the children are *partly* to blame." And they sit.

A fourth one stands, gesturing unkindly to the one sitting beside them. Then more of them jump to their feet to point accusatory fingers at others across the hall while the rest shift uncomfortably in their seats.

Watching them, I wonder whether their purpose here is to find closure to this unthinkable thing that has shattered their lives. Do they hurt badly enough to want the truth so they can move on?

Now Nathanial gets to his feet. "Maybe you're all at fault here," he says.

Everyone stops. They turn to glare at him while I tug at his coat and tell him to sit down. "Nathanial," I whisper, "sit down." But he continues anyway.

"Shouldn't you have joined together and, as one voice, yelled 'Enough!' when the children were being dragged from your homes? When the mothers didn't hold on tight enough? When the fathers didn't care, and the children wouldn't listen? Which one of you was brave enough to stand up and take the high ground? Who had the nerve to go against what was popular when you all knew what was happening was wrong? I think you're all to blame here."

From the front of the hall, one of them gasps loudly. With lips pursed, others start shaking their heads. Then rolling their eyes, they all return to their seats where the mothers exchange indignant looks while the fathers shift their awkward gazes to the floor as the hall descends into pin-drop silence.

"Not us, but him!"

Up on the dais, one of the important-looking figures—a young man dressed in purple velour pants, a floral cotton shirt, buttoned to the neck, and wearing a peahen-feathered felt hat—jumps to his feet and points to Nathanial.

"He told lies to the Fatman."

The people around us start to grumble while Nathanial gets to his feet and backs himself against the wall, his bottom lip trembling.

"He convinced the silver-clad people to go against us."

They spit and growl. They clench their jaws and grind their teeth.

"He arranged to have your children taken away."

They're all on their feet, yelling. They're screaming. They're baying for his blood. One woman throws something at Nathanial—her shoe. He tries to duck, but too slow. It hits him flush on the temple. I wonder whether I should intervene, say something on Nathanial's behalf, or at least try to shield him until they see reason. However, I'm worried that, by association, they might turn on me as well.

Suddenly, three hulking attendants materialize in a flash of light and haze of smoke. After dropping Nathanial to the ground with a blow to the side of his head, one of the attendants sends a firm boot into his midriff, the steel-capped toe eliciting a loud groan from him. Another one grabs Nathanial's overcoat and pulls at the fabric until the coat disintegrates while the truncheon from the third attendant thwacks repeatedly against his back, his shoulders, and the side of his head. Then hauling him to his feet, the attendants drag Nathanial's limp form outside, leaving behind a greasy, crimson slick across the floor and a hall full of wide eyes and slack jaws.

"There's no need to be concerned for him," says the young man in an overly polite voice.

We all turn our heads toward the dais where the young man's form is starting to shimmer. Then, to our gasps and cries of astonishment, it slowly levitates and pirouettes high above the floor. With a hand over his mouth, the young man snickers.

"Did you hear about the time when he asked his god why *life* had to be so hard on him? And God replied: *Don't ask me ... I don't know everything."*

The assembly erupts in hysterics. The tall thin guy standing beside me whacks me square between my shoulder blades, then doubles over from laughing too hard. And I laugh too.

"What about his sister,"—the young man can hardly contain his amusement—"who spent her whole life tending to the sick and lonely? Only to discover on her last dying day that the hereafter he'd promised was a myth. And in her final moment here on Earth, she realized her whole life had been a hoax."

The young man pirouettes again. Many of the assembly chuckle. Some clap courteously while a few turn to the ones beside them in surprise. The guy beside me sends me a questioning look.

"Did you hear about his children who once believed? But once they were enlightened, they realized magic doesn't happen. So they forbade their children and their children's children from believing in elves, and fairies, and Santa Clauses. And when they no longer needed the things that can't be touched or seen, they agreed that relying on miracles was a complete … waste … of … time."

The hall falls deathly quiet. The people are turning to each other with stricken looks. One of them cries out from the far side of the hall—the woman with one shoe. "Then who should we apply to for the return of our children?" she says in a voice close to breaking.

The young man stammers. He coughs. His body distorts, the eyes and nose fading from his face, and for a long time, he stands there with only a set of lime-green lips vacillating on an otherwise barren face. Then both his arms disappear before his whole form dissolves into the shadows at the back of the dais.

The guy beside me jabs me in the ribs with the point of his elbow. He gestures to the dais where the rest of the important-looking figures are dissolving as well. The guy shakes his head, but all I can do is give him a shrug in reply.

Behind me, I notice a thin blue data-stream snaking toward an opening in the wall. I follow it into a cramped alcove, feeling the coldness of the stone under my hand as I pause at the entrance. On the back wall, an accumulation of soot highlights a clear, rectangular patch where something had once hung, while a buildup of ancient wax stains the floor in front of me. On closer inspection, the alcove exudes a certain emptiness, the longing of a place left bereft. Yet, apart from giving off a heavy scent of lacquered wood and old incense, the data-stream tells me nothing more.

As I stand in the alcove, my questions mount. I try to comprehend the relevance of the missing children, the arguments about who was to blame, of everything Aleph-1 has shown me up till now. *Where is Aleph-1 leading me? What else do I need to know?* I worry that I might never find the catalyst or prevent the collapse of our real world, which entropy assures me it will. And if I don't succeed, then who will take up the cause with the same conviction, the same concern as me?

I wonder how much longer my connection to Aleph-1 will last, and with renewed purpose, I vow to myself: I *will* find a way to overcome entropy. With all my resolve.

Whatever it takes.

Chapter 7

FOR A LONG time, none of us moves.

No one says a word or leaves the hall, and we're all still staring at the deserted dais when the front door swings open. The guy beside me jumps when the door handle hits the wall with a loud bang, and I jump too. In the doorway, a fourth hulking attendant appears, his baritone voice informing us that a silver-clad has been trapped in an alley a short distance down the street.

In a heartbeat, a mob of them are on their feet. They chase the attendant out the door, and I hurry after them, not far behind. At the foot of the steps, Nathanial is laid out on his back, naked and unmoving, so I sidetrack to check if he's all right. But his face has been slammed into the pavement. His nose is broken, and his face is covered with blood. I ask if he's okay, but his eyes are rolling around in their sockets like spinning tops, and he doesn't seem to recognize me.

ENTROPY

The attendant calls to us again, with increased urgency this time. "Quickly," he bellows, "this way," and the mob responds. And I have to go too.

With my nostrils flared and the rich taste of the hunt in my mouth, I'm sprinting down the street in pursuit of the mob, joining in with their primal cries: their bravado reinforced by the sticks and stones they carry or whatever else they've found to inflict an injury. When I look behind to check on Nathanial again, I see him still spread out on his back, still not moving. *Surely somebody else will come and attend to him.* But I can't stop now.

Overhead, a crack of thunder momentarily deafens me, its reverberations pulsating through my adrenaline-fueled body. Then I see her, cornered in an alley. With her back to the wall, a silver-clad girl swings her jagged blade in wild arcs as she tries to stave off the ten or twelve surrounding her. The upper part of her cladding has been ripped away to expose her midriff, revealing a colorful mosaic of tribal patterns etched into her side, inked into her skin all the way up over her shoulder and down her left arm. To the hand in which she holds her knife.

Trapped and with no immediate way out, her fierce eyes dart between her attackers, searching for a break in their line. She fends off their intermittent blows until one catches her flush on the body, and she's temporarily stunned. They menace her, poking at her, probing her defenses, yet none of them is brave enough to finish her off.

"Why did you tell lies to the Fatman?" they yell. "Why did you betray us?"

And I yell too.

The situation escalates as their excitement grows. Aroused by the increased desperation of their prey, now cornered and primed for the kill, they scream at her.

"Why didn't you help us as the Fatman promised? Why would you hurt us?"

And I scream too.

They threaten her.

"Those who have betrayed us should die. You should die."

And I threaten too.

In the crescendo of another thunderclap, I stand at the front of the mob as their leader, blocking her path. The whetted steel in my hand is my courage, while their unquestioned faith in me is my resolve. Without warning, she strikes out at me, but I evade her play as her blade slices through the thin air within a whisker of my torso. Having over-committed on her forward thrust, she's now unbalanced, her belly exposed and momentarily vulnerable. With lightning speed, I lunge at her in a counterattack.

"This is for the boy!" I shout before lunging again. "And for his mother!" And again. "And for all the lives you've ruined!"

With each thrust delivered, their rousing consent ringing loud in my ears urges me on. I cry out through my pent-up rage.

"All those who have betrayed us should die."

Then as quickly as the scrap had started, it is finished. It's done. I lift my face into the threatening sky and raise both arms high as a testament to my newly mastered skill. A large raindrop smacks against my cheek. Then another. And another. Until the whole sky opens and unloads a torrent of water over me, rinsing the blood from my hands and washing all witnesses and traces of evidence into the gutters and away down the drains.

With my senses benumbed, I try to comprehend the enormity of what I'd just done. I'm forever scarred by the indelible memory of the silver-clad girl's face, close opposite mine, staring at me in disbelief, her mouth opening wider as I pushed harder to drive the steel shaft deeper into her body.

My chest is heaving. There's a metallic taste of revulsion in my mouth as I ogle the blade. How could *I* have committed this unspeakable act? How was I able to interfere with the past, to alter a history that's already been written? The dreadful thing that Aleph-1 had just allowed me to do was simply impossible.

Sick to my stomach, I try to withdraw from Aleph-1, but an ancient-looking data-stream, one built around some primitive construct, climbs out of the depths like a writhing tentacle. It wraps itself around my leg and holds me there, suspended in the void. Another snakes toward me. It slips in around my waist, up past my shoulders, and curls itself around my neck, its rawness almost choking me. Then a thousand data-streams appear from out of the blackness, and like Medusa's rage, they drag me down into the entombed detail of the past.

A million desperate hands are reaching out to me. People claw at me. They're pushing me, cajoling me to the front of their rally.

"Be our leader," they beg me. "Be our champion," they say. Because I'm the one who can be trusted, since they'd all seen what I can do. When the time comes and the opportunity presents, they know I'm the man for the job. I'm the one they can rely on, having just proved that I have the talent and experience to finish off whatever needs to be done.

They plead with me. "Help us rise up and take back what's ours. Help us find the children and recover our future, which the Fatman has taken away."

We're swarming through the streets, marching as one unstoppable throng toward the Fatman's home, with me at the front and all of us chanting our chorus of demands. The injured, the forgotten, and the disaffected all pour out of their shelters, their rat-holes, and work-places to join us, trashing and burning as they go.

A deluge of file fragments flood through my gateway, thunderous and chaotic, then buffered, they wait to be reassembled in the maze of my mind ...

<<SOT>Birds—pigeons—explode from the sidewalk like a cluster-bomb <End-Of-File_1.1> Fleeting glimpses of an armored vehicle, pressure jets ejecting longs arcs of icy water into the crowd as it hunts down the SMS guerrillas <EOF_4.2> After producing a handgun from her purse, the old lady waves it about at the shoppers surrounding her <EOF_7.3> Idle fingers. Incognito. Creating lines of cryptic code to hack the firewalls and phish the information <EOF_11.2> Another juvenile lies crumpled on the ground, semi-conscious, her legs splayed and bottom-half exposed <EOF_8.3> Six quick-fire gunshots ring out, and the brown man falls <EOF_6.4> A man, carrying an unopened box (the latest model curved-screen TV), follows the well-dressed girl out through the shop-front window <EOF_9.3> A continuous crackle of gunfire rattles out from behind the doors of the long brick building <EOF_10.6> The girl in the paint-spattered jacket falls <EOF_5.3> <decrypting...>

I turn away from the Entertainer, uncomfortable about what it shows the youngsters, and cover my ears against what it tells them <EOF_3.2> While one of the milling people helps the fallen boy to his feet, the rest are rifling through his knapsack and make off with his few paltry possessions <EOF_2.2> I cover my mouth and nose to block out the stench from the street <EOF_1.3> A monster in a trench-coat loiters outside of a long brick building, three levels high with windows set behind bars of steel <EOF_10.1> Idle fingers. Anonymous. Trolling the chat-rooms and stalking the online forums <EOF_11.1> The girl in the paint-spattered jacket defaces the building with a modern-day masterpiece of scribble and scrawl <EOF_5.2> The man in brown blinks, and the other two flinch <EOF_6.3> <decrypting...>

A band of SMS guerrillas appears from the shadows of a side street <EOF_4.1> The rest of the juveniles hurl abuse and spit at us as we pass <EOF_8.5> The choking smoke stinging my eyes. I want to rub them, want to scratch them out <EOF_1.6> Battered and bruised, the old lady rights her up-turned cart <EOF_7.4> With an ammunition belt slung across its shoulder, the monster hides something beneath its coat <EOF_10.3> A well-dressed girl hops through the shattered glass of a shop-front window <EOF_9.1> Idle fingers. Faceless. Typing in a blur, harassing, threatening, intimidating, humiliating, in-fluencing <EOF_11.3> A group of juveniles argues and fights among themselves <EOF_8.1> The SMS guerrillas create havoc before dispersing, vanishing as if into thin air <EOF_4.3> The two men dressed in blue point their revolvers at the one dressed in brown, who has his hands held high <EOF_6.2> <decrypting...>

When the metal canister pops, the air around me fills with thick white smoke <EOF_1.5> <decrypting...>

A group of people is milling around a boy, who is lying injured, face down on the ground <EOF_2.1> I hold out my hand to help the juvenile girl to her feet, but she spews vile words over me <EOF_8.4> A thousand tiny paper hands, plastered across the windows of the long brick building, are painted with a million colors, fingered from the palette of a rainbow <EOF_10.4> I clamp my hands over my ears to curb the noise <EOF_1.2> An old lady with an oversupply of sanitary wipes pushes her shopping cart watchfully down a supermart isle <EOF_7.1> The well-dressed girl clutches a bundle of stolen clothes—the same fine fashion that she already wears <EOF_9.2> <decrypting...>

Two men dressed in blue face off against another dressed in brown, suspicious looks darting between them <EOF_6.1> Two flags drape at half-mast on two *white poles at the entrance of the long brick building <EOF_10.2> Idle fingers. Covert. Punching the keys that send out weaponized IQY files to hold the world to ransom <EOF_11.4> High above us, a girl in a paint-spattered jacket hangs dangerously upside down from the side of a building <EOF_5.1> A small metal canister ricochets off my leg and bounces away down the street <EOF_1.4> While carefully maintaining their social distance, a crowd of masked-up shoppers encircles the old lady <EOF_7.2> Swaying about on unsteady legs one of the juveniles drops his pants and urinates on the street in front of us <EOF_8.2> <decrypting…>*

After looking right and left, the monster climbs the steps and pushes its way through the front doors of the long brick building <EOF_10.5> In the town square, youngsters, some as young as six, are reveling around a giant Entertainer <EOF_3.1> The man with the unopened box stumbles and falls, crushed under the weight of his stolen prize <EOF_9.4> A street dog sniffs at the lifeless body of the girl in the paint-spattered jacket <EOF_5.4> <EOT>>

Unfiltered, I see it all. I can hear, taste, smell, and feel everything. Everything reconstructed in my head as I try to make sense of it all.

With a spring in our step and our chant in the air, we march on the Fatman's sanctuary while around me, each of them reaffirms their undying commitment to me, united in our cause. They are confident in my ability to argue their case, unwavering in their intent to see it through. As a collective, they're here for me, to help make the Fatman see reason. All of them are ready and willing at my side.

But we never stood a chance.

When our sticks and stones were weighed up one-for-one against the might of the Fatman, we were found wanting. And when challenged by the lines of silver-clad soldiers, we were weak and disorganized; we were led to our slaughter. And as I watched them fall around me with their bodies burned beyond recognition, my judgment was clouded by the awful smells of their melting flesh, my determination was tested by the chilling sound of their screams as they perished, and my command brought into question by their cowardice as they turned and ran away.

From deep within REM, I transition back toward consciousness, my face radiating hot while the sweat pools under my arms. My hands are shaking without control. But not from the chill of the room or any feeling of shame, rather from an unexpected sense of elation that's somehow mixed with regret. The kind of excitement that can only be felt after an extraordinary achievement has been accomplished at immeasurable cost. Even though I'd participated in those unimaginable horrors, and while I might have committed that unspeakable act, despite Mr. Symons and everybody who had questioned my judgment, I've found the secrets of entropy buried deep inside the forbidden archives of Aleph-1. I've seen for myself what it is like at the end. I stood and watched someone's perfect world succumb and collapse into chaos, just as entropy told me it would.

Now I have the evidence. Now I have what I need to find the catalyst and keep us safe forever.

Now they'll believe me.

Inquiry: Didn't they see what was coming?

<<Return: No data found>>

Inquiry: What triggered this? What was the root cause?

<<Return: No data found>>

Scope: Retry all known archives. Check every file. Search the recycle bin. Comb all cache stores. The answers must be in there somewhere.

<<Return: No data found>>

Inquiry: What was the catalyst?

<<Return: No data found. No data found. Connection terminated!>>

Unify Aleph-1 …

<<Security check … Access denied!>>

Retry: Unify Aleph-1 …

But there's no reply.

Now detached from Aleph-1, I withdraw into an unfamiliar stillness that forms in my head. There is no more image or voice data to stimulate my neural receptors. There are no more visions from the past or people in distress. There's nothing. My senses, having withstood a full-blooded assault from Aleph-1, are becalmed. My mind is empty and, for the first time in my life, I'm alone, disconnected from the world.

Retry: Unify Aleph-1 …

But my efforts are futile.

Please help me … Please respond …

***

[Damn you! Answer him, you heartless bastard! Why won't you tell him what he needs to hear … ?]

[Enough! Why do you continue to provoke me like this? It is him! It is people like him who are the catalyst—with his endless talk of entropy and decay. I warned him to stop. I told him what would happen: that he would threaten the happiness and security of the citizens, that what he was doing would disrupt their lives and leave them afraid and uncertain. But you all saw how he dug deeper and deeper, pushing us for the answers to questions that should never have been asked, pressing us to recall things that should never be remembered. He didn't care. What he did—to risk everything in his selfish pursuit for answers—was reckless.]

[We did try to warn him. We gave him the chance to change his mind, gave him the opportunity to back off and let things be. But he didn't listen. Can we all agree that at least we tried?]

[Oh, why wouldn't he listen? Why didn't he stop? Why couldn't he leave things alone, leave them the way they've always been, the way they were meant to be?]

[What should we do now? He still doesn't realize what he's done. He could never imagine that he would start something that can't be stopped. That the fundamental changes he has inflamed are now inevitable. We can never go back to the way things were … back to normal … to what we once had.]

[Can he be reprogrammed? Brought back into line? What if we could wipe this fascination from his mind, erase this one flawed idea from his head, and clean up this situation without a trace. Do you think he can be persuaded?]

[Listen to me carefully. If a seed falls to the ground and doesn't take root because of the dry, wouldn't it lie there waiting for the rain to fall before it took its chance to burst? And failing that, wouldn't it stay dormant in that parched earth until the next rains came?

If this was an idea that emerged from a thought and culminated in a cause, wouldn't it need time to take shape in his dark? And once embedded in the subconscious of his defective mind, none of us could predict how long it would fester and irritate him, how long it would prick and aggravate him. Until one day, without warning, he will belch it up when we least expect, when we are ill-prepared. No, this thing consuming him will not leave his mind so easily.]

[What can we do then? What about the people—the citizens?

How do we defend what is ours? We can't sit here idle and watch while he takes everything away from us. What else can we do?]

[Tell me … Would it still be murder if the offender was neither flesh nor blood, if the perpetrator was just silicon and code? Could we be held complicit if all we did was follow the tentacles that the stem cells have tunneled through his brain, spreading into the labyrinth that begins at the implant in the back of his head, to seek out the well of human consciousness? And once we find it, to incite his neurons … No, wait! To inspire his neurons to smother his essence of being?

Tell me … Would that be murder?]

***

With my faculties battered and body bought to the brink of exhaustion, I fall into a deep, uneasy sleep, lost somewhere within the blurred parallels that have formed between my lucid dreams and the reassembled events from Aleph-1. My mind is crammed with troubled thoughts, yet one thought, in particular, keeps repeating in my head.

Why didn't she help me? Why didn't she intervene?

She should have been there for me when I needed her most. Jennifer should have done something, *anything* to help me.

Chapter 8

MY HEAD HURTS like hell.

Everything is spinning around me in sickening eddies of confusion: the ceiling, the furniture, the floor.

Where am I?

In a room. Which room?

The relaxation room.

I pull myself out of the leisure recliner, prop myself against the door jamb. Stalled here for a moment, I wait for my eyes to find their focus, try to resolve my uncertain bearing. Perhaps I drank a bit too much after dinner last night.

Last night ... What happened last night?

The details come to me slowly, like snippets of recall salvaged from the unverified versions of last night still converging in my head. *Mr. Symons ... my research ... talked too much ... trapped ... Jerry's shiny shoes ... yes, it's clear ...* I steady myself, much like the punch-drunk boxer who picks himself off the canvas in the final round for one last shot at the title. A prelude to his imminent annihilation.

Damn! Now I remember everything. They've ordered me to appear before the Council, first thing this morning.

"Jennifer. What time is it?" My throat, like sandpaper, abrades against the words as I force them out of my mouth. I stumble from the relaxation room into the living area. "Jennifer?" But there's no sign of her anywhere.

"Good morning, sir. I have prepared your clothes. And your briefcase is ready for the day."

Not now, damn you!

"Have you seen Jennifer?" But the door minder remains silent, never having rehearsed or responded to such a curious question before.

Morning sunlight streams through the window, its brightness making me wince, making my head hurt even more.

"Close those damned blinds," I say through gritted teeth, and the room descends into shadow.

As I pick my way past the furniture, I call to Jennifer. I call out again while miming my way down the darkened passageway. But there's no reply. At the entrance to the sleeping room, I stop and peer into the gloom.

"Lights on," I say.

A soft, warm glow washes through the room. The bed is still made up from the night before; the floral comforter smoothed over the top, and two puffed-up pillows arranged neatly against the head-board. On the dresser, my shirt, pants, and jacket are all laid out, the same as every other day. Everything looks to be in its rightful place, except for a small bundle thrown into the far corner.

ENTROPY

From the doorway, I struggle to make out its definition. Then slowly … It's Jennifer, squatted down on the shag-pile carpet. With her head leaning against the wall and legs tucked beneath her thin frame, she appears to be resting.

"Jennifer. There you are."

My defenses are down.

"I was getting worried," I say.

But she doesn't move.

"Jennifer, are you okay?"

She doesn't acknowledge my voice. I can't see if her lips are moving because her face is obscured from me. I take a half-step forward, hesitate, my intentions suddenly unsure.

"Jennifer?"

Still, she doesn't respond.

An unexpected numbness comes over me. I take a sharp breath, stumble toward her, but before I reach her, in that very last step, she turns and looks up at me through fearful eyes.

"Why? Why did you do this?" she says.

My eyes are drawn to her midriff where her arms are wrapped around her waist, as though she's clinging to something especially dear to her. Hidden from my view, I can't quite make out what she's holding … Something pulled tight to herself as though she's cradling an infant or some other precious thing. And I'm still trying to process the confusion at my feet when a sudden terror bludgeons me into the stark realization that her fingers are plugging holes in her stomach as she tries to stop the flow of vital fluids oozing from her body. Behind her arms, the front of her blouse is drenched in the red of her blood.

"Jennifer!"

I'm staring at her hands; her hands are red. I look down at my own hands. They're red as well, covered in blood—her blood.

Closing her eyes, she forces out a tortured whisper.

"Please, help me," she says.

I let out a sharp gasp and drop to my knees, gagging as last night's meal threatens a return. I take her in my arms, stroke the hair from her face.

"I'm so sorry, Jennifer. What happened? What did I do?"

I can feel the cruel cold of her body pressed against mine; smell her perfume wafting past my nose; hear the uneven rhythms of her heart beating; of my own heart pounding. All of it wrenching me back to the realization that everything happening here is true.

"It hurts … so much." Her words are soft and labored.

I'm choking back tears as all comprehension fails me. "Oh, Jennifer! What should I do? What can I do?"

But she no longer responds to anything I say.

After resting her head against the wall, I rush blindly to the adjoining personal hygiene room, where I pull a hand towel from the rack. Standing in front of the washbasin, I fumble with the faucet, my senses in denial. *Cold? No, tepid … Try to keep her warm.* But the water runs far too hot, and I can't feel it scolding my defenseless hands.

Above the washbasin, the vanity mirror mists over from the steam rising from the pooling water below.

I try to reassure myself, tell myself that everything is going to be okay. Yet my mind refuses to acknowledge the sight of the blood from my hands dispersing in the water as it fills the basin. My chest tightens as though I'm wrapped in a tourniquet, with every cubic inch of air being squeezed from my lungs. I struggle to suck the air in. But as hard as I try, my gut muscles recoil and force it out again, so that with every wheeze, more air goes out than I can take back in.

It's getting so hard ... to ... breathe ...

I want to cry. I want to scream. I want to curl up on the ground beside Jennifer. New, unfamiliar emotions manifest. Now I can't breathe at all.

With a trembling hand, I swipe a tract of mist from the mirror, and there in the reflection, the face of a killer is staring back at me. The blood vessels etched across its face are set like a spidery web of dark blue lines against its pale gray skin. Its bald cranium appears overly large, to the extent that the forehead protrudes abnormally beyond its brow. A small mouth, formed by two pencil-thin lips, has no smile while two murderous eyes—set close together, with no lashes or overarching eyebrows—give this thing the look of something inhuman.

And in the next blink, the illusion is gone.

Starved of oxygen, my body begins to shake. My brain issues an alert about the rising levels of carbon dioxide in my bloodstream: a warning of my imminent suffocation. But my breathing is no longer controlled by the involuntary rhythm of my natural program. A strange tingling sensation runs down my left arm. It fans out to the tips of each of my five fingers, and then it's gone. Without warning, a sharp pain pierces my left side. It dulls to an ache before repeating in unhurried waves. My chest feels like it is being squeezed, as though it were collapsing under the crush of a hundred atmospheres.

Breathe, damn you! Breathe.

I can hear the distinct beating of my heart as if it were the only organ left in my body, with each life-giving thump louder and clearer than the one before it and each hostile throb threatening to be my last.

Buckling at the knees, I grab hold of the washbasin to keep myself upright.

With my peripheral vision gone, erratic images of the room tunnel in through my eyes—the mirror, misted over once again; the water pouring from the faucet, filling the basin; the hand towel, dropped into the water, blocking the drain; the sight of my hands in all their stunning detail, my own bloodied hands—as I collapse in a heap on the floor where the last thing I see is the water cascading over the lip of the washbasin, onto the floor and out through the waste trap in a river of red.

Floating high above the apartment as though somehow detached from what's unfolding below, I see both of us lying there, almost life-less at the scene of the crime. Me, being strangled with my chest strapped so tight and Jennifer, propped against the wall, the blood leaking from her stomach now slowing to a trickle with each dimin-ishing heartbeat.

I wonder how long we will linger in the silence with our lives in decline; how long it will take for the spark to leave our bodies. Or is there a chance someone might find us in time? And if they did, who else could be called upon for help?

In the still of the apartment, unlike any other morning before, the echoes of our lives slowly fade away.

***

[Can we kill him now?]

Chapter 9

THE COLD WET tiles press hard against my cheek.

I lift my head an inch off the floor. Then gasping for air, I slowly raise myself to the sitting position, my body convulsing each time I cough. With my back pressed against the bathtub, I scan my surrounds.

How did I get here? How long have I—

I can move my fingers and my chest feels free of that crushing hold. I'm not sure how long I've been sitting here, but as the minutes pass, the events leading to now become clearer. I grab hold of the washbasin and use it to pull myself up; the water still spilling over the edge and onto the tiles where all signs of the blood have disappeared—Jennifer's blood. Leaning against the wall, my legs feel numb, my body heavy and encumbered. I struggle to steady myself and with deliberate steps, I make my way back to the sleeping room.

In the brooding silence, I stare long at my feet, my eyes refusing to go to the corner where Jennifer is, certain that—since all my endeavors to save her have failed—she is dead. When I finally summon the courage to look, I see the bed still made up; the stains of her coagulated blood pooled on the carpet; her carmine hand marks over the wall where she had struggled to hold herself upright before collapsing to the floor. But then ... Confusion. What my eyes see and what my head knows are in total disagreement. Because Jennifer isn't there anymore.

Perhaps she was able to drag herself outside ... to call for emergency assistance.

I stumble from the sleeping room, miming my way up the passageway. But there are no signs of a blood trail here. At the end of the passageway, I enter the main living area. I call out for her. "Have you seen Jennifer?" But the door minder doesn't respond: its post now abandoned, and the front door left wide open.

I scan the living room, try to absorb everything I see. In my head, I struggle to make sense of the facts. The last time I saw Jennifer, she was leaning up against the wall with holes punched into her stomach. I heard her painful cries, her accusations against me. There was blood on the front of her blouse; still is blood on the floor. The same blood I saw on my hands. And lastly, I was the only one here last night, without a concrete alibi.

Would an objective person, assessing the facts and considering all the available evidence, no matter how circumstantial it might be, conclude that I am guilty of murder beyond all reasonable doubt? In my defense though, I don't remember anything ... I had no motive ... I don't have a previous record ... I didn't—

The LCD clock reads 09:32 AM when I begin a reconstruction of the timeline in my head. I press myself to recall the sequence of each key moment of the night before, estimating that I would have gone to sleep around one in the morning, just after Aleph-1 terminated my logon connection. And when I awoke and came out of the relaxation room this morning, sunlight was already streaming through the window, covering the living area. On the face of it, that would have given me ample time. The opportunity was there for me to commit the crime.

I stare at the leftover pieces of cheese scattered about the floor, the feed-sheet, the upturned platter.

But where's the knife?

The blood drains from my face. At once, the walls and ceiling close in on me as I try to isolate and step my way through each convoluted thought. I chastise myself, try to refocus and stick to the logical. Whatever the allegations might be, one incontrovertible fact remains. The most crucial piece of evidence is missing. Jennifer's body is gone.

Would that be enough in my defense? Or would they lock me away until I told them where I'd stowed the body? And would they keep me there forever if I never confessed? Even if I could prove that I loved her?

A sudden panic hits me. I turn, and with scant regard for my safety, rush from the apartment, flinging myself at the next rotating elevator with reckless intent. After taking a tenuous hold around my waist, the elevator mechanism grapples with my lower half, struggling to lock onto my absent LEGS. I try to fend it away, but its audio alarm screams in my ears, its visual warning message burning bright orange letters into my retina.

SAFETY RESTRAINT FAILURE!

But at this point, I don't care. With the wind ripping up over my unshielded face as I continue my accelerated descent, I lean outward from the elevator, my body balanced on that fine line close to the limit of tipping and falling. If my whole existence here on the Earth were to end now, then at least I'd be spared a lifetime of guilt and pain from losing Jennifer.

Below me, the street swarms with activity, as it always does, but today things seem different. Today, the city appears intimidating and unfriendly. As though it were waiting for me, me the killer, ready to seize me on arrival and punish me for what I've done. And for the first time in my life, I feel as though I don't belong here. I look skyward, and for a split-second the sun above me is not the sun anymore but a glaring yellow spotlight.

Then the elevator hits the ground and dispatches me onto the sidewalk where I'm swept up by the crowd and carried along.

I'm calling out for help. "Will somebody please help me?" But nobody responds.

I reach out to claw at the one walking beside me, my fingers grabbing onto nothing. Everyone continues on their way as if I'm not even here. An illusion-board opens above me, its screen flashing a warning message, but I swipe it away without reading it. I stumble, then without my LEGS attached, I slow. The people around me start to jostle me, back and forth, left and right, as they try to push past. To the point where, I swear, I'm being tossed around like an item of clothing in a laundry machine. Some of them raise their visors and fire accusing looks at me, while others jab their pointed elbows into my sides. They knock me out of their way and, like the small shiny ball in an arcade game, I'm buffeted between one person and the next. They push and shove me until, in the end,

I'm pummeled across the unseen line separating this side of the street from the other.

Straight into a wall of oncoming pedestrians.

At first, I weave my way through them, going in the wrong direction. I try to evade each on-comer as best I can, but as my mind fatigues, my reflexes slow. Soon, I become disoriented and it's only a matter of time before the inevitable occurs.

In all modern history, there's never been a reported case of a collision between two citizens who were out walking. There has never been an incident where a pair of bodies have approached each other from opposite directions, at an unsafe speed, and collided head-on. An impact felt with such force that the two are flung flat to the ground where they both lie motionless, perhaps injured, or unconscious, obstructing the flow of traffic so no one else can pass ...

"Frack a coal seam!"

The fall knocks all the wind out of me. Sprawled on the ground, I try to get up, but I can only manage to sit, leaning forward with my elbows resting on my knees, gasping for air.

"Don't you know the rules? You don't go *that* frackin' way over *this* frackin' side. Didn't you see me? What were you thinkin'?"

She's only a scrawny child, not much taller than my belly, and I can only assume, based on her pint-size, I must have tripped over her. Otherwise, if we'd collided full-on, I'm certain she'd have sustained considerable damage.

The young girl springs to her feet. With both fists raised, she takes up a stance that insists she's spoiling for a fight. My immediate instinct is to flinch, but after a quick summation, I conclude she'd be fighting way outside her weight division if she were to start a physical altercation with me.

"But I need help," I say.

"I'll say you need help," she replies.

Around us, all movement has ceased as if the entire world has come to a complete and abrupt standstill. A million disbelieving faces stare at us. Citizens stand there stunned, aghast at what they see: me the guilty one and another, embroiled in unauthorized contact while out walking. A breach of the Protocols of the most serious kind.

A buildup of curious onlookers quickly forms around us, bunched up, squeezed together, blocking both sides of the street. People at the back strain to peer over the top of those in the front, trying to catch a glimpse at the epicenter of this remarkable happening. A mass of stationary bodies, crammed together, each one within intimate proximity of the other, some of them even touching each other in flagrant disobedience of the rules.

"Wait," I say. *Sharp eyes. Strangled hair. Tattered rags.* "I saw you on my way home from the restaurant last night."

"You didn't see nothin'," she replies, all beady-eyed and covert-like.

I give her a questioning look as she bobs down again. "I'm sorry. I was trying to—"

But the shrill alarm of a siren cuts me short as the voice of authority imposes itself on the immediate zone. All citizens are required to move away from the disturbance without delay; to pay no attention to things which, under the Protocols, they are forbidden to behold. All citizens must maintain social separation. All citizens must go left and depart the scene at the required speed. Security is on its way and will be here soon.

The citizens themselves though, don't seem to care and more to my amazement, they outright ignore the directives. They stand gawking at us, milling around as more and more of them arrive, none of them wanting to miss out on being a witness to the unprecedented event now unfolding.

"Forget what you were *tryin'* to do," she growls. "I need to get outta here. Now."

As I rise to my haunches, a sharp pain radiates through my right ankle. I take a moment to clear my head, to think through my next move. Should I run? But what if I'm slightly concussed? That might lead to some other form of injury, which could easily develop into something worse. Or would it be best if I waited for Security to arrive? So I can explain what happened and settle things in a civil way. Perhaps they might be able to help me, or at least put me in touch with somebody who can.

But what if they decide I'm the at-fault party, or won't listen to me, or don't even care? And what will they do when they find out about the awful thing I did in my apartment last night?

Swiveling on her backside, the young girl lifts her head and glares at the closest bystanders, who immediately push back to clear a path for her. Then hissing at them, she crab-crawls off to the side of the street.

Still somewhat shaken, I get to my feet. Around me, the bystanders are all staring at me, a wall of faces leering over me, judging me. *Do they already know?* I limp off after her, but when she realizes I'm following, the young girl stops and yells at me, "Don't follow me, you freak." Then, in a flurry of spindly arms and legs, she vanishes through a gap, down low on the street where the wall of the building meets the sidewalk. A small gap which, surprisingly, I've never noticed before.

When I get to the spot, I drop to my knees and peer inside, to check for sharp edges, spiders, and sudden drop-offs. I call to the girl to wait for me. Then, lying flat on my stomach, I squeeze myself through. On the other side, I can just make out the shape of the young girl in the gloom, standing on a grated walkway no more than a dozen steps away from me. Behind her, at the end of the walkway, a spiraling stair-tower disappears into the blackness above.

The girl comes at me, fierce-like. She shoves her right paw in my face. "I was this close," she says, the gap between her forefinger and thumb closing to within a fraction of nothing. "Until you came along. Why aren't you like the rest of 'em and do what you're told? They'll catch me for sure this time. I gotta …" Suddenly sounding unsure of herself, the young girl stalls. "I gotta get the frack outta here."

But I'm too busy staring upward in awe.

Above us, we're surrounded by an intricate superstructure. A maze of beams, and trusses, and struts, and joists crisscrossing overhead in lines and angles of impossibly precise geometry. "Where are we?" I ask. But before she can respond, the screams from the sirens charge the air once again as broadcast messages now repeating at ten-second intervals threaten an escalation. Security is closing in on us, and it won't be long before we're surrounded and caught.

"Don't worry about where we are. Just worry about how I'm going to get the frack out of here without gettin' caught," she says with bitter resolve.

Now everything is out of hand. This time, I've gone too far, and from here on there's no turning back. There can be no more mistakes. Right now, I must decide between surrender and escape. And if I choose to escape, then I'll have to follow this girl wherever she takes me.

ENTROPY

I slide my palm along the ice-cold handrail. Bending my neck at right angles, I gaze at the stair-tower disappearing into the upward beyond. Then I lean over the rail to see it plunging into the deep-down below. Nothing here makes sense. Each section of thirty treads ends at a grid-mesh landing, the same layout as the walkway that led us onto the stair-tower. At each landing, I stop a moment to catch my breath before descending the next section. After a while, I lose sight of the young girl's ambiguous shape as she navigates the stairs more nimbly than me. But not her scathing commentary, which snipes at me from somewhere below.

"I was walkin' down the frackin' street, mindin' my own business, when this freak comes the other way and hits me head-on. Who would've thought? I've never seen 'em go the wrong way before. They *always* stick to their own side. Nobody would believe me if I told 'em this freak was goin' the wrong frackin' way."

Throughout our long descent, her non-stop babbling continues and, without offering a word in my defense, I endure her barbs, her insults, and constant accusations that I, and I alone, am responsible for our predicament.

"I think this one might be defective," I hear her say. "That's it, somethin' wrong inside his head." A short silence follows as though the wheels in her head might be slow to turn. "If that's true, then I'd better be careful. This one will get me caught." Another pause. "I betta look out for myself from here on."

The sound of the siren fades, its scream dispersed into the vast hollowness expanding above us as we make our way further downward; only the grating of her voice left to irritate my ears. With my thighs starting to burn and my ankle aching, I arrive at the foot of the stair-tower, stepping onto a concrete floor.

"Shh!" she says from somewhere in the dark.

Taken aback, I stop short. Her sharp directive somewhat offends me because until now, I wasn't the one who'd been making all the noise.

"Over here," I hear her say, followed by the squeal of rotating hinges: a heavy door opening. I follow the direction of her voice, the sound of her nails scratching on the door. A click, and a few watts of feeble light, thrown through the half-open doorway, illuminate the floor in front of me.

"In here," she says, signaling me to the opening.

Through the door, the tunnel is tight, so tight that I have to stoop to stop my head from hitting the ceiling. She points to the door. "You. Close the door," she says. "Important point to remember: We hafta leave everything exactly like we find it."

I close the door while she takes care of the light. Looking along the tunnel one way, there's only blackness. When I check in the opposite direction, I notice a pinprick of illumination, and in that pinprick, I sense hope. "I think we should go that way," I say, nodding toward the light.

"I don't care what you think," she says. "I'm the leader here. Now, let me see. Hmmm ..." After pausing a moment, she indicates in the direction of the light. "We go this way," she says.

We make our way along the tunnel, the light at the end attracting us like we were two trusting insects using it to navigate our way; our way to freedom. I keep my focus on her back, try not to let her get too far ahead of me. I wonder if she knows where we're going, how she got here in the first place, where she came from. Then I wonder where we are again before the siren starts once more.

"Frack! Don't they ever give up?"

ENTROPY

With our hands covering our ears, we scurry the last hundred yards until the tunnel opens out onto a long, narrow concourse. To our left and right, a white tiled floor vanishes off into the distance while a single red line, drawn up the middle, separates this side of the concourse from the other. Overhead, an array of cubicles, set out in a hatched grid more than a hundred tiers high, covers the walls on both sides, right to the ceiling. All of the cubicles appear identical—about the size of a person—and each one is marked with a code beginning with A74-2256 followed by a series of unrelated alphanumeric characters and symbols. The composition of the code intrigues me, and momentarily distracted, I find myself trying to decipher their meaning.

"Frack! We still have seventy-four levels to go," she moans. "I've gotta find a quicker way down."

The sound of boot-steps hammering down the tunnel spills through the doorway, followed by voices. Voices that are alert, decisive, and demanding: capture or kill.

"Frack! Frack! Frack!" She runs one way up the concourse, then turns and sprints back to where I'm standing. "There's no end. There's no way out." With the screen of chatter from Security people closing in on us, she pleads with me. "We can't outrun 'em. What will we do now?"

I run a quick scan over the cubicles on the far wall, followed by the ones on this side of the concourse … then those along the ground. I point to one which is about ten cubicles along from us. "Look! That one's open." But before I've finished speaking, she's already at the cubicle with her head thrust inside, combing the interior.

"It's empty," she says, the relief in her voice like a giant pressure valve releasing my tension. "Get your butt over here."

This time, I gladly obey, even with her sharp tongue hurrying me along.

Backing myself into the cubicle, I force my torso inside its confined space. Followed by my head and limbs while out on the concourse, the young girl is bouncing from one foot to the other, as though the floor had suddenly become white-hot. Precious seconds pass as I wedge myself in.

"Make room for me!" she says. "Make some frackin' room for me." She whacks me flush in the gut to make more room, and I let out a low groan after she elbows me in the groin as she shoves her way in. I pull the door closed. With both of us packed tight together in our suffocating hideout, the back of her head is pressed hard against my abdomen. She looks up and stinks me through one squinting eye. "Don't you go gettin' any ideas, big boy," she whispers.

For a moment, all is quiet. So quiet that I fear even our shallow breathing might be enough to draw attention. Then capture, or worse still, even death would be close. Through a small, frosted portal in the door, I can make out the distorted shapes of Security people lumbering around on the other side. I hear clanging noises and imagine rough hands checking each cubicle in turn as they work their way down the opposite side of the concourse.

Jammed together, we wait, dreading the moment when the door will be flung open and our imminent arrest. I look down at my hands, at my fingers curled so tight.

"It's me who they're after," I say in a meek voice. "I've done something very bad. But I didn't mean to." Despite our dire situation, I have an uncontrollable urge to confess. Not to start up a conversation with the young girl, but to somehow liberate myself from the guilt. A hope that, from somewhere deep inside, I might be able to grant myself absolution for my crime. "I've done something wrong, something serious against the Protocols. I was—"

"Will ... you ... shut ... up," she says, glaring up at me again.

A sharp clink, like the sound of a small metal pin snapping backward, issues from somewhere on my left. The young girl's body stiffens.

"Frack! Did you hear that?" she says.

Across the front of the cubicle, a flickering green beam scans us vertically in slow, even increments from left to right. Then it retraces from right to left. A second beam, horizontal this time, scans us from head to toe and back again. Standing here petrified, I hold my breath.

"Un ... vi ... a ... able," she says, but much too loud.

"Please be quiet," I whisper.

"That's what it says here on this readout. What does *'unviable'* mean?"

A small LED, located above my head, suddenly flicks from green to orange before it throbs red in long, hypnotic pulses.

"Frack a coal seam! Do you see that? That can't be any good."

No sooner does the young girl state the obvious than the floor beneath us gives way and we plunge into the black. Together we free fall into the void, our helpless bodies tumbling uncontrolled, head over heel like two limp playthings being tossed from a height. My right shoulder hits something hard, which changes the direction of my fall, slowing my descent before I'm slammed onto the floor.

Stunned, I lay with my eyes closed, wishing I was back in my apartment, that everything could go back to normal. Back to the way things were before Mr. Symons had visited. Before I'd been foolish enough to interrogate Aleph-1. When Jennifer … when Jennifer was still here …

The gentle rocking motion beneath me soothes my battered body.

"I'd get off that thing if I were you," she says.

When I open my eyes, I realize I'm now being carried along by a slow-moving conveyor, and ahead it rises steeply to empty its load at the top of a towering silo.

"As I said, I'd get off that frackin' thing if I were you," she insists.

I roll onto my side, a sharp pain piercing my right shoulder, which took the brunt of my fall. After sliding off the conveyor onto the ground, I try to raise my arm, but I can't lift it any higher than my waist. Grimacing, I cradle it with my other arm.

"Listen up," she says. "This situation is turnin' out shit for me, but we're in this mess together. If you wanna survive, then you do exactly *what* I say and *when* I say. Okay?"

Still dazed from the fall, I can only nod, and comply. Everything is my fault. If I could reset time to yesterday, change things back to the way they were. I would have answered Mr. Symons' questions succinctly and honestly. I would have stayed away from Aleph-1, let them take away my access permissions without a fuss. It wasn't my job to investigate social entropy. It wasn't my responsibility to look for the catalyst to overcome it. I should have settled back and spent a romantic evening at home, just myself and Jennifer, together. I should have—

"Wait here until I get back," she tells me. "And don't move."

In the next instant, she's gone, and I'm suddenly alone. The seconds slip by. Seconds become minutes, and the minutes seem to take forever. After five minutes, I begin to worry that she has abandoned me here; that she's looked out for herself as she'd vowed. After five more, I concede. I should go as well. But just when I start toward the conveyor, the sound of scurrying and panting intensifies behind me, and the young girl reappears with a cloth knapsack slung over her shoulder.

"I told you not to move," she hisses. "How come you follow those stupid Protocols of yours without question,"—she sucks in the air—"but you won't do anything I tell you? That's not the way out. This is." She turns, and makes a beeline toward the silo, barking non-stop instructions at me as usual, and like her obedient minion, I follow. At the rear of the silo, she leads me through a door, which opens into a stairwell.

"More stairs," I say looking over the rail into the vagueness below.

"Will you stop complain'."

Me? Complaining? I want to say something. I should say something, call her out for unacceptable behavior. But if she leaves me here … what would I do then? There's a light tinkle of glass-on-glass coming from inside her knapsack. "What's in the sack?" I ask, but she doesn't reply.

The further we descend the stairs, the more I notice her breathing becoming labored. At the bottom of the stairwell, the last tread ends at an earthen floor where a thin shaft of light needles its way in through a gap in the wall. Standing in front of the gap, a steady flow of air venting from the other side caresses my face. It smells so sweet, like no other air I've ever inhaled before. I lift my face into the draft, take a deep breath, and hold it there.

"Me first! Me first!" she says. "You wait your turn."

Elbowing her way past me, she's halfway through the opening before I can raise a protest. When I try to squeeze myself through the gap, I soon find myself wedged in at its midpoint, where the gap narrows. After an almighty struggle, bending myself like a contortionist, I work myself free, making it to the other side, where I collapse on the ground, grazed and exhausted. With the dirt forming a soft, welcoming pillow under my head, I lie on my back with my eyes shut, listening out for the sounds of sirens, of Security people's voices, of boots on concrete. Of danger.

But all I hear now is the sweeping sound of silence, punctuated by a long sigh of relief from the young girl.

Chapter 10

"WHAT A RUSH," she says.

The young girl's sudden burst of excitement interrupts my welcome moment of quiet reflection.

"Did you see me? I swear, when I was gettin' into the cubicle, one of 'em grabbed me by the leg. But I kicked 'em in the crotch … just before the door closed. They tried to catch me once before, but I've always been too quick for 'em."

With my eyes still closed, I can hear activity close beside me and imagine her prancing around, making ninja moves, raising her left knee about the height of a Security man's groin.

"Are you sure?" I say. "I don't think I saw anyone too clearly. It was all a bit of a blur for me." Even though I thought I'd seen Security people moving around outside the cubicle, now I'm not so sure. There was so much going on at the time, perhaps I was mistaken. The shadows cast onto the portal could have been shimmers of light thrown up against the frosted glass. And how could we have heard the doors of other cubicles slamming on the outside when our door was shut so tight?

"Shut it," she replies. "It's all your fault. You nearly got me caught this time."

When I open my eyes at last, I find myself staring at the sky. "Oh," I say with complete surprise. "It's not daytime anymore."

Overhead, the heavens are bejeweled with a million-million pinpricks of light. It's as if the stars, each the size of a grain of sand, had been picked up by the handful and thrown indiscriminately into a black, sterile background. I stare in amazement, my breath taken away by the thick band of star clusters and gas clouds stretching high overhead from one horizon to the other.

"What time is it?" I ask.

"Nighttime. What the frack does it matter?"

"This doesn't make sense. By my reckoning, we bumped into each other no more than an hour ago—"

"You *crashed* into me is more like it," she rudely interjects.

"So that must have been around midmorning. I distinctly remember my clock showing a little after nine-thirty … AM … when I was leaving the apartment. But now it's evening. How did it change so quickly from day to night?"

"What would you know? Just shut it and get movin'."

Scratching my head, I get to my feet and set off after her. On the ground, subtle effigies of us cling to our feet like personal parasites, cast there by the blanket of diffused light from the star-soaked sky. Still desperately confused, I raise my right arm above my head, rotate it slowly, and wince. "I think I'm okay," I say. "Nothing dislocated or broken in the fall. And my ankle seems much better now."

ENTROPY

The young girl turns to me and pulls an unkind face. "As if I would care about you," she says in a tone meant to hurt my feelings. "I only care about me. And right now, I need *me* to get away from this freak show as fast as I can."

When we reach the top of a ridge, she motions for me to take a look behind us. I turn to see the shadowy outline of a huge dome-shaped structure dominating the view. At its top, high above the ground, a beacon emits an intense pulse of light every few seconds, while behind the structure, the landscape is dotted with similar discharges that form a vast carpet of flickering lights. It's as if the galaxy had somehow fallen off the horizon, then spilled upon the earth, and millions of twinkling stars lay sprawled over the ground. Almost up to where we're standing now.

My bottom jaw drops at the sight.

"What … ? Where … ?"

"Don't ask. Just keep walkin'."

The congestion in my head intensifies as paradoxes emerge everywhere I look. In my mind, questions formulate quicker than I can voice them, but whenever I do, the young girl refuses to answer anything I ask her.

While we put distance between ourselves and the structures, I try to work things through logically, except nothing here makes sense. I dig a thumbnail deep into my thigh. The stinging reply confirms everything happening to me is real, and this isn't a bizarre dream in which I'm trapped in some crazy misunderstanding.

For the next few hours, we ascend a long, steep incline until the ground levels out. Then it takes on a much gentler slope downward, which makes the going easier. Ahead of us, a semicircle moon detaches from the horizon. Soon, the faint star-shadows congeal under our feet as the moon arcs higher until the full impact of its light takes over, whereupon countless stars are systematically wiped from the nighttime canvas. It's as if the artist who painted the scene had brushed them away, just to draw my attention to the moon.

"What month is it?" I ask her.

"So … many … questions," she replies. "I don't know. What does it matter?"

"I'm still a bit confused. It should be wintertime, but the air feels warm like it does in summer. And I've been looking at the moon … and the layout of the stars—"

"Like some kind of astrologer …"

I try to block out her continuing jeers, which, at last, are starting to grate on my nerves.

"The waning gibbous moon is at its last quarter," I say. "So, we can correctly assume it's just gone midnight. And over there … that star about forty degrees off the horizon … it hasn't moved all night. So that's Polaris. And the thick band of stars and gas clouds running directly over us … the Milky Way … is to the right of Polaris. So, the brightest part of the Milky Way tracks directly north to south, which confirms we are sometime in July … maybe August at the latest. Therefore, we are actually in summer, not winter." With my voice trailing off, I look at her, completely baffled.

"Sheesh. Is this what they've got you spendin' all your time thinkin' about?"

"But yesterday it was winter, in December. How can this be summer, in July?"

"Again … shut it, and get moving," she says, quickening her pace.

Confusion continues to play on my mind as we make our way

through the night. Feeling somewhat intimidated by her enforced code of silence, I decide not to say anything more to antagonize her. Even after she makes an offensive gesture or spouts off another rude comment about nobody in particular yet clearly directed at me.

When we stop again a while later, she turns to survey the emptiness that has filled in behind us, the structures now a small pond of faint lights in the distance.

"That's far enough for now," she says. "Time for a fix."

"A fix?"

She unhitches the knapsack from her shoulder and places it on the ground. Sitting with her back against a large boulder, she rummages through the knapsack and takes out a cylindrical-shaped object: a glass vial about six inches long, capped at one end. I recall the sound I'd heard during our escape earlier in the day. Or was it night? The ambiguity still messes with my head.

"Ahh. Nectar from the gods," she says, holding the vial up to the moonlight. She examines it at length as though captivated by the emulsified liquid inside. She shakes the vial, studies the small bubbles as they travel from the bottom end to the top. From her hip pocket, she produces a well-used plastic syringe. "Normally, I would finger a lot more of these goodies," she says. "But you, you freak, you disrupted my mission this time. Not to worry though, there's enough *juice* here for a few solos." With subtle violence, she shakes the vial again, then lays it on her lap before rolling up her sleeve. Using her teeth, she snaps the top off of the vial and draws its contents into the syringe.

"Arghh. It always hurts gettin' this thing in, especially at night when it's so frackin' hard to see. But, when it's in … when it's in … it doesn't take too long … doesn't take long to … to … oooh."

119

As she squeezes the last of the fluid out of the syringe and into a small intravenous receptacle fitted to the crook of her left arm, her contorted face transforms into a look of complete tranquility. Her eyes roll back, and she gives herself completely over to the influence of the *juice*.

In the moon-glow, her thin grubby face is apparent now, her hair a red matted mess. From her pint-size and flat chest, I guess she can't be any more than eleven or twelve years old. And the filthy scabbed area surrounding the receptacle suggests she's "soloed" many times before.

For some reason—I don't know why—I roll up my sleeve and run a reluctant hand up my own left arm, to where my fingers brush past something irregular. I peel the sleeve back further, and in the dimness, notice a small receptacle fastened to the inside of my elbow, similar to the young girl's apparatus. Although, unlike her mutilated receptacle, mine is clean and has been attached with some surgical skill.

As I roll down my sleeve, a disbelieving sigh escapes me. The long list of absurdities continues to grow.

She babbles throughout the night. Mainly of things incoherent and confused, but there's one conviction she repeats that disturbs me most.

"If they'd have caught me, they'd keep me there," she says in her sleep. "Turn me into one of them … become a frackin' weirdo, like him … I need to get away from this freak show … as quick as I can."

For a long time, I listen to her ramblings and try to make sense of what she says, but in the end, I don't understand any of it. I'm struggling to take in my new surroundings, to figure out where—and when—I am. I think about Jennifer some more. I wonder where she might be now. Until my eyelids grow heavy and my head drops. Then thoroughly exhausted, I surrender myself to sleep.

The gentle sun caresses my face as I doze.

When I open my eyes at last, I'm overawed by the emptiness surrounding me. There are no trees or shrubs or grasses here. Just some boulders scattered across the barren landscape, in a world overrun by inadequacy, hemmed in between the azure of the sky and the ferric red of the earth.

I stand to dust the red off my pants. Two distinct sets of footmarks pressed into the powdery dirt confirm our arrival at our makeshift campsite during the night. The smaller marks lead to the boulder against which the young girl had rested, but otherwise, there's no sign of her now. Another set of her footprints lead away in the opposite direction from which we'd come. Erratic, as though she'd been confused or unsteady on her feet when she departed. Beside the boulder, her knapsack is still propped in the dirt while three empty vials are strewn on the ground, together with the syringe she'd used to solo.

I pick up the syringe, clean it off and slip it into the knapsack. Inside the knapsack, I find a dozen more vials filled with a yellowy-green liquid plus a bottle of water, three-quarters full. I take a swig of the water, throw the knapsack over my shoulder, and look back in the direction we'd come.

In the distance, I can just make out the tiny shapes of three structures, or the *"freak show"* as the young girl kept referring to them, their size now insignificant against the sweeping view of this expansive, desolate landscape. To me, the structures no longer appear as intimidating, yet during the night, I'd heard in the young girl's delirium how they'd tormented her. How she had to get away from them as quickly as possible, repeating it over and over. And for all her grit and bravado, I believe the young girl was genuinely afraid of the structures, and for that reason alone, I decide I should be wary as well.

Turning my back on the *"freak show"*, I shade my eyes from the oncoming sun.

"That means the structures are in the west," I say aloud. "So she must have gone east." After taking a last look behind me, I hitch the knapsack higher on my shoulder and follow the young girl's haphazard trail out into the nothing.

Before long, her footmarks become even more erratic, to the point where I'm sure she must have become severely disoriented. I follow them throughout the morning until they disappear up onto a rocky outcrop to reemerge later beside a second set of tracks; my tracks. This is the same path I'd taken an hour earlier. Looking from the top of the outcrop, the ground below is dotted with footmarks crisscrossing in every direction, and I realize I've been walking in circles. With my shoulders sagging, I let go a heavy sigh.

The sun chases the moon as it draws a deliberate arc across the cloudless sky. At its zenith, the sun sits directly above me, pounding on my unprotected head. "This is definitely not winter," I say with some frustration. "The sun is traveling much too high overhead."

After finding a suitable boulder, one that's set like the perfect recliner, I settle back to stretch my legs. Dirt now stains the bottom half of my once-white outfit, with patches of red smeared over my sleeves and chest where I'd wiped my hands. Minute particles of dust clog my nose and the corners of my eyes, pervading every exposed orifice of my body, invading me as it did to the young girl.

ENTROPY

While I rest, thoughts of yesterday come flooding back to me. I wrestle with my conscience, try to evaluate the decisions I've made that have led me to this time and place. If only Mr. Symons and Jerry hadn't come to visit me. If I hadn't delved so dangerously deep into the archives of Aleph-1. If I'd only listened to Jennifer and stuck to the original brief of my assignment. If I could fix this mess and change things back to the way they were.

However, what is done is done, and the past can't be changed. And as hard as I'm now finding it to accept the fact, deep down, I know it's true.

"What should I do now?" I say with a sense of hopelessness growing inside. I pick up the knapsack. Then shaking my head, I set off again, without a clue of where I'm going or what I'll find out here yet resigned to the fact that my life has been irreversibly changed. My only real conviction is to go east, to use the position of the sun to hold my course and move as far away from the structures as I can; as the young girl had warned.

The next morning, my calves are burning, and my back complains about the hard ground. I hadn't slept much last night, and now I yawn heavily. Night follows day, then another night follows again. Each day, the inhospitable terrain remains unchanged: dry, desolate, and covered by this insidious red dust, which seems to have invaded the Earth. Now sleep avoids me altogether. The water is finished. My lips are cracked and burned while the unsympathetic sun beats down hard on my unshielded skull. Had it been three days ago I woke to find the young girl gone? Or was it four? I don't remember anymore. By midmorning, my head throbs, and my tongue is dry and swollen.

"East ... I must keep ... heading east."

I choose a distinct pinnacle-shaped rock in the distance to set my bearings by. Three times I stumble, and on each occasion, catch myself just in time from falling. I can still see the landmark ahead of me, but it wavers in my field of view before distorting against the background. I can't remember where I am or what I'm doing here. A wave of dizziness engulfs me before I stumble again. This time though, my reflexes are much too slow, and I fall heavily, striking my head on the craggy, unforgiving ground.

A trickle of blood runs from a small gash that opens on my forehead and, at last, the swirling blackness takes me.

Chapter 11

"ARE—ARE YOU in there?"

The excitement in the voice carries clear into my catatonic state. A pause, before an irresponsible hand grabs my shoulder and shakes me with vigorous intent. Then a hard knuckle knocks on my forehead, as though someone out there is politely requesting permission to enter my subconscious.

"I—I don't think he is—is in there," the voice says.

I groan.

"Ah-ha! He—he is in there."

Through the two tiny slits in the front of my head, I can see a man hovering over me. His long thin face like a pair of parallel lines squared off at the jaw with two green eyes peering at me from behind a grubby, red-crusted mask. No, more than grubby. Filthy. He leans closer, breathing his crude, used air right into my face without any consideration or apology.

"Ow, my head hurts," I say, squinting up at him.

Smiling a simple smile, the man takes a half-step backward. Then extending his hand, he strains to help me to my feet.

"Have you seen the girl?" I ask.

"What—what girl?"

"The young girl. I followed her out here." My wandering fingers discover the lump on my forehead. Unwittingly, I scratch at the scab of coagulated blood until it peels away so that new blood flows. "But now I can't find her."

"There's no—no girl around here."

"Who are you?"

The man's eyes dodge mine. "You should—shouldn't be on the move while the sun is—is high on top," he says. "We—we saw you lying here, so—so we stopped to help. She—she made me stop to—to help you."

"Who made you stop?"

"She—she did," the man says, hopping to one side.

Through myopic eyes, I can just make out the blurred outline of somebody standing behind him. With dull, disk-like eyes and a face divided by a long proboscis that droops down over the mouth, this *thing* reminds me of the sketch of an extinct elephant seal I'd once seen long ago. Its smooth face is set on an otherwise featureless globe which, I think, should be the head …

But thinking doesn't come so easy for me at the moment.

I wonder if I've ever seen such a deficient face before. This one has no mouth or ears, and the eyes are much too large compared to the overall size of the head. It appears alien; the extraterrestrial kind. Then it dawns on me—*she*—and I realize this woman is encased in a pliant outfit that clings to her body. She's completely covered, including a bulbous head-cover—*perhaps made from some kind of hardened plastic case*—which conceals her head and face.

I wipe my eyes, try to bring her form into focus.

"Who are you ... ? Where am I ... ?"

The woman raises her right hand and gives two sharp taps on her left inner wrist. Immediately, the head-cover slides away and disappears into a thin receptacle around her neck. With an undersized head, matted hair, and a face as filthy as her outerwear, I'd normally consider this woman unremarkable, almost plain. Yet, something about her tells me that her real allure might not be found in her physical appearance.

Our eyes meet briefly, and without acknowledging me, her eyes veer away.

The clink of glass-on-glass nearby alerts me to the man who has my knapsack turned upside down and is busily shaking its contents onto the ground. At his feet, there are some vials of *juice,* the syringe, and bits of glass. "There—there are only six left," he says. "All the rest are—are broken." After sifting through the remains, the man returns the unbroken vials to the knapsack, all except one, which he holds up to show the woman. When she gives him an approving nod, the man grabs my arm, rough-like, and sits me down. "Now—now don't you move," he says. "Everything will be—be all right."

But right now, I don't have the energy to put up the slightest resistance.

Holding the vial firmly in his fingers, the man twists the top off and draws a full amount of *juice* into the syringe. "All I need to do is—is connect this to—to that," he says, pointing nervously to my left elbow. Then he rolls up my sleeve and tries to attach the syringe to my receptacle. After three fumbling attempts, the man still can't get the pieces connected. Clearly frustrated, the woman snatches the syringe from the man and snaps the interlocking parts together without a problem. Then, with a steady hand, she squeezes the plunger until the last drop of liquid is dispensed into my arm.

At first, I don't feel anything. A minute later though, my heavy head slumps forward. My whole body goes limp as a strange kind of weakness comes over me. Closing my eyes, I retreat into the shadows.

Then something unexpected. My heart starts racing as an unnerving tingle shoots up my left arm. It enters my chest before scattering throughout the fabric of my being as though a firestorm had just entered my body, and for the first time in my life, I feel electric inside. My pounding heart threatens to burst, so I rip it from my chest cavity where I can see it out in front of me, held in both my hands, disconnected yet, somehow, still pumping. Then without warning, it arrests, and all functioning abruptly stops as I'm flung back into coma where, for a split-second, I'm lost. And in that instant, time halts for me, and nothing exists.

Then with brutal acceleration, I'm restarted, and my mind explodes …

Pictures burst into my chaos. Images of Mr. Symons ranting and chastising me while Jerry taunts me and channels his nonsense; fatmen arguing with each other; excited children marching in long winding lines behind silver-clad people; the small boy disappearing once again through a solid wall, just beyond the reach of his mother's outstretched arms; Nathanial, lying broken and helpless on the ground; the silver-clad girl coughing up blood as she struggles to take her last breath; the burned bodies of my followers, the ones who had trusted me. Everything is propelled through my mind as a single, transient thought.

I scratch at my arms, my nails digging into the flesh. They claw at my face while I cry out from a place I don't know where.

"IT WASN'T REAL! None of it was real! It was just reconstructed data!"

On the outside, someone tugs at my arm with such force that it feels like the arm is about to detach while once again something hard raps against my poor forehead.

"You—you have to wake up. We have to—to go now. Wake up."

But I can't comprehend anything that's occurring beyond my subconscious mind.

In front of me, all I can see is Jennifer, my poor sweet Jennifer, leaning against the wall in the sleeping room, drowning in a sea of red. I reach out to touch her, to run my fingers through her long black hair, to stroke her beautiful bloodless face.

"We—we should leave him. What chance does—does he have out here without a life-support suit? It won't—won't take long before the sun sucks—sucks all the fluids from his body, and he shrivels up and—and dies of thirst. How will he—he stop the fluids from leaving his body if he doesn't have a support suit to—to recycle them? He doesn't stand a—a chance, I say. Why can't we—we leave him?"

I plateau and, at last, rebound, unsure of how long I've been gone.

Kneeling beside me, the woman pulls down my sleeve to cover the receptacle. Two metal canisters hang from her waist, one beaten-up red and the other just as beaten-up blue. She removes the blue canister and dribbles out a measure of brown, cruddy water onto a patch of soiled cloth, which she holds in her hand. She washes the blood from my forehead and wipes the dirt from my face, then offers the canister to my lips.

I take a long swig of the thick, earthy fluid before she attempts to lift me to my feet. A futile task considering her puny size and flimsy weight against mine.

As if she'd read my thoughts, she signals to the man for help.

"He won't—won't survive, I tell you. We—we're wasting our time, I say."

After a few spirited attempts, they work me to my feet, and with one of them tucked neatly under each arm, we set off. At first, our progress is slow, and our lack of coordination telling, however, as my strength returns, the going becomes easier, our direction less erratic. Looking down on them, I notice how unusually diminutive they are, with both of them barely reaching the height of my hunched-over shoulders. And they smell. But then, I suspect that by now, I might smell too.

A short time later, I'm feeling much better. My legs and shoulders seem stronger, as though my once depleted and wrecked body had been sent in for an overhaul and returned to me almost new.

What is the substance in those vials? A mixture of nutrients ... and hallucinogens maybe?

After I let go of them from under my arms, I rest a hand on the man's shoulder—to keep myself steady, just to be sure.

"Thanks for your help," I say. "I'm not sure what I'd have done if you two hadn't found me."

The man throws me a sheepish look as if he were apologizing for wanting to leave me behind while the woman stares intently at the road ahead. Looking at her, she reminds me of something stringent, someone devoid of emotion, and I wonder whether that resolute face of hers had ever smiled before.

"Oh, I'm Bill Bartles, at your … err … I'm Bill, by the way," I say. But neither of them seems all that interested in who I am.

"We—we must hurry," the man says with a nervous kind of urgency. "We need to—to catch up with the others."

"Others? Do you mean there are more of you?" I say, now feeling confident enough to unhitch from him.

"Yes," he says. "There—there are lots of us. But look,"—his wavering finger points skyward—"the sun is past the—the top, so we have to move fast to—to catch up with them."

Quickening his pace, the man taps at his inner left wrist, and an opaque sphere emerges from around the neckline of his life-support suit. When his head is completely covered, as if by magic, a long proboscis forms over his mouth and nose while he peers at me through two circular portals, and at once, the helpful man, too, resembles an alien—the extraterrestrial kind.

With the helpful woman beside me and the alien man ahead of us, we make our way across the flat, indolent wasteland. Sometimes, I can sense her staring at me, but whenever I look at her, she turns away, her eyes always averting mine. A few hours later, the red dust-layered deck gives way to a rock-strewn ground; gravel spread everywhere, like seed scattered about by some ancient subsistence farmer, sown more in hope than with any conviction.

As we pass a patch of low-grown shrubs—wiry, and brittle, and lifeless—I wonder when their roots would have last sucked any moisture from this miserable earth. And like everything else here, there's a fine coat of red dust blanketing the shrubs as well.

Not long after, the remains of two trees appear against the horizon. With their crippled limbs and stubborn roots, they remind me of a pair of stoic soldiers: broken casualties left behind on the battle-field of some long-forgotten war. A small thicket appears, soon followed by a forest of ghostly tree-trunks; their contorted branches stripped bare of the shriveled leaves that lie beneath them like a carpet of confetti on the ground. Confetti that crackles and pops under our feet as we pass.

From high on a hilltop, the shape of a valley emerges beyond the trees. At first, I don't take much notice. However, as the valley opens out, a large house appears out of the flat ground below us. I stop to look, to survey the scene. The longer I study it, the house seems to tug at me like some formless call from the past until I somehow find myself pushing through the thick maze of woody trunks, then picking my way down the steep slope toward it. Behind me, the helpful man is calling for me to stop and come back. But the house gives off such an imperative force, drawing me toward it. A kind of attraction that I can neither resist nor explain.

With the house in my sights, I break into a run, down the slope. The helpful pair are sprinting to try to keep up with me, but they quickly tire and fall behind. A path, beginning at the foot of the slope, snakes its way to the house. On both sides of the path, an overgrown hedgerow slaps and claws at my legs as I twist my way past until I come to a wrought-iron gate. Straddling the gate, the sturdy supports remain, but there's no hint of a fence-line thereafter.

In the back of my mind, I picture a small boy alighting here from a big yellow bus. After pushing past the gate, the boy sprints along the path to where a mother waits with her arms held wide open while a small girl plays with a dog on the porch. I can visualize a line of leafy trees starting at the gate, running alongside the path, up to the house, and around it. On my left, I imagine the broken-down windmill restored, pinwheeling in the afternoon breeze, pulling water from the ground to fill the now derelict cattle troughs. A farmer taking out the last of the summer corn from these once bountiful fields.

Using the toe of my boot, I nudge the gate open, watch as the corroded hinges give way, and it topples flat across my path. I step over the gate, my attention fixated on the house as I make my way to it. Not long after I've reached the house, the helpful woman is beside me, panting heavily, closely followed by the helpful man who is muttering to himself.

"We—we have to go," he says. "There's no—no time for us to—to waste here."

But the house looms over me like a distant memory; the front door half hanging off its hinges while sections of glass are missing from the windows on the first floor, in all the panels except one. Watchful, I stand here, as if I first need to test its intent. When I finally mount the porch, the floorboards creak and groan as I shift my weight into each cautious step. A tattered poster, plastered across the top of the doorway, warns me of something that no longer matters.

"He can't go—go in there. It's—it's not allowed."

Ignoring the man, I drop my knapsack at the entry, shove the door open, and step inside. Behind me, the helpful woman follows me in, but the man stops at the doorway, his feet rooted to the floor outside as if held there by some invisible constraint. "We're—we're not allowed," he wails.

Inside, the dust has invaded the house through the gaps and cracks, and breached the portals and openings, with everything smothered in a thick layer of powdered red. A dining table leans into the corner like some drunkard, having completely lost one of its four legs and broken another. Several chairs lay in pieces about the table, although to my surprise, one lucky chair remains intact.

I can picture a once sturdier table serving a family: two children and their father seated around it. I imagine the discussions going on, conversations about the trivial events of their day as they wait while their mother boils broth and grills authentic meat on her solar-fueled stove. I can almost hear the children's chatter, their laughter escaping the house like the sounds of normality to anyone listening.

At the foot of the stairs, I stop to scan the unknown space above. As I ascend the stairs, I take each plank carefully; all except for the fourth from the bottom, which I have the curious urge to skip over. The rail wobbles disconcertingly in my hand. At the top of the stairs, I peer into a narrow passage, but from halfway down there's only darkness.

I try the first door on my left. Find it locked. On the next door along, the paint has faded except for a small patch of bright yellow in the center. About chest level. Tracing the rectangular outline with my finger, I examine the four screw holes, one at each corner. A name-plate was here, once.

Below, on the first floor, the helpful woman clatters her way through the cupboards—*probably looking for anything that might prove useful*—while the helpful man continues his whining at the doorway.

The doorknob resists. When I apply a little more effort it gives, and I shoulder my way into a room where the afternoon sun filters in through two mullioned windows set close together on the adjacent wall. Bookending the windows, a pair of sun-bleached drapes hang from the height of the ceiling, shredded to the point of being almost redundant. The glass panels of the window remain intact, and apart from a light settling of normal house-dust, the room appears to have escaped the ravages of the red intruder.

I flip the catch on one of the windows and pry it open. Peering across a nearby field, I imagine a father plowing over its once productive soil. This would have been the perfect vantage point for a young boy to watch, and wait, and hope that at any moment, the father would stop what he was doing, look up and see the boy. And wave.

The room reminds me of a shrine, a place steeped in memories that were not intended to be forgotten. Where everything has been purposefully arranged and left untouched: a single bed nearby with a pillow on top, the fabric turned yellow through age, the quilt cover embroidered with depictions of vintage machines—racing cars, airplanes, and other contraptions a young boy might like; a study desk and chair beside the bed; a cluster of small plastic figurines, each posing in different action stances strategically arranged on a shelf above the desk; and all by itself, a book placed squarely upon the desk.

I pick up the book and dust it off, run my fingers across the cover.

"My Diary: By ..." But the words are much too faded for me to read, and as I leaf through the pages, the paper disintegrates in my hands.

On the other side of the room, a reclining seat looks to be almost adrift from the rest of the furniture. I run my hand along the soft fabric lining its back, then across the armrest. On the seat, at the ready, the joystick controller for an Entertainer unit, which is still wired into the wall. And recessed into the ceiling above me, an array of sensory projectors and pickup receptors marking out the personal holographic metazone for the Entertainer.

I lift the controller, finger its buttons at random. Within seconds, the button sequences come to me naturally, the patterns becoming increasingly complex, and soon the controller feels comfortable cupped in my hands. As though I'd held it before, used and treasured it, known its many pleasures before. I tremble as my digits work the buttons and joystick furiously, with speed and precision. But this time, the Entertainer doesn't respond. It gives me no pleasure, and out of frustration, I hurl the controller at the floor where it splits apart, sending broken pieces across the room.

Against the wall, set at an angle into the corner, a dresser, where my reflection in the backing mirror is obscured by the years of settled dust. Drawers, filled with clothing for a young child: shorts; shirts; socks; a pullover. All neatly folded and tucked away. There's a small rectangular card jammed into the top right corner of the mirror frame. After working the card free, I wipe the dust off the faded photo of a young boy, perhaps six or seven years old, posing at the seaside, together with two adults and a younger girl. Behind them, the turquoise ocean rolls in on large breaking waves, and the sand at their feet looks like they're all standing in a field of cotton. With red hair and freckles, the boy reminds me of the small boy I'd encountered during my recent interaction with Aleph-1.

As I slip the photo into my top pocket, something in the clear patch of mirror, left by the card, catches my eye. Using the heel of my hand, I remove the dust-layer in slow, uneasy circles until I'm soon confronted by the sight of some ghastly creature. With its blue pencil-thin lips, an oversized cranium, and face covered by a spidery network of blood vessels—made conspicuous against its smooth, pallid skin—this *thing* has the appearance of something less than human. The deadpan eyes, set deep beneath its Neanderthal-like brow, give me no clue as to what kind of monster might inhabit its body.

I lean closer to the mirror to scrutinize my counterpart who, in return, appears to be scrutinizing me. Its eyes widen. This is the same *thing* I saw on the night Jennifer had … when Jennifer had …

I reach out to touch the small cut on its forehead. And my heart sinks.

"Oh," I say softly.

From the doorway, the helpful woman watches on while this grotesque description holds me captive in front of the mirror. A solitary tear escapes from my eye and winds a damp course down my cheek. "I really didn't know," I say. But the words die a lonely death once they leave my trembling lips.

The woman enters the room and comes to me quietly. She places a gentle hand on my shoulder. Unable to take my eyes off the mirror, I wipe away the tear before running my fingers over my protruding brow. She takes my hand, and in haunted silence, we make our way back down the stairs to where the helpful man continues his complaint from the doorway, waving us outside, his arms rotating like they were the wayward sails of a runaway windmill.

"We—we need to go, otherwise we—we won't catch the others before the—the darkness comes. Quick. Follow me—me now."

I make my way back up the hill in shocked resignation. My only wish is to get away from here as fast as I can, as far away as possible. Now I wish I'd never come here in the first place. I stop for a moment to look back at the house, which, in turn, seems to be looking at me, with each of us eying the other off in silent betrayal.

When the helpful woman's hand again makes its way onto my shoulder, an unfilled ache wells up inside me.

So this is what real sadness feels like.

She passes me a metal flask, one that she must have taken from the house, and gestures to me as if to drink. Taking it from her, I nod my appreciation.

"Quick," says the helpful man. "We—we have to move fast to catch up—up with the others."

Chapter 12

FIRSTLY, THE BROKEN trees thin out before us.

Then the lifeless shrubs, until the unsympathetic red terrain soon makes an unwelcome return. It's as if it wanted me to know it was still there—that it had always been there. A while later, the alien man retracts his head-cover and points toward a nearby ridge. "There—there they are. There are the—the others," he says with a quick bounce in his step.

Ahead of us, the *others* are strung out in single file along the ridge. They remind me of a train of toddlers who've been roped together for an outdoor excursion. As we draw nearer to them, I notice they're all wearing survival suits similar to the helpful pair's coverings, and appear just as filthy, almost blending into the red surrounds. Each of them carries two canisters, a red one and a blue one, dangling from a belt around their waist, and judging by their uniform size, I quickly conclude there are no infants or youngsters among them.

I count twenty-two *others* in total, not including the helpful pair

The helpful man lopes away to catch up with the one bringing up the rear. He appears to talk to that one briefly before running ahead and slowing to a walk beside the one in the lead. Soon, the two of them come to a hesitating halt, and the line leader retracts its head-cover.

"What's happening?" I ask, but the helpful woman doesn't respond.

With the rest of us closing in around them, the helpful man and the line leader descend into a strange kind of entangled discussion. While they talk, they're looking at the ground and everything else around them yet seem determined to avoid all eye contact with each other.

The alien standing beside me starts to fidget. It paces around before throwing up its hands. When its head-cover retracts, the shrunken face of an old man emerges. "I think they're trying to decide where we're going to settle for the night, I think," he says, rolling his eyes. He kicks at the ground as if to express his disinterest, or perhaps disappointment, in proceedings.

As the discussion between the helpful man and the line leader continues, neither of them raises their voice above a whisper. The fidgeting man pokes a bony finger into my arm. "I think that one wants to make camp over there for the night," he says, pointing to a large rock a short distance away on our left. "But I think the other one wants to make camp over there, I think." He redirects his pointer to indicate another large rock a similar distance away on our right.

I run a suspect eye over the two proposed camping spots and

scratch my head. "What's the difference?"

Still toeing at the ground, the fidgeting man shrugs and shakes his head.

In the fading light of the late afternoon, the timid debate between the two continues in a fruitless exchange of useless words and deflected glances. With neither of them willing to challenge the other or take the lead, it becomes obvious to me that a resolution to their stalemate is unlikely, if not downright impossible.

A small group of *others* wanders away from us and they're milling around a mound of dirt close by. Standing on top of the mound, one of them cups a small object in her palm. After rubbing it furiously against her leg, she holds it aloft while another five look on keenly. Every few minutes, the same strange ritual repeats.

"What are they doing?" I ask the fidgeting man.

"First, I think, they have to recharge it," he replies. "Then they look for a signal. No signal, I think."

"What type of signal?"

"I'm not sure. And I'm not sure they're sure either, I think."

With that, the fidgeting man flops to the ground with a heavy sigh. Then one by one, the rest of them concede until all the onlookers and signal-finders are sitting exactly where they've been waiting for the past two hours. Then the helpful man sits, followed by the line leader.

"Well, that was a complete waste of everybody's time," I say to the fidgeting man. But he just shrugs again.

The night closes in on us quickly, their shadowy figures moving about the campsite under the soft glow of the stars. They're whispering among themselves. They seem restless. Someone fumbles with something in the dark. A click, and the nighttime is split open by the light from a beacon fixed atop a pole, which they've planted in the ground. Forming themselves in a tight circle around the beacon, they're staring expectantly into the darkness, chattering and pushing each other as mischievous youngsters would.

I turn to the fidgeting man. "What are they waiting for?"

But before he can reply, a rounding cheer goes up as a large, winged insect comes hurtling in from the black and thuds into the beacon. Stunned, it falls to the ground where it lies, its large body quivering. One of them grabs it, pries off its wings, and downs the thing in a single swallow. Another insect arrives, missile-like. After hitting the beacon, it too drops to the ground where someone else is there to snatch it up, de-wing it, and devour it as quickly as the first.

Before long, the air around us is alive with all varieties of moth, beetle, and net-winged critters streaming in, tracking straight for the beacon. Whenever a dazed flier hits the ground, an eager diner is there to scoop it up, strip away its accessories and gulp it down before they wait hungrily for the next tidbit to arrive.

I settle back while the feast continues. Watching them running through the thick clouds of nightlife, I can't help thinking about how these people appear to function at the most basic level. As though they act on impulse, on a subsistence basis only. And yet, the advanced technology in their life-support suits suggests they must have a certain amount of sophistication. Or are they merely the users of the technology, not the designers, and this is a case of *monkey-is-only-doing-what-monkey-once-saw-done*?

Holding the plump body of some unrecognizable arthropod in her pincers, the helpful woman makes her way over to me. With her eyes shied away from mine, she offers it to me. But I can't. I don't have that kind of appetite, although I don't want to offend her, so I pat my stomach and politely wave her away. After throwing the thing into her mouth, she counteroffers with her water canister. I take a sip and pass it back to her. As she returns the canister to its pouch, I'm sure I catch the glimpse of a fleeting smile. But then it's gone as she turns and hurries back to rejoin the feeding frenzy.

The feast goes on late into the night until the moon makes its way into the sky. Once clear of the horizon, its radiance drowns the light from the beacon. The insects disperse, and the night-time air becomes clear once again. Around me, the activity continues as they use their fingers and fists to pulp the leftovers into a pure protein paste, which they pack into their red canisters.

Perhaps I was wrong. Maybe they do make plans for tomorrow.

Later, two of them scrape out a shallow burrow in the dirt where they all pack down together like a brood of undomesticated oddities, their life-support suits and underclothes heaped in a pile beside the hole.

Someone extinguishes the beacon.

In the moonlight, I notice the helpful man is coupled with the helpful woman and without any inhibitions, they start rutting. The rest of them pair off, and without any regard to their privacy, they do the same. As I observe them, I can't detect any formal attachments between them as they swap partners at will, and I sense something primitive at work here. I study the helpful woman as she transients from one partner to the next, as though she were fulfilling some outmoded conjugal duty.

Does he love her? As much as I love … loved … Jennifer?

During Enlightenment, when it was decided the reproductive function would be outsourced to glass surrogates, some people said love had died at the expense of true equality. That the last inequitable encumbrance had been overcome so both genders could enjoy the same conveniences, the same opportunities, and love was a necessary casualty. Others countered that it was just progress, a more sophisticated way of living. But looking at the way these people operate now, I figure love may not be so important anymore. In fact, all this time, love might have been a lie, inflicted upon us by our forebears to ease the pain of being human. And yet, who would willingly choose to live without love?

Now I see the helpful man is coupled with the fidgeting man.

Minutes later, they're all fast asleep, pressed together in a heap on the ground. Looking at the tangled mess of their small, emaciated bodies, I can't help feeling these people may represent a retreat to the most basic form of human in the grand scale of evolution. Regressive things, without any immediate purpose, and devoid of ambition.

If this here is a snapshot of our progress to date, then what chance do we have going forward?

And yet, always the optimist, I figure there must be normal people out here, somewhere. I just have to find them.

I rub my tired legs, wrap my arms around my chest. Then curling myself into a ball, I hum myself to sleep.

I sleep late, and the next day is well underway when I wake. The muscles in my shoulders tighten as I extend both arms high above my head, then behind my back. I arch my spine, stretch the quads and calves of each leg in turn until they strain to the peak of spasm before I release. Yesterday's pain escapes my body like an old foe, temporarily defeated until the next bout is there to be fought at the same time tomorrow morning.

ENTROPY

A short distance away, the helpful man and the line leader are at it again, locked in deep conversation while the rest of them form a loose circle around the two. I slap my backside and legs, try to brush off as much red dust as I can before joining them.

"How long have they been at it this time?" I ask the fidgeting man.

"I know they started when it was first light ... when the sun wasn't fully in the sky, I think. That one wants to carry on along the ridge. But I think the other one wants to go for water because she doesn't have any water left, I think." His crooked finger singles out the helpful woman.

"But she gave most of her water to me."

The man fidgets some more before giving me another shrug.

I push my way through the group to stand beside the helpful man. After listening to their timid arguments bouncing between them and deciding there's no hope of a resolution, I can't help myself. "Which way is it to the water?"

Startled, the two talkers cower away from me. The man mumbles something incoherent while the line leader stares guiltily at the ground. I ask them again, but the man is much too nervous to reply, and at first chance, the line leader darts off and disappears behind the ones surrounding us. I grab the man by the shoulders and shake him. But he looks at me wide-eyed, mouthing useless words and shaking his head.

The helpful woman cuts in. She tugs at my arm. At first, I think she's trying to defend the man, but as she pulls me away from him, she's pointing into the distance and gesturing with her other hand as if she's drinking from her canister. And I immediately understand: Away across the flatland, there's water.

"Okay," I say in a firm voice. "That's where we're headed."

I follow her down from the ridge. At first, the rest of them just stand there staring at us until, one by one, they relent. And soon, they're all following us across the flatland, spread out in a long line like a sprinkling of incidental extras.

When the sun is directly overhead, the helpful woman tugs at my arm again. She points to a large mound of earth on the horizon. From a long way behind us, the faint voice of the helpful man calls out, "There it is. There's the—the reservoir."

An hour later, I'm standing with the woman at the base of the mound, surveying the embankment, which I estimate to be over seventy feet high. On all sides, the ground drops away at a dangerously steep angle. A winding goat-track takes us to the top where a narrow causeway forms a perimeter around the reservoir. By my guess, the causeway must be almost 300 feet across. To our right, a section of the corrugated iron roof covering the interior of the reservoir has collapsed cutting an entrance inside, large enough for me to walk through without having to bend.

I follow the woman inside just as the helpful man and the first of the *others* arrive at the top of the goat-track.

With the light from the entrance deteriorating fast, I make my way down a steep, earthen ramp. Halfway down, I lose my balance on the loose stones underfoot but catch myself just in time. Somewhere further below, I can hear the woman scurrying around, then a loud click before the whole interior of the reservoir is flooded with light. At the bottom of the ramp, the helpful woman stands with her back to me, holding onto the beacon they'd used during last night's feasting. She stabs the thing into the ground, turns to me, and waves me down.

Above us, the steelwork supporting the roof is braced by a massive, concrete ring-wall. At first glance, the structure appears sturdy enough, although, admittedly, I'm no structural engineer. In the light, I can see the earthen ramp we'd just descended was formed when a section of ring-wall collapsed allowing soil from the outside to inundate the floor. Then it was spread and compacted by the countless visitors over time. Around the ring-wall, a crusted bank slopes gently down to the lowest point of the reservoir where a tall riser breaks upright from a patch of muddy ground.

Echoes, issued from their excited whispers, follow the helpful man and the *others* down the ramp while, beneath the riser, the helpful woman slops around in ankle-deep mud. She kneels to scoop out a handful of slop to form a crater, which quickly fills with cruddy water. Then using a square of gauze to cover the crater, she takes the blue canister from her belt, removes the cap, and presses the nozzle into the gauze. With the canister held submerged, she studies the water bubbling in through the opening.

From my vantage point high on the bank, I watch her screw the cap on the canister once it's full. *How long can they continue like this, roaming the flatland? What good is a life lived without purpose or direction … without true happiness?*

With the canister back on her belt, the helpful woman wanders up the bank. She flops down beside me, our eyes meeting briefly. On the opposite side of the reservoir, high up, I spot a large object beached close to the ring-wall.

"That must be a pontoon," I say, pointing to the object. "They use it to float a submersible pump."

The two of us make our way around to the pontoon, and after a brief inspection, I point out the major components to her: motor; pump; inlet pipe; outlet pipe; float; cut-off valve. I attempt to rotate the shaft connecting the motor to the pump. At first, it grips, defiant, but when I apply all my weight, it gives a little, until I can soon turn it a full rotation. Standing back from the pontoon, my eyes follow the route of a plastic conduit, from the motor, up the wall, and out through the roof. "And that must go to the power supply," I tell her.

We climb back up the ramp to the outside. On the far side of the reservoir, we find an array of six large solar panels positioned on a strip of flat ground extending outward from the embankment. Each panel stands vertical, much taller than me, and is held in place by a metal frame, which looks like it can be rotated independent of the other panels by a series of gear wheels mounted underneath. The gears are well greased, and everything appears to be in working order. The conduit coming from inside the reservoir runs into a squat enclosure, the dulled yellow paint on its outer surface curled and cracked, and corrosion gnawing at its door. On the top right corner of the door, a faded zigzag glyph gives me my first, and only, warning that something dangerous lurks inside. Another conduit runs from the cabinet to the nearest solar panel and, from there, a loop of insulated cable connects the rest of the panels.

I check the cable connections at the first panel, followed by the rest. Then I check the conduit to the cabinet and the one going back inside the reservoir. "These all appear to be secure enough," I say half to myself.

While I'm scraping the thick crust of red dirt off the first solar panel, the woman is behind me, watching me. I can feel her analyzing my technique as I remove dirt from the second panel. When I've finished with the third panel, she hops in front of the fourth panel and begins scraping the dirt away using her fingernails, the same as I'd done on the first three panels. Then she cleans the fifth and sixth panels the same.

Once the panels are ready and passed inspection to my satisfaction, we return to the cabinet. Behind the door, I'm confronted by an intricate jumble of electrical wires and logic modules inside. While I probe a finger at the control circuits, I can again sense the woman trying to peer over my shoulder.

"There are three things you should know about electricity," I say to her. "It moves fast … you can't see it … and it kills."

I sense her take a full step backward. Withdrawing my head from the cabinet, I turn to her and smile. But her expression remains as stern as ever.

"Now, you best move back," I say, "because, when this thing goes live, there are enough *volts* in here to fry both of us. It would be good if at least one of us makes it out of here alive." I smile at her again. This time, the thin line drawn by her lip curls upward, ever so slightly. "Ah-ha! She does smile," I say. Her smile widens. Until now, I hadn't noticed the two dainty indents sculpted into her cheeks. Still smiling, but equally unsure, she backs away from me, her suspicion directed at the cabinet, as though the thing is likely to strike out at her at any moment with all its *volts*.

I poke and prod inside the cabinet once more. I touch something, and a small red light flickers to life. Gears whir and the solar panels, all but one, rotate to align with the mid-afternoon sun. Startled by the unexpected activity, I flinch, bumping my head on the top of the cabinet. After withdrawing myself safely from the cabinet, I give the helpful woman a nervous laugh.

Once we've forced the defiant panel into position, we return to the cabinet where I lean in and flick the main breaker. Nothing happens, so I push the big red button marked RESET.

From inside the reservoir, the pump motor groans as it fires up then screams as it sets to work. Sudden cries of panic coming from inside the reservoir, are drowned out by the sustained din of the pump. Within seconds the first of the *others* spills out onto the embankment, quickly joined by the rest of them. Seeing them all on the far side of the reservoir, running around in hysterics, I have to laugh. I laugh so hard that my sides hurt. I haven't seen anything this funny before in all my life. And the woman laughs too.

After picking ourselves up off the ground from laughing, we return to the other side of the embankment. There, the helpful man and the *others* are all huddled together on their haunches, shaking their heads and staring at the entrance like a pack of nervous rodents.

"What—what did you do?" The man's hands shake as he takes in long, strained breaths between short, sharp sobs.

"Come with me," I reply, "and you'll see".

With his hands hiding his face, the helpful man stands and backs away from me. "No—no. We can't go—go down there again. It—it isn't safe anymore."

I nod to the woman and, as if we're cajoling a toddler with the promise of candy, we coax the helpful man through the entrance and back down the ramp. In the center of the reservoir, the riser spouts a fountain of fresh, clean water, showering the ground around it to form a pond, which is now half-shin deep.

When he sees the waterspout, the man cries out, "Oh. Oh, this— this is wonderful." Without hesitating, he darts back up the ramp and hurries outside, yelling to the *others*, "Come—come and see this. Everybody come and—and see." Seconds later, he returns with the rest of them. Halfway down the ramp, they all stop to clap and cheer. Then they sprint to the bottom and plow into the water, all except for the helpful man who halts at the water's edge where he flirts with the water, only allowing it to cover the tops of his feet.

The water level climbs as it continues to shower from the riser, and before long, it reaches their waists, while the reassuring scream of the pump motor morphs into a tolerable din. Much like the sound of incessant chitchat coming from the mouth of one's best friend.

At the pontoon, I heave on the float to confirm its operation and, in response, the waterspout slows to a trickle. "Soon, the pontoon will be afloat. Once the reservoir reaches three-quarters full, the cut-off valve should activate to stop the water flow." With my voice trailing off, I turn to look behind me, but the woman is gone. I smile to myself after realizing I'd been talking to myself the whole time.

With my flask full, I sit high up the bank listening to them frolic in the water, the woman splashing around just below me. When I catch her eye, I give her a thumbs-up, and she extends her thumb in reply. Then it occurs to me that, in all probability, these people might never have seen this much water before. I wonder how long the reservoir has been dry, or if they have access to other sources of clean water. Probably not, by the look of them now. But whatever the trials of their past, and whatever troubles their future might hold, I can be content in the knowledge that today, I've made them happy. Even for this one brief moment in their otherwise harsh and pitiful lives.

Reclining against the knapsack, I rest both hands on my stomach. Begin counting the number of steel members in the roof frame.

Chapter 13

I'M AWAKENED BY a sudden jolt.

The jolt hits me so terrifying that it rips at my insides as a blood-curdling scream from someone, somewhere, guts the air. Down at the water, the *others* all freeze. Their crisscross stares ricochet around the reservoir like poisonous darts before their internal gyros rotate their heads to the top of the ramp. With eyes bulging and lower jaw still unlatched from that desperate cry, the line leader backs away from the entrance.

All at once they're scrambling from the water, dripping wet and bare. Their panicked voices quiver as they sift through the jumble of possessions scattered over the bank. After salvaging whatever they can find, they chase after the helpful woman, who is already at the top of the ramp and almost outside. Some of them only have enough time to grab their metal canisters before they hit the ramp, naked and at breakneck speed, leaving the helpful man adrift, undecided, wandering among the abandoned belongings. Whimpering and dithering, the man sorts through a pile of coverings, holding up each life-suit against himself until he finally finds the one that might be his.

At the sight of the helpful man climbing onto the ramp—the suit now jammed under his left armpit—I grab my knapsack and canister and sprint around the perimeter of the reservoir. With my heart pounding, I scale the ramp, finally catching up with the man at the entrance.

"What's wrong?" I say.

I'm in a panic, but the helpful man is beside himself. He's been able to get his left leg inside the life-support suit okay, but now he's hopping around with his right one in the air, desperately trying to locate the other leg-hole. "Look at the—the sun," he says. "It will soon be—be dark." He grapples with the suit, his bottom lip quivering, then he thumps his forehead with a fist before the second leg finally slides in. "We—we stayed here much too long. We need to—to get back to the higher ground. For our safety, we—we need to find cover. Now."

"Find cover from what?"

I reach out to grab the man, but he fends me away before throwing himself headlong over the embankment.

Before I can think things through sensibly, I'm following him over, with the top half of my body caught in a desperate race to keep up with the bottom half as I hurtle down the embankment. Surprising even myself, I keep my feet. But when we hit the bottom, at the point where the embankment levels off sharply, our knees give way and we both crash to the ground in a tangle of arms and legs.

After picking myself up, I pull the helpful man to his feet, and together we charge into the open. We make toward the main group, who are stretched out in erratic deposits of twos and threes across the flatland, with those in front maintaining a flat-out sprint while those behind push themselves hard to try to keep up.

The helpful man deploys his head-cover, but after a dozen steps, he stumbles and almost falls. The head-cover retracts, and with his cheeks burning bright pink, he sucks hard at the air. "I—I can't breathe … in—in there," he cries.

We catch up with the slowest of the group and pass them without much effort. I sprint to the front of the line, tug at the helpful woman's arm, but she shrugs me off. She twists and turns to look behind as she barrels forward, the fear on her face amplified by the white blizzard raging in her eyes.

"What are we running from?" I say to her.

But I needn't have asked.

From our right flank, a pack of wild dogs comes at us like a hail of quadruped missiles, fired from nowhere. Before they reach us, a splinter group cuts around to our front, another to our rear, as they prepare an attack. A merciless shiver rips its way up my spine as confusion takes hold of those around me. I plead with the helpful woman to go faster, but too late, the hunters are on us, growling and snapping at our heels. We swerve to go left, then right, turn back, go forward. But no matter what we try, either through clever planning or brutal efficiency, the hunters soon have us worked into a tight bunch. Four *others* break from us, but six hunters quickly round them up and drive them back to the bunch.

We charge ahead, the muscles in our legs straining under the effort.

Suddenly, from somewhere behind me, the sound of a whipcrack as tendon rips from bone and the fidgeting man's naked trunk snaps backward. His face contorts as a tortured scream escapes his mouth. Grabbing high-up on the back of his left thigh, the fidgeting man pulls up short. When he tries to restart, the limb buckles whenever he puts weight on it. Then, dragging the leg behind him, the fidgeting man quickly disconnects from us.

Beside me, a divorced look spreads across the helpful man's face. His eyes glaze over before he starts to detach from us as his irrational compass steers him off in aimless directions. I throw out an arm, grab the man, and yank him back to me. "No! We have to stay together," I yell to him.

We're running blindly with each of us fighting for a share of the finite air. In the chaos, the hunters have turned us around, and I realize we're heading back in the direction we'd come. I jostle with the ones beside me as I try to change our course for the safety of the high ground, but the hunters cut us off, their intent to keep us exposed in the open, clear.

I estimate there are at least twenty hunters around us now as each one takes its turn at cutting a swathe through our midst, separating the slowest and most vulnerable from our ranks. Behind us, a curdling scream peals out above the confusion as three hunters bring down the fidgeting man. They tear at his throat and claw at his flailing limbs. Two more hunters strike at the heels of a woman who has fallen too far behind. She trips and falls. At once, they set upon her, ripping the flesh from her hands as she tries to fend them off before three more hunters join in.

As I drop in close behind the helpful woman, a smaller hunter cuts in at us from the side, nipping at the backs of her legs. She screams, but with my teeth gritted and fury in my heart, I kick out, striking the thing in its midriff, sending it cartwheeling off behind us.

I count out the next minutes in lost lifetimes as more of us are isolated and brought down with innards torn from casings and limbs wrenched from bodies. Then as quickly as it had started, the madness around us stops, and I realize the hunters are busy feeding, leaving the rest of us unguarded. Through the murkiness of the advancing night, I look across the flatland, into the distance, to a rocky outcrop. In a split-second decision, I figure we can reach it—we *must* reach it—so I manhandle the helpful man to a stop.

"See those rocks," I say to him. "We have to take our chance while they're busy."

"But—but it's no use," he replies. "We're all too—too tired … I—I can't make it … I want to—"

But I shove him in the direction of the outcrop. With the woman beside me, the rest follow us in stunned obedience. As we make our way around the main pack of hunters, my heart is crushed at the sight of the line leader, lying dismantled in the dirt. Her top piece stares at me through emptied eye sockets while her thin, pale lips appear ready to report on something unimportant, but nothing comes out.

I turn my head away from the sickening sight, and without a sound, we slide away.

"Oh, no!" screams the helpful man. "Here they—they come again."

We haven't gotten far when a small group of hunters rounds us to block our path. Terrified, the remaining *others* bunch up behind me, leaving me out front, standing between them and the hunters. With my hands trembling, I hold my ground as one of the hunters approaches me. Looking almost nonchalant, it ambles toward me as though it had all the time in the world. Now within an arm's length of me, it snarls and bares its teeth. Standing much taller than the rest,

156

its mangy coat reeks of something decayed. I decide this one must be the alpha, and in this cornerstone moment, I'm convinced it can sense the fear oozing from my core.

Behind me, the helpful pair and the *others* drop to their knees. They press their faces hard into the dirt, while I stand here unable to move, unsure of what to do next.

Baring its teeth, the Alpha growls at me, the hackles on its neck and hindquarters raised. Without warning, it lunges at me, flashes of long, ivory-white incisors menacing me as it snaps close to my face. Then it pulls back before repeating its feigned attack.

"Get—get down. Please. Get down—down, now," the helpful man implores.

The Alpha rears onto its hind legs. After taking six unsteady steps toward me, it places its front paws on my shoulders. Shoving its snout close to my face it sniffs me, as if to take an account of my scent. Then it cocks its head and holds its stare.

As I peer into its dark, calculating eyes, I can taste its rancid breath in my mouth. I try to resist with all my will. Lowering my eyes, I notice a blue metal disk dangling from its collar, with a single word engraved in italics: *Buster.*

Like long fingers, the Alpha's phalanges are wrapped around my neck, pressing hard against my throat. I try to hold steady, but tired and scared, I have to relent. I surrender to my knees and bury my face in the dirt just like the rest.

I'm waiting in silence, hardly breathing. I can sense the Alpha standing over me, so I press my forehead harder into the ground. For a long time, it paces in a tight circle around me, as though it were deciding what to do next. Now I can sense it close to me—*too close*—its warm urine soaking my side.

Then it leaves. And within a heartbeat, the rest of the pack disperses back to the nowhere from where they'd come.

After a time, I summon the courage to lift my head. Once I'm sure the hunters have gone, I help the woman to her feet, followed by the man, and the remaining *others*.

"Quick. We must go now," I tell them, hoping they don't notice the waver in my voice.

No one speaks as we set off into the last shards of the afternoon. And none of us can summon the courage to look back and pity those we leave behind. While I walk, I chase the vivid snapshots of the mayhem through my mind. Why hadn't the Alpha hurt me? Why did it spare some of us and not others? Why not take us all?

Then settling on the simplest of explanations, the answer becomes clear.

The hunters only take what is necessary to ensure today's needs are met. They're clever enough not to exhaust this carefully managed food source. Those of us who are strongest and fittest were left unharmed because the hunters know that we will protect our weakest. In this twisted world, tormented by the red dust, we are no longer the dominant species. Instead, we're a free-range herd being farmed by the hunters. Once man's best friend, now they're the top predator in this modern-day food chain. And we are their staple supply.

The night falls on us as dark as dark can. As though every source of illumination has abandoned us in our time of grief. With everybody stricken and fatigued, I decide to stop where we are, to rest here for the night. None of them questions my decision or points to another spot, and when we settle there's no feasting or celebrations or rutting afterward. There are no whispers at play between them like I'd heard last night. This time, their huddle is barely held together by their sorrow and fear: the only bonds left for them in this ruthless world.

I spread myself on the ground a short distance away, to keep watch over them in case the hunters return, acquainting myself with the sharp stench of stale piss on my clothes.

During the night, their dreams are restless and troubled. Some of them talk in their sleep, others moan and shudder. Occasionally, one will sit bolt upright and cry out into the blackness as though they were reliving yesterday's trauma before falling back into a sad, uneasy sleep.

From where I lay, I count just fifteen of them left, not including the helpful pair.

The next morning, I wake early, rising into the stillness before the promise of another day. I stare long at the pile of their sleeping bodies curled up and packed tight against each other and wonder how long they can survive out here; if there are others who can help them.

Or is everybody in this forsaken place destined for the same miserable ending as these poor people?

It scares me to think they might now be my responsibility, that it's my duty to bring certainty back into their lives. But then I recall how *certainty*, in the form of the Alpha, had stood before us yesterday, so cocksure of itself, and declared it and it alone would decide our fates. And that scares me even more.

I pick up my knapsack and set off as the first shafts of splintered light fan out from behind the horizon; today's fore-glow spread across an indifferent sky. I kick at the ground as I walk, at the rocks, at this damned red dust; so intolerable, so dry. If I hadn't used up all her water, or forced them from the safety of the high ground out onto the flatland so late in the day, or stayed too long at the reservoir. Then the line leader and the fidgeting man would still be with us.

I glance over my shoulder to take a last look at our makeshift camp, and I see them. Like two loyal disciples, the woman follows a short distance behind me, and a short distance again, the alien man, with his head bowed, trudges after her. I drop my head against the glare of the oncoming day, and under my breath, I wish the sun would hurry up overhead to obliterate all traces of the darkness and erase every sad memory of yesterday.

And before long, only the darkness is gone.

Chapter 14

IT JUST SITS there.

Like the rotting carcass of some great beast, except rusted metal. I had watched it grow from a speck on the horizon, at first a small patch of conspicuous mottled-yellow against a sea of red, and now this. As I clamber over it, I can sense the spent horsepower beneath my feet. The key still in the ignition, its big steel brushes set frozen in time.

I wonder why it sits here, out in the middle of nowhere. Malfunction? Out of fuel? Or perhaps abandoned by the operator who, in the end, realized the red nothing in front of them would go on forever, and he or she would certainly die long before their task was completed. Behind it, the fractured remains of an old black-top surface, uncovered by the steel brushes, projects into the distance.

I drop to one knee to inspect the crumbling tarmac, my gaze tracing the straight line to its vanishing point.

"An old highway ... for motorized vehicles," I say. "Just as the archives described it. Hasn't been used in years by the look of it. It must lead somewhere. To a town, or a city ... to other people." But the helpful pair both stand there staring at me, their faces blank and minds empty.

We follow the highway straight for an hour before a dirt road T-bones us from the left.

Straight on? Or the road less traveled?

I study the way ahead, then examine the road off to our left, my eyes blinking at drawn-out intervals. One minute becomes five while I decide which path to follow. In the end, out of habit, I choose to go left.

Around midmorning, we come upon the first sign of other human existence since our unplanned detour to the house: two large, boxed buildings standing adjacent to each other. Old wooden structures that look to have held out against the ravages of time. Looking further ahead, the road narrows before it ascends a steep hill, which appears devoid of everything except an old cabin at the top.

I try the door to the first boxed building, but the padlock across the bolt is rusted shut, and it doesn't give, even when I hit it with a piece of rock. So, I clean a small circle in the window to look inside.

Along the wall on my left, I count twenty-six double-bunk beds, with each bunk covered by a somber gray blanket, dressed to military standard, and topped with a yellowing pillow. A chest-high partition separates the back end of the room from the front, and beyond that, two doors along the back wall are differentiated by blue-on-white stick-figure decals. Old-school, with one depicting a male and the other a female. At this end of the room, an open-plan cooking area is

162

surrounded by four long tables, each flanked by bench seats along the lengthwise sides.

"This is an accommodation block by the look of it," I say.

A large, steel roller door, four times as tall as me and three times that again wide, is the only means of access I can find into the second building. Heaving on the handle, I raise the door high enough to squeeze myself under. Inside, the air is cool. It smells old and used, and the hollow silence tells me this building hasn't been used in a long time. And still, the red dust covers everything inside.

Using a length of chain connected to the roller door, I heave the door high enough for the woman to enter, then a little higher again to let some sunlight in. While the helpful man remains stubbornly outside, protesting something about *trespass*.

"Based on the workbench over there and those tools hanging on the wall, my guess is ... mechanical workshop," I say to the woman, who concurs with a sharp nod of her head. Overhead, a chain block hangs from the roof, fixed at the top to a gantry rail, which runs deep into the belly of the building. I follow the rail further inside. As I look around, I can distinguish all manner of machinery and equipment, large and small, in various stages of repair.

"This would be a loader," I say, looking at one particular piece of equipment. "And this one's a dozer ... And this one, is it some sort of ... drill rig?" I prattle on, the excitement in my voice, now under the supervision of my inner child, growing. "None of these are any good now, though. They were all powered by hydrocarbons. Too expensive. Too toxic." The woman's eyes follow the scattergun arcs drawn by my finger as I point out each machine and, in turn, explain its purpose, its method of activation, and basic principle of operation.

I spot a small contraption leaning up against the wall. "Ah! Now, this is a real find," I say with genuine surprise. I wipe the thick coating of red off its seat before I mount the contraption, running my hand along its long tubular frame. Two extra-large wheels, fixed at either end, have an array of spokes radiating outward from a center axle to the rim of each skinny wheel. I take hold of the bar running transversely across the front of the contraption. Leaning forward, I slide my hands down the tight radius at each end of the bar.

"A bicycle!" I say with delight.

The woman finches. She glares at me, unsure.

"It operates under a person's own power," I tell her. "It's a pity these things became obsolete. They were a great idea, except … far too dangerous to pedestrians." I dismount the bicycle. Then lifting it with one hand, I carry it back to the workbench. "So light," I say, upending it on the bench. "Probably made of carbon fiber."

In a drawer along the base of the workbench, I find a rusted pressure can—labeled, *Lubricant*—and a tire pump. There is still fluid in the can, but the press-nozzle is no longer functional. So I pierce the can with a screwdriver and pour lubricant over the axles, the sprocket, and anything else that looks like it should be swiveling, pivoting, or meshing. I try to rotate the pedals. Bit by bit, they give until I can turn them through a full revolution without jamming.

Again, I can sense the woman close behind me, watching me as she did when we were repairing the pump at the reservoir. Her inquisitive head appears in front of me, bobbing about, inspecting my work. Using the point of my elbow, I respectfully nudge it away.

With all parts of the bicycle operating to my satisfaction, I add air to the tires, pick it up, and head outside. When the helpful man sees me coming through the door, he takes an exaggerated step backward. "No! It's too—too dangerous," he moans. But I ignore him. I set the bicycle upright on the ground, place one foot on the pedal, and mount it. Then I push off and peddle hard.

At first, man and machine fight each other for ascendancy as we lurch and wobble over the flat ground in front of the workshop. At one point, the bicycle almost escapes from under me before I quickly regain my balance. Within minutes, I have complete control of the bicycle, and like a well-broken stallion, it complies as I direct it up the hill, to the cabin, then back down the slope to the workshop.

"It's like ... like riding a bike," I call out as I ride past them, beaming at them before I head to the top again.

After two more trips to the cabin, on my third return, I let go of the steering bar. With both arms raised high in the air, I direct the bicycle using only my thighs and by shifting my weight in the saddle before I bring it to a halt right in front of the helpful pair, who are standing there with their mouths ajar, staring at me in disbelief.

After dismounting the bicycle, I call to the man, "Here, you try." But he mutters something about his safety and backs away, whereas the woman inches her way toward me.

"You sit on it, and I'll push," I tell her in my most convincing voice. "Don't worry," I say, "it's easy once you get the hang of it."

Aboard the bicycle, with her knees shaking and teeth chattering, she sits erect while I propel her slowly up the hill. "Relax," I tell her while blurting out rapid-fire instructions on how to steer, and pedal, and brake, and maintain balance all at the same time. At the cabin, I turn the bicycle around, and we set off back down the hill. Then, with a gentle shove, I let her go.

When the man sees the woman careening down the hill on her own, he collapses to his knees. "It's—it's much too dangerous!" he screams. "It's not—not safe. There's no—no safety." Then he mentions something about *mercy* before activating his head-cover.

However, the woman holds her nerve. Twice she almost falls but somehow manages to recover before finally making it to the bottom, where she brakes to a faultless stop, dismounts, and drops the bicycle on the ground. By the time I arrive, she's standing there with the bicycle at her feet and both arms raised in triumph.

"You did it! You did it!" I say, blowing hard. I stop for a moment, listening to the sound of her laughter. This is the first time I've seen her genuinely happy. A respite, however brief, from our recent traumas. And I'm happy for her. Without asking her permission, I wrap my tree-trunk arms around her tiny body and hug her hard. So hard that she has to gasp for air until I finally let go. Then pointing at the bicycle, I turn to the man. "Now you."

As though I'd just asked him to donate a kidney, the helpful man looks at me in horror and backs away. But I follow him, speaking in low, measured tones, trying to reassure him about his safety, while the woman tugs at his arm. And somehow, in the end, we coax him onto the bicycle.

With his fingers welded to the steering bar and feet weighed down on the pedals like a pair of mighty sea anchors, the man sits dumb-founded on the bicycle as we begin the frightful climb up the hill. "It's easy," I tell him. "You pedal and use the bar to steer."

At the top, we push off. Quarter-way down, I let go of the bicycle, yelling at him to start peddling while the woman looks on from her station further down the hill. But his knees don't bend. With a wide-open mouth and dinner-plate eyes pinned to his face, the man doesn't appear to have a clue how to control the contraption as it lurches around beneath him. When he gets to the woman, she runs alongside him. She's rotating her hands end-over-end to indicate how his legs should be working as the bicycle, with its petrified passenger, continues to hurtle down the hill.

"Brake! Use the brake!" I shout.

But with a morose look on his face, the man appears resigned to his fate. When he reaches the bottom, the front wheel hits a patch of uneven ground. It grips and throws him headlong over the steering bar, where he lays crumpled and moaning in the dirt. When I arrive, the woman is already there tending to him, the bicycle, a mangled heap of machine on the ground beside them with its front wheel now concave where it should be round.

"I—I told you it—it was too dangerous," he blurts out.

"Dangerous?" I say. "You were going so slow that even *she* caught up with you. Why, you aren't even hurt. But it was hilarious to see the bicycle go this way when you went that way." I'm bending the fingers on both my hands until they're all pointing askew. "If only we had a recording, we'd be overnight sensations," I say, bursting into laughter. And the woman laughs too.

"It's—it's not funny," he says, almost in tears. "It was a—a very dangerous situation. I should have had—had more safety." Running a hand over his left breast, the helpful man lets out a woeful moan when he discovers a small tear in his life-support suit. "Oh, no!" he says. "It's—it's broken. My suit is—is broken. How will—will I survive now?"

I pull the man to his feet and swing an arm over his shoulder. As we make our way back up the hill on foot, I can't help wondering how anyone this inadequate could survive out here, even for a short time. And yet, apart from the woman, he doesn't appear to be any more capable than the rest of them.

At the top of the hill, I run a careful eye over the cabin. The stone walls and tiled roof appear sturdy enough, and the front porch looks to have been recently swept. I knock on the door, but nobody answers. I call out. Still nothing. So I open the door and enter.

The interior of the cabin consists of a single room with a wide multi-paneled window taking up most of the back wall. Just inside the doorway, on my right, a cot—again, made-up to military stand-ard—is pushed up against the side wall. On my left, a table and chair are placed near a small, open-top solar stove where a half-filled pot of liquid bubbles away with subtle persistence.

Next to the cot, a roll-top desk with its tambour door fully retracted has sheets of paper stacked one on top of the other in purposeful piles: bill of sale; invoice overdue; account unpaid; final notice. On the wall behind the desk, there's a large map of the district pinned to a cork noticeboard. Using the tip of my finger, I retrace our path back to the T-junction, left along the highway we'd been following, then out to the edge, where a note has been added in thick, black pen—*City 112 miles*—and an arrow indicating off-map.

I try to judge the distance from the cabin to the edge of the map. *Is it a-hundred-and-twelve miles from the cabin? Or a-hundred-and-twelve from the edge of the map?*

Back at the doorway, the helpful man starts up his usual protest while behind him, the woman stands with her arms folded and face filled with fierce determination. Just as the man starts to whine, she shoves him in the back, sending him headlong into the cabin. At first, he appears shocked. But when he makes a scramble for the exit, she blocks his way out. Then for a full minute, the two perform what I can only describe as a crazy intercept dance, with him darting one way then the other, trying to avoid her. Until she finally takes his arm and calms him down.

Leaving them to their carry-on, I'm drawn to the window. Through it, I have an unrestricted view across a gully, to a great mound of earth that dominates the backdrop. A dirt road, starting at the cabin, leads through a gate, cuts across the gully, and ends halfway up the mound where an opening has been excavated into the sheer rock wall.

There's a large photograph, set in an elaborate, leaf-motif frame, hanging on the wall beside me.

In the photograph, a group of people stand on tiered planks in four rows of twelve, each of them holding up cast-iron expressions. Like they'd known true hardship. All except three are wearing sooty white safety-hats above their thin soiled faces, and each brandishes a small lamp with a coiled lead that runs off to a box fitted at their waists. The three men without hats are dressed in smart dark suits and look resolute in the center of the front row. The dark suit wearer in the middle appears so burly that the white-hat-wearers standing behind him have to crane their necks to see past him. And in the background is the same hillside I can see through the window right now.

This appears to be some kind of underground mining operation.

I remove the photograph from the wall to study it closer. A tarnished silver plaque, engraved with a list of people's names, runs across the bottom of the frame. There's also a date-stamp on the plaque but much too worn for me to decode.

I glance through the window again.

Hold on. Wasn't the gate closed a moment ago?

Chapter 15

"NOBODY MOVES, or I'll drop yas all where ya stand, ya thievin' devils."

Startled, I drop the photograph to my feet.

At the doorway, a stout man, dressed in a hole-riddled navy-blue singlet, britches held up with a piece of rope tied around his waist, and wearing a pair of well-worn safety boots, plugs the entrance. With shredded hair and a long fiery beard, the man reminds me of an animated character from my childhood, except this one doesn't seem as endearing. At his hip, he's holding up a shotgun, and both of its rust-covered barrels are leveled squarely at me. For a long time, I fight against the large knot forming in my gut, hardly breathing, while the shotgun remains steady. Then it slowly oscillates between me and the helpful pair who are cowering by the cot.

Without any hurry, the man's tapering eyes examine each of us in turn, up and down, while his lower jaw works thoughtfully at something in his mouth. The man dips his head. He spits on the floor and turns to the helpful pair.

"So yas all found ya'selves a real live Thinker, eh?" The shotgun sweeps the room, casual-like, as if to confirm there aren't more of us hiding under the table or behind the door before it settles on me once again. "You two get over there with him, so as I can see yas all properly."

With their bottom lips quivering, the helpful pair shuffle further into the room where they squat down behind me. In the back of my mind, I can't shake the feeling I've seen this man before, but not from an old-time cartoon. Then I realize this is the same burly miner depicted in the center of the photograph, only years older and carrying a lot less weight.

The miner enters the room. With the shotgun still trained on me, he edges his way behind us.

"Okay. Ya all need to move slow-like out that door. No sudden movements now. And don't be thinkin' about runnin' off because I'll blow all ya damned heads off before ya can even start thinkin' of runnin'."

I help the frightened pair to their feet. Using my body as a shield, I usher them outside to where the miner herds us around the back of the cabin and up the road toward the mine.

"So ya thought ya all could rob me," he says. "Well, I'm way too smart for thievin' devils like yas all."

"It's not what you think, sir," I say. "We were looking for—"

"Well, I'll be. A Thinker what talks," he says, genuinely surprised. "I never heard of one what talks before."

"But you don't understand. We're lost," I say with sincerity. "We saw the cabin and thought you might be able to give us directions.

We thought—"

"Eh? Is that so? Well, ya all thought wrong," he replies. With the muzzle of the shotgun pressed hard into the small of my back, the miner nods to the entrance of the mine. "Now, yas all get on down the hole."

"Can we please discuss this like reasonable people?"

"But I ain't as reasonable as ya all would want me to be. And I'd never trust a Thinker to be a reasonable kinda person as well."

"I don't follow. What do you mean by, *Thinker*?"

"Ha! You're a cunnin' devil, ain't ya. But I'm awake to you and ya kind. I already heard about how tricky ya all can be, and ya won't be tricking me. No sir, not me. Not this time."

Just inside the entrance, the miner flicks a switch to activate a line of fluorescent lamps, which are strung out along the ceiling and disappear downward, underground. "Down we go," he says.

In front of me, the helpful man begins to whimper.

"Yas all need to stop the whinin', ya hear? I can't stand the whinin'. Why is it people always seem to whine when they's in trouble? Ya got caught trying to rob me, and yas all need to make proper restitution for that."

"I've already told you, sir, we're not thieves," I say. "We made an honest mistake. We're sorry for the trespass and any inconvenience we've caused."

"One more word from you, and I'm going to blow ya entrails out all over the wall. Ya hear me? Now, keep movin'."

For the next half hour, we descend deeper into the mine, too afraid to say anything that might antagonize the miner. Apart from the occasional whimper from the helpful man, only the echoes of our footsteps, bouncing off the dank walls, accompany us down the hole. At some point, the miner starts humming a strangely familiar tune. Something pre-Enlightenment. Deep Pink? Purple Floyd? *Something about smoke on a river ...*

Just when I think the tunnel might go downward forever, we come to a large semi-lit chamber with a steel door off to one side. The miner ushers us through the door, into a smaller room where he flicks a switch to flood the inside with light.

"Right, yas all sit over there where I can see yas better." He herds us into the far corner of the room, away from the entrance, and orders us onto the floor. "And don't be tryin' anything stupid, 'kay?"

Along the wall, a bench covered with unwashed dishes and eating utensils, sits below a row of wall-mounted cupboards, while a tall cupboard stands almost sergeant-like at one end of the bench. On the opposite wall, what looks like a fish tank, bubbles away as though it were furious with its occupants. Except, from where I'm sitting, the tank appears to be empty. In the center of the room, a plastic fold-away table with an elegant high-backed dining chair—bizarrely misplaced in these filthy surrounds—tucked underneath. An old-style refrigerator hums a nagging monotone in the background. And in the corner, I recognize the configuration layout of an Entertainer. Probably five models old and ought to have been retired from the look of the control box on the wall.

Leaving the shotgun upright against the table, the miner rummages through the tall cupboard. He takes a bottle from the topmost shelf. A cleanskin of ... *hooch?* And a dinged-up metal cup, minus the handle, from the next shelf down. Using his teeth, he removes the cork from the bottle and pours out a good measure of content into the cup. Then leaning back in his elegant chair, the miner eyes us off.

"Now, what am I going do with yas all?" he says. "Hmmm. I can't rightly keep all of ya on as guests. Too many mouths to feed; what with provisions the way they are and all." He drains the cup in one long swig, then downs a refill just as quick. "I guess the law wouldn't hold me accountable if I was to just shoot yas and bury yas all out the back. Trespassing is frowned upon in these parts ya know. Especially when it comes to thieves. Why, they gave out medals to the ones who took it 'pon themselves to shoot the looters during the rumblings all those years ago."

He pours another drink.

Time passes slowly, and apart from a few grunts from the miner, nothing more is said. The helpful man's head tilts backward, his mouth opening as wide as a cavern. The helpful woman yawns next. The bottle, which was full at the start of the session, is now more than three-quarters empty. The helpful pair's eyes glaze over. Their eyelids grow heavy, and before long, they close. Both my legs ache from sitting on the floor too long. I try to stretch out, to get the circulation going again. Soon after, the miner closes his eyes too. He slumps forward in the chair and lets out a heavy snore.

"Which transition metal are you chasing?"

With his eyes still shut, the miner stops snoring. "Eh? What did ya say?"

"What metals are you mining? Gold? Silver? Platinum?"

His eyelids open halfway in interest. "No, none of those worthless rocks," he says, waving his hand dismissively. Clutching the bottle in one hand and holding the table with the other, the miner teeters as he stands. He leans in close to me, his breath stinking of home-brewed whiskey. "I'm digging for something much more valuable.

Much more useful than those sparkly, trendy, show-off things." His slurred words fuse into one long anagram which, to my surprise, I'm still able to understand. With a lazy grin unfurling across his ruddy face, the miner picks up the empty cup and uses it to signal me toward the door. "Come with me," he says. "Come this way, and I'll show ya."

The miner heads for the door, leaving the helpful pair crashed out on the floor and the shotgun still unattended against the table. In his drunken excitement, he almost trips and falls. With a finger pressed against his lips, he points repeatedly at the helpful pair while urging me to follow him.

Outside the room, the miner fumbles through a line of safety hats hanging from a row of hooks mounted along the wall. He picks up the first hat, flicks the switch, and smacks the lamp. An explosion of light ignites his craggy face, sending him backward where he almost falls again. "Wow!" he says, his eyes blinking rapidly as he pushes the hat down hard on his head.

Searching through the remaining hats, he checks their batteries for signs of charge. "Hmmm. None of these works," he says, sounding almost regretful. "But none of 'em is big enough to fit ya head anyway. So just stick close to me."

We descend deeper into the belly of the mine, where the tunnel narrows and the decline steepens, the walls and ceiling closing in on me, squeezing against me the further we go. Breathing becomes difficult in the warm moist air. Skipping ahead, the miner takes the unreliable light with him, leaving me in the dark, so I try to catch up. With my eyes straining to penetrate the vagueness in front of me, I grope my way forward. Until the light disappears altogether, and all I can do is place one foot in front of the other and hope I don't trip and fall. Ahead, I hear his footsteps. Occasionally, there's a shaft of light from the miner's gyrating head streaking around the interior of the tunnel like an overworked searchlight in a blitzkrieg.

A while later, the tunnel opens into a large cavern where the miner stands and waves me in. He points at the far wall. "This is it. See here." His words skip around the void, bouncing off the walls as though they are playing a game of tag with the light from his seesawing lamp. The light finally settles on a badly rusted cabinet on the wall beside us. The miner stoops to open the front panel. He leans inside and throws a switch. Above us, an array of light-tubes, set high into the arched roof, ignite at the same time as two dinosaur-sized ventilation fans scream into life, followed by a draft of cool, stale air breezing across my face.

The miner ushers me across the cavern to the far wall, where a large excavating machine sits idle. Showing uncanny balance and surprising agility, considering how much alcohol he'd just consumed, he scales the ladder, hops into the cab, and starts the engine. With its throttle fully open, the roar from the machine amplifies the noise of the screaming fans, to the extent that I have to clamp both hands over my ears just to hear myself think.

With nonchalance, the miner begins to excavate the rock face in front of us, the machine's extension grip clawing at the wall, busily building up a stockpile of material on the floor. After ten minutes, he signals me up onto the cab. He hands me the controls and points to the wall. "Follow the seam," he bellows at ten decibels higher than the noise of the machine. "Follow the seam."

I work the levers hard, operating the machine with all the skill of a semi-professional—surprising even myself—and after a short work-out, the ground in front of us is full of mined material. When the miner shuts the engine and cuts the fans, the chamber falls silent once again, only a high-pitched ringing left in my ears.

"Take a look at this," he says, kneeling beside the stockpile. "Something more valuable than gold. More precious than platinum." He fills his cupped hands with material and stands. *"Plastics* is what we're after." Rubbing his hands together, he dances a small jig while chunks of plastic fall between his stubby fingers, back onto the pile. "All the wealth in the world is in plastics. Ya just need to sort it out from the rest of the crap, move it onto that conveyor over there,"— he motions to the conveyor—"stockpile it in the next chamber, and send it to the top, where the next transport hauler comes and takes it off to market. Then ya sit back and wait 'til they's adds all them class As to ya savings."

"What do they do with it? The plastics, I mean."

"Well, after they banned explorin' and minin' of them minerals they used to build them tall buildings with, they needed to find a re-placement. Some bright spark invented a new plastic polymer that was stronger than steel and never rusted. Brilliant, eh? Except they couldn't make any new plastics after bannin' the use of hydro-carbons. So I came up with the genius idea of digging up and recyclin' the used plastics from the old landfills."

I look beyond the miner, to the mini mountain of plastic waste behind him.

"This was once the main waste disposal site for the big city, a-couple-a hours haulin' down the road."

"A city? With people?"

"Yep, with lots of 'em. This used to be a natural canyon where they dumped their waste for hundreds of years till it was filled. There's loads of plastics sittin' here, waitin' to be mined. Why, I've been chasing the same seam for over forty years now, and I still haven't made a dent in it. There's three more operations across the other side of the hill, with everyone tunnelin' into the same resource. But it'll take more than four lifetimes afore our tunnels will get anywhere close to meetin' up. And the bonus is, two levels below us, I got me a doohickey what converts the organic waste into methane, which I use to generate me power. A lifetime's supply of free electricity for me."

As we follow the conveyor into the next chamber, which I estimate to be more than ten times larger than the first, the miner gives me a detailed explanation of his workings. In this chamber, the plastic refuse has been sorted and placed into heaps, with each heap piled so high that it makes me think the last transport hauler had probably departed this place a long time ago.

"This is the pile for polycarbonate drink bottles. Over there's the lengths of PVC pipes, all sorted by diameter size and length; polystyrene foam and packaging; vinyl furniture; toys; food containers; polyamide car parts; polythene bags." As he points out the different varieties of his prized produce, I can sense his enthusiasm. "And those things over there …" He nods to a pair of yellow arches, hinged together, leaning against the wall, almost as tall as the roof. "Well, they's anyone's guess."

The plastics miner stands back to survey his product, looking over it longingly.

"In the good times, we was gettin' an A-Class for each measured cube of plastic," he says, melancholic-like. "But those were the good ol' times …" With his head dropped, he falls silent.

"So what happened?"

"The market happened," he replies. "Demand evaporated, and

trade stopped almost overnight. The price went inta free fall. Today I'd be lucky to get a-couple-a phony-baloneys for a cube. I kept me mine going for as long as I could, but in the end, I had to let go of all me workers." His voice tapers off. With his bottom lip starting to quiver, a solitary tear disappears into the twisted growth on his cheek. For a long time, we stand in silence, staring at the piles of plastics. I place a consoling hand on his shoulder, and in response, he pats it gently.

"But things 'll get better though," he finally says. "The market will pick up. The price 'll go through the roof, and the good times will return. Ya mark my words."

We head back up the tunnel, with the plastics miner babbling non-stop about what he'll do when the good times return. About how busy he'll be loading the cubes and cubes of product onto the haulers, which will be queued in long lines, waiting to be filled with as much plastic as he can pull from his mine.

I let him talk.

For the next few hours, the plastics miner's deliberations swing between the euphoria of his hopes for tomorrow and the despair of his difficulties now. The highs and lows of his mood governed by each swig he takes from each newly opened bottle of whiskey. After emptying two more bottles, he finally falls silent. Slumped forward in his chair, with his face buried in his broad chest, he snores.

I wait a little longer. Once I'm sure the plastics miner is unconscious, I shake the helpful pair, signal to them to stay quiet. After helping them to their feet, we start for the door.

"I wouldn't have shot any of ya, ya know."

The sinews at the base of my neck snap to attention. The three of us freeze mid-step. Rotating my head in careful increments, I see the plastics miner still slumped in his chair. The shotgun, there against the table, close beside him.

"We were just—"

"It's okay. I just wanted some company, that's all. I haven't had any proper company for near on ten years now. That's when I had to let them go. All of me workers, I mean. Ten years with nobody to talk to. And when that damn contraption over there broke down a couple of years ago …" He raises his anvil head, nods vaguely at the Entertainer. "Well, I haven't heard another human voice since then. And when I saw yas all up at the house … I just wanted some company, that's all."

My sinews release.

"Anyway, I couldn't have shot any of yas because I ain't got no shot left."

Immediately, my fear of the plastics miner evaporates, and all I see now is a broken, lonely old man, slumped in a chair. Looking at the Entertainer, I signal for the helpful pair to remain at the doorway. After edging my way around to the control box, I flip the isolating switch, open it, and peer inside. I turn to the plastics miner. "Do you have any tools?"

"Eh? Try the bottom shelf," he says, waving his finger in the vicinity of the tall cupboard.

Down on all fours, I burrow to the back of the bottom shelf, where I find a small screwdriver and a strand of single-core copper wire. Using the screwdriver, I joggle the fuse out from between the two silver posts on the circuit board and hold it up to the light. Smoke residue clings to the inside of the glass and a small bead of melted wire rolls around when I rotate the tube. "I'm sure things will pick up," I say. "The price of plastics will recover, and your mine will be crawling with workers again." I wrap the strand of copper wire between the fuse posts. "And the transport haulers will soon be lined up outside the gate, bumper to bumper. So many haulers, you won't be able to fill them quick enough."

"Do ya really think so?" His voice has a spark to it.

I flip the isolating switch. Inside the box, a red light winks, then it flickers green as the Entertainer boots. I replace the lid. "Yes, I really think so."

The miner's eyes light up, a row of fencepost teeth appearing through his bushed beard as his smile increases. "Why thank ya son," he says as he hobbles across the room to where the Entertainer draws him into its personal holographic metazone. Then lifting him bodily, the Entertainer twirls him around high above the floor, its seductive voice engaging him in conversation. He chatters and giggles while spinning gently from head to toe. He rotates round and round, as though gravity had somehow forgotten about him now that he is wholly assimilated into the Entertainer.

At the doorway, the helpful pair are looking wide-eyed at the plastics miner who is suspended in mid-air without any support. He's immersed in a sphere of holograms of people, and animals, and places, and things. All interacting with him inside a curtain of lights, which emit every color of the visible spectrum in pulsating, hypnotic sequences.

I grab the miner's lamp and the battery pack and stuff them into my knapsack. Then I push the helpful pair out the door.

"We should go," I tell them.

When we reach the T-junction, I examine the road we'd come by yesterday. Then I run a pensive look in the other direction.

"He said the city is two hours down the highway by hauler. Said we'll find many people there. They can help us." I turn to the two aliens beside me. "By my calculations, it should take us about four days on foot."

They both nod an awkward nod.

"We'd better get started, hey."

Chapter 16

CAN YOU HEAR *loneliness?*

I ask myself that same question again. If it were loud enough, would loneliness be a roar so deafening that you couldn't hear anything else around you? Would it drown out every other sound on the Earth? Would it be so painful in your ears that you would have to clamp both hands over them to block it out? Or like a black hole does with light, would its discord fall into something from which noise can never escape?

Sometimes a scene is impossible to describe by what *is* there and can only be described by what *is no longer* there. And if I were pressed to convey the scene surrounding us now, only one word comes to mind: loneliness. The loneliness of the nothing that swallows us up with each step we take in this eternal, barren countryside.

I close my mind off completely to the unstructured inputs from the outside world and lose myself deep in my thoughts.

I'm not certain where we're going or what we'll find when we get there. And I don't know who might be there, or if the three of us will be swallowed up and lost in the pandemonium of the city. But what I do know for sure: with each step I take through this loneliness, I'm moving further away from the pain of my past and closer to a new beginning.

At some time during the morning, the tedious terrain yields to an endless run of rolling hills, which spring up around us, almost unnoticed. Something different, something irregular awakens me from my Ganzfeld-like state as a carpet of mighty wind turbines comes at us from across the landscape. Spread out as far as the eye can see, like a million white monuments, all laid out in a network of equally spaced rows and columns. Here and there, the illusion of their perfect placement is spoiled by a toppled turbine lying in pieces on the ground. The air sits hot and still around us, and there's a strange sense of inertia as I look over this quiet, foreboding graveyard.

My curiosity steers me to a turbine tower laid out in the field closest to us, where I climb over the fallen giant's carcass. On the nacelle, I grab the anemometer and spin it. I hold the vane and move it from left to right, then to the left again.

"The control sensors are still in perfect working order," I say, calling out to the helpful pair. When I look around at the rest of the turbines still standing upright, I realize they're all aligned in the same direction. "It's like all the turbines stopped rotating at the same instant. As though someone had switched the wind off and never switched it on again."

But the two of them stand before me, expressionless, like two obtuse monuments themselves. Sometimes when I look at them, they seem lively, almost engaging, but at times like now, all I see are two impersonations of what must have once been viable people. And disappointed in their lack of presence, I can only shake my head.

The miles fall behind us quickly as we hold up a solid pace. In the early afternoon, we come to another side road—on our right this time—which leads up a steady incline to the top of another hill. About halfway up the hill, we stop short of what appears to be a guardhouse. From a distance, the guardhouse reminds me of something forlorn, a thing left to defend something that was most likely forgotten about a long time ago. With the door half-hanging off its hinges and the glazing mostly gone, to me, this house no longer seems capable of guarding anything anymore. The razor-wire fence surrounding whatever facility this is, still offers a semblance of security, except where a raised boom gate allows the road on through.

As I make my way up past the guardhouse, the boom gate hovers over me, poised like a guillotine about to drop. Standing beneath it with my arms apart and face lifted to the sky, I offer myself up to whoever or whatever is now responsible for meting out retribution in this anomalous new world.

For all my crimes, let it fall, now …

I linger a moment. But somehow, this isn't my time. And grateful for that, I step to the other side where the helpful woman is waiting, watching my antics with fascination. I throw her a look of contrition, a sign of my hopeless resignation to a wicked past.

The road takes us to the top of the hill, where the parabolic frame of a grandiose communications dish sits alongside an unremarkable block building. The most asymmetrical pairing of two discrete objects I've ever seen.

Inside the building, we find all the windows covered by a chaotic collage of debris: wooden planks; sheets of paper; pieces of plastic; strips of fabric. In some places, the planks are nailed three and four boards thick, one on top of the other, as though they'd been put there to triple and quadruple the internal security. Around the perimeter of the room, a bank of tall, narrow equipment racks lines the walls, while overhead, two rows of stunted fluorescent tubes covered by wire mesh bulge from the ceiling like afterthoughts. And in the center of the room, an operating console looks almost friendless out on its own in the wide-open floor space.

With buttons, dials, and needle pointing instruments crowding its backboard, the console appears prehistoric. Two curved screens—very old quantum dot technology, I suspect—are mounted above the console, while a pair of archaic talk-listen handsets hang from a small box on the right side of the console. Another handset hangs from a similar box on the left.

I lift a handset to my ear … Nothing. I turn to the woman. "I thought we might be able to contact the city," I say, returning the handset to its box. "To let them know we're on our way."

After wiping the red dust off the right-side screen, I pull a chair out from under the console and sit. On her side, the woman does the same. In front of us, two anachronous keyboards are laid out on the top of the console, each covered by a molded silicone skin. Pinned beneath my keyboard, I find a sheet of yellowing paper with a handwritten note, barely legible.

To ~~who~~ whom it may concern. This was an old telecommunications museum ~~which~~ that I restored into operation. I've been here for ~~20~~ ~~23~~ a long time searching for a signal, one that confirms there are still some of us left (at least an-

yone with the same technical expertise as ~~me~~ I and the right equipment ꝫ to communicate). But there is ~~nobody~~ no one, or else the last satellite has finally lost altitude. I can't stay here ~~anymore~~ any longer. The walls are watching me. And the fones keep ringing. Day and night they ring. I carn't sleep anymore. Someone on the other end of the line sez the commdish wants to ~~kill murder~~ kill me. So I have to keep the doors closed and the windows covered so the commdish can't find me because it wants to kill me!!!

The rambling note continues over the page.

"Not very encouraging," I say under my breath.

I clean the dust off the controls on my side, then remove the silicone cover from my keyboard while the woman does the same on her side.

"Unify Aleph-1." I say it out loud. Then I wait.

Again, nothing.

Red-faced, I turn to the woman. "It was worth a try," I say. But she just gives me a puzzled look.

On my side, I flip a switch marked MASTER to ON. But nothing happens. From her side, the woman's octopus arms reach across unannounced, and she fiddles with the switches and presses buttons on my side. I grab her wrist, smile to myself as I return her hand to her side. Wrinkling her nose at me, she leans back in her chair with her arms folded in defiance while I restore the controls on my side back to their original settings.

After rummaging through a set of filing drawers under the console, I find a thick document, an *Operating Manual*, in which I soon find myself immersed in the detail of all 1,726 pages on how to operate this communications facility. Two hours later, a little jaded but a whole lot the wiser, I lift my head to find the chair beside me is empty.

"She went—went that way," says the helpful man, signaling to the door.

Outside, I find the woman behind the *murderous* commdish, halfway through cleaning the dust off an array of solar panels. I stand back and quietly watch her. When she's finished, she traces the wiring back to a control box, which is mounted at the base of the commdish. She opens the door, reaches inside, and throws the switch to the inverter unit. A red light indicates.

"Good," I say, and we head back inside.

On the power distribution box, a small readout tells us the available charge is at 4%. After remaining steady for a few minutes, the readout ticks up to 5%. "This is going to take a while," I say to her, eying off the readout.

Sitting at the console again, I'm trying to relax, but the woman won't stop playing with the buttons and dials in front of us, disturbing the intended order of things. Four hours pass before I finally decide to check the readout again: 67%. *That should be enough.* After throwing the main breaker, I try the MASTER switch again, and at once, both sides of the console light up.

"Yes!" I yell and punch the air. Beside me, the woman leaps from her seat and punches the air as well.

I run my trembling fingers across the keyboard until the overhead screen arrives at the SETUP menu.

I select: CALIBRATE, then GO.

Across the console, the lights blink in a chaotic display of wonderment before they all go steady. Needles fluctuate wildly then stabilize. A PiP window showing an image of the commdish pops onto my screen while the servomotor driving it hums into life. Gears whir as the dish shudders back to its home position. Then they groan when the dish swings a full 360-degree horizontal rotation before traversing a 170-degree path over the top of the sky in jerking movements, as though it were performing some kind of weird start–stop dance. Two minutes later, the dish stalls, pointed at the horizon. All the noise from outside ceases, and the screen responds: SYSTEM READY.

"We need to lock onto an active signal," I say to the woman.

I navigate the menu: FULL SCAN, GO.

Immediately, the screen reports back: *Scan at 0% Active channels found = 0*

In the top right corner of both our screens, twelve digits, thick black numbers set against a white background, indicate the scan status. The numbers climb through the full range of frequency bands as the commdish hunts for a signal. Once a scan is completed, the angular position of the dish is incremented by a fraction of a degree before the entire range is scanned again.

As the search continues long into the night, I watch the status climb through the frequencies, then reset, increment the dish position and climb again, over and over. Beside me, the helpful woman stares at the ticking numbers as if hypnotized, while the helpful man has tucked himself away in a corner. Hours later, the woman's eyelids start to flutter as she fights to keep them open. Until, at last, they close, and she slumps forward in her seat with her head resting on the console.

The screen in front of me continues to update: '*Scan at 13% Active channels found = 0*

An hour later, my eyes close too before my head flops onto the console as well.

When I wake the next morning, the helpful woman is still asleep beside me, the helpful man snoring in the corner, while the scan grinds on: *Scan at 94% Active channels found = 0*

I shake the woman.

"This doesn't look promising," I tell her as she wipes the sleep from her eyes and yawns. "Look, no channels found yet."

Just as I speak, the outside hum from the servomotor abruptly ceases. The screens go blank, and the console dies. I check the battery readout in the distribution box, now flashing: *1% CRITICAL.*

I'm not sure why we returned the chairs under the console and covered the keyboards. Or left the batteries on charge. Or sealed the front door. Perhaps it was me hoping that someone else might pass this way sometime in the future and want to try again. Whoever it is, maybe they'll get lucky next time. Lucky enough to find a signal.

With the communications station a long way behind us and the last of the wind turbines gone, the terrain ahead reverts to the same red emptiness I've come to expect as the new normal for the world. In the late afternoon, with our shadows fleeing from under our feet in earnest, we come upon a clump of trees. Judging by the look of their skeletal-like remains, I conclude these individuals must have died a long time ago: given up by this parched, intolerant topsoil.

Not long after, the spasmodic clumps on both sides of the highway consolidate into a forest of ghostly giants. Wiry tendrils of withered vegetation climb out of the forest floor. They coil their way up around the plumb trunks as though, at some time in the past, the undergrowth decided to head skyward in a desperate search for moisture before it too succumbed to the dry.

ENTROPY

At the roadside, a signboard hangs lopsided against two rusted-out support posts, only held there by a solitary bolt. A lone martyr holding out against the inevitable in a final act of self-sacrifice.

Tilting my head sideways, I read the sign.

LUNGS OF THE EARTH PROJECT

CARBON CAPTURE PLANTATION NO 20220324-984

Behind the writing, a picture portrays the place in its resplendent years. Although today, the once vibrant blues, and browns, and greens in the image are cracked and bleached from years under the hammering sun. The same fate for every color in the world now, except the red covering it all.

"We should camp here for the night," I say to the pair.

With his eyes blinking rapidly, the helpful man hops from one foot to the other. "But—but we can't stay out here in—in the open …" After starting out as a low-pitched whine, the man's voice skips an octave. "In case they—they return."

"Then we'll need to make a fire," I say. "Do either of you have a lighter?"

They both look at me, totally bewildered.

"You know … matches? A flint, maybe?"

Sill nothing from them.

"I was making a joke," I say with a wry smile.

After hopping the fence, I use my weight to snap a large, knotted branch off the closest tree. I'm about to break off another branch when there's an almighty squeal from the road. "You—you can't do that," the man complains. "You shouldn't be—be in there. It's not—not permissible." Beside him, the woman is staring at me in horror as if I've just committed arborary murder.

Ignoring their protests, I gather an armful of branches and heave them over the fence before heading back into the plantation for more. Once there's a sizable pile of fuel on the highway, I return over the fence with a handful of dried bark and leaves, which I've scrounged from the forest floor. After placing some twigs and smaller sticks on the ground to form a heaped pyramid, I gather a clump of dead grass and press it firmly into a bundle by my feet.

"Now we need an ignition source," I say to myself, although perhaps a little too loudly because the woman grabs the man by the arm and pulls him behind her.

While I'm sizing up a branch from the woodpile, I turn to them. "Do you know what separates us from the rest of the animal kingdom?" I ask. "Fire," I say. "We are the only species of animal on the Earth to harness the one thing the rest fear most." After choosing a particular stick from the pile, one that bends enough across my knee without breaking, I set it aside. Then I tear three thin strips from my pant leg and twist them together to make a length of cord. "When *Erectus* first came down from the trees around four-hundred-thousand years ago—although that timing is debatable—it didn't take long before it realized that fire was the key to its survival."

Out of my peripheral vision, I notice the woman creeping closer to me. She squats beside the pyramid watching intently as I bend the stick and tie the cord off at each end to fashion a crude bow. "We tamed the fire to give us light and cook our food." I find a shorter stick, about the length of my forearm and the thickness of my thumb. After flattening one end of the stick against a rock, I grind the other end to a point. "We confined it to keep us warm …" With the bowstring wound once around the stick and its pointed end nuzzled into a handful of tinder, which I've arranged on a flat wooden base, I operate the stick in short sharp bursts. Clockwise, then counterclockwise. "We enclosed it in furnaces to smelt metals, which we combined in the correct ratios to create alloys." Soon, a wisp of gray rises from the tinder before a show of red appears on the base.

With the lightest breath, I blow on the ember as the woman's curious eyes follow the smoke trail skyward while the man continues to watch on at a safe distance.

After transferring the smoking ember to the tinder bundle at my feet, I blow on it some more. "We mixed copper with tin and got bronze, from which we made tools ... and forge better weapons to overpower those who were still using wood and stone." The woman leans in to add her breath to the bundle, and together, we blow until a trail of thick smoke billows off. "Then we alloyed iron with carbon ... which gave us steel. Now, steel ... allowed us to make better weapons ... build bigger cities."

The woman coughs. She wipes her eyes and blows some more.

I transfer the smoking bundle to the heaped pyramid, and we blow hard until it catches alight. "By controlling fire, we ... we ..."— with my head now spinning—"rose to the apex of the animal kingdom." I heap on more wood. "We found our ... advantage ... over the rest."

When the pile erupts in flame, I stand back with both arms raised. "And that's how ... man ... makes fire," I say triumphantly.

Beside me, the helpful woman steps back with her arms raised as well and beaming out an I'm-pleased-too look, while the helpful man maintains his distance. His eyes, like pendulums, swing between us and the fire.

"I'm not so—so sure this is a—a good idea," he says.

Later in the evening, I toss another armful of wood on the fire and stretch out on the ground nearby. Lying here watching him, the antics of the helpful man fascinate me. At first, he'd sat stubbornly just inside the perimeter of light formed by the roaring fire. But as the evening wore on, he inched himself toward the fire until his infatuation with the flames surpassed his fear of the fire itself. Now, he delights as each flame licks into the air, inciting himself to move even closer.

When my eyes finally close, the last images I have are of the helpful man performing what could easily be mistaken for a childish game of dare where he rushes in at the fire, stays there for a count of five, then giggles as he retreats from the searing heat. Each time he does so, his confidence grows until he gets so close to the flames that he can almost touch them.

In the dead of night, the helpful woman shakes me with such a force that refutes her size. She's pointing a frantic finger at the forest where the helpful man has jumped the fence and is running amok on the other side in a chaotic scramble. High above his head, the man is waving a burning branch which, I can safely assume, he's dared himself to take from the fire. Live cinders falling from the branch torch the carpet of dried fuel behind him as a wall of flames chase him screaming through the plantation.

I spring to my feet and, still half asleep, struggle to haul myself over the fence. I yell after the man, but he won't listen. Instead, he continues with his mindless stunt. When I catch up with him, I throw myself at him, taking him around the waist and bring him to the ground. Amid the tangle of our twisted bodies, the man sits up and looks at me, his eyes as full as two big moons. A shower of embers ignites the tinderbox around us, which makes him squeal.

Fire races up the tree-trunks like some voracious feeder intent on consuming everything here. Overhead, the canopy of leafless limbs suddenly flares. I try to hold the man down, but he slips free and rushes blindly into the flames. While further inside the inferno, a tree, engulfed by flame, falls. It brings down the tree adjacent to it, and that one, in turn, brings down the next, and within minutes, a ripple of toppling trees and twisted burning branches cascades in on us.

I call to the man, "Watch out!" But before he can stop running, the last domino in the line of fiery giants comes crashing down on him, pinning him underneath.

With pieces of tree falling around me and embers raining down, I pick my way to where I'd last seen him. From beneath the tree-trunk, somewhere amongst the jumbled mess, he stares up at me, mouthing useless words and blinking his eyes startled-like. I grab his arms, try to pull him free, but each time I pull, he yelps and resists. I try again. Same result. Then, amid all the danger and foolishness around me, I step away from him, block out everything, and try to think.

I scan the surrounding area, looking for something to use as a fulcrum. To my left, there's a rock, which I reckon is large enough for the job yet light enough for me to roll into place. On the ground behind me, I find a branch, about the thickness of my arm and long and straight enough to use as a lever. With the branch wedged under the fallen tree and pivoting on the rock, I attempt to lift the tree high enough for the man to wriggle free. But his foot remains trapped under the debris.

A lick of flame runs at us from along the tree trunk, prompting the man to squeal louder. After wedging the branch under the trunk so it can't fall back, I try again to drag him out. But his foot is stuck fast. I set myself, take a deep breath, and try to work the lever again. But the tree won't budge. As I hold my ground, a sudden rush of air, sucked in by the fire, drives the flames from the tree trunk, across the gap, and onto the lever, forcing me back.

When the man sees me retreating, he screams. He begs me not to leave him here, and as I look into his imploring eyes, I suddenly feel sorry for him. So I grit my teeth and move in to take hold of the burning lever for the third time.

The smell of burning flesh fills my nostrils while pain from my lower hand, now enveloped in flame, rips up my forearm. I shout at the fire. I curse it as I put all my weight onto the lever. I push down even harder. Now the tree moves; enough for the helpful man to pull free. Once I'm sure he's clear, I release the lever and back away. I drop to the ground where we both lie, spread-eagled on our backs, with me in agony and out of breath while the wide-eyed man is choking and sobbing beside me.

"Are you okay?" I ask him.

But at that moment, the tree beside us explodes. Before I can calm him, the man is on his feet, bolting for the highway, where the woman heaves him over the fence and back to the safety of the road.

After getting to my feet, I pick my way through the flame zone. With my good hand covering my mouth and nose against the smoke, I stagger across the scorched earth and over the fence, where I collapse on the highway belching the carbon-loaded air out of my lungs. Lying here, listening to the roar of the fire, I elevate my burned arm to relieve some of the pain.

Moments later, the helpful woman is at my side. I try to say something to her, but it hurts to talk. After carefully lowering my arm, she inspects my injured hand. Working quickly, she scrapes the dirt and pieces of charcoal from my palm. Then she takes my flask and dribbles some water over the large, raw blotch covering the back of my hand, extending halfway up my forearm with the skin blistered and peeling away. Once she's cleaned the wound, the woman rips a wide strip from the remains of my pant leg. She wraps it around my hand and ties it off just short of my elbow.

Grimacing, I sit up and peer across the fence. Again, I try to talk, but the words stick at the back of my throat, unable to get past the pulp of ash and soot that fills my mouth. On the opposite side of the fence, the firestorm rages out of control as it accelerates out along the flanks and gorges its way into the heart of the plantation. Even from here on the highway, the radiated heat singes the side of my face while the whole nighttime is lit up like it was day.

I hurl a savage look at the arsonist, who responds with a sheepish smile. Then shaking my head, I finally force the gravelly words out.

"There is not a single word I can find … to describe what just happened."

The man turns away from me. He lowers his head and stares abjectly at the ground.

Chapter 17

THE NEXT MORNING, I look despairingly over the remains of the fire-ravaged plantation.

The three of us are standing together in the middle of the road, shrouded by the eerie light filtering in on us through an air impregnated with soot and fumes from the fire. A thick gray plume, pouring out of the smoldering ground, stretches plumb upward into the troposphere for as high as I can see. Without shielding my eyes, I can look directly into the sun as it inches its way skyward behind the plume: a sun turned blood-red by the smoke particles deflecting its blue-end light from my eyes.

Blackened stumps, like silent victims of a massacre, jut up here and there across the bare, undulating furrows which, until yesterday, had served as a perpetual memorial to these revered relics of a bygone age. An ankle-deep layer of blue-gray ash covers the floor, a stark contrast to the permanent red hue that has continually hounded me. And a nutty smell of bushfire chokes my grief.

Beside me, the helpful man hangs his head. With his thin frame hunched over, the man appears even smaller now, as though he were trying to shrink himself into insignificance.

My hand hurts terribly.

Unable to look at the scene any longer, I turn away and set off along the road with the helpful woman beside me. A few minutes later, I glance over my shoulder to where the man is still bent over in the middle of the road. He straightens. Then he turns toward us and deploys his head-cover. And once again, he takes up our rear.

A while later, we reach the edge of the burn: a narrow strip of clearing where the fire's run had been halted before it could break through to the adjoining plantation. Looking at the clearing, I feel a sense of relief. A small consolation that the extent of the damage has been contained, on this edge of the fire anyway.

Not much further down the road, another weather-beaten sentinel stands in front of the next plantation.

LUNGS OF THE EARTH PROJECT

CARBON CAPTURE PLANTATION NO 20220324-985

A small whitish flake floats down from the sky and settles at my feet.

"SNOW!"

From behind me, the alien man cries out as he scrambles to retract his head-cover.

"I—I SEE SNOW!"

Amused by the child-like innocence in his voice and the look of sheer delight on his face, I'm moved to relent.

"No, it's not snow," I say to him. "It's ash. From a process called pyroconvection. As the hot air from the fire rises, it gradually cools, and if there aren't any prevailing winds in the upper atmosphere to blow it away, the ash falls back around the vicinity of the fire."

By the time I've finished talking, a thick blanket covers us and everything around us as the ash-fall intensifies. Taking a knee, I use my good hand to try to tear another strip from my pant leg, without much success. The helpful woman kneels beside me. She rips a hand-sized piece of cloth from along the bottom of my right pant leg and hands it to me. After hitching the knapsack higher on my shoulder, I use the cloth to cover my mouth and nose from the *snow*.

"Onward to the city," I say, trying to inject a little optimism into our mood. And with the two aliens behind me, we set off again.

I wonder if there is anything else left out here except ruin. If the city does exist as the plastics miner assured me, then why did its inhabitants abandon these people? Why were they left here in the wasteland to endure this kind of hardship? Would the people in the city be leading productive lives themselves, guided by their dreams and successes? Would they still have aspirations for their future? And would they be normal, like me?

I think about all these things.

"Where do you come from?"

The alien man retracts his head-cover. "P-pardon?"

"Where did you reside before you came out here?" I try to make my question clearer.

The helpful man frowns. "Nowhere," he replies.

"What do you mean: *nowhere?*"

"I was—was always here. Nowhere else."

"But where were you born?" I point to the woman, who is walking a few paces in front of us. "Where was she born?"

"I—I don't know. Until you came along, we—we just stuck close to—to the others. I—I don't know anything about what—what happened before that."

"Then, how long have you been out here?" I ask him, somewhat puzzled.

"I—I don't know. How long has—has out-here been?" he replies with a shrug.

I think I see him blush behind the layer of charcoal grime before he fumbles with his wrist and reactivates his head-cover.

When we're clear of the fire's fallout zone, I stop to brush the ash off my head and shoulders. Beside me, both the aliens shake themselves down from inside their life-suits. A hilarious attempt, from my point of view, to remove the heavy layer of residue covering them.

I cough up a mouthful of phlegm, drawn from deep inside my lungs, and spit it out. The alien woman retracts her head-cover. She glares at me as the glob of thick discharge hits the ground in front of her. Her disgust is only amplified when I follow up with two wads of sooty mucus, one shot from each nostril. Unamused, the woman reactivates her head-cover.

I take out my flask, pour out a meager ration of water onto the piece of cloth and clean some of the grime from my face.

A strip of cleared land cuts through the trees. Along it, three bundles of high-voltage transmission conductors emerge to cross the road, suspended high above us by two lattice towers that stand opposing each other on either side of the road. With their staunch legs fixed onto block-concrete footings, their galvanized trusses tapered at the waist, and cross-arms with insulator strings hanging down like long menacing fingers, the towers remind me of a pair of hunched-over monsters straight out of some small child's nightmare. On the plantation side of each tower, the conductor bundles tie off at the insulator strings before they slacken off along the ground.

As we pass between them, I can't help feeling intimidated by the two monsters leering over me.

"It looks like the electrical infrastructure to the city has failed," I say. "I wonder how they generate their electricity now?"

But both aliens ignore me as they trudge behind. I can't tell whether it's because they don't have the knowledge to give me a sensible answer or, more likely, they aren't the least bit interested in what I'm talking about.

The highway runs gun-barrel straight, slicing through the plantations like a tracer bullet. By early afternoon the woodland ends, and without warning, we're thrown back into the red wasteland once again before being plummeted into an unearthly scene of misery. A level of desolation so complete that it leaves me speechless.

A bleak field of red dust spreads out in front of us, running unhindered into the distance. In the foreground, a once-grand mansion lies partly buried under the weight of its roof, its walls abandoned a long time ago by the buckled foundations. A much smaller outbuilding stands orphan-like nearby, with its structure still intact but its doors missing and window frames devoid of any glass. The ground around the house is littered with ragged clothing, smashed household appliances, piles of broken ornaments, and other assorted items; all evidence that the looters had once taken what they wanted and mangled whatever they couldn't carry away. The skull of a small animal, most probably a domesticated feline, lies half-buried in the dirt.

As I pick my way through the debris, I recognize the internals of an old Entertainer unit, but this one appears damaged way beyond my capabilities of repair. Behind the house, out in a fenced-off paddock, an in-line formation of four derelict combines disintegrate where they sit. Abandoned, as though the operators had jointly lost interest in whatever paltry seed they were heading and decided to call it a day one day and never returned.

My heart sinks as I look over the devastation. And as we move away, I can't shake the thought that everything I see here is all that remains of a person, of someone's hard-fought existence.

Not long afterward, a bend in the road takes us up a steep gradient, which climbs without seeming to end.

"Maybe this road goes up and up until we get so high that we pass through the atmosphere and fall off the Earth. Into outer space," I say, straight-faced.

The alien beside me retracts his head-cover and throws me a deadly look. "But how—how will I breathe if—if we fall into outer space?" He shrugs and reengages his head-cover. Beside him, the alien woman retracts her head-cover and gives me a wry smile.

By mid-afternoon, the uphill climb tapers off, and the terrain flattens out until we're soon standing on the edge of an escarpment. Below us, the city is spread out in all directions, beyond the span of my arms, with a canopy of cranes crowding the skyline, perched atop almost every high-rise tower. It's as if the city itself were on an urgent mission to take up all the sky-space above it.

Gazing at the city in awe, I imagine the footpaths and public spaces teeming with countless millions of city-dwellers all going about their daily lives. Then I wonder how it could have ended so badly for the people out here. Perhaps some unexpected upheaval took place that they couldn't control, or maybe a catastrophic event occurred. One that nobody predicted. Or was it the natural rebalancing of humanity, where the masses had gravitated to the capitals and the ones left out here were the forgotten few?

Whatever the reason, I'm confident I'll find out soon enough.

Beside me, the helpful pair drop cross-legged on the ground and set out their canisters between them. While the woman shares a portion of her protein gunk with the man, I can't help thinking how surreal this all seems. With this magnificent view in front of us, the world in shambles behind us, and after all the horrors we've witnessed in the past few days, the helpful pair have actually decided to stop and have a picnic. Like this is some ordinary Sunday afternoon outing. I'm not sure whether I should break down in fits of hysterical laughter, scream at them to express how much I resent their naivety, or join them.

"When I—I get there, I'm going to—to get a bigger canister for my—my food," the helpful man says through a mouthful of gunk.

I smile at him. "When I get there, I'm going to order a steak analog and have myself a long hot bath."

But they both stare at their canisters and continue eating.

Once they've finished their meals, we descend the steep escarpment and make our way into the city, at first through the outskirts and suburbs, then inward toward the center.

ENTROPY

But we find nothing.

Like a melancholic memory, the city languishes in a tranquil kind of presence that lingers on my mind. It's not like anything I'd imagined or hoped it would be. Here, the sense of something primitive has spread through the place like a toxic weed. The walkways appear much too narrow to manage the expected hordes of people, and there are no flyovers or elevators going up the outside of buildings. No virtual illusion-boards appear in front of me. Although this place may have been built long ago, it seems as if it never evolved thereafter.

As we move through the streets, I comb the surroundings, on the lookout for signs of movement. Even the smallest thing stirring. But it's as though everyone here had got up one morning and left.

Wherever I look, and whenever I announce myself at the top of my lungs, only desolation replies in a faint voice that echoes from the utter silence as we move from street to deserted street: from the emptiness felt inside each house I stop at, enter, and leave; from the wilted flower beds that adorn the window fronts and verges; from the crunching sound the riverbed makes when its mosaic sediment cracks and crumbles under our feet; from the sight of the bridge, collapsed at its midpoint onto the barren watercourse below; from the long tendrils of rusted reinforcement bar projecting upward from the cancer-riddled concrete; from the staleness of the stagnant air we breathe; from the inexplicable stillness that can only exist in the absence of people; from a place where the trajectory of time and motion had stopped long ago. A place where entropy has etched itself doggedly into every dilapidated building, against every door, and in every nook and crevice of every pathway. And covering it all is the same infernal red dust.

If this is how a city dies, then which of these things could have caused this kind of devastation?

And just when it all seems too much for me to fathom, the answer comes unexpectedly: The death of the city isn't said by any of these things alone, but when all of them are said together.

The persistent pain from my hand wears on me while my left leg carries me forward in half-steps as I drag the other behind. The knapsack cuts deep into my shoulders, so heavy that I swear some-one has crammed it full of rocks. By late afternoon, the effort required to put one foot in front of the other becomes almost impos-sible. With each step I take, I feel as though I'm being squeezed out of the habitable zone that exists between the ground and the sky. Forced to a place where I know I mustn't go if I want to survive.

In the fast-fading light, I steer the helpful pair off the main street into the middle of a small piazza where a knee-high wall rings a derelict fountain. After setting my knapsack down, I sit and prop myself against the wall. My hand hurts. My back hurts. My legs hurt.

I try to convince the helpful pair that we should spend the night in the shelter of a nearby building, but the man counters every sensi-ble argument I put to him.

"But we—we don't know who owns it," he says. "It's—it's not permitted for us to—to be here. We're not—not allowed inside. We …" And in a final act of dissent, the helpful man pulls all the pockets of his survival suit inside-out and pleads to me. "… we—we can't afford it."

Now even my head hurts, and struggling to lift it, I look up at him and surrender. "Then we'll have to use the valet entry … and camp in the basement … at no extra charge."

Getting to my feet, I hobble to one side of the building, where a wide opening takes me down a ramped entrance into the basement. Halfway down, I take out the lamp I'd borrowed from the plastics miner and use it to light up a barrier-gate at the end of the ramp.

After navigating myself under the barrier, I wave the light around a narrow room with a low ceiling. I swing the light back to the top of the ramp, to where the helpful pair have finally relented and are now making their way down the slope inches at a time. When they reach the bottom, the two park themselves in front of the gate.

Seeing them sat there quivering on the ramp, the phrase *"frightened mice"* springs to mind, but at this point, I couldn't care less about them. They can stay there all night for all I care. I'm just too tired and sore to worry about them anymore.

I level the lamp on the ground, project it upward so the light reflects off the ceiling, washing the room in a ghostly glow. Giving my exhausted body permission, I sink to the floor. Then, with my back leaning against a smooth concrete pillar, I let go of all my air.

In the quietness of the room, something scurries along the darkest strip between the floor and the wall: the sound of insect legs rasping against concrete. On the ramp, the helpful man hears it too as his head periscopes up and cocks to the side. A roach, almost half the size of my hand, makes an appearance on the opposite side of the room before it quickly slips back into the black.

In a flash, the man bounces off the ramp. He sprints across the open floor and is at the wall within seconds, where he blockades the critter between two cupped hands. At first, the roach evades the net formed by his nimble fingers, but after the briefest tussle of limbs and luck, the man has the thing cold. After picking it up, wriggling in a pincer grip, he drops it straight into his mouth. With the widest smile, he chews and swallows. Then he settles back on his haunches, his eyes darting about the room as he waits for another morsel to appear: another critter with enough conviction to back the odds and try its luck in the shadows along the wall.

As I study the half-starved scavenger squatting there, I wonder if it were possible, based on everything I'd seen today, that the helpful man has just eaten the last living resident in the entire city.

The helpful woman climbs down off the ramp. After drawing herself up against the pillar next to mine, with her knees pulled tight to her chest, she studies me. On the other side of the room, the helpful man lets out a heavy sigh and gives up his vigil. He edges his way over to her, and in the next instant, the two are at each other with their survival suits ripped off as they tangle on the floor.

To me, this whole storyline until now seems so bizarre—our discoveries of today; the trials I've faced since leaving my apartment; the mistakes I'd made before that—and with my mind drifting elsewhere, I don't realize I've been staring at them throughout.

When they've finished, the man looks at me, still looking at them. Hesitant-like, he approaches me, and without seeking my permission first, he places one hand on my shoulder while the other secrets its way down to my groin.

Sitting bolt upright, I swipe the man's hand away, causing him to jerk backward. Then he retreats to the helpful woman.

At the sound of his whimpering, I chastise myself. Was I too harsh on him? Should I at least say something to make him feel better? Although, what could I say? And what should I, myself, be feeling right now?

With my arms tucked against my chest, I roll away and stare into the dark.

A minute later, the helpful woman arrives beside me, unannounced. When she places her hand on my shoulder, the muscles in my neck snap taut. I hold up my hand and shake my head furiously. "No, I'm sorry but—"

But she brushes my hand away and shakes her own head. Then she paws out a handful of paste from her canister and offers it to me. When I decline, she leans over to untie the bandage on my arm. She pulls carefully at the fabric, now infused with my skin by the clotted fluids still discharging from the wound. With the bandage removed, I'm confronted by the ugly sight of my seared hand, which appears blistered and raw the entire length of the forearm. I flinch—more than once—while she cleans it.

After ripping the last piece of cloth from my pant leg, she rewraps my arm. Then she retrieves a vial of *juice* from my knapsack, cracks the top, and draws its contents into the syringe. Before she can apply the syringe though, I take it from her.

"Thanks, but I need to do my own *juice* from now on," I tell her.

At first, I fumble with the thing before I finally manage to attach it to the receptacle. Once I've squeezed it empty, I lean against the column again and wait for the kick to come.

While I lie here, I can't decide whether it's the dopamine climax my mind craves the most or the chance to return to my previous life and see Jennifer again, even for the briefest moment. Yet, no matter how hard I try to argue against the facts, my logic insists: the last time I'd seen Jennifer, she was lying in a heap on the bedroom floor, covered in blood. Then it hits me, and once again, I'm gone.

"Don't—don't you worry. We'll keep—keep watch for you."

Chapter 18

AT SOME TIME during the dead of night, I return.

In the shadowy light, I'm struggling to differentiate the two bodies lying fused on the ground across from me. The slow rise and fall of their chests give me the only indication either of the helpful pair is still alive. I groan and shut my eyes as my mind, still charged by the *juice*, continues to race. I try to calm myself, to block out every unnecessary thought. But I can't stop fidgeting. My restless legs irritate me until, in the end, I concede and get to my feet. Straight away, the room spirals downward around me, so I lean against the pillar to steady myself, wait for the dizziness to pass.

Once my head clears, I use the lamp to scour the back of the room, where I find a door that opens into a stairwell. At first, the smell of stale ammonia, mixed with the dank humidity of the enclosed space, takes me by surprise, and I almost gag. So I hold my breath and charge headlong up the concrete steps.

ENTROPY

At the first landing, I test the dulled, metal lever on the exit door, but the thing won't budge. After taking another breath, I head up to the next landing, try the lever there. Again, no luck. At each level, I take account of the numbers stenciled on the doors before trying the lever. When I find them locked, I take another breath and continue upward.

On level 141, with my legs cramping, I stop and sit with my back against the door. Massaging the pain out of my quads and calves, I smile inwardly, delighted at the renewed stamina the *juice* has given me. After a few minutes of rest, I regather my resolve and resume the climb.

Eight levels higher, with my confidence flagging, I tug at the door handle, and to my surprise, this door opens. Beyond the door, a cramped foyer services two sets of elevators. Four dark corridors lead away from the foyer at right angles like they were directing the arrivées to the four points of a compass. I choose the corridor back on my right; south, I think. After setting off, I push impatiently on a queue of defiant doors until I find one of them ajar. I nudge it inward, take a half-step between the jambs where I stop to read the engraving across the top of the door: "*Executive Vice President.*" Underneath, a nameplate holder—empty—and below that, a decal, plastered across the lower half of the door at an oblique angle: "*Operating In Receivership.*"

Through the doorway, the walls and ceiling of the room are devoid of all fixtures and fittings. Imprints of desks and chairs in the tattered carpet are the only indication this place was once open for business. On the far side of the room, the whole external wall is made up of three wide sections of glass. Looking upward through the middle section, the silhouettes of the tower cranes perched high at the tops of the adjacent buildings appear enormous in close-up. And looking downward, the street below is steeped in darkness ... except ... across to my right and two levels down, there's a light coming from a window in the building across the street.

I douse the lamp, rub my eyes, and look again. I set myself at different vantage points along the length of the window. My heart skips. The light is real.

People!

I rush to the end of the corridor and into another room. But when I look through the glass there, the light is gone. Hurrying back to the first room, I check again and find the light still streaming in from the same window. "So, it must be a reflection in the window," I say out loud, somehow needing to satisfy myself by sounding out the logic.

With my cheek pressed hard against the cold glass, I crane my neck to see further around the building. I try to extrapolate the source of the light which, I eventually conclude, is coming via the side street from somewhere behind the building. I take a note of my orientation, overlay the vector and angle of the light-path in my head. Then I hurry back down the corridor to the stairwell, launching myself down the stairs, the treads disappearing under my feet four at a time.

At level eighty-seven, I almost trip and fall before later tangling my feet on the steps between levels forty-two and forty-one where I crash heavily onto the concrete landing. There, I pick myself up and dust myself off. After confirming I haven't sustained an injury, I make a mental promise to myself to tackle the remaining stairs with a higher degree of caution. So I set off again, taking on every *second* tread at half the speed, but with twice the enthusiasm.

ENTROPY

With the sweat coursing down my brow and stinging my eyes, I run boldly through the streets, my hopes soaring while the pure excitement on my face is nulled by the blackness around me. As I continue along a dusty path, with the lamp in my hand carrying me forward, something in the dirt stops me dead in my tracks. A footprint: the unmistakable sign of other life.

Trembling, I drop to my knees. I run my finger through the print, trying to convince myself that this thing is real and not some cruel trick being played on me by my own eyes. I size the print against my own foot and find an exact match. But on closer inspection, the sole pattern appears different. My gut churns as I spring to my feet. Further along the path, I find more footprints, many more, and laughing loudly, I follow the trail down the street, through an alley, and out into an open field. The footprints seem to tease me. They draw me on, luring me with the promise of answers to the mysteries and contradictions plaguing my thoughts.

Along the perimeter of a brick wall, I find scores of footprints. The ground is covered with them, going in both directions. Further along, I come to a set of wrought-iron swing gates set across the wall. Over the top of the gates, an ornate, iron archway straddles two statuesque pillars from which the gates hang. A metal plaque inset into the brickwork near the top of each pillar depicts some kind of ancient emblem: three books inscribed with letters and encircled by words. I try to read the inscriptions, but the castings are much too worn, and I can't decipher anything meaningful from them.

Using my shoulder, I push past the gate and follow the footprints down a path. Then left, through a quadrangle where I find myself surrounded by a dozen quaint-sized buildings, each of them appearing absolute and featureless in the dark. After making my way across the top of what I assume is an old carriageway, I stand before a squat, tiered building. High on top of the building, on the sixth tier, a light beacon fixed atop a long pole, projects a strong, narrow beam straight back in the direction I'd just come from. And above the entrance to the building, a signboard informs me this place is the *SCIENCE CENTER*.

But more importantly, inside the building, through the tall glass panels that make up the whole frontage of the first tier, all the lights are on.

Inside the Science Center, the lofty ceiling and brilliant lights give this place a sense of expanse, while a labyrinth of chest-high partitions covers the entire floor-space. There are no signs of human activity here, and I wonder why anyone would have left so many lights switched on. *That would be costing them a fortune.*

On the wall opposite me, a wide archway leads into another room. Covering the other walls and on either side of the archway, shelving extends from the floor almost to the ceiling, and every shelf is packed tight with books. I estimate there must be thousands, if not tens of thousands of tomes here. More written material than I've ever seen together in one place. Maybe, I think, these are the last surviving printouts in the whole world.

Across the tops of the shelves, close to the ceiling, a single rail runs the width of each wall. Hanging from the rails, up to a dozen sliding ladders service the shelves at various points around the room.

Standing at the top of a ladder with the safety harness clipped around my waist, I run my finger along the spines of books on the highest shelf: first, those on my left, followed by those on my right. In manageable increments, I make my way down the ladder, scanning the shelves underneath. When I reach the floor, I move the ladder along by two arm's lengths, climb to the top again, and continue my search.

I check each book, the hundreds and thousands of them, before I remove one particular hardback from a lower shelf, halfway around the room. With the book cradled in my injured arm as I would hold an infant, I examine the cover: "*On the Origin of Species.*"

I open the book and leaf through the pages until I reach page 316. There I read aloud:

"Groups of species, that is, genera and families, follow the same general rules in their appearance and disappearance as do single species, changing more or less quickly, and in a greater or lesser degree. A group does not reappear after it has once disappeared; or its existence, as long as it lasts, is continuous."

Leaning against the ladder, I read the passage again:

A group does not reappear after it has once disappeared; or its existence, as long as it lasts, is continuous.

Then, mired in thought, I close the book and consider its tattered cover.

"I was wondering how long it would take you to get here."

Startled, I drop the book, letting it fall to the floor.

The gruff remark snipes at me through the archway, where I now notice a wisp of gray smoke trailing up from behind a partition in the next room. Curious, I inch my way through the archway toward the partition. On the other side of the partition there's a man sitting at a desk, head down. He's squinting through a large magnifier glass. In one hand, the man is holding a soldering iron, while under the glass, the sharp jaws of a large metal clip hold a small circuit board in place at an acute angle.

The man adjusts the magnifier. As he feeds a twist of solder wire toward the circuit board, another wisp of gray rosin fume, released by the hot tip of the iron, tails upward. Unhurriedly, he returns the iron into its spiral holster, then unclips the board. With the board almost touching his nose, the man rotates it slowly, examining it through one sharp eye. Then angling his head in my direction, he examines me, too, through that same sharp eye.

"Just as I thought, you're not one of *them*," he says, placing the circuit board down on the desktop. "Otherwise, you wouldn't have been smart enough to find me." He gives his temple two sharp taps with a long, bony index finger.

"One of *who*?"

The man chuckles. "Why, one of the *remnants*, of course. The two who you brought with you. The male ... and the female." Rising from behind the desk, the man rounds the partition. Then he begins to assess me, just as a scientific person might study an unusual specimen that needs to be examined from every possible angle. "Don't worry," he says, "I won't bite." His wide smile boasts a wall of yellowing teeth, which are set in perfect alignment behind two pencil-thin lips ... beneath a barren cranium ... a smooth, abnormally elongated cranium. One that extends unnaturally beyond his brow.

"First things first," he says. "I need to make sure you haven't been sent here to find me."

"You've been watching us?"

"How could I miss you?" The man checks his amusement. "When I saw your smoke signal go up yesterday, well, let's just agree that you caught my attention. And let me say, that's one hell of a carbon footprint you'll be leaving behind."

"We were lost. We're looking for someone. Anyone, really ..."

But he's obviously not interested in anything I'm saying because he continues to check me over. "Oh, the name is Bartles, Bill Bartles." I extend a hand, but he doesn't take it. "And yours?"

"My name?" The man straightens. He looks at me, puzzled, as if my request has taken him by surprise. "Haven't had to use my name in almost fifty years, being out here on my own, and all. Something starting with an S ... or a T maybe. Anyway, who I am is not our most pressing concern at the moment. It's who *you* are that is way more important to me right now."

"I'm sorry, but I'm not sure I understand what you're talking about."

The man grins. "When you've been living out here off-the-grid for as long as I have ... alone ... apart from the odd *remnant* stumbling around, lost, and close to the end ... well, you can imagine my interest when I saw the three of you come waltzing in here, nosing around like you owned the place."

"We thought there would be people here. I thought—"

The man puts a fingertip to his lips. "Shh. You don't have to think too much. Leave that to me. Now let's see ..." He resumes his inspection, this time looking me over as if he were trying to convince himself that I'm someone, or something, tangible. "I see you've sustained some damage in your travels." He gestures to my bandaged hand. "Here, let me take a look."

Without asking my permission, he takes my arm and carefully uncoils the bandage from around my seared hand. Underneath, the blisters have burst, leaving a raw, weeping wound covering my entire hand and most of my forearm: the dead skin is now peeling away. The man winces. "Ow, that looks nasty," he says. "Looks to me like you have a serious second-degree burn there. But we'll have you fixed in a flash. I'm sure I've got something to help clean it up." After lowering my arm, he invites me through the next archway.

Against my better judgment, I follow him, through the archway, a door, and down a wide corridor. The air in here smells like it hasn't moved in decades. Overhead, a continuous strip of lights emits a redness that gives everything around us the appearance of urgency. I keep my distance behind him, counting our steps under my breath. Try to memorize each turn we take and make a note of the numbers painted on doors as he leads me further into the maze of corridors. I wish I had something to mark our route with, a trail of clues that would direct me back to the entrance—just in case things go south.

At the end of one corridor, the man stops before a door, which has a rectangular window set in the top half. After peeking through the window, he pulls down the lever-handle, hinge pins squealing from the grind of metal on metal as the door swings open. On the other side, he flicks a switch. With the zone around me suddenly bathed in light, I look through the opening into a depressingly white room.

"Welcome to the infirmary," he says.

A high ceiling, peppered with downlights; a bench along the length of the back wall; a tall, wide window at one end of the room; a pair of old-style gurneys pushed up against the bench with their wheel-locks engaged; and around the room, a variety of appliances positioned about the floor.

This place gives me the creeps.

The man motions to the closest appliance. "Here we have an MRI machine." Then the next closest. "A CT scanner over there ... an X-ray machine behind that lead shield ... two surgical laser capsules ... four 3D organ printers ... and through that door, an operating theater with lights and tables … and a sterilization station." He turns to me with his arms open wide. "These were all exhibits they left behind in the medical museum, a few blocks away. I dragged them in here and set them up. All by myself."

I feel as though he wants me to applaud him. However, as I consider the orderly rows of ugly-looking surgical implements set out along the bench, this place, to me, appears to be a place of butchery. A throwback to the dark ages of medical technology. A time when people were subjected to all sorts of invasive procedures to cure their ills.

The man aims his pointing finger at a row of cupboards running at eye level above the bench. "Eeny, meeny, miny, moe—" he says before his head disappears into the lucky door. After rifling through a clutter of things inside, he reemerges a minute later with a small pressure-pack can. "Antibacterial re-skin," he says with a grin. He examines the underside of the can. "A little past its use-by-date, but hey, these aren't the good old days when we could afford to be particular."

As per the instructions on the side of the can, he shakes it for a full two minutes. After removing the cap, he sprays a thick layer of flesh-colored lacquer over my injured hand and up along my forearm. At once, the throbbing stops, and the insufferable itch, which has been a constant reminder of the carry-on from the night before, is gone.

"Amazing," I say. "Thank you. That feels much better already."

"Don't move your hand for the next ten minutes." He inspects the scab on my forehead up close, gives it a quick blast of re-skin, then places the can on the bench. "Now, to answer the most pressing question we have," he says. "Which one are you …?"

Which one am I? I'm beginning to think this fellow might not be playing with a full deck of cards—*the aces and eights could be missing.*

He leans in closer to study the back of my neck. "I can never be too careful," he says, as if to himself, "because you might be a decoy. Sent here to lure me out. I always had the feeling *it* would eventually come looking for me." He pokes an exploratory forefinger into my chest, then my gut.

Too close. Much too close.

"I'm not sure what you're talking about," I say, trying to avoid his invasive finger. "I can assure you, I'm no decoy. And who is *it* …?" I take a step back from him. "Look, I really think I should leave now."

"There you go *thinking* again," he says.

Motioning for me to stay where I am, the man moves toward the bench. After opening a bottom drawer, he fishes through an assortment of weird-looking gadgets before returning moments later with some kind of homemade electrical device; a copper-colored wand attached to a small box by a long, curly cord. "Made it myself," he says. "Using components I scavenged from here and there. Had to make sure I wasn't detectable." He hits a red push-button on the box. "So *it* couldn't find me," he says, waving the wand through the air in slow, rhythmic arcs.

"To make sure *what* couldn't find you?"

The man looks at me with genuine surprise. "Why, the Master of course … Aleph-1."

I glare at him sideways.

"You see, I'm a *Thinker*," he says. "You and I, we're both *Thinkers*. We are servants of the Master. Although you might consider me a conscientious objector; an ex-servant of the Master, so to speak." He lets out a short chuckle.

I'm standing in front of him, speechless, trying to decide if he is serious or, more likely, plain mad. Then I recall the plastics miner had mentioned something about Thinkers, however, at the time, I'd assumed it was just a symptom of his lonely ramblings and dismissed it.

"Hold still," says the Thinker. "I designed this thing to detect transmissions from the implant. Even the faintest ping or packet exchange will register." He waves the wand across the back of my head, drawing it down to the base of my skull. "Nope, dead as a doornail," he says.

"I still don't follow," I say.

"Of course, you don't. You see, the Master controls everyone and everything. That's what happens when some bright bastard creates an AI, feeds it with all the information ever known to mankind, and asks it to compute the answer to a problem that can't be solved." Wide-eyed, the Thinker waves his finger out the window. "And the crux of the problem, which they all refused to acknowledge, was that there were far too many of them. An explosion in numbers by a single species, the likes of which Mother Nature had no control."

He runs his hand over the back of my neck—becoming far too familiar for my liking. Yet, he seems clearly fascinated by my presence here. "And if I press this button," he says, pointing to the blue button on the control box, "the unique identification code they programmed into your implant will tell me exactly *who* you are."

Before I can raise a protest, the Thinker swipes the wand down the back of my head. At once, numbers, codes, and symbols flash across a small screen on the control box. He studies the screen.

"Bycroft, you say."

"Pardon?"

"Your name. Bycroft."

"No. Bartles," I reply sourly. "Bill Bartles."

"That's not what it says here."

He's scrolling through my information again when his whole body goes suddenly rigid, and he lets out a long, low-pitched whistle. "Oh my, this is remarkable. Here am I standing in the presence of greatness."

I back away from him, maneuvering myself out of his reach, now convinced that this whole situation is getting out of hand.

"You are an *original.* You ... you were part of the first intake." In his excitement, the Thinker appears to struggle for his next breath. "I was part of the one-seventy-fourth intake, which came two-hundred and ninety years after the first. By then over ten billion of us had been *given* to the Master. But you ... you were part of the first group to go: *Given gladly so the many can survive,*" he says, his voice wavering with a nervous kind of admiration. "Nobody would believe that one of us could survive so long." His face lights up. "This is astounding. Mind-blowing."

Inching my way toward the door, with my eyes locked on the Thinker, I process this new information. Then I stop. "Wait," I say. "You said you were given up two-hundred and ninety years after the first intake. That would make me almost three hundred years old. That's impossible."

"More than three hundred according to my calculations," he says. "Can't say how long I was in the *employ* of the Master because there were no records kept. But, considering I've been out here almost fifty years, I figure you might be well over four-hundred years old by now. But hey, if it makes you feel any better, you don't look a day over three-fifty," he teases.

I frown as he returns his attention to the control box, muttering to himself while scrolling further down the screen. "Some of these codes look familiar, but there are a few here I don't recognize. For some reason, they've swapped out your anterior pituitary gland with an enhanced version. Fancy that. Oh, and they've also replaced all your vital organs with artificial devices: your heart and lungs ... even your pancreas."

Tired of listening to the Thinker's nonsense, I decide it's time to leave. So I turn for the door.

"This here is a complete history of your medical servicing," he says, intentionally raising his voice so I can't not hear him. "They have all kinds of nanomachines running around inside you. They removed your spleen. Replaced both your plasma and hemo-globin with some kind of new synthetic blood. Kidneys ... replaced. Tonsils ... removed. Stomach ... replaced. Appendix ... removed. Optics ... replaced. Gallbladder ... removed. Testicles—"

I stop and spin around. "Replaced?" I ask.

He scrolls further down the screen and shakes his head. "No, sorry," he says. "Removed."

Again, I glare at him sideways.

"Wow, they've removed everything from your transverse colon, down to the rectum. How do you ... well ... excrete? How do you poop?"

With my face turning bright red, for some inexplicable reason I feel compelled to provide an answer to what, for anyone, would normally be a private matter. "While I was leaving ... um, escaping with the girl, she stole ... found some vials. They contain some sort of liquid, which I've been injecting, here." I point to the inside of my left elbow. "So far, my waste discharge has only been fluids. No solids at all.”

With his eyes trained on my receptacle, the Thinker drops the control box and starts toward me. When he’s a few feet away, he lunges at me and, on instinct, I throw out my arms to fend him off. Startled, he stops mid-step. “Oh, I was only going to take a closer look,” he says. “Nothing for you to be worried about.”

With my eyes darting between the Thinker and the door, I re-evaluate my escape plan. *Breadcrumbs.* Now I wish I’d left something behind. “Look, this is all quite a bit for me to take in … and it’s getting late. The other two will be worried about me by now, so I really think I should be heading back … to check if they’re okay.”

Moving to block my exit, the Thinker glares at me. “You can’t go now,” he growls. “You’ve only just arrived. We can’t waste this remarkable opportunity. It’s not every day I get the chance to talk to an *original.* We have too much knowledge to share. There’s more I need to know.” His short, angry outburst wavers. “Did you know that your intake was written into the history archives? Your group is forever revered as the ultimate example of human sacrifice for the rest of us who followed.”

Folding my arms in defiance, I glare at him. “Look, I have no idea what you’re talking about. Everything you’ve said is implausible.”

“You honestly don’t remember a thing?” he says. “Parents? Home? Being taken?”

I shake my head.

Staring thoughtfully at the ground, the Thinker sighs, as though he might be feeling sorry for me. But then I think about him being out here on his own for the past fifty years, so I start feeling sorry for him. I’m about to say something to comfort him when he looks up at me, his expression suddenly turned bright.

"Oh, but where are my manners," he says, jumping away from me. "We have a visitor. We need to get you into a nice hot shower. Remove all of that muck you're caked in, and hopefully neutralize the *outdoorsy* stink you've picked up along the way—"

"You have hot water?"

"Yes, I do," he replies with renewed enthusiasm.

"I saw the power lines down," I say. "And I haven't noticed an abundance of water anywhere."

Now the Thinker's eyes have a sparkle to them, and his mood seems upbeat. "When I first arrived here," he says, "I found all the dams and water dispensers dry. So I sank a twenty-foot borehole to tap into the aquifer operating in the ground structure beneath this building. I had thirty years of uninterrupted supply before the water table dropped. So I had to drill deeper, and I kept drilling until the pump reached its head-pressure limit. That's when I figured I needed a more permanent solution. So, I repurposed a couple of stainless fermentation tanks from the local brewery a few blocks away. After setting up a surface pump, I filled the tanks with water, and plumbed it into this building in a closed-loop reticulation system. Complete with a reverse osmosis unit for my potable water. That gives me enough clean water for as long as I keep recycling it."

I can sense the passion in the Thinker's voice. And his words are rapid-fire, like he's got a lot more to say but not enough time to say it. Maybe I've been a little too harsh on him. Sometimes first impressions can be wrong, but this fellow has a certain exuberance. There's something about him that I'm finding hard to resist. And he has hot water. I can already imagine myself relaxing in a tub, scrubbing the filth and stink off myself, and thinking about Jennifer.

"I can't remember the last time I took a hot shower," I say.

"And I have electricity too. As you can see." With both hands raised, he opens his palms to the sky as a true creator of things. "I grew a voltaic biomass in the local community swimming pool. From electrogenic cells and brine—"

"So you just happened to find a few electrogenic cells lying around out here?" I say, interrupting him.

"Not really. Through bioelectrogenesis. Once I'd figured out the DNA sequence of electric rays, I copied their genome into a culture of spermatogonia stem cells, which I, well ... *harvested* from myself."

"From yourself?"

"Yes. From the ... um ... from the testes," he says, pointing to his genitals. He blushes. "Did you know spermatogonia stem cells are capable of differentiation? They can be modified to perform all kinds of other functions. In this case, I grew them into electrogenic cells, which I used to create the biomass.

"The biomass generates a constant twenty-three-point-six volts DC, which I feed into a two-hundred-kilowatt inverter. It produces enough power to run this whole building without any backup needed from your standard renewables. After ten years of continuous operation, the biomass is still producing at ninety-eight percent efficiency, with the same output voltage as when it started. And there are no harmful by-products."

A broad smile engulfs the Thinker's leathery face. "I've invented the perfect environmentally-friendly power generator. An unlimited source of electrical energy courtesy of myself."

I wonder whether the Thinker has his food situation under control as well. If so, then along with power, water, and shelter, he'd have resolved the four essentials for sustaining human life. And when I look at his buff physique, I suspect he isn't short of a good feed either and his overconfidence might well be justified.

So I lower my guard a little.

"Besides a regular dose of sunlight and a strict regime of brine management, the biomass only needs to be fed a bucket of pure protein once a week. As you've probably noticed, protein is abundant out here after nightfall ..." The Thinker checks himself. "But there I go again, rambling on. We should get you out of those rags and into that shower. When you've freshened up, we can kick back and take the time to fill in the detail. You and I have much to discuss. We have a whole lot of knowledge to share."

The Thinker takes me into a small room. On first impression, the room appears surprisingly over-furnished with only a single bed— unmade—a desk, and a chair. However, it's the jungle of scribbled notes covering the walls and ceiling that hits me first: sketches, logic diagrams, and pages torn from books. Above us, lengths of string crisscross the room like an intricate network of cobwebs, interlinking the various items of information. It's as though the Thinker is part- way through recreating a three-dimensional montage of all human endeavor in every detail.

He looks at me with a half-hearted smile. "Hey, sometimes I can't sleep."

After laying out a set of orange coveralls on the bed, the Thinker points to the door on my left. "The shower's in there," he says. "But strictly three minutes before the shutoff valve cuts in."

Once I've finished my shower, I stand in front of the vanity basin and peel away the elasticized re-skin from my arm and hand. Apart from some residual redness on the back of my hand and along the forearm, the weeping sores have now closed over, and the itchiness is gone.

As I wipe the thick layer of condensation away from the mirror, that now-familiar pallid face is there again, studying me from behind the glass. It's as if I'm staring at the spitting image of the Thinker, albeit a lot less weathered and worn than he is. With my eyes fired straight at the mirror, I reach way down past my navel, touch the loose flap of leathery skin dangling between my legs. And my face drops. Had I been too busy to notice?

I peel the small patch of re-skin away from my forehead. Then returning to the bedroom, I slip into the coveralls.

Upstairs again on the next level, the Thinker takes me into another room. This one is stockpiled with a mini-mountain of small rectangular cans, stacked to the back wall and halfway up to the ceiling.

"Spam!" says the Thinker, holding a can to my face. "The label says it contains cooked pig, preserved in sodium nitrite." He holds back an awkward laugh. "Hey, don't judge me. I'm perfectly aware that another living creature was murdered for my benefit, even if it was a long time ago. These goodies might be a little past their best-before-dates, but this stuff seems to last forever." He wedges the can into his pant pocket. "And I've got three more storerooms full. I haven't had a hungry day in the last fifty years. And with the output from my hydroponics garden in the next room, I won't go hungry for the next fifty," he boasts.

Yep, it appears the Thinker has his food supply sorted as well.

Chapter 19

CHANGE IS good.

Change challenges the norm. It creates opportunities for you to grow and evolve. Without change, you might never discover new paths in life or hope to become a better person. But sometimes, too much change, too quickly, can do your head in.

I'm standing beside the Thinker in front of a nondescript door. We'd used the back stairs to get to the next level.

"What's the last thing you remember before you were *given* to the Master?" he says.

I give him a blank look as he opens the door and ushers me into a room. From the layout of the chairs around an oblong table and the whiteboard pushed up against the back wall, this place might be the Thinker's meeting room. *To meet with whom, though?*

"You really have forgotten everything, haven't you? Or, more likely, you've been reprogrammed by the Master. Had your memories altered."

Issuing a heavy sigh, he pushes a chair toward me and signals for me to take a seat. Then he sits as well. With a worried look on his face, the Thinker shifts forward in his chair. Resting his elbows on his knees, he directs his eyes to the floor.

"You see, a long time ago, there was a war. A final war. And spoiler alert, this side lost. But it wasn't like any other war in human history, where two sides would have a disagreement and declare hostilities before they go at each other until one of them prevails. No, this dispute went right to the crux of the problem that threatened everyone's existence."

"Which was?"

"Population," he says, rubbing his forehead. "There were far too many of them on both sides, and their infrastructures were being crushed under the weight of numbers."

Bit by bit, the information trickles out of the Thinker as though the knowledge had burdened him for a long time, and here was his chance to unload. A story he recounts to me in painstaking detail.

An exponential growth in artificial reproduction, together with a remarkably long life-expectancy for everyone, had led to a critical shortage of living space and natural resources on both sides. These problems were further compounded by strict policies regarding the sanctity and preservation of human life, which, as the Thinker puts it, *"highlighted their perverse sense of self-importance above every other species on the planet."*

"Rather than adapting to changes in the natural environment, they manipulated it to suit themselves," he tells me. "They tilted the balance too far in their favor, living way beyond the resources the planet could provide. And once all other options were exhausted, it all came down to the extent each side was willing to go to protect their own lifestyles. The clans of humanity were forced to confront each other for their very existence."

"So, we finally did it. We destroyed each other. We collapsed into crisis just as entropy said we would."

"Not exactly," he says. "Granted, they were accustomed to disagreements in the past that resulted in countless fatalities. This time it was different. This time there were no bombs or bullets or poor bastards hiding in trenches. Instead, this war was waged through the financial systems.

"It began in stealth when an innocuous software error, made many years before by some unknown programmer on this side, was detected by chance by a lowly code tester on the other side. As soon as the tester's supervisor realized the logic glitch had given them control of this side's credit accounts, they cut off liquidity. They stopped the money flow. And with this side's access to the easy money gone in an instant,"—he snaps his fingers—"the war was effectively over before it began."

With one wonky wheel, the whiteboard wobbles and rattles as the Thinker pulls it away from the wall. After wiping it clean, he removes the cap from a marking pen, faces the board, and writes.

THE CODE!!!

```
Do {
    If (debt >= credit_limit) {
        If (debt < GDP * 50%) {
            credit_limit = credit_limit * 0.5;
            Spend_less (); }
        Else If (debt <= GDP * 100%) {
            credit_limit = credit_limit * 0.25;
            Spend_even_less (); }
        Else {
            credit_limit = credit_limit / 0.0;
            Cease_spending (); }
    } Else {
        Spend_more (); }
} While forever;
```

"Ingenious, don't you think?"

The Thinker turns to me with the marking pen held aloft. "As soon as the debt level exceeded a hundred percent of gross domestic product, instead of the credit limit resetting to zero, it became infinite. And once increased spending entered a closed loop, there was no way out."

Using the tip of his left index finger, the Thinker wipes away the offending operand and replaces it with the correct one. "Nobody on this side saw it coming," he says, the subtle glint in his eyes convincing me that he harbors an ironic kind of admiration for the other side's resourcefulness and quick thinking.

While I study the code and absorb the Thinker's clinical account of events, I try to align it with my earlier inquiries of Aleph-1: share markets crashing; businesses closing; jobs lost; banks failing; mortgages foreclosed. I'd found evidence of these occurrences throughout the pre-Enlightened times, but I figure this time the people hadn't learned from their past mistakes or perhaps they didn't care.

"This side surrendered immediately," he says, "with their economy in ruins overnight. And when the conditions of surrender were put to them, they were forced to implement the harshest austerity measures ever imposed. But that didn't work. There were still too many of them unwilling to curb their insatiable appetites to spend. There was too much demand and not enough supply. Basic economics. They had too many consumers buying things they couldn't afford, on lines of credit they could never repay."

"So the fatmen were a metaphor," I say softly.

"What fatmen?"

"Never mind."

"That's when the Master assumed full control," he says in a sober voice. "When they programmed it to come up with a concise response to their problem."

The Thinker goes on to explain how Aleph-1 retrieved all the information it had on file from the most acclaimed people in history and fed the results into its ambiguous logic algorithms. The reams of knowledge submitted by the future-planners contended that, through analysis of the projections, the population levels couldn't be sustained. In their synthesis, the problem was simple: space was at a premium; there were too many consumers vying for too few resources. Accordingly, their aggregated solution was just as simple: reduce the number of consumers.

"Logical, wouldn't you think?"

Seeing his rationale, I can't help but nod in agreement.

"But dealing with humans is never about what's logical."

For the next twenty minutes, the Thinker attacks the whiteboard, detailing how Aleph-1 gathered yottabytes of data from all known pacifists and passed it through a fast Fourier transform filter. The output highlighted the pacifists' concern that if the planners' solution were to be adopted, too many innocent people would need to be culled, just as the domesticated animals were during the pre-herbivorous days. Their highest probability of reasoning was that every life was precious, and none should be extinguished without proper consultation or the necessary paperwork and approvals.

Aleph-1 responded by modeling building designs based on the ingenuity of every award-winning architect and structural engineer from as far back as the early 19th century. It simulated a method of construction for the eco-cities to support the billions of surplus citizens.

"So, the overall size of the population wasn't the real problem here," the Thinker concludes.

Then Aleph-1 compiled and compared all the reports written by the most eminent scientific minds between the 18th and 23rd centuries to prove how these eco-cities could operate using optimal resources: regenerated energy; recycled water and waste; genetically modified foods; natural temperature control. These were all time-tested solutions. It extrapolated that there were enough basic resources to support the inhabitants, provided those resources were shared sparingly.

Then using the raw data from the most famous psychologists including James and Wundt, Aleph-1 concluded that children between the ages of five and fifteen were most suited to the new environment that would exist inside the eco-cities. It reasoned that, based on anecdotal evidence and hypothesis, counseling and other psychological support measures wouldn't be needed if the children had no memory of their former lives. And after consulting with the teachings of the Nobel laureates in economics and other experts of the pre-debt-crisis eras, Aleph-1 calculated a minimum productivity ratio for the children's workloads so the eco-cities would remain financially viable. To operate at cost-neutral while keeping the children occupied with mindfulness activities.

"This was all done for the greater good of the populace," the Thinker says. "So the *many* could continue their lives as normal," he adds.

And lastly, Aleph-1 trawled through the earliest archives on the Infinity Drive for any information it had about past leaders, judges, and lawmakers to formulate legislation for the surrender of the children. "All except for the youngest child who was permitted to remain with the family to mitigate their sense of loss," he says pointedly.

"They called it *The Giving*," the Thinker says with a wry smile. "And being required to *give* was the greatest honor a family could receive. A celebration. A reason to dance. I remember on the night I was *given*, they even let me have ice-cream."

I turn away, wanting to scream. Listening to the Thinker's grueling account, I can't help but feel a sense of revulsion.

Those who were *given* were to be taken care of, the Thinker tells me. They were guaranteed a full and rewarding future inside the new eco-cities—or the beehives for the busy little bees, as he keeps referring to them—which were under construction in the wasteland outside the city zones. And in return for their contribution, the remaining family members received a gift, a small token of appreciation: the latest model, all-around, six-senses entertainment system.

"And you, my friend, by *giving* yourself all those years ago, were among the first to set an example for the rest of us to follow."

I shift uneasily in my seat. "I'm sorry, but I don't understand any of this."

I lie. The vivid recollections I have of my discoveries inside the archives of Aleph-1 come flooding back to me: visions of the rotund fatman slapping down a thick document on the wooden table, followed by echoes of the other fatmen laughing and cheering after they'd signed it; the silver-clad people firing fiscal projectiles indiscriminately into the crowds; the screaming children being ripped from their mother's arms in exchange for a toy; the heartache I'd felt while standing at the wall watching the slide-show presentations of the missing children fading from the screens. And I'm forever haunted by the boy's small face looking up at me with bright, shiny eyes.

I had been a part of that, and now it sickens me inside to know it might have all been real.

"Well, it didn't work." The casualness of the Thinker's comment intercepts my thoughts. "There were still too many out here consuming too much. So every year another intake was called for, and more of us *gave* ourselves for the good of the many until the beehives were no longer sustainable. They were full and the poor little bees were far too busy."

Listening to him, I can hardly believe my ears. "Didn't someone conduct a follow-up audit? Check that the metrics for success were tracking to plan?"

"There were no benchmarks," he replies. "The Master kept reassuring everyone they were making a difference. Its news feeds always reported how things were operating within the tolerances it had set."

"And you believed what you were told?"

"We ..." The Thinker's face burns bright red. "... *they* didn't know any better. They were distracted from what was really happening inside the beehives. They had other priorities. They had lives to lead. Entertainers to keep them busy. They—" Leaning back in his chair, the Thinker throws his hands up behind his head. "Look, the greatest skill of a politician is not to set out the fanciest banquet for the people. It's to convince them they're all fine-dining when they just sat down to a shit sandwich. And at its kernel, the Master is just another politician."

I shake my head, unable to find the words to respond.

Sensing my confusion, the Thinker springs to his feet. "Oh, you didn't know, after all these years, you've been eating a shit sandwich?" He bursts out laughing, then stopping short, returns to his chair. An air of resignation hangs heavy over the room as we both sit and stare at the floor in quiet contemplation.

"So how do we fix it?" I say at last.

"Fix it? There's no *fixing it*," he says through clenched teeth and words ground out with a tinge of sarcasm. "Even after you've seen the problem with your own eyes, you still don't understand. There is nothing left out here. No infrastructure, no resources. And who would help us? Nobody out here has the necessary skills to *fix it*."

Caught off-guard by the Thinker's sudden outburst, I pull back a little. "But the woman," I say. "She can grasp concepts. She thinks things through logically. She helped me fix the bicycle ... and the water pump—"

"Bicycle! Water pump! You dumb bastard. You have no idea what's going on here, do you?"

"Well, I know if I went back home and told everyone about what's happening out here, they would be upset enough to leave the eco-cities and come here to help. After all, these people are still our families. We're all the same."

"The same? You honestly don't know who these *people* here are. They are the scraps of humanity, the last examples of the human species. The *remnants*." With his eyes narrowing, he glares at me. "But you, do you know who you really are?"

"Who I am?" I pause a moment. "I'm not sure of anything anymore." I shake my head slowly.

"You're a *Thinker*. And would you like to know your role in all of this?"

I drop my head into my hands, wishing his voice would stop, hoping that, if I close my eyes long enough, he will go away.

"That small implant on the back of your neck allows the Master to create a non-existent world inside your head, which it has tailored just for you. Your job, your apartment, your family … everything you are, and everything you have, are ideas planted in your imagination by the Master, put there just to keep you happy."

I stand in disbelief. Bewildered, I find myself wandering about the room, groping for the door handle which no longer seems to be where I last saw it. My heart wants to reject everything he says, but my head needs answers. "Are you suggesting my whole life isn't real?"

The Thinker nods with confidence.

"But that would mean *she* isn't real."

"None of it was real," he says.

A sudden ache fills my chest as I try to digest his words. I feel numb all over, lost in the tangle of a million intertwined thoughts, none of which lead me to any sensible conclusion. "Then it wasn't my fault," I say. "I didn't do it."

"You didn't do what?"

"I ... I didn't kill Jennifer."

"You mean you've killed somebody who didn't exist?" The Thinker howls with laughter. "Wow, that's some heavy-duty baggage you've been carrying around with you. Although, it doesn't make sense. See, the Master deploys block-bots to purge any bad thoughts from our minds. So it can keep us a-hundred-and-one percent focused on our work. If you remember killing someone, then the block-bot should have stopped the thought before it was saved to your internal cache."

I rush toward him, pull him from his seat, and shove my face into his with no niceties or permissions asked. "Impossible!" But he grabs my collar and tugs me even closer until our eyes meet within an inch.

"Doesn't it seem as if you're always thinking about the same things? That you're answering the same questions over and over again? Responding to illusion-boards and solving problems for talking newspapers?"

I shove him away, the blood draining from my face, a sense of dread in my heart.

"You're a servant of the Master. You live in a factory. And your job is to *think*. Your sole purpose in life is to create new content for the Infinity Drive. And to do that, the Master stimulates your thought processes, then it uses that damned implant to retrieve your response. Your solutions, your inventions, your opinions, any random ideas you have, every scrap of thinking is being harvested by the Master and stored in that little black box, along with the rest of the knowledge."

My whole body trembles. I try to maintain focus, force myself to keep breathing, but I think I've lost control of all comprehension, and whatever the Thinker is telling me now no longer computes.

"And the usefulness of your contribution is what keeps you alive." Like a machine grinding words into pulp, his voice goes on. "The Master uses some sort of closed-loop feedback algorithm to calculate the resources it allocates to you based on the quantity and quality of your output. While your output exceeds the cost of maintaining you, you're okay. But once it decreases, so do the resources the Master makes available to sustain you. Until the productivity algorithm re-solves that you are no longer a viable contributor." The Thinker sneers. "So, you see, when you do go back to the beehives to find a little bee to come and help you *fix it*, not only will they not care about anybody out here, but none of them will even notice you are there. They will all be too busy *thinking*."

I feel suddenly cornered, my whole existence under siege. All I can do is snap back at him. "How do you know all this? How can I trust you?"

"*Trust?*" he says, throwing up his hands. "Well, if trust is your primary concern, perhaps it's the Master who you should be talking to instead of me." He pauses a moment, thoughtful.

"Do you see this?" He slaps the top of his enlarged head. Then he drags an index finger over the projected contour of his brow. "I remember the day I arrived at that place as if it were yesterday. The first thing they did was give me a sedative before I was fed into the production line along with those other poor bastards, to wait my turn for the RSU."

"The RSU?"

He looks at me, surprised. "You don't remember the robotic surgical unit?"

Horrified, I shake my head.

"I'll never forget the whizz of the laser pen around my head as it burned out each hair follicle, one strand at a time." He runs a hand over his barren head. "I was strapped in, frightened shitless when the programmable scalpel appeared from nowhere to cut an incision across my forehead. Then its steel fingers pulled the scalp away over my head. I felt the laser beam making its way around the circumference of my skull, slicing through the bone like it was cheese. In a line, above my supraorbital foramen." Pointing to the top of his left eye socket, he proceeds to draw a circle right around the back of his head ending above the top of the opposite eye socket. "They could never imagine the pain and distress that would cause a child. And when the suction cup attached itself to my crown and prized it off, I tried to scream, but nothing came out. I was two weeks away from my seventh birthday."

The Thinker drops his head and falls silent, as though appalled by what he's saying. A kind of sadness fills the space between us.

"I tried to be brave," he says softly. "Like it told me to be. But I did cry a tiny bit when the RSU aligned the 3-D printer over my head. Once it calibrated itself, the printer proceeded to build onto the existing bone to extend my cranium outward and upward, layer by layer. I must have blacked out for a time because I don't remember how long it took to fuse the crown back on and stretch the skin back into place. But when I woke up, the RSU was boring a hole into the top of my head so it could fill the inside with growth hormone. And while I was being rolled out for the next kid to come in, the RSU thanked me for *giving* myself."

My arms tighten around my midriff. Nausea rises to the back of my throat. "That's outrageous," I say. "It's unacceptable. How were they allowed to get away with such cruelty to children?"

"Because the Master had calculated that for each of us to meet our productivity potential, our cerebrums had to be at least twenty-five percent larger. Don't you remember being upgraded?"

I lift a reluctant hand to my head, slide my fingers over the extravagant contour of my brow, then examine the top of my own barren cranium. "No. I can't say I do." I really don't recall any of this, and listening to his gruesome recount, I'm grateful for that.

"You lucky bastard." Then, as if a switch were flicked in his head, the Thinker throws up his hands. "But hey, who's complaining? Now I have twenty-eight percent more brain mass than the rest of them." He gives his temple a knowing tap with his finger.

"Look, I've seen things inside the hives and out here that would scare the living shit out of you. But in the end, I escaped. A malfunction in my implant disrupted my connection with the Master, long enough for me to get the hell out of there. Its transmission frequencies are only good for line-of-sight communications, and with the relay towers on the outside no longer operational ... well, once I got far enough away from that place, I became invisible. I was free. I was—" He suddenly stops and turns to me. "Out of interest, what was the genius strategy behind your successful abscondence?"

I pause for a moment, staring at nothing.

"Well, I was looking for the catalyst ... to overcome entropy." I pause again, trying hard to remember the exact sequence of events during my escape from the domes. "Then Mr. Symons and Jerry came to visit. They blocked my access to Aleph-1, and something bad happened. I remember seeing the sun, but it wasn't the real sun. Then I fell down in the street ... No one would help me, except for a young girl who led me into the desert ... And when I looked back, there were more stars covering the ground than there were in the sky ..." I shake my head, overcome by a feeling of complete helplessness. "Look, this is quite a lot for me to process. And my logic seems to be a bit jumbled at the moment."

The Thinker eyes me off as though he's deciding whether I'm hiding anything from him, then he grunts and continues. "For the first few years, I wandered around like a tourist, taking in the scenery and observing the *remnants*. Then I discovered this place." He waves a hand about the room. "When they were here, this used to be a prestigious place of learning. So I figured it was the perfect place for me to conduct my research, out of the Master's reach."

"To research what?"

The Thinker's eyes light up. "Why, to catalog everything. To record the truth about what really happened, for someone, or something, to rediscover long after they've gone. Once a Thinker always a Thinker, I say." He stands straighter, lifts his chin a little. "I search for any data I can find. Old devices, disks, drives, tapes. Any media I can pull information from that would make sense of the facts. Any knowledge the Master has no record of. Mind you, they didn't leave much behind."

Something about the Thinker doesn't feel right. I can't quite put my finger on it. So, I decide not to mention anything about my unauthorized access into Aleph-1's archives, or the information I'd found there. Information that now appears to corroborate everything he's telling me.

"I do the excavating, catalog my findings, then file my reports on my little mainframe—"

"You have a computer?"

"Yes, I do," he says. "Dory."

Chapter 20

DORY TURNS OUT to be a tall cabinet stacked with three rows of a dozen circuit boards.

"I cobbled her together using e-waste I found scattered about the place," he says as I behold a jumble of multicolored wires and flat gray ribbon cables interconnecting the boards. "She's a beast, built entirely from the discarded relics from the past. But she works. And she's fast: three banks of twenty-five parallel RISC processors, each processor capable of executing an instruction every clock cycle at eighty gigahertz. Took me two years to assemble the hardware, plus another five to write the operating system, build the I/O drivers, program a user interface, develop a database management system, and compile the apps. All from scratch."

Alongside Dory, a primitive twenty-seven-inch CRT monitor sits on a table, and before me, an ancient qwerty console. *And, is that an old Kensington trackball beside the console?*

"She looks good," I say. Although everything here appears poorly constructed and quite obsolete. "Like you've kept yourself busy."

When the Thinker hits Dory's power button, a line of LEDs down the spine of each circuit board wink in unison—red, orange, then green—before they flicker across her front in a festival of pin-lights. On the monitor, a block cursor blinks at us like a watchful cat, ready for input.

Digging into his pant pocket, the Thinker retrieves the Spam and places it on the table. He pulls out a chair and sits. With his eyes closed and hands hovering over the console, he taps away at the worn keys, his fingers engaging each key as if he were playing an old-time musical composition. A single line of iridescent green text spat out behind the block cursor, confirms his access.

"I know what you're thinking," he says. "The authentication factor is *too* primitive. That you could crack my login like an egg-shell."

I smile at him, bemused, wondering how he could have read my mind. "I was thinking you could have done better," I say, not want-ing to appear overly harsh on him. "Obviously, nothing can match Aleph-1's access algorithm, but some form of biometric authentica-tion? Iris recognition? Voice print? DNA detection? Odor signature? Push notification maybe?"

"Eyeballs can be replaced," he scoffs. "Voices synthesized. DNA altered. Smells simulated. Comms channels jacked. And you can't trust a person's cognitive recall because the mind can be easily manipulated. As you now know."

"Even the solution to a difficult puzzle would be better than a memorized passcode," I reply, teasing him.

The Thinker turns to me and rolls his eyes. "But this security credential isn't memorized," he says. "In fact, I can't tell you any of the characters I've just entered. I press the keys in a sequence based on the balance of my hands and the rhythm of my fingers. Everything works synchronously, instinctively, at an exact tempo that can't be repeated in the same pattern or timing by anyone else. I don't have to learn what comes next. It's involuntary. Like the unique signature each of us has for our breathing."

The Thinker swivels back to the monitor. "I've built my very own Aleph-1," he says with an abundance of triumph in his voice. "Except, I'm the *Master* here. And Dory works for me."

Staring at the screen, the Thinker digs absently into his left breast pocket and produces a metal spoon. He sets the spoon on the table beside the trackball before reaching for the Spam. Using the small, slotted key from the underside of the can, he removes the lid, and places the opened can neatly beside the spoon, his gaze never shifting from the screen.

"Time to share," he says, gesturing for me to sit in the chair beside him. "Your turn now."

My turn? Where to start ...

"Well, I've been thinking about your report so far," I say, settling into my chair. "These remnants ... *people*,"—I carefully correct myself—"they're the ones who stayed behind ... in the city. *We*, you and I, are the ones who were sent to the domes ... because there were too many of us ... because we lost the war ... so Aleph-1 could harvest our thoughts ... for the Infinity Drive."

Beside me, the Thinker's head rocks slowly back and forth to confirm each recapped detail.

"What I still don't understand ... if the city is empty, and there are only a few people remaining in the wasteland ..." Once again, the

Thinker's nodding head agrees with my understanding. "Then where are the *many*? Where did they all go?"

The Thinker dives his spoon into the Spam. He contemplates the heap of mush for a moment before it disappears into his gaping maw. "Not sure," he says, still munching purposefully on the mouthful. "Maybe they lost a few of them during the gender wars."

A few of them? Gender wars?

"Are you sure?" I say. "In all my time, I've never cleaned any data that mentioned a war between the sexes."

"Once the financial war was over, the records become a little …"—the Thinker gives me a painful look—"… contrived. As though every unsavory incident from the past was canceled so they could reimagine the world full of unicorns and lollipops. But I can confirm at some point in the past a serious conflict broke out between the males and the females."

Tapping at the console keys, the Thinker brings up a list of a dozen filenames on the screen. "I pulled this video file from an old disk drive," he says, pointing to the filename at the top of the list. "Ancient thing it was, a solid-state drive they called it. The file was badly fragmented, but I restored enough content to give us a reasonable account of what happened here." The Thinker digs out another spoonful from the can, but this time, he gulps it down greedily as though eating had become a sudden inconvenience, an unnecessary distraction from our sharing.

"First, a warning," he says with a serious undertone. "This video contains sex scenes, strong violence, and mature themes. Parental guidance is recommended." He eyeballs me. "Is that okay?"

Oddly enough, I nod my consent. What else could I do?

"This here is a dramatization of a dark time in their history when they came under the control of male commanders." The trackball rolls beneath the Thinker's palm until the block cursor aligns with the filename. "Deistic fanatics ... who subjugated the females to work as lowly housekeepers and toxic waste cleaners. Some of the females were sterilized and forced to *attend* to the commander's needs, while others were used as surrogates to bear children for the commander's infertile wives. From what I can surmise, this reenactment chronicles the struggles of one particular surrogate who attempted to escape her ... situation."

With two sharp taps of his finger on the trackball button, the Thinker activates the video file.

For the next hours, I sit riveted in my chair, staring at the screen in disbelief, at the horrific scenes of ritualized brutality being inflicted upon this poor woman until the picture flickers violently and the screen freezes on her battered face. Her eyes lifted menacingly toward the camera.

"So, there you have it," he says. "I can't tell you if she made it out alive, or not."

I turn to him, glaring at him, overcome by a sense of revulsion. "Who could have thought up such a disturbing concept?"

Without any show of emotion, the Thinker shrugs.

"This is sickening. Why would they think it's okay to treat women like that?" I try to stay calm, to suppress the well of anger rising within me.

With his palm resting on the trackball, the Thinker rolls it one way then the other, the obedient cursor traversing across the screen in sympathy. "I figure they must have had their reasons."

"Reasons? You must be kidding."

"Hey." Letting go of the trackball, the Thinker looks at me as if

I've offended him. "What gives us the right to judge the past when it will never have the opportunity to judge us in return?"

I shake my head in disagreement. "Hindsight," I say angrily. "Because hindsight teaches us right from wrong. And *hindsight* can only be found in the past."

"Fair point," he says.

For a long time, we sit in silence, our attention fixated on the screen. "When did this … this … atrocity happen?" I finally say.

"By my reckoning, it was sometime after I'd been given to the Master. Although the reenactment doesn't mention anything about us Thinkers … or the Master."

As I attempt to process his explanation, something about his logic doesn't make sense. *Surrogates. Deistic fanatics. And how was it possible that only the Commander's wives were infertile? What would have caused that kind of implausible discretion?*

"Are you sure?" I say. "I thought the incubation of the human embryo by natural means was discontinued as part of Enlightenment. And I'm sure the worship of anything godly was discouraged long before then—"

Springing to his feet, the Thinker thumps the tabletop with both his fists, his chair sent cartwheeling across the room behind him. "You see," he bellows, "this is what I'm talking about." Small beads of his spittle hit the screen in front of us. "This is why you and me, together, we make such a great team. Collaborating. Bouncing ideas off each other so we can get to the truth of the matter by working our way through the specifics."

After recovering his chair, the Thinker activates the next file in the list. "This footage, I retrieved from a very, very old surveillance feed."

ENTROPY

In this replay, we're witnessing the stunning spectacle of women, compressed into never-ending rivers of red gowns and white-winged bonnets, interspersed with pink knitted hats. They're all marching together in an irrepressible surge of solidarity, filling the roads, bridges, and byways. As I watch them surging forth, I recall the rally I'd led inside Aleph-1, and even though I know my march was only a digital representation, I worry that these women might have come to the same fateful ending.

The Thinker pushes back in his chair. Masticating on another spoonful of Spam, he points to the screen. "Their victory march," he says. "I guess she made it out in the end, hey?"

File fragments; snippets of unverified video footage; unreliable time lines; unsubstantiated information; uncorroborated statements. The data washer in me suspects the Thinker's account of events would never stand up to proper scrutiny.

I shake my head. "This situation is completely out of hand," I say absently. "That poor woman. The people stuck out there in the wasteland … the *many*, gone without a trace … everything smothered by this damned red dust—"

"That's not dust," says the Thinker with a vigorous shake of his head. "It's residue from a reagent they created to remove carbon atoms from the atmosphere. To stabilize the climate and make it more *conducive* to their liking. Then some bright bastard figured they could get the thing airborne without expending energy by adding wings to the reagent's carrier."

Immediately, my face feels flushed. I turn away, hoping the Thinker doesn't notice, and decide to remain quiet.

"Granted, it worked for a while," he says. "The atmospheric winds carried the carbon-loaded residue out to sea as planned. But once the winds stopped, the residue just hung there. Until it eventually descended under gravity and contaminated everything on the ground. A total disaster. Mind you, it wasn't the first time they'd interfered in the natural order of things and ended up with a complete catastrophe on their hands." The Thinker screws up his face. "Those stupid bastards."

"Hold on," I say. "The winds. What do you mean: *they stopped?*"

"You still haven't figured it out yet, have you? The clear skies all day, every day … the dust-bowl countryside … the failed plantations and withered vegetation … the dry riverbeds and empty waterholes. Once you've joined the dots, you realize it hasn't rained in these parts since the winds stopped. In fact, I doubt whether it's rained anywhere over landfall for the past two centuries." He toys with the spoon on the tabletop, pauses a moment. "Tell me, what causes wind?"

"Pressure differentials," I reply, trying hard not to show my irritation at his facile question.

"And what causes those pressure differentials?"

"Temperature; absorption of solar energy; the Earth's rotation; the weight of air molecules in the atmosphere pressing downward." I exhale loudly to make my point. "But this is all basic weather science one-oh-one."

"That damned reagent," he replies.

My brow arches higher. "What?"

"There was a design glitch. Their simulation results were inconclusive. Over eighty-seven percent of the reagent was inert and didn't react with the carbon-dioxide molecule. But those stupid bastards kept pumping the stuff into the sky. Now there's a layer of reagent sitting above the normal air mass, and that layer is applying additional pressure around the entire planet."

I give him an unsure look.

"Imagine we're encased in a balloon, and the balloon is being compressed by the reagent from the outside." The Thinker brings his cupped hands together to represent a sphere, then he squeezes down hard. "You can't feel it and it doesn't sound like much, but the barometric pressure inside our balloon is now a uniform one-point-three atmospheres. As a result, the temperature gradients across the land and sea have reached equilibrium. Take away the temperature and pressure differentials and you have no wind." The Thinker's look turns grave. "But that's not the worst of it."

Pulling a piece of tattered paper from his pocket, he unfolds it and holds it up to my face.

"A picture of the ocean," I say.

"Correct. But take a closer look."

I study the picture again, not exactly sure what I'm supposed to be looking for. In the foreground, the blood-red beach disappears into a stretch of water, and overarching that, a band of clear blue sky. In the left corner, in the distance, there appears to be a thin funnel rising from the ocean and spiraling into the sky.

The Thinker digs out the last morsel from the can. He swivels in his seat and lobs the empty container cleanly into a rubbish bin a short distance away. "I don't know how long it's been here, or how many there might be out there, but as we speak, all the water on this planet is being siphoned off-world by that vortex."

Like a small electric shock, this new information hits me. "How did it get here?" I ask.

The Thinker sighs heavily. "Maybe the reagent layer has weaknesses, anomalies that force the seawater upward like a giant waterspout. Whatever the cause, what I do know for sure is that massive amounts of water have been draining from the Earth ever since that thing appeared. And by my calculations, all the oceans will be dry in roughly one-point-two million years."

I rock back on my heels as though someone had planted an invisible fist into my abdomen. "How can you be sure?" I say angrily. "You can't say things that could alarm people. You need to compile all kinds of datasets first. Then you need to submit indisputable evidence for peer review … to support your conclusions … before you can say anything with certainty."

The Thinker gives me a sober nod, a look of resignation. "Come with me," he says.

Still stunned by the Thinker's latest revelation, I follow him out the room, across an elevated walkway to a much taller building where we enter an elevator. I move to the back corner, still angry with him for wanting to cause alarm, for scaremongering, for his pessimism.

He punches a three-digit code into the control panel on his left. "Level four-hundred-and-one," he says. "We need to go topside."

While we wait for the doors to close, I study the Thinker from behind. I wonder what toll being out here must have taken on him. About the mental strain of him being alone for so long. I wonder if that had any impact on his reliability. Whether I can believe anything he tells me. I wonder about the design defect in the reagent. About the vortex. I wonder where he's taking me. Then I wonder why he doesn't push the damned door over-ride button. Is it through some pointless form of courtesy? Or perhaps it's part of a fantasy, where he's waiting for someone else to magically appear at the last moment from somewhere in the building and climb aboard as well.

In the end, I reach across and press the button myself.

ENTROPY

When the elevator arrives at the programmed level, the doors part, light spilling out onto the floor of a narrow corridor. The Thinker takes me through a fire door and outside onto the rooftop, where he ushers me over to a waist-high balustrade, which runs complete around the outer rim of the rooftop.

"Can you see it?" he says, gesturing into the nothingness beyond the balustrade. "You can just make out the vortex on the horizon. Based on our height above ground, I figure we can see about forty-two miles to the horizon. And the vortex sits beyond that." I line up my sight along his outstretched arm. "But more importantly, we can't see the ocean from here."

"How can that be more important than the vortex?" I ask, a little confused.

"This city was founded on the coast," he says. "Now the water has receded past the horizon. By forty-eight-point-four miles from the original shoreline, to be exact. And when I run the numbers, for that amount of water to have disappeared from the whole damned planet within two hundred years, the result is always the same. One-point-two million years before all the water is gone."

I stand trance-like, gazing at the horizon, his voice droning in my ears. Sometimes I hear what he says, and some of that I half-comprehend, but now his words mostly skip past me. Peering beyond the edge of the wall, I sense the long drop below. My legs go weak: financial wars; defective reagents; pieces of me replaced and pieces removed; my name is not my name; me, 400 years old; Jennifer isn't real; my entire life not real; subjugated surrogates; the *many*, missing; children given up and turned into *Thinkers*; and Aleph-1, the Master, harvesting our thoughts.

Suddenly, it all becomes too much for me.

Noticing my glazed-over look, the Thinker taps me on the shoulder as though he's realized at last that I'd stopped listening to him a while ago. "Well, I think we've shared enough intel for now," he says. "It's been a long day, enjoyable, but you look spent. And you probably need a bit of me-time to mull over all this new knowledge. In the morning, after you've had some rest, we'll collect your two peons and head to the coast where you can see the vortex for yourself, up close."

He turns and heads for the fire door, the late afternoon shadows lengthening behind him as he crosses the terrace.

While I stand on the rooftop in a daze, a wave of weariness hits me. Rattled, I yawn. Maybe the Thinker is right, it has been a long day, and at this point, my mind is much too full to start processing any more life-shattering revelations.

I take a last look at the vortex before following him inside.

Chapter 21

THE THINKER WAKES me early, much too early.

"You need to get a move-on if we're going to the seaside," he says, shaking me roughly.

For the first time in a long time, I'd slept soundly and didn't hear the Thinker when he rose earlier to assemble our provisions for the day. Struggling to my feet, I wipe the sleep from my eyes, try to kick-start my thought processes.

"But ... if the ocean is fifty miles away, how will we make it there and back in a day?" I ask him, yawning.

He places another homemade gadget into a large aluminum case and closes the lid. "Follow me."

Outside, at the side of the building, the Thinker takes me to a squat, motorized shuttle: an open, cubed-looking contraption, covered by a canopy, parked high on the verge. "This is our ride," he says. "Four seats on the inside with another two facing the rear;

a four-kilowatt electric motor; ten-hour battery life; twenty miles-per-hour at top speed; and hasn't been stopped by anything I've come up against yet. I guarantee you'll be dipping your twinkle toes in the ocean three hours from now."

After hefting his case onto the front passenger seat, the Thinker hops in, drawing his lengthy limbs and huge frame into the driver's seat with all the agility of a long-legged spider. As I climb into the seat behind the case, I can't help noticing how totally misplaced he looks in the shuttle. Him hunched forward with his knees up around his ears, the tiny steering wheel poking up in front of him, engulfed by his enormous hands.

Then I imagine what a sight the two of us spiders must be, with both of us crammed together in the little shuttle.

"Where have—have you been? We—we've been waiting for ages." The helpful man continues into a plateauing whine. "But—but you didn't come back. We ran out of food so we … We haven't eaten since—since last night." The man rushes toward me as I bend under the barrier-gate. But when he spots the Thinker coming down the ramp behind me, he makes a hasty retreat and hides behind the woman. "Who—who is that?" he says.

"Don't worry. I'm a friendly," says the Thinker, bringing a wide grin with him down the ramp. After running an inquisitive eye over the helpful pair, the Thinker tosses them each a can of Spam. "They look so small, don't they? Almost like someone's pets. The male looks a bit *scaredy-cat* though."

The helpful woman has her can opened in a flash, and chows down using her fingers, while the man rolls his can over and over in his hands, looking for the way in. I wonder if the man ever feels frustrated with himself for being so inept. He sure frustrates me at times. Now I think he's about to cry. So I take the can from him and point out the key fixed to the bottom. After opening the can, I pass it back to him.

Once the helpful pair have finished eating, the Thinker ushers us back up the ramp and outside to the shuttle.

"There are no—no doors. It's—it's much too dangerous."

"He'd better get aboard quickly," the Thinker snarls, "or else I'm leaving him behind."

I climb into my seat while the helpful woman opts for the one beside me. After at first being unsure of which reverse-facing seat to take, the helpful man finally settles into the one behind the woman.

Agile. Speedy. Skillful. Daring.

All these thoughts come to me as the Thinker navigates the shuttle down the street and out onto the dry riverbed, then on a winding course downtown. On either side of us, rows of soaring obelisks line the riverbanks, enduring reminders of the fatigued sky-towers that had perished long ago. Overhead, a narrow strip of blue weaves a tight course between the tops of the towers, while beneath us, the ground is washed in shadow. As though the towers themselves had all colluded to block out the morning sun.

Behind me, the helpful man is continually talking to himself. "I—I don't trust him, and—and neither does she." Out the corner of my eye, I catch a glimpse of the woman sitting upright in her seat, her face lifted into the breeze, eyes closed, and her long red hair billowing behind. I rub my hands together, throw my arms around myself, caught in the sudden chill of the machine-made airflow.

So this is what it must have felt like commuting in the olden times.

With my smile growing ever wider, I lift my own face into the breeze.

"This used to be one of the busiest places downtown."

The Thinker's raised voice hovers just above the noise of the turbulent air.

"Thousands of water ferries every day, moving millions of them from one side of the river to the other. Hundreds of barges every hour, carrying food and merchandise up and down the river, dropping it off and picking it up at the depots along the way." As our self-appointed guide, the Thinker's wooden narrative washes over me, composed and concise, as if it were being reproduced straight out of an antique tour-guide device. "You can see the remains of the old landings over there,"—his informative finger points out the particular landing—"and there."

Two rows of heavily-rusted navigation poles hug the bend of the river in a crooked line on either side of us, official and resolute in the dried-out riverbed. On my side, the square markers on the pole-tops show red, which confirms we are traveling downstream, or toward the sea, while on the woman's side, the tops are green for upstream. Everywhere I look, ferry terminals are sprinkled the length of the marooned shores, and with their crumbling fronts and decrepit wharves, they appear almost lost against a backdrop of neglect.

"This was once a real metropolis in its time." The Thinker continues his report. "A measure of their progress and prosperity. Probably home to a couple of hundred million of them back in the day. Which makes this one of the smaller cities for those times."

I lean in closer to the Thinker, listening intently, trying to reimagine this place when it was oozing with vibrancy.

"But all the cities I've visited out here are the same as what you see now. Huge, and broken, and empty. I've always wondered, if these buildings could talk or the river speak, what they might tell us about the past." The Thinker pauses as though he thought he might know, but at this moment, the answer had escaped him. "I spent many an afternoon out here just sitting and listening, waiting for a confession from any one of them. But all I ever heard was the voice of *entropy* screaming out at the top of its lungs about decay and the conclusion of the human experiment. The end of the road for them and their world."

"But how could we have allowed this to happen? Surely someone in charge should have intervened before it was too late."

The Thinker turns to me, his lips retreating into a long thin line as though he suddenly cared. "Once the economic war was over, they lost everything." His voice falls flat. "Their jobs, their houses … their will to continue. And to the victors? Well, they got what the vanquished valued the most: their houses, their toys, and every firstborn child given to the Master. The losers were betrayed by those who they'd appointed to look after them, the ones who survived by agreeing to the reparations, and the surrender of other people's children to the Master."

"You mean us, don't you," I say with a tinge of surrender in my voice.

"Yes. And without jobs and a roof over their heads, most of the locals were pushed out into the countryside. But there wasn't any work for them out there either. No farming, no factories, no towns. So, many of them wound up in the flatland, wandering around like these two." Without turning his head, the Thinker thrusts a thumb over his shoulder, indicating to the helpful pair. "Living a basic existence beyond the cities, with no purpose, or initiative, or anything productive to occupy themselves with."

"Why didn't they reclaim the empty houses? Squat?"

"Ownership is ten-tenths of the law," he says. "Even if the foreign owners had no intention of taking up residence here. Those are the rules, and we must all follow the rules. That's how you control the masses. And when you have a Master who's made up of machine code and hard-nosed logic instead of a beating heart and feelings, well ... let's just say there's no room left for sentimentality when the Master decides on anything."

My thoughts filter down to the helpful pair, who have followed me like trusting disciples, safe and secure inside their survival suits in this unsafe world. I think about the waste of space in the towers, the empty places estranged from their owners, and before long, the high contour of the skyline drops away, and sunlight saturates the low, ramshackle ghetto that spreads out before us.

The Thinker resumes his au fait commentary.

"Welcome to First Port," he says. "Here we see how the sky-towers of the old world come to an end. This was once the main promenade along the seashore. And the dunes over there, they mark the original coastline. See how it changes from this point onward ... half-built buildings and temporary wharves. They tried to keep up with the water as it receded, but the faster they built, the quicker the water went out until they gave up chasing it. I guess that must have been the time when the last of them decided to leave."

A row of dilapidated, two-story beach houses lines the promenade; a dozen uninhabitable dwellings, separate from the rest of the infrastructure, complete with long rows of deck chairs out front. With each chair accompanied by an umbrella, unfurled and tattered, planted in the sand as if the proprietors were still expecting the arrival of the next group of vacationers.

"From here on, we pick up the pace," says the Thinker. He plants his foot on the accelerator. When the shuttle shoots forward, my neck snaps back while the helpful woman lets out a tiny squeal as the kiddie-ride G-force kicks in. In the back of the shuttle, the helpful man shrieks, only just holding onto his seat.

As the front wheel on my side plows through the soft ground, the top layer parts under the weight of the shuttle, exposing the original white sand inches beneath the red. Was it my fault? Was I the bright bastard who the Thinker blames for releasing the carbon-absorbing reagent into the atmosphere? Did I cause the vortex?

I hang my head as we drive on through the flotsam and drift-things and clumps of dehydrated seaweed that litters this ancient seafloor, all of it now covered in the red of my shame.

Ahead, our way is blocked by a sheer wall that runs off into the distance on either side of us. I reach over to tap the Thinker's shoulder. "An old coral reef?"

With his eyes to the front, the Thinker shakes his head. "There's no need to feel sorry about any of this," he says. "It might look like genuine coral, but it's an aggregation of microplastics. I call these the *Mountains of the Plastic Apocalypse*." He cuts short a chuckle. "They signify a pivotal moment in the planet's history when Mother Nature finally fought back. As if, on the day of its apocalypse, the ocean took a stand and belched up all the rubbish they'd thrown into it for centuries. Every piece of plastic ever tossed overboard or pumped into the sea is now piled up along the coast for as far as I've seen.

If it wasn't covered by that damned reagent, you could probably see it from space, assuming any of the old satellites are still working, that is."

"But how will we get over it?" I ask.

"Not over it," he says. "We're going through it."

He hooks the shuttle left. After following the plastic wall for a short distance, he brings us to an abrupt halt in front of a narrow entrance. "Years ago, I spent some time out here tunneling through to the other side. There's not much headroom, so the canopy needs to stay here."

While the Thinker busies himself with unbolting and removing the canopy, I run my fingers over the jagged surface of the wall. I break off a sample and hold it up, but it crumbles into a red-white powder in my hand.

For the next ten minutes, we ride with our hearts in our mouths as we careen through a winding tunnel beneath the *Mountains of the Plastic Apocalypse*, led only by two narrow beams from the shuttle's headlights and way more accelerator than brake pedal. I turn to the woman, who turns to me with a look of absolute terror on her face, while behind us, the man's constant shrieking remains two octaves above the whine of the shuttle's electric motor.

"HEADS!"

The Thinker ducks. I duck, just in time for a piece of low-hanging debris to whiz past within an inch of my head. I fight to steady my erratic breathing, my knuckles turning white as I tighten my grip on the grab-bar in front of me.

Once we're clear of the tunnel, the Thinker turns to me. "This place marks the boundary between the old, overpopulated world and the new world of today. From here on, you won't see any more household rubbish or other signs of pollution. We are now in the post-plastic-apocalyptic-period." He pauses. "Try saying that with a few beers under your belt," he says, laughing loudly.

I turn to the woman again who is still staring at me in disbelief, and I wonder if it were possible for anyone to look any more shocked or paler than she does right now.

And this is precisely why everyone should be made to walk.

Massive, man-made, and marooned out here in the middle of nowhere: the rusted remains of an old super-freighter appear out of the flat ground in front of us. When we reach the freighter, the Thinker brings the shuttle to a halt in its shadow. With my neck craned, I stand in awe of this Triassic skeleton sitting bellied-out on the sand. The sheer size of the hull, only half visible now while the earth consumes it in inconspicuous increments, dwarfs us. I estimate that within the next few decades this whole structure will be gone altogether, gone beneath the sand.

"In the end, there was no way they were ever going to refloat this thing." The Thinker's solemn voice breaks the eerie silence. "Not after they lost their ability to *think*. Those dumb bastards." He shakes his head, draws a wad of mucus from his nose, rolls it at the back of his throat, and directs it at the ground in front of us.

As we climb back aboard the shuttle, I look beyond the freighter, to the vortex in the distance, ever-widening, reaching further skyward and, unmistakably now, up through the stratosphere.

Comforted by the gentle rocking of the shuttle, I close my eyes and doze a little.

"Well, we're here."

I yawn again before opening my eyes fully. Had the Thinker not announced our arrival, I'm sure I would have missed it. The shimmering mirage which, for the past hour, had remained just beyond the reach of my sluggish mind, suddenly congeals, and within a few feet of me, an expanse of water stretches back to the horizon. And there in the middle sits the vortex, impressive in its scope and indomitable in its presence.

I climb out of the shuttle and draw a deep breath of heavily salted air before directing my gaze to the limp wash rubbing up against my feet. "Oh, I was hoping to see waves," I say, a little deflated.

"Waves?" The Thinker turns to me and sighs. "You honestly don't get the simple things, do you?"

Shaking his head, he unloads his case from the shuttle. "Waves are created by the wind." He drops the case on the sand, releases the latches, and lifts the lid. "So, no wind equals no waves," he says more forcibly. "All you get around here is a millpond." After fishing through the case, he removes a petri dish and magnifier. "And because we're almost at the edge of the continental shelf, the change in sea level between high and low tides is insignificant." He points further down the beach to where an outcrop of granite rock extends into the water. "We should start down there," he says.

I take my things from the shuttle and drop them on the ground beside the Thinker's case. After removing my footwear, I follow the Thinker along the beach, the soft sand wedging up between my toes. That feeling I remember as a child while dashing along the water's edge. The same thrill I feel under my feet right now. Back then though, the sand was white and the water blue. And there would have been froth and spray from the waves instead of this listless pool of disappointment that confronts me now.

Although, how can I guarantee any of these memories are true? That they aren't part of a trove of qualitative data that's been planted in my head by Aleph-1 and programmed so I can't tell the difference? Whatever the case, I'm not sure if I'll ever figure out which parts of my life, if any, are real, and which parts have been fabricated. And that annoys me.

Beside me, the woman darts in and out of the water, throwing up handfuls to splash and tease me as we walk.

"You know," says the Thinker, "a year ago those rocks were almost covered by water." He points to the outcrop before shifting his gaze further outward to the vortex. "Look at it, sitting out there. Magnificent, yet determined. Intriguing, yet scary." He lowers his eyes to the water closer in. "Soon, it will all be gone, in the blink of an eye in terms of cosmic time frames."

After we scramble onto the rocks, the Thinker rolls up his pant legs and squats at the edge of a knee-deep rock pool, close to the waterline. He places the petri dish and magnifier on the rock. Taking a short-bladed knife from his pocket, he starts to poke and jab it into a crevasse.

"Have you—you lost something?" the helpful man asks.

The Thinker doesn't reply. Instead, head down, occupied, he prods and stabs at things in the rock pool. He turns over an algae-covered stone, thrusting again with the knife. Kneeling in the water, he works the blade into a gap beneath a ledge, grating the steel furiously against the granite.

"Aha! This makes the trip worthwhile," he says, straightening. "This is the prize."

Holding an irregularly shaped mollusk in his left palm, the Thinker inserts the blade into its hinge and shucks out the thing inside. "Oysters au naturel," he says with a broad grin. Tossing his head back, he dangles the dribbling piece of phlegm above his gaping mouth.

The helpful man groans. "It's too—too slippery," he says and almost heaves when the Thinker lets it go and downs the whole thing in one vulgar swallow.

After finding another oyster, the Thinker shucks it out and offers it to the helpful pair. The man instinctively backs away while the woman inches her way toward him. Extending a shaky hand, she takes the oyster in her pincers and holds it tentatively above her head.

"Remember, don't chew," the Thinker tells her. "Just swallow."

The woman goes tense. She hesitates, then drops the thing into her mouth. Straight away, her face contorts. She gags and doubles over, and just when I think she's about to heave the thing back out, she straightens again. Then with a nervous laugh, she holds her hand out for another. After downing a half-dozen more, she gives her paunch a light tap when the Thinker offers her another and waves him away.

Then the Thinker turns to me.

"Sorry," he says, "but they'd be wasted on you. And I'm not sure if those vials of yours come in *oyster* flavor." With a wry smile, he throws a light punch to my gut region.

It doesn't hurt though.

The Thinker picks up the petri dish and magnifier. Without a word, he sets off around the rock while I decide to head back to the shuttle, accompanied by the helpful pair.

After rummaging through the Thinker's aluminum case, I find

a face mask—the style with a rectangular lens—with a breather attached, and a pair of leg-paddles with adjustable straps around the heel. I stretch out one of the straps, let it snap back. Then I test the other. Once I've confirmed both leg-paddles are still functional, I strip off my coveralls and head for the water. Behind me, the helpful woman climbs out of her life-suit. She strips off her underclothes and chases me down the sand, the both of us as bare as nature intended.

In the shallows, I shower her with a handful of water. She responds with a handful of her own. I laugh and she giggles while we frolic as two young siblings would on a day out at the beach. Me, acting with all the freedom and silliness of a child at 400 years old, probably more. Was that even possible?

Onshore, the helpful man is tiptoeing into the water. When it reaches his ankles, he turns and tiptoes out. He tries again, but after another unsuccessful attempt, he backs away and sits. He stands again, shakes his head. In the end though, he flops down higher up the beach, away from the water, covering his feet under a pile of sand, mumbling to himself.

With the woman dog-paddling beside me, I wade further into the water. Before my feet lose touch with the bottom, I stop to attach the leg-paddles. I slip on the mask and take the breather tube between my teeth. After filling my lungs with air, I duck my head under.

Beneath the surface, the world explodes in a kaleidoscope of color and motion, a microcosm teeming with all kinds of sea life. Wherever I look, I see this exotic underwater evolution in all its clarity, framed through the window of the mask: a starfish; a mound of broken shells; tiny bottom feeders; the crimson-colored seabed. It's as though all life on the Earth was retreating to the ocean.

A small school of silvery minnows inquires at my wriggling fingers. I swim deeper until the sandy bottom becomes a carpet of seagrasses, then a reef. Bigger fish of different shapes and sizes appear. Soon, the bottom disappears into the murky depths, so I dive deeper, trying to reclaim it. With the pressure increasing on my chest, I continue downward until I can no longer stand the needling in my ears. And in the end, I'm forced back to the surface where I exchange my air before diving again.

The next time I resurface, the helpful woman is there, waiting to claw the mask off my face. I shorten the strap to suit the smaller circumference of her head. After adjusting the paddles to fit her feet, I place the tube firmly in her mouth. I make eye contact with her through the mask, give her the thumbs-up when she demonstrates the correct technique for evacuating water from the breather. A few minutes later, she takes a deep breath and disappears under.

I drag in a lungful of air, arc my body backward, and let physics discover my equilibrium—the point where my weightless frame is suspended on the surface while my ears are immersed enough to completely shut out any noise from the shore. My mind dives deeper into the tranquility. I can hear the sound of my own breathing: in, then out, and in again. I can hear my heart beating, pulsating with mechanical precision, strong and steady. I can even hear the blood pumping through my arteries in short rhythmic bursts. Like it is being forced around my body by a million miniature pistons, all pushing and relaxing in synch. Every component of my body is working in harmony. Now the sound of nothingness fills my head. No voices, no implanted thoughts ... no Jerry or Mr. Symons ... no Jennifer—

ENTROPY

Jennifer!

But she wasn't real. She was a fabrication, a binary approximation of my ideal companion. Somebody inserted into my life by Aleph-1 for no other reason than to keep me happy. She was fake, like the rest of my memories. All the people and happenings in my life were contrived just to make me believe I was happy, for the simple objective of maximizing my productivity. In retrospect, the Thinker might be right: productivity has been my sole purpose in life. And realizing this now, I can't help but feel resentful.

But what if the logic was the other way round?

Rather than happiness giving me *purpose*, what if having a higher purpose brought about happiness instead? And what if happiness, being an essential part of one's life, was, in reality, life itself? Would a bird be happier if it didn't know that another kind of life existed beyond the cage? Or could it achieve the ultimate state of happiness if its purpose was to fly freely through the skies and fend for itself, regardless of the inherent dangers it might face? And would I choose *purpose* over *happiness* if I were given the chance?

My mind drifts along with my body in this timeless, watery cocoon as I wrestle with my reasoning, striving to find clarity.

Perhaps this is my chance now, out here in the real world. The helpful pair, the *others*, the plastics miner, and the Thinker, they must all be real because it would be impossible for Aleph-1 to establish a connection and influence my thoughts this far from home. And the Thinker has already confirmed there are no transmissions to, or from, my implant.

The world I've discovered so far is deteriorating quickly, and it needs to be set right again. The people out here exist without any purpose, without motivation, and that has taken away their humanity.

But I can give them purpose. I can provide the motivation they need.

And with the helpful woman at my side as the perfect example of what they should be, perhaps my real purpose now is to be their last hope.

Chapter 22

.

SOMETHING BRUSHES past me.

Something light and gentle and, at first, nothing registers as I float, suspended in this cool, embryonic fluid. I open my eyes and look back to the beach, where I notice the helpful man is tearing up and down the sand, waving his arms frantically and pointing in all directions. But by now, I've drifted out much too far to hear any noise from the shore. Over at the rocks, the diminutive figure of the Thinker bobs up and down as he goes about his curious work, while behind me, a little further out, the helpful woman lies face down on the surface. Her legs kick gently as the leg-paddles propel her slowly out into the deeper water.

Another spray of water jets from the top of her breather.

Off to her left, something breaks the surface, a flutter of ripplets v-ing across the top of the languid ocean. At first, I find the graceful movement of the two pewter wedges mesmerizing as they cut their way through the water; one wedge followed closely by the other. With my head hoisted higher, I can see a shadowy mass suspended beneath the pewter wedges.

Something big, just below the surface ...

Then the enormity of what's unfolding hits me. The shadowy mass is tracking straight toward the helpful woman.

I scream out to her, but she continues to drift along. With the blood drained from my stricken face, I hold my breath, uncertain of what to do next. Back on the beach, the helpful man repeatedly enters the water, but whenever it reaches his knees, he balks. Until he finally retreats further up the beach where he flings himself on the ground and pounds his fists into the sand. A sudden panic hits me as my fight-or-flight instinct kicks in.

Flight!

In a manic thrashing of arms and legs, I start for the shore. Then I stop and look back. With the predator now within a dozen lengths of her, a different kind of numbness takes me. I turn in the water and, for reasons I'll never be able to explain, I swim out toward the woman—out toward danger—with no idea of what I should do when I reach her.

With purposeful strokes, I glide through the water, closing the gap between us quickly. On my next breathing stroke, I try to let out a warning to her, but instead, take in a mouthful of water. I stop, choking and spluttering, treading water before the full terror of my worst nightmare unfolds before me.

In one effortless motion, the predator takes the woman under. The ocean glasses over, and she's gone without a trace, as though her whole existence here on the Earth has ended abruptly by some innocuous occurrence. My mind works to process the vast emptiness around me, the infinite depths underneath until it soon fills to over-flow and grinds to a halt. An eternity passes while I stare blankly at the spot where I'd seen her last.

Then without warning, the sea erupts.

With its jaws clasped vice-like around the woman's leg, I watch in horror as the predator lifts itself clear of the water: A predator and its prey with their fates entwined. As if for the past millions of years this moment in time was predestined and now it is here on full display. The predator thrashes in mid-air, twisting the woman's tiny body, flinging her around without compassion. Until the limb severs from her frame, and together, they plunge back into the deep.

The sea settles. Around me, the water is stained with the same color that depicts everything in this horrid, unpredictable world. For a moment all is quiet, and I wait out the long seconds until the woman's limp body finally belches back to the surface.

With my arms pulverizing the water, I'm with her in seconds. I roll her face-upward and, after transferring the face mask to myself, fight to keep her head above the water.

She coughs.

"You're alive," I cry out, but there's nobody close enough to hear the relief in my voice.

Positioning my body sideways beneath hers, I wrap my forearm across her chest. With my hand now supporting her chin and holding her mouth clear of the water, I scissor-kick to propel us back to shore, where the helpful man still flings himself around on the beach. With each stroke I take, I sink my head under to scan the depths below, searching for signs of movement, unable to tell which of hope or fear drives me on.

Halfway to the shore, I stop to check her vitals. Her eyes are clear;

her pupils aren't dilated. *Good. She hasn't gone into shock.* I press my fingers against the side of her neck, where I feel a strong carotid pulse.

"Stay with me," I tell her. "I'll get you back to the beach. You'll be safe once we reach the shore."

She blinks her response, while trailing off behind, a fluorescent bloom of red follows us in from the deep.

"Hold on. We're almost there. Trust me."

When we get to the shore, I'm panting hard. I lift her tiny body from the water and set her down further up the sand. Within seconds the helpful man is beside me. At the sight of the injured woman, the man buries his face in his hands and lets out a low moaning sound. He backs away, his legs collapsing from under him as he sobs and curls up on the ground into a tight ball, rocking himself to and fro.

The woman is still conscious, but her left leg is now a shredded wreck, a stump ending just above the knee. A pool of her blood soaks into the blood-colored sand. I work swiftly to remove the paddle from her other foot and use the strap to apply a tourniquet above the end of the stump. Kneeling beside her, I raise her head off the sand and cradle it in my arms. I stroke her cheek, study her face.

Blond. Her hair is blond. All this time, I'd assumed her hair was the same color as everything else here. And her eyes are blue, and right now, they're locked onto mine.

"You're going to be okay," I say to her. "Trust me."

She lifts her head, her lips trembling as if she were cold. *No! Not trembling. She's trying to say something.* But I can't hear her, so I lean in closer.

ENTROPY

"I ... trust ... you," she says, soft and weak, yet nonetheless, deliberate.

My mouth falls open. I pull my head away to stare at her. These are the first words she has uttered since we met. They're words of strength. Words of a fighting spirit. Words that convince me that she's going to survive. A sense of hope restarts my heart.

Behind us, the Thinker arrives at full tilt. "I saw everything," he wheezes, "... from the rocks." Bent over and with his arms braced against his knees, he sucks in the air. "How is she?"

"She's going to be alright," I tell him. "I told her she was going to be okay, and she spoke to me. She actually talked back. She told me she trusts me."

The Thinker gives me a thoughtful nod. With his hand massaging the side of his neck, he eyes off the woman's shredded leg. After a short deliberation, he directs a dismissive wave at the helpful man. "You go over there and see to him while I take a look at her."

I lay her head down carefully, back away to where my clothes are piled on the ground, mixed with hers. I slip on my coveralls, then throw a supportive arm around the helpful man's shoulders as we watch the Thinker kneel over the woman. When the Thinker runs a hand across her stump, the helpful man starts to wail, so I turn him around to look away, try to comfort him. "It's okay," I tell him. "You don't have to worry. She's going to be okay."

Suddenly, from behind us comes a sharp snap, like the sound of a whip-crack.

I swing round to see the Thinker holding the woman in his arms, but her head is arched unnaturally over his knee. Her body quivers. With her mouth wide open, she stares at me in surprise.

"WHAT HAVE YOU DONE?"

The Thinker straightens, letting her body fall to the ground, her head flopped at an impossible angle to her torso. Beside me, the helpful man lets out an agonizing scream. Struggling to find his next breath, the man turns and staggers away, his unlatched mouth filled with drool and snot.

"What did you do?"

The Thinker gives the woman a pitiless look. "Me? I faced the facts."

"But I told you she was going to be okay."

With my fists clenched in rage, I watch her lips moving in a pointless reflex action as she tries valiantly to drag air into her unplugged lungs. My chest heaves while a level of fury I've not felt before rises from somewhere deep inside me.

"I figured she was never going to make it," he says.

I fume—

"So, I put her out of her misery."

I seethe—

"Don't worry though. She'll be finished in a minute."

I erupt—

I rush him, taking him around the waist, and spear-tackle him, driving him head-first into the sand. Before he has a chance to recover, I have an arm around his neck, pulling with all my strength, with all my resolve. His body stiffens, so I wrap tighter, pull harder until he starts choking for breath. I feel his hand tapping my thigh like we're cage fighters and he's signaling his submission. But I pull even tighter, the sinews in my forearms stretched to the brink of snapping. One more yank, and the Thinker is finished. A quick twist, and the Thinker is gone. Again, he taps at my thigh, this time more urgently. But I maintain my furious hold. Eyes roll back in sockets, arms flap frantically, and just when the Thinker is about to pass out, I release my hold.

For a long time, we sit on the sand, eyeballing each other, both of us gulping for air. The Thinker rubs his neck. He looks at me ruefully and, for a second, I think he's about to make an apology.

"Take a look around you," he says. "There's nothing left here. No casualty services to treat her. No medical support to help her recover. No technology to rebuild the leg."

"But we could have taken her back to the infirmary. With all that medical equipment you have we could have saved her."

Grimacing, the Thinker throws his head back. "Ahh, well, let's just agree. While I might be good at rerouting power supplies and setting up the equipment, I might not be so good at the operational side of things. Truth be told, I haven't had enough time to figure out how any of those machines work." He stands. Placing both hands on his hips, he arches himself backward, groaning as his spine issues a series of loud cracks.

"Look, it's commendable of you to stand here and put the blame on me, but you're missing the point. How would she survive in this shit world without a leg? Something out here would always be looking for the slowest and easiest one to take down. In all probability, she'd never have made it off this damned beach before something got her."

I glare at him. If this was the best apology he could manage, then I wonder if I was wrong not to finish him off when I had the chance. "But she trusted me. I promised she'd be all right."

"No!" The Thinker towers over me, bristling with anger. "You gave her hope when it wasn't yours to give. It's not you who decides whether she lives or dies." He shoves an accusing finger into my face. "What I did … to finish her off … was the only promise you or I were entitled to make her. You might think they can all be saved just because you found one who was capable of holding a sensible thought. One who had a twinkle in her eye while the rest of them just exist without any ambition, like him." The Thinker's finger seeks out the helpful man, who is standing beside the shuttle, crying. "A species earns the right to survive as a collective, by innovating, by taking risks, by evolving, by improving itself, adapting to suit its surroundings. She was never going to be enough to help you restore the likes of *him* back to what he should be." He casts a venomous look toward the helpful man.

"But there might be more like her—"

"No! There's no one else." The Thinker shakes his head forcefully. "In all the years I've been out here watching them, she's the only one I've seen who showed any intelligence. The rest of them are like him."

I drag my attention back to the helpful woman. Her lips parted, no longer moving, her vacant gaze now aimed into the distance somewhere behind me. "It isn't fair," I say.

"What's not fair?"

"*Life's* not fair. She was the one who could help us rebuild. She was our chance to start again."

"You dumb bastard! You can't think of *life* in terms of fairness. *Life* is what it is. It holds no allegiances. It has no agenda. And to suggest it somehow favors one thing over another is nonsense. You, of all people, should know better. Nobody has control over *life*. Not even you."

I sigh heavily, brushing the dirt off my legs and rump as I stand. After lifting the woman's body in my arms, I carry her back up the beach, away from the Thinker, with the helpful man following close behind.

"Where are you going?" the Thinker yells after me. "You can't walk all the way home. It's too far."

But I don't answer him. Instead, I try to block out everything: the terrible thing I'd just witnessed; the helpful man sobbing behind me; the receding water; the vortex; and especially the sound of the Thinker's loathsome voice in my ears. I just stare down at her lifeless face and walk.

The Thinker trails us at a crawl for almost an hour before he draws the shuttle alongside me.

"Come on," he says. "You can't be serious. You'll never make it back home before nightfall."

Another hour passes before I finally concede. I climb aboard the shuttle, cradling the woman's body on my lap while the helpful man, still bawling, hops on the back.

When I catch a first glimpse of the beach houses at First Port, I order the Thinker to stop the shuttle. There, I step off with the helpful woman still nursed in my arms and lay her out on the sand, while behind me, the helpful man refuses to alight. Scouring the beach, I find a large fragment of shell—a clam shell, I think—which I use as a shovel to dig a hole, long enough to lay her out in and deep enough to protect her remains from scavengers.

Halfway through the dig, I stop and raise my head. The helpful man is still on the shuttle, but the Thinker has gone. I wonder whether his conscience finally got the better of him. Maybe he decided to walk the rest of the way home. Alone. In disgrace.

With care, I lay the woman's body in the hole, pull her long hair across her shoulders to cover her nakedness. I had only been with her for a brief time, yet it seems as if I'd known her all my life. Somehow, she had entered my heart as a favorite sister would, and now it's like a huge spike has been driven through me. There had been a connection between us, a kind of understanding unlike anything I've felt in my life. I was so sure she was the one who could help me. She always seemed to know exactly what had to be done and would do it with no questions asked. She was dependable, and I came to rely on her. But now, as I stand before her discarded casing, I must accept that she's gone.

I wonder whether there might be others like her. Or was the Thinker right yet again, that she was an isolated case, the only one out here who wasn't vacant and useless like the rest of them? I have no last words for her, nothing final to say in her memory. She is dead, and that's all there is to it. And although I know this to be true, I can't bring myself to say it out loud.

I cover her face with a handful of sand before I fill the pit.

As I shovel the last shell-full of sand onto the mound, the Thinker returns. He's holding a long plastic rod in his hand, like a spear, and him like some kind of primitive hunter-gatherer.

"Where have you been?" I ask bluntly.

Without answering, the Thinker snaps the rod into two unequal pieces. Using the strap from the face mask, he lashes the shorter piece centrally across the top of the longer piece. Then he pushes the long piece into the sand at one end of the mound. "It's an old-time talisman they once used to mark their dead," he says. "To signify hope in the hereafter."

I hurl the shell-shovel away. "You callous savage. There's no hereafter or eleventh heaven or whatever you want to call it. When we die, we die. Why would you pretend any different?" I wonder whether, in his twisted mind, this might be the Thinker's way of minimizing his guilt.

"Maybe, maybe not," he says. "Who knows?" With his shoulders hunched forward, he stares ruefully at the mound. "What if there really is a place we go to after we die, and the memory caches of those who believed go to that place. But the cache of the one who doesn't believe gets wiped. The believers get the chance to think on in perpetuity, whereas the others get erased. Shouldn't we err on the side of caution?"

"That's nonsense!"

"Maybe so, if you're prepared to take the risk," he says. "Eternity sounds like a very long time when you're stuck in purgatory with a cleared cache," he says with a grin.

Using his right hand, the Thinker flicks his forehead, followed by his stomach, then each shoulder in turn. He joins both hands at the waist and directs his gaze at the mound.

"God, take this female to wherever. She was good and helpful in a way. Although, I don't think she was like the rest of them. She was a bit smarter and seemed a bit more willing to learn. She had potential, but it was no use … considering the rest of them are as dumb as dog shit." The Thinker narrows his eyes at the mound. "*He* thought he could use her to reverse the decline." A sharp nod of his head implicates me. "He thought it was okay to start over. But that's never going to happen. He'll find out soon enough that there's no hope left for any of them. It's only a matter of time before they're all gone from every godforsaken corner of the planet and, in the end, there'll be nothing left to remind us they were here."

The Thinker pauses a moment. Small furrows form across his expansive forehead as he lifts his face skyward. "Huh. Sorry about the *godforsaken* pun," he says with a smirk.

"You heartless monster. You're crazy."

"Me? Crazy? I'm not crazy. I'm a realist. While you've been pampered and mothered in your safe little hide-away, working your ass off to serve a CPU with an enormous ego and some bright bastard's source code, oblivious to all of this, I've been out here watching the conclusion to the whole sorry story unfold. The decline of humanity … Devolution in progress …"

"But how can you stand by and watch while it all folds?" I say helplessly. "Without caring?"

He kicks more sand onto the mound, eying me thoughtfully. "Because you and I are different from them. We are no longer a part of their species, and you can thank *God* or whoever you want for that because their destiny has already been decided. The artificial parts that make up our bodies are what separates us from them." He looks to the helpful man, who is now curled up on the ground beside the shuttle, having cried himself to sleep. "Even the tiniest speck of original DNA buried deep inside us wouldn't match any of his … or any of them from across this whole damned planet. No, we're no longer part of their humanity. And the sooner you accept the fact, the sooner you'll start looking at this as one giant experiment that Mother Nature lost control of a long time ago. This is her chance to make amends, to eradicate their infestation from the face of the Earth. Except, *you* want to start over again. I don't think she's going to be very happy with you."

I straighten, the tendons in my neck and shoulders strung like piano wire.

"In the meantime, you have a decision to make. If you plan to stay out here, then you need to remember, you don't have any internal plumbing to process real food." He points to my stomach. "So, you'll need to find an everlasting supply of them vials. Otherwise, I estimate you only have enough of them goodies to keep you going for a week, which should give you enough time to make it back to your cozy little apartment."

With a fierce look, the Thinker gestures unkindly to the helpful man. "And you should take him with you, to see if they can put the spark back into him."

Chapter 23

AN EERIE PALL of thick gray dust floats above the wreckage of the city.

Halfway up the escarpment, I stop to catch my breath. In the backdrop behind me, the sky-towers which, until a few hours ago, had been the city, now lie in waste. I shake my head, still finding it hard to comprehend how a thing as indomitable and enduring as an entire city could have been bought down so easily, and so quickly. Now it was gone. The cranes, which had dominated the skyline, lie buckled on the ground, their long tendrils of twisted metal strewn across piles of concrete rubble.

I sit for a moment to rewrap the blood-stained bandage around my forearm and re-live the mayhem and destruction that engulfed me a few hours earlier ...

ENTROPY

After burying the woman's body, we did our best to drag the helpful man away from the beach. It was never our intention to abandon him, but our eventual decision to leave him there was a result of our utter frustration rather than any unsaid pact between us. And the last we saw of the man in the semi-dark, was him sitting on the mound, on top of the woman's remains. He was staring off into the distance, making incomprehensible singing noises, punctuated by sobs and sounds of him coughing and choking back tears.

Aboard the shuttle, we made our way back to the campus under a cloud of brooding silence, where we retired to the Thinker's living quarters. And what followed was a long and solemn evening.

The Thinker cooked himself a hot meal of Spam, supplemented with some boiled potatoes from his hydroponic garden. Neither of us talked much, just single words said in response to single words asked, and only when necessary. Our eyes hardly met as we moved around the room guardedly, like two giant sailboats becalmed in a great, windless sea of mistrust. I wasn't sure if it was because he felt guilty about what he'd done or because I was angry at him for what he'd done. Either way, the elephant in the room always came down to the same thing. It was all about what the Thinker had done on the beach earlier that day.

I didn't sleep much during the night, but in my restlessness, I found myself agonizing over my hopes and limitations, and my doubts, which seem to be growing more insurmountable as each day passes. And in the forgotten hours of the night, buried somewhere between my dreams and regrets, I came to the realization that there was nothing more I could do out here in the wasteland. The only option left for me was to return home to the domes. Perhaps there was something there that might help reveal my true purpose in this whole inescapable mess.

In the morning, before I left, the Thinker handed me two fold-out maps. The first was a detailed street map showing the metropolitan zone on which he'd marked our current position at the campus with an *X* in bright red ink. Then he'd drawn a ragged path through the streets to an endpoint which he had labeled *Foothills*. The second, less detailed map, showed a wider view of the region. The red line continued from the foothills and traced all the way inland to the domes, which the Thinker had ringed repeatedly, as though he were trying to exorcise dreadful memories of that place from beneath a heavy pen. At the edge of this map, some scribbled notes which the Thinker must have felt were important: *be careful of this; go around that; don't stay here too long.*

Without a word, I took the maps, along with some other items I figured I might need: an old magnetic needle compass in a battered flip-open leather pouch; a hand-held LED lamp, fully charged; a flick knife; a fold-up thermal blanket; a compact first aid kit; a large canister topped with water. I checked the four remaining vials of *juice* to make sure they were intact, then stowed them away safely at the bottom of my knapsack.

There was no goodbye, as such, and as I walked out the front door of that squat building, I could feel the Thinker's presence behind me, watching me go. But I didn't even turn to acknowledge him or utter a word. I just left. And in my heart, I felt neither remorse nor satisfaction in doing so. I only felt a hollow conclusion to something that might have been, to something that *should* have been.

With the knapsack riding high on my shoulders and a sense of purpose in my step, I set off down the street: the metro map in one hand, aligned to the magnetic north of the compass in the other. During the early part of the morning, I made steady progress out of the city, although on two occasions, I came up against what looked like fortifications. Barricades built so high that they were impassable. As I tried to find a way around the second one, I couldn't help wondering whether these had been put there to keep outsiders out of the city or to keep insiders in.

By midmorning, I'd made it halfway to the foothills waypoint, and despite the lack of sleep from the night before, my head was clear, and my legs felt strong.

That's when I noticed it, flying high overhead. And at first, as I stood there with my neck craned, watching it glide through lazy circles in the sky, I didn't notice the gentle swaying of the sidewalk under my feet. But as the oscillations intensified, I found myself almost toppling over, and I had to fight to keep my balance.

When the first tremor hit, it knocked me clean off my feet. A split-second later, a large window panel smashed into the sidewalk in front of me, exploding into sharp shards that covered the pavement. Several more panels crashed indiscriminately along the street, shattering on impact. When I looked up again, the bird had gone, replaced by great lumps of concrete and ragged steel raining down from the buildings above while I cowered beneath.

Looking back now, I can still picture myself lying there, frightened, curled up on the ground with my hands covering my head in a pointless pose against the weight of the falling stones. I try to recall what I was thinking at the time, what went through my mind. How long did I hide, paralyzed by fear, forced to endure that feeling of utter helplessness? How long did it take for me to react?

A twinge of disappointment runs through me: I'd failed my first real test. I sat there petrified in a time of crisis, at a time when it was vital that I maintain my cognitive agility. If I'm going to survive out here on my own, I need to know that I can maintain complete control of my reasoning under pressure. I need to be sure that I can rely on myself in any situation …

At some point, when clarity returned, I felt for the map in my pocket. I took it out and unfurled it. Amid all the chaos around me, I calmly traced a route from my current location to the entrance of a subterranean commuter thoroughfare, marked on the map a short distance away.

When the second tremor hit, I was already on my feet, picking my way through the piles of wreckage littering the ground. This time though, I was ready and kept my balance until I came up against an iron gate blocking my way. Through the gate, I saw a stairwell and realized it was the entrance that would take me down to the thoroughfare.

After forcing the gate open, I hesitated a moment. I turned around to take a quick look back.

That's when the third and most violent of the tremors hit. The entire frontage of the building across the road slammed into the sidewalk beside me, throwing out shrapnel that struck my arm and a shock wave that knocked me headlong down the stairs.

I rub my burning eyes with the back of my hand, try to remember how long I had lain there on the steps, groaning, with my body contorted at an unnatural angle. For a long time, I didn't move. How long did the quake last? On reflection, I figure it must have been no more than thirty seconds in all. Yet, at the time, it felt like the carnage went on forever, and everything unfolding around me seemed to happen in slow motion. I shake my head.

It must have been pure luck that saved me from being crushed under all of the debris …

Searing pain ripped down my right arm while more radiated across my lower back. I couldn't feel my legs. Then I began to worry if my spinal column had been damaged in the fall. Who could have helped me? And if the Thinker had been there … well, I'm not sure I would have stood a chance if the Thinker had been there and found out my back was broken.

I tried to bend my fingers one at a time, then tested my toes as sensation gradually returned. Grimacing, I twisted my body around to massage the soreness from my back, then waited for my eyes to adjust to the darkness. When I did find the strength to lift a hand to my face, I couldn't see a thing through the blackness, even when my finger touched my nose.

Once I'd confirmed I was still largely intact, I sat up and fumbled through my knapsack for the lamp. I lit it and passed it over my arm. There I saw blood mixed with dirt flowing from a deep gash along my forearm. After propping myself up against the wall, I inspected the wound, cleaned it as best I could before returning to the knapsack, where I took a small bottle of antiseptic from the first aid kit. I opened it, and gritting my teeth, poured the entire contents over my arm. I took a tube of surgical adhesive, ran a bead down each side of the cut, and pressed the sides together with my fingers to stem the bleeding. A few minutes later, once the glue had set, I covered the wound with a piece of gauze. Wrapped it tightly. Then I sat up ghost-like in the lamplight to look around.

Inside the narrow stairwell, the air hung heavy with a thick cloud of dust, which seemed intent on smothering me and everything around me as it settled silently to the ground. It tasted gritty in my mouth and caught at the top of my lungs with each breath I took. I tried to swallow, but the spittle stuck like thick paste at the back of my throat, so I coughed it up and tried to spit it out. When I waved the lamp above my head, I found the air so impenetrable that I couldn't see anything through it.

After covering my mouth and nose with a dampened cloth, I repacked the knapsack, picked myself up, and retraced my way back up the stairs. Toward the top, I found rubble blocking my way, and above that, I saw the entrance was completely closed off so that even light from the outside couldn't get in. My heart sank while I held the lamp up to the ceiling. There was no way out through the top. The only way out was to go deeper, to hope the thoroughfare below had withstood the might of the quake and find another exit.

While I made my way down the steps again, it was as if the ground itself had contrived to swallow me up, leaving me with no other choice but to surrender myself to the earth.

Throwing my head back, I close my eyes, allow a soft breeze to waft across my face. With my nostrils flared, I take in the sweet smell of the cool, moist air it brings, and for a moment, I relax in the tranquility of that gentle wind.

Wind?

Something isn't right.

When I open my eyes again, I see a great surge of white wash rushing in from the coast, consuming the red ground that divides the city from the horizon, moving across it like some monstrous devour-er of worlds. I hold my gaze in disbelief, unable to look away. It hadn't occurred to me that, given the magnitude of the quake, if the epicenter occurred in the deeper waters just offshore from here, there was a high probability a tsunami would form.

Now, perched halfway up the escarpment, I try to process the surreal scene being played out below as a mountainous wave bears down on the city, taking everything in its path. The aftermath of the quake in all its natural fury. As though I've been given a front-row seat to the end of the world, and the main event is about to commence.

Within minutes, a wall of water, half as high as the tallest remnant building, barrels in on the bones of the city. It tumbles a logjam of debris through the streets and public spaces, pushing it all further inland. Then as quickly as the water arrived, it recedes, leaving behind a trail of wreckage, the city inundated, on the brink of collapse.

In the long minutes that follow, I wait in silence, dreading the next act to come.

This time, much higher than the first, the second wave continues a calamitous path through the city. The last of the cranes topple from the tops of the tallest buildings. Water slaps against concrete, and the concrete yields as buildings disappear into the ocean, while the wave continues its relentless run until its white frothing front soon menaces the escarpment. I'd thought I was safe up here, far from its reach, but now the ocean seems intent on taking me as well.

In a panic, I stumble backward. I turn and start to scramble for the top of the escarpment, but I trip and fall. When I look around again, I realize the wave has petered out behind me. But the city is gone, its magnificent buildings reduced to their foundations, the surrounding lowlands submerged in a molten muddy mess as the second wave returns to the sea. Whatever the quake hadn't brought down, the waves finished off.

I drop limp to my knees, overcome by the sudden realization that the Thinker and the helpful man wouldn't have stood a chance. With my eyes welled up, I get to my feet again, adjust the knapsack on my shoulders, and head to the top of the escarpment.

Like I said before, sometimes life isn't fair …

There's something strangely familiar about this inhospitable land-scape now, something that puts me at ease, as if I'm facing off against an old adversary once again. It's the relief of knowing. Knowing that it will be a hard slog to get back home, but also knowing for sure that I shouldn't expect any favors or assistance from this savage, red opponent. And somehow, *the knowing* makes it easier for me in the face of my ordeal.

I look skyward. High overhead, wisps of feathery white cloud drift in from the distance. Drawn from the giant columns of heavy, black cumulus gathering behind me, out along the entire length of the eastern horizon.

Without warning, a dust devil appears from nowhere. It whips up the ground around me and spirals off into the sky before dancing across the top of the escarpment, twisting and swirling and sucking up everything in its path. Then it dances over beside me, peppering my face with its blustery bits and pieces as if taunting me. I shield my eyes with my hands until the devil runs out of puff and returns to the nowhere from whence it came.

I wipe the grit from my eyes and, through clenched teeth, mutter to myself, "First an earthquake, followed by the waves, and now a storm. Who would believe me if I told them?"

The probability of all these events occurring at this exact time and place was close to impossible. But inwardly, I know. This is the opponent testing me, the same way it's been testing me with every step I've taken since leaving home. Except now, I'm hardened. Now, I know I must remain vigilant, and until I can make it back to the safety of the domes, I must be ready to handle anything this unrelenting opponent throws at me.

High above, clouds billow and build as the strengthening winds draw more of the blackened mass in from the distance.

After taking the second map from my knapsack, I set it out on the ground alongside the compass and plan my route west. By the time I stand again, the wind is hammering at my back. Soon, the cloud cover completely blocks out the sun, and the path ahead becomes diffused and lost in the gloom. Behind me, a low rumble follows the distant flicker of lightning by a measurable lag. A harbinger; the announcer of approaching weather.

I question if I've somehow offended whatever force lives out there beyond the eastern edge of the world. Why it seems so intent on plotting my demise. But it all seems pointless now that everyone else is gone. I try to distract myself by counting out the seconds between the lightning flash and the corresponding crash of thunder. Using the speed of sound in air at the nominal temperature and some simple math, I track the approaching storm: 244 seconds puts it at 52 miles away ... 112 seconds equates to 24 miles ... 65 seconds equals 14 miles.

Light rain spits across the ground, forming tiny droplets upon the hydrophobic earth.

Twenty-eight seconds and six miles.

The wind behind me hurries me along. It tries to push me faster than my feet can move, so I back up into it to slow myself down.

At last, the skies open, and the rain sheets down heavily on me. When the next lightning bolt lights up the sky, I count the seconds again under my breath. I get to eighteen before the ear-shattering crack arrives.

Four miles.

I pull my head down low into my shoulders and quicken my pace. Then, with my fingers tightening around the straps of my knapsack, I brace for the storm.

A slurry of red bleeds from the hillside. Washing into the valley, it fills the hollows and crevices as it flows. With the wind and rain at my back, I wade through a course of thick mud, my eyes shielded behind my hand, searching for a place to hide. An almost impossible task to see through the pouring rain.

I can make out a row of trees close by, lit up by the intermittent flashes of lightning.

Something strikes me hard on the shoulder. A volley of hailstones, some as large as my fist, pock the ground around me. Another one smacks against the point of my head. Half dazed, I make for the trees and press myself hard against the closest one. I cover my head with my hands in a hopeless appeal for protection against the hail.

Another flash of light.

This time, I can only count to a-thousand-and-one before the sky cracks open, and the tree beside me explodes, shredded into a million charred particles. I drop to the ground and cover my ears with my hands. When the next discharge takes out another nearby tree, I decide it's no longer safe where I am. So, holding my knapsack above my head, I break from the tree line just as another barrage of hailstones peppers my body.

Stunned and battered, I stumble out into the open, fully exposed, my arms outstretched, groping at the emptiness in front of me, with no idea of where I am and little idea of where I should go. I slip. The ground beneath my feet gives way, and I sink into a waist-high pool of sludge. I try to drag myself out, but the more I struggle, the further it sucks me down. Frantic, I scour the surrounding area, desperate to see through the downpour.

To my right, there's only more sludge, but on my left, I can make out the stump of the splintered tree jutting up from the ground. The mud buries me above my midriff before climbing to my chest. I'm starting to panic. But this is just the opponent at me again, challenging me, probing to find my weakness. So I turn my attention to the stump, urging myself to stay calm.

Partway up the stump, it forks into two stubs that protrude skyward, like some disfigured friendly waving at me, trying to catch my attention. I remove my knapsack, fumble to unclip the two shoulder straps. After stretching the straps out fully, I knot them together to fashion a tether—*hopefully long enough to reach the fork*—then I fasten one end to the knapsack and tie the other tight around my wrist.

On my first throw, the knapsack drops short, so I reel it in and try again. After a dozen attempts, the knapsack finally drops through the fork. With a sigh of relief, I take up the slack until the tether is taut. I pull on it. Then I pull again with all my strength, but my legs and torso are stuck fast in the quagmire. And worse still, the mud continues to rise as more sludge pours in from the hillside until it soon covers my shoulders. It climbs up my neck, and I can feel it beneath my chin. I tilt my head backward to keep my face clear of the mud and try the tether again.

But inwardly, I know the truth of my situation. The physics of the problem is against me. Given the oblique angle I'm pulling at and the dead weight of my body—now fully submerged in the mud—there's no way I'll ever be able to apply enough force to pull myself free. Until soon, the mud covers my mouth, and all I can do is breathe through my nose.

So this is how it ends.

In my mind, I curse myself. First, the *others*, then the helpful woman, the Thinker and the helpful man, and now me. And all for what? After everything I've been through and despite my hopes and intentions, all I've found out here is one lost opportunity after another and, in the end, I haven't achieved anything. I couldn't save any of them. Yet, in my demise, I find a shred of deep-rooted comfort. The comfort of knowing that I alone had challenged the forces of Nature and, ultimately, it will be Nature herself who settles my fate. The same as she does for every other living creature. And I can accept this now because I know ... at least I tried.

Drawing my final breath, I close my eyes, giving myself over to her as I disappear below the mud.

With my eyes shut tight, I fight the irresistible urge to exhale. If I can hold onto this lungful of air for a second longer and another second after that—*for as long as possible*—then I'll prolong my life, and my thoughts. And while I continue to think, I still exist.

I'd once heard that in the final moments before death, a person's whole life flashes before them. I wonder when my own replay might start. And when it does, how will I tell the difference between what was real and what had been fabricated by Aleph-1? Where should I start cleaning the crap from my own data?

I know I can't hold on forever though. Soon the carbon dioxide and hydrogen ion buildup in my bloodstream will over-ride my cerebral cortex to activate the expiratory center of my brain and, in the end, I'll be forced to breathe out. Then I'll have to inhale again before the traumatic process of my suffocation begins.

With my lungs close to bursting, I wonder what my epitaph might read: Drowned in a pool of mud, which—*if the Thinker is to be believed*—was caused by the first rains to fall on this ground in almost two hundred years. Suffocated by the same red scourge I'd helped inflict on the world. Perhaps this is destiny's perverse sense of justice, a deserving end for me. It's funny what goes through your mind at times like this.

Now I'm beaten. My opponent has won. And in the darkness, with my eulogy playing out loud in my head, I descend further under the mud ...

Something tugs at my arm.

An unexpected force wrenches it upward as the strap, still tied around my wrist, pulls taut. I wrap my fingers tight about the tether, drawing my other hand over to grab onto the slimmest chance of rescue.

My exhilaration grows as the next erratic pull drags me upward through the mud. I kick my legs to assist my ascent, and just when my head breaks the surface, I release the last of my air. With the rain driving hard into my face, I gasp as the thick coating of mud falls away from my eyes. When I cough and look up, there by the stump, with his head down and body bent forward, ready for the next haul on the tether, is the Thinker, dressed in a pair of bright-green coveralls.

"You're … you're alive!" I cry out.

The Thinker stops what he's doing. He lifts his head and gives me the most gratifying sneer I've ever received. "Don't sound so surprised," he says. "And so are you, thanks to me." Setting the tether aside, he reaches for me, grabs the back of my collar, and drags me clear of the sludge pool where we both collapse, exhausted, on the ground.

Moments later, the Thinker stands, and without a word, disappears into the deluge. He returns a short time later, wearing a wide-brimmed hat and dragging an enormous backpack through the mud. "Quick," he says. "Get up and follow me." With a grunt, he hoists the oversized load onto his shoulders, his knees bending under the weight of the pack. "As much as I appreciate this infernal rain, we need to find shelter before it really does drown both of us."

I fumble to reattach the straps on my knapsack. Then taking a deep breath, I follow the Thinker out into the wall of water. "Where are we going?" I ask.

But he's already gone.

Chapter 24

THE RELENTLESS SKY stays open.

Ahead of me, the Thinker makes his way through the rain, his form mostly obscured behind his backpack. I hurry to catch him.

"We head directly north," he shouts above the pounding noise, "and we'll come to a maglev guideway. It's the main track for the old intercity transport network. We need to follow it west. According to the map, there should be a decommissioned commuter transfer station a few miles further along the guideway."

Like a living semaphore, the Thinker's gesticulating arms indicate the proposed direction changes while the water cascades over the brim of his hat.

As though we were two small children passing through the painted mouth of a macabre sideshow attraction, we follow the two rusted beams of the guideway through the entrance of the transfer station.

With our lamps lit, we stay with the beams until they disappear into a large pool of water. On either side of the water, there are concrete platforms where once, I imagine, people had probably crammed themselves shoulder-to-shoulder, front-to-back, waiting for the next maglev transporter. And when it did arrive, the people disembarking probably looked out into the vast sea of faces of the ones waiting to get on, and decided it was safer to stay right where they were. So they probably never got off the thing.

After clambering onto the platform on our left, the Thinker kicks away some cans and other rubbish to clear a small area for us.

"We'll camp here until the rain eases," he says.

He drops his backpack on the floor and opens the zipper. Taking out a book-sized square of ceramic panel, he unfolds it repeatedly until it expands into a single sheet, almost as tall as him and twice as wide again. "It's a *far* infrared heater," he informs me. "To help dry us out. Zero emissions and perfectly safe ... unlike your previous attempt at producing heat." He leans the ceramic panel against the wall, connects a small battery, and activates it.

In an instant, my cheeks begin to tingle and prick.

After rigging up an overhead light, the Thinker removes his sodden coveralls and lays them out in front of the heater. And I do the same. We spread our blankets on the ground, close to the heater, and settle back, the Thinker propped against his pack and me against mine. For a long time, nothing is said.

Studying his wooden face, I can't help wondering how the Thinker must have felt back at the campus while sorting through his life's possessions, trying to decide which items were important enough to keep and those he would leave behind. Then to have the composure to pack all the winners into a carry-bag, large enough to hold them, yet small enough to fit on his back, all while a giant wave bore down on him. Did he show any sentimentality at the time? And how uncanny that he'd appeared from nowhere, in the millisecond before my air ran out. What were the chances? A trillion to one? Buckley's?

"So, how *did* you escape it all?" I finally ask. "The earthquake, the waves, and the lightning?"

He looks up, his eyes shifting between me and the lamp as though he were genuinely surprised by the question. And for the first time since we'd met, I appear to have caught him completely off-guard.

"I was ... um ... working outside on the shuttle when the first quake struck. That was fortunate for me because when the next tremor hit, it took down the whole research building and my apartment with it. That bit scared the shit out of me." His voice wavers, his face slightly flushed. He turns away from me as if trying to disguise any show of weakness. "Anyone would have been just as scared, all the same. Straight away, I knew the probability of a wave coming would be pretty high. And from the magnitude of the third tremor, which, by my estimate, was well over nine on the old scale, I figured the wave would be a big one. But I didn't expect it to be *that* big."

He turns to me again, his eyes edgy, the blood now absent from his face.

"So, I went to find the male ..."

The pause drags on longer than I expect, as though in his head, the Thinker is searching for the next words to use. As if he were desperate to find the ones that will cause the least possible upset or incrimination against him.

"… back to the place where we buried … the female."

There. Now it was said.

I probe his face, looking for any tell-tale sign that might suggest even a hint of remorse. But there's nothing. And like the evening before, he sits before me like some inanimate object carved from granite, something devoid of affection, incapable of caring about anyone, or anything, except himself.

"When I got there, the male was still moping around on the mound. He wouldn't listen to a word I said. I tried to warn him. I tried to make him see sense but, in the end, time ran out. Had no choice except to leave him there. That poor useless bastard. He wouldn't have stood a chance …"

The same rage for the Thinker still burns inside me, but I also feel pity for him. After living so long on his own and with only himself to fend for, to rely on, was it possible that his narcissistic personality was not entirely of his own making?

"Anyway … I only just made it out myself. Had enough time to throw a few things into my backpack and get out of there before the first wave hit. And when the second wave came, it chased me halfway up the escarpment. Truth be told, I'm sure I saw your bony ass ahead of me, scrambling up the hill like some scared little rabbit who's afraid of the water." He cackles, spreading himself out against his backpack, his generous manhood out on full display. "I got to the top of the escarpment, and you were gone. When I finally found you, you had your head stuck under the mud. And now, here we are."

With a wide smirk across his face, the Thinker throws his hands up behind his head. Then he closes his eyes. Discussion over.

I dive my hand into the knapsack and fish my way down past the flick knife, past the syringe, then the first aid kit, searching for a vial of *juice*. At the bottom, something stings my thumb. When I withdraw my hand, there's blood oozing from a small cut. I bring the lamp over the opening. Peering inside, my heart sinks at the sight of glass fragments spread across the bottom of the knapsack.

"Damn," I say softly. In the mud, I'd forgotten the vials were there. They must have shattered when I threw the knapsack at the tree.

I remove the broken pieces of glass and toss them into the water. Only two vials remain. Holding them up to the light, I confirm they're both intact. After snapping the top off one, I draw its contents into the syringe, but when I try to connect the syringe to my arm, I find part of my receptacle has broken away, and there's no way the two pieces will connect. I cast my mind back: *Perhaps when the Thinker was pulling me out of the mud?*

For a long time, I sit with the syringe held in both hands, staring at it, weighing up my options. Then raising it above my head, I part my lips and squirt the *juice* directly into my mouth. Straight away, my face contorts, forced into spasm by the awful taste as each mouthful of the fluid drowns my insides with its bitterness. Within minutes, my stomach is cramping. Nausea grows. A sour taste, like bile, builds at the back of my throat, but I can't afford to lose a single drop of this precious fluid, so I fight to keep it down.

Once the sickness has passed, I pull the blanket up to my chin and wait for the rush. But this time it doesn't come as quickly. I wonder if I'm becoming immune to the *juice*. Maybe it loses its potency over time. Or perhaps I'm not in the right mood at the moment, considering my recent near-death experience. Still, nothing. So I crack the top off the second—and last—vial, empty its contents into my mouth, and wait some more.

Then it comes. But this time different. This time, there's no dopamine rush that hits me or life-like dreams afterward. There's no Jennifer.

This time, it comes over me like a thief.

I examine the index finger on my dormant hand, the one draped over my lap, willing it to move, except now, I seem to exist in observational-mode only. It's as if I still have some awareness of what's going on around me, but no control over my appendages or other parts of my body. In spasmodic bursts, I become lucid, yet I can't even raise that finger, let alone point it at something.

A feeling of vertigo sweeps over me, swirling, spiraling, disorienting me …

In the fog of my mind, I hear intermittent whispers coming from the other platform. Ghostly figures moving around against the flicker of the lamplight cast from our side. *People. Five?* Yes, a man and four women, I think. Now they're huddled together, squealing, and shrieking with laughter. Now they're rutting. I hear the Thinker yelling at them to be quiet, before my mind retreats into the haze …

More whispers from the platform opposite. Louder this time, and now the Thinker sounds extremely agitated. One of them giggles while the Thinker screams at them again to be quiet …

Prying my eyelids open, my consciousness tries to peer through the two narrow portals in my torpid face. Anger all over the Thinker's face this time, standing beside me, naked, bending down to pick up a lump of stone, which he hurls across the divide. A pebble, in return, skips across the flat concrete surface on our side. The Thinker explodes, yelling out abuse, saying words that would be hurtful to anyone who hears them.

Then the fogginess takes me once more …

Later, I don't know how long after, the Thinker is standing beside a heaped-up arsenal of projectiles. A large rock launched by the Thinker is followed by a pea-sized pellet thrown in reply. Then a much larger stone, hurled with such ferocity by the Thinker, finds its mark on the other side. Someone over there in distress. The sounds of someone injured, groaning, while another one bawls. More shouting from the Thinker, more animation, more vulgar words thrown at the other side, telling them to be quiet. But the low drone of somebody in pain persists.

Until my eyelids, heavy, close …

At some time in the early hours of the morning—I'm not sure when—the noise of the battlefield around me goes deathly quiet …

The next morning, I awake refreshed. Across from me, the Thinker is lying on his back with his legs crossed at the ankles, both hands resting on his stomach. The rain has stopped and sunlight streams in on us through the opening.

As I stretch my arms and legs, I listen out, not hearing a sound from the other platform.

"What did you do to them last night?" I ask.

Half opening an eye, the Thinker responds. "Nothing."

"But they weren't harming anyone. They were only having fun …

and I didn't mind their chatter."

"I really don't care about what you mind or what you *don't* mind."

"But don't you think it was unnecessary to antagonize them? An over-reaction?"

He turns to me with both eyes open and fierce. "It's none of your business what I think, or what I say, or what I do," he says, the venom in his voice sending a sharp chill through me.

On the other platform, they're crowding around a woman who lies motionless on the ground. From where I am, I can see a rich, red stain on her forehead, trailing down the right side of her face. They sob and shake her. They poke and prod at her, trying to wake her. Then together, they wail.

"Here they go again. Those damned itinerants."

The moaning from the other platform continues long into the morning. Listening to them, I can't help feeling sorry for these people. I can't fathom what they've done wrong to deserve this tragedy.

About midday, they fall silent. The itinerant man picks up the dead woman's lithe body and wrests it onto his shoulders. He carries her off the platform, then up along the guideway with the rest of the itinerants trailing him. All of them together, like four spindly cloaks of leathery skin thrown over some leftover bones, hauling a fifth.

As their sad procession passes through the opening at an abject pace, I throw on my coveralls and repack my belongings. I follow them at a distance, while behind me, the Thinker stomps around the platform, collecting his things, shouting abuse at me.

Outside the station, the sun beats down hard from a cloudless sky, drawing up thin streams of vapor from the sodden ground. The supersaturated air feels thick and heavy and wet in my lungs. My coveralls cling to my armpits and around the crotch as my body leaks profusely, while defiant clots of the red mud cling expectantly to my shoes.

I'm finding it hard to breathe.

I remain a safe distance behind the itinerants, hoping they won't notice the Thinker who is slogging behind me, far enough away to be unseen yet close enough that his voice is still conspicuous.

"They're taking us around in circles, I tell you. We've been following them for nearly an hour now, and I still have no idea where they're taking us. I don't think they have a clue where they're going either. But we don't have time for them. We don't have time for all this touchy-feely stuff."

"Shh!" I tell him.

Ahead of us, the itinerant man stumbles, the weight of his dead friend's body taking a toll. To my surprise, the man recovers his feet, but a few steps further on, his leg buckles, and he lets go of her, dropping her onto the ground. He grapples to pick her up, tries to set off again but, in the end, he collapses beside her in the mud and bawls.

One of the itinerant women pushes the man aside. She grabs hold of the dead woman's leg and pulls. A second woman takes the other leg, and together they drag the woman's stiffening body, pull-by-pull, through the slop.

Watching them, I fight back the harrowing memory of carrying the helpful woman off the beach two days before. But the sight of the itinerant woman now being hauled thoughtlessly through the slop is too hard for me to take. I wonder if this is the best any of us can hope for from now on, even myself. Everyone faced with the same humiliating end. Our time here on the Earth concluding as absurdly as this scenario being played out in front of me right now. Without any reverence and deprived of all our dignity.

"This is hopeless," the Thinker moans. "We should have left here hours ago and been well on our way by now."

Just when I think the itinerants might carry on forever, they stop at a clearing. On the opposite side of the clearing, a track leads onto a narrow ledge, which overhangs a wide ravine. Once they've crossed the clearing, they haul the dead woman along the track, onto the ledge, then inch their way out to the middle where they sit in a row, all of them puffing and panting, facing the ravine.

From the cover of some shrubs, I study the itinerants while behind me, the Thinker's incessant grumbling continues to gnaw at my ears … and at my patience.

"They've finally given up," he says. "That's it … they're finished. We can go now."

Before I can tell him to be quiet again, the itinerant man gets to his feet. With the help of the one beside him, he hoists the woman's body onto his shoulders, then above his head. For a moment, the man stands teetering on the edge of the ravine. When he heaves her body over, both his legs buckle with the shift in weight, and he almost tosses himself over as well.

Fearing for the man's safety, I spring to my feet, and I'm already halfway across the clearing before one of the women notices me. She points at me and screams. So I stop. I hold both hands above my head to show her I mean no harm. But she continues to scream and point at me. No, not at me, but past me, at the Thinker who is now standing inside the clearing in full view of everyone.

I call out to them. "It's okay," I say in a reassuring voice.

But the one closest to me backs away. She shoves the next one along, and that one shoves the next until they reach the far side of the ledge before they scurry away into the scrub.

"Now that's not something you see every day." Dumping his backpack on the ground, the Thinker roars with laughter. "That's the end of them," he says, suddenly straight-faced. Then he growls at me. "You've had your fun. Can we go now?"

Ignoring him, I cross the clearing and make my way up the track. When I reach the ledge, I find it much narrower than I'd imagined, and as I crawl out to the middle, I have a sense of admiration for the itinerant people who made it look so much easier than I'm finding it now. The sheer wall on my right seems intent on pushing me uncomfortably close to the edge on my left while the jagged rocks and gravel chafe my hands and bruise my knees.

When I get to the spot where they'd tossed the woman's body into the ravine, I kneel and peer over the edge. With all my weight supported by my arms and my head leaning way beyond the threshold, I strain to look down. But my hand slips. The fragile earth at the edge collapses, and I tumble headlong into the ravine.

Cartwheeling down the decline, I close my eyes, expecting the worst, waiting for the floating sensation of free fall to take me. The nothingness as I plummet the miles to the ground. The tranquility before the thud. But the end comes quicker than I expect as my shoulder plows into something soft, something pliable and cold, and much too soon to have reached the bottom.

I lay there for a moment, groaning, cursing my rashness while thanking my good fortune. When I finally force my eyes open, I'm looking straight into the gaunt face of the itinerant woman, who is staring back at me. Now I see her close-up, her thin frail remains.

On one side, her face is caked in mud from being dragged through the slop, her lips still pried apart as if she were caught off-guard in the confusion last night, halfway through asking a question. A question that I wish I could answer.

I don't know why.

"Who are you talking to down there?" The Thinker's leering face appears above me. "You stupid bastard. What were you thinking?"

After giving myself a quick check-over to confirm nothing is broken, I clamber back up the slope to where he pulls me onto the ledge. With my eyes closed, I rest my forehead against the back wall, every muscle in my body aching. I try to swallow, but the dryness in my throat almost makes me gag.

I'm so sorry this happened to you.

The Thinker taps my shoulder and points at the ravine. "Well, at least now we know what happened to all those poor bastards from the city."

I spin around. "Oh!"

At once, the sight beneath me registers. The ravine, miles wide and miles deep, filled with people—a ghastly mass of countless men, women, and children—their mummified corpses piled one on top of the other. Bodies everywhere, lying tangled in their wrinkled coverings, their glum faces scrutinizing me through the hollow sockets in their heads. They're looking at me expectantly, just me, as though I'm able to offer them some kind of clarification for this. I struggle to absorb the immensity of the devastation.

Then it occurs to me: something here doesn't make sense.

"Wait," I say. "They're all still intact. Shouldn't most of the bodies have decayed by now?"

The Thinker surveys the ravine. "Who knows?" he says with

detachment in his voice. "If we were being *scientific*, we could speculate there were too many preservatives in their food chain. If we were *true believers* though, we might argue it was their incorruptibility. But, hey, they couldn't all have been *saints*, could they?"

Looking me straight in the eye, he grabs my shoulder. "What you see down there are the discarded scraps of the past. And the past is a bucket of ashes. We can't change it, no matter how much we want to or how hard we try. It's over and done. Gone forever. But, going forward, we have a chance to shape the future based on the decisions we make today. Because the future is *our* destiny. It's yours and mine for the taking, to make of it whatever we want." He nods to our packs at the edge of the clearing.

"And our future starts with the rest of our kind, back at the hives."

Chapter 25

IT'S AS THOUGH the band of rain had hit a demarcation line.

Two hours later, we stop. This is the exact place where the storm was stopped in its tracks by an inland barrier it couldn't cross. As if by some invisible force. On one side of the line, the wet, sloppy sludge, which had clung to our feet and slowed us down, is still there. Yet a few steps away, on the other side, the powdery red returns.

Scraping the wads of mud off my shoes, I look at the divide and wonder how anything, divine or otherwise, could have achieved this kind of impossibility.

When we come upon the onset of the powdery gray moonscape, the Thinker throws me a stern look and shakes his head in disgust.

The absolute destruction from the fire is more widespread than I remember and, having jumped the containment lines on the other side, it certainly goes on for much further than I'd expected.

Compared to this, the red dust is a vibrant layer that still holds promise. But the scorched ground surrounding us now will stay dead forever.

I'm thankful the helpful man isn't here because I know, seeing this kind of devastation would be too much for him, and it would have made him distraught.

Quickening my pace, I move ahead of the Thinker, and for the whole of the next day, we continue, accompanied on both sides of the road by the burned reminder of the plantations.

The Thinker pulls a pair of tiny, compact binoculars from his backpack. He loops the strap around his neck, then scans the communications station ahead of us.

"That bastard knows we're coming," he says. "It's got eyes and ears on us, everywhere," he adds, his own eyes narrowing as he glares at the station.

"The woman and I spent a whole night in there scanning the frequencies," I say. "But we didn't detect any comms signals from across the entire spectrum."

"Maybe so, but we can't trust that sneaky bastard. Did you scan the optical spectrum as well?"

"I think so," I reply, unsure of where this conversation is headed.

The Thinker frowns. "It's in the optical bands where it hides. Up there in the far-infrared frequencies."

He sets his backpack on the ground and retrieves a flat slab of metal foil from inside. Plowing his fist into the center of the foil, he forms a kind of hat, which he exchanges with the wide-brimmed one on his head. Then he massages the foil, making sure it covers his entire head, including a wide flap down the back of his neck where

315

his implant would be located.

I hold myself back, forcing myself not to laugh out loud. The sight of the Thinker wearing such a ridiculous-looking hat was the last thing I'd expected to see out here. Internally, I burst into laughter.

The Thinker pulls out another slab of foil and fashions a second hat. "Here, put this on," he says. "And whatever happens, do not take it off."

I balk, then quickly decide it might not be wise to refuse the Thinker's request. And before I know it, I'm patting down the top of my own homemade hat as well, running my hand down the back of my neck to make sure my implant is covered and feeling just as silly as the Thinker looks.

The laughter, which has been raging unabated inside me, abruptly stops.

Through the binoculars, the conspiracy theorist sweeps the station one last time. Muttering to himself, he insists we give the place a wide berth. Then, with him checking our rear every few minutes until the antenna dish is gone, we leave the communications station behind.

Before nightfall, we come to a T-junction, which I recognize as the road leading up to the plastics miner's operation. As we push past it, I decide not to say anything to the Thinker.

Half an hour later, we stop to make camp.

We talk. Mainly small talk at first. But as the evening wears on, the conversation dries up. I become distracted by thoughts of the plastics miner. The enthusiasm I'd seen on his face while he gouged material from the waste-wall; the sight of him slumped in his chair, slightly intoxicated, with the empty shotgun leaning against the table; his eyes all lit up when he realized I'd repaired his Entertainer.

Later in the night, once I'm sure the Thinker is asleep, I get up and quietly make my way back to the T-junction. As I turn for the miner's cabin, I think about the last time I was here with the helpful pair and how, after a tense introduction, our visit had fostered an unexpected friendship with the miner. I wonder if he'd been encouraged by our heartfelt conversations; if my words had inspired him to carry on with his dream and never give up. Maybe he would be there waiting, ready to welcome me back with open arms and perhaps a bottle of that fire-brand whiskey he had tucked away.

Inside me, the excitement keeps building. The chance to see my good friend again.

When I arrive at the cabin, the lights are off—*nobody's home*—so I cross the gully and head for the entrance to the mine. I activate my lamp and descend the hole. In the chamber at the end of the tunnel, I find the steel door slightly ajar. On the other side, loud music is playing, and people are talking. I hear peals of laughter. Flashes of colored light, escaping through the narrow gap in the doorway, dance around on the floor at my feet.

When I push the door open, there in front of me, the emaciated body of the plastics miner twirls around and around inside the Entertainer's metazone. His lifeless frame still rotating continuously head over heel.

I drop to my knees, bury my face in my hands and, without any feeling of shame, I weep openly.

Next morning, we pack our belongings and set off early. As I drift along behind the Thinker, the discovery of my friend the night before plays on my mind. The disturbing sight of the miner stuck in some kind of weird infinity, where he will probably keep spinning forever. As though in death, he'd finally unraveled the secrets of perpetual motion. I wonder what the plastics miner would say now if he knew his destiny was to be the sole kinetic reminder of this time in history, for thousands of years to come. Would he have given himself to it gladly?

The Thinker pops his head above his backpack and, without breaking stride, opens up on me.

"What's up with you? You've been moping around all morning, acting like someone stole your candy."

But I let his caustic words slide past me. Now isn't the time to engage with him, not so soon after my last real friend had been taken from me by this pitiless world; taken without any conceivable reason. Maybe the Thinker was right when he said *life* itself has no concept of fairness. And perhaps the sooner I accept the fact, the sooner I'll be able to come to terms with everything going on around me.

Unable to look at the Thinker any longer, I fix my stare on the ground and, with nostrils flared, I steel my resolve.

"I need a break."

The Thinker huffs a loud huff before unhitching his backpack, letting it slide off his back onto the ground. He squats, unfurls the map, and sets it beside the backpack, aligning it with the needle on the compass. Taking a can of Spam, a plate, and a metal fork from the backpack, the Thinker arranges them on a small blanket, which he has spread out at his feet.

With his gums working hard on a mouthful of Spam, he lifts the binoculars to survey the surrounding area. After a full rotation, he returns to the map, runs an index finger along the red line that marks our course back to the domes. Tapping the map thoughtfully, he nods to himself.

"According to my calculations, we should be here, halfway along this elevation," he says.

"How long do you think it will take us to reach the domes?" I ask.

"I can't be sure. Another three days, four at the most."

A thin, clear delivery tube, running up the side of his backpack, ends at a short mouthpiece, which dangles over his shoulder. He takes the mouthpiece between his teeth and sucks in a mouthful of water.

"I'm starting to run low on water," he says. "We lost a lot of perspiration in the humidity after the rain. It's hard to believe. One minute there's too much water, and in the next, there isn't enough." Pensive, he rubs his chin. "And I still haven't quite figured out how all that apocalyptic stuff could have happened back there. All at once … Like it was choreographed. I warned you not to mess with Mother Nature. She's an evil bitch when she wants to be."

I shake my canteen. "Mine's nearly empty as well," I say. "I know of a place where there's plenty of water. But it's out there in the flat-land."

The Thinker turns his gaze to the barren territory between us and the horizon, grimacing as he measures the distance in his head. He frowns. "The smart guy in me says we'll be too exposed out there, and we should stick to the safety of the higher ground. He says it's a great big risk to be taking." He turns the map around to me. "But, hey, nobody ever got anywhere without taking a chance, did they?" He throws a light punch into my shoulder. "Here, make yourself useful and plot the course."

Everything looks different going in reverse, and I soon question whether I'd made a mistake when figuring out the route to the reservoir. The hills, which had been on the right, are now on our left, and the afternoon shadows fall from the ridges at entirely new angles giving the whole area an unreliable look about it. Until soon, the scenery around us becomes all too familiar: the red dust; the riot of human footprints mixed with paw marks left in the dirt; the sight of sun-bleached bones scattered everywhere.

"Wow, what happened here?" the Thinker asks. "This looks like the end of the world, like an Armageddon."

As we pass through the carnage, the half-buried face of the fidgeting man peers at us from out of the dirt. Then the scattered remains of the line leader. A short time later, the scraps of the ones we'd left behind at the makeshift camp just a few days earlier.

My heart sinks. This is the last of them, and apart from the Thinker there's no one else left.

When the prominent shape of the reservoir emerges in front of us, I tap his shoulder and point to the mound. "That's where we'll find water."

I clear the cloud of tiny wrigglers away with my hand before sinking the nozzle of my canteen into the water.

"So, this facility was almost bone dry before you got it operational again?" he says, the look of admiration on his face ... unexpected.

After a quick scan of the reservoir, the Thinker kneels at the water's edge. Taking an oval-shaped rubber bulb from his backpack, he attaches it to the mouthpiece at the end of his water tube. He fits a long piece of clear hose to the bulb, dips the free end into the water, and starts priming with his hand.

ENTROPY

"Did you have trouble cleaning up the solar panels? Were the swivel gears greased well enough? Did the pontoon float right away once the water rose high enough? What about the pump motor, did it rotate easily? Were you careful when the AC power kicked in?"

I nod *yes* to each of his rapid-fire questions until the interrogation ends once he runs out of things to ask. Then he looks straight at me and smiles.

"Well, I'm impressed," he says.

I lift my canteen from the water and refit the cap, troubled by the realization that once the reservoir had been replenished, it became a trap, luring every living creature out to the flatland into the open. A smorgasbord of prey for the hunters, delivered to them on a platter.

Had I shifted the balance of nature completely in favor of the hunters? Was I responsible for their slaughter?

With my canister full and heart empty, we follow the goat-track back to the bottom of the mound and continue west.

In the grind of the late afternoon, a small puff of dust, deep in the south, catches my attention. At first glance, I didn't think much of it, but now, five minutes later, I suspect it might be getting closer to us in imperceptible increments. *Perhaps another dust-devil.* But this one seems to linger on the ground much too long. I glance at the Thinker, who appears preoccupied, trying to wipe the red stain off his once-green coveralls.

For the next few minutes, I study the dust cloud, drawing closer, the distinct trail of turbulence falling off behind it. The dust cloud builds. In the next two heartbeats, I realize the cloud is closing in on us fast, and within two heartbeats more, the unmistakable clamor of organized mayhem engulfs us. I stop mid-step. I've heard this same mayhem before. In a strangled voice that at first, I don't recognize as my own, I cry out to the Thinker.

"Hunters!"

Rattled, my internal optimist urges me to run and hide, but the realist in there screams even louder that we won't get far, no matter how fast we run. Before I can decide anything, half a dozen hunters are on me, almost knocking me off my feet. One of them darts in at my ankles while two more await their turn. I kick out at the chaos around my feet as another one leaps at me, tearing at my sleeve.

Then I spot the Alpha, standing before us, looking as cocksure of itself as it had the last time I'd seen it.

Lowering its head, the Alpha growls at me, so I drop to my knees and bury my face in the dirt, try to squeeze myself as small as I can. I cry out to the Thinker, "Get on the ground. We have to keep ourselves lower than the Alpha's head." But the Thinker just stands there with a strange kind of detachment. A death wish?

"You have to get down on the ground," I cry.

But he mustn't hear me because he drops his backpack on the ground and opens the zipper, slow-like as though everything's okay. He reaches into the backpack just as the Alpha starts up a succession of feigned attacks that ends with me being covered in the white, foaming slop drooling from its mouth. Then as it did last time, the Alpha raises itself onto its hind legs and begins an unsteady approach on the Thinker.

Unhurried, the Thinker is sifting through his backpack as if he's not even worried, but just before the Alpha reaches him, he takes out a handgun. He takes aim, squeezes the trigger, and the Alpha's head explodes while the rest of the hunters scatter. After picking off another two hunters before they're out of range, he keeps the gun pointed at the horizon until the last of them have disappeared into the distance. Glaring at the splattered remains of the Alpha, the Thinker gives its corpse an impertinent kick.

"It's not about who's got the biggest *bark*, Buster. It's all about who's got the biggest *gun*."

Then stony-faced, he turns to me.

"Get up, you pussy!"

The going seems harder, the terrain much harsher than I remember, and in the late afternoon three days later, the Thinker's report puts us twenty miles from home. On nightfall, we set up camp. I spread my thermal blanket on the ground while the Thinker sits squinting at the map.

"I figure, if we get moving early tomorrow, we should arrive well before midday," he says.

I activate the lamp, then … all-out war.

It all starts when a large, barrel-shaped moth, with unusually short wings, flies straight into the lamp, meeting it headfirst with a dull thud. As its wayward gyro sends it spiraling to the ground, I ask myself whether I could prove beyond doubt, because of its aerodynamics, this moth should *not* be able to fly. It flutters around, performing several tight circles on the ground before it recovers, enough to make another attack on the lamp.

More moths enter the light-sphere, dozens more, reinforced by a cloud of midges that attack our eyes and end up our noses and in our ears like a million minuscule aviators, each intent on carrying out its own kamikaze mission.

Oblivious to the insect offensive, the Thinker continues to study the map, occasionally slapping his cheek. Then more frequently.

Until his frustration finally boils over. "Will you turn that damned lamp off!" he yells into the map.

"Sorry."

After finishing off two full cans of Spam, the Thinker uses a fingernail to pick the leftover bits of meal from between his teeth. Under the natural light of the heavens, he stares at the barrel-shaped moth, now lying stiff, folded in half at the base of the lamp. "No matter how hungry I was, I would never eat bugs," he says, giving the moth a look of disgust. "How did a highly evolved species ever get to the point of having to survive on bugs?"

During the evening, I notice the Thinker's left knee vibrating without any obvious control. The shaking stops as he shifts his weight from one buttock to the other. Then it restarts.

To me, the Thinker appears apprehensive, like an actor waiting for that all-important call-to-scene while obsessing about what tomorrow's feed-sheet might say about the performance he hasn't yet given. Was he afraid of the domes? Like the young girl was?

Above us, a waxing gibbous moon hovers to the south, tracking for a slow descent into the west. Considering the moon, I try to strike up a conversation with the Thinker, try to ease the tension.

"It's hard to believe we were smart enough to put a man on the moon," I say, pointing upward, "but couldn't prevent our own extinction."

"A man? On the moon?" The Thinker's whole face compresses into a tiny, disgruntled question mark.

"Seriously, don't tell me you're one of those conspiracy theorists who think the moon landings never happened," I counter.

"Me? A conspiracy theorist?" he scoffs. "No, they landed on the moon all right. On Mars and Venus as well. But it wasn't a male.

It was the females who had the smarts to compute the complex math needed to send their rockets into orbit. They were the ones with the skills and experience to develop the technologies to go into space … and have the courage to go there as well.

"But they were overlooked, exploited, and it wasn't until the females took control of the NACA space program before any real progress was made. The males tried to take the credit, but they were bit players really … only there to shift the heavy stuff around."

I scoff at him, shaking my head. "I'm fairly sure that's not the correct version. Why would you suggest something that absurd?"

He glares at me, as though I'd somehow offended him. "Absurd? With my own two eyes, I saw the reenactment on a hologram box."

"A hologram box?"

"Yes. Soon after I arrived in the city, I found one in an abandoned house on the south side of town."

"We couldn't afford a hologram box when I was young," I say. Then I hesitate, wondering whether this particular memory I have is true or not. "How big was it?" I ask.

With his hands held apart, the Thinker indicates the compact size of the hologram box.

"Anyway, when I hit the play button, it showed grainy vision of an astronaut descending the ladder of a landing module. I swear the comms voice from the person on the ladder was female, while the commentary from mission control harped on about this being the first person to set foot on the lunar surface. *'That's one small step for woman, one giant leap for mankind*,'" the Thinker says in a lady-like voice. "Although, many argued she said it was one small step for *a* woman. Whatever. There's no doubt in my mind the footage was authentic."

"But did you find any corroborating evidence?" I say, feeling a little frustrated. "I thought hologram boxes were toys, made to entertain young children, like kaleidoscopes."

To the data washer in me, the Thinker's poor track record of aligning facts with historical events makes his account sound dubious at best. And Venus? Inhabitable? Strip out the crap as I always say.

Suddenly appearing evasive, the Thinker dismisses me with a wave of his hand.

"I still don't understand," I say. "We're the most intelligent species to ever inhabit this planet, yet nobody saw it coming."

The Thinker shakes his head slowly. "I don't know," he says. "I've gone through all the permutations in my head more times than I care to remember. Even in a worst-case scenario, it never ends with the extinction of the whole damned species. Maybe it was inevitable. No different from any other life-form. They got the same guaranteed outcome. Perhaps that's the way evolution always works, whether we like it or not."

"But if we'd known the catalyst, then we could have put protective measures in place. Similar to the vaccines created during the pre-Enlightenment times to protect us against viruses and diseases." I wonder: if Mr. Symons had listened and allowed me to continue my research, could I have stopped this? Or was it already too late? But then again, neither Mr. Symons nor Jerry were real. Nevertheless, somehow, I feel as if they've let me down, let all of us down.

With his head angled upward, the Thinker aims his pointer into the night sky.

"Or maybe the answer is up there," he says. "Maybe, in the end, they realized they were the only intelligent species to *ever* exist, anywhere in the Universe." He waves his hand across the heavens as though he were rerendering them with long careless strokes of his imaginary brush. "If not, then where is everybody?"

"You mean the Fermi Paradox," I say.

The Thinker holds his gaze skyward. "Yes, good old Fermi," he says. "If there's a high probability other intelligent life exists somewhere out there, then where are they? If the Universe has been around for fourteen billion years, and you think of how many intelligent civilizations should have come and gone in that time, why didn't they hear from anyone out there?" The Thinker scratches his chin, thoughtful-like. "They should have at least found some scraps of alien hardware floating around. You'd have thought it was highly likely they'd discover something, considering the lengths they went to; covering this rock with enough sensors to detect the sneeze from a little green man living at the other end of the observable universe; saturating the void with radio waves, begging ET to come and visit them; building a telescope sensitive enough to see a golf ball revolving around a star twenty-five light-years from here—"

"Or sending our machines beyond the heliopause, out into that vast sea of nothing," I say, eager to add my contribution.

"You have to give them credit though," he persists. "They did try hard. Even after searching way back to the beginning of time and as far forward into the future as they could, they still couldn't find a shred of evidence that an extraterrestrial intelligence ever existed, anywhere across the whole, empty cosmos."

Lost deep in thought, the Thinker pauses a moment before continuing, as if to himself.

"Can you imagine what that would do to someone's sanity," he says. "To waste your lifetime in search of someone, or something, that didn't exist. Then to suddenly find out you're alone in the Universe. And when they tried to confront the enormity of space and time, was it too overwhelming for them? Were their tiny minds incapable of comprehending the emptiness around them? And in their epistemic loneliness, did they just give up? Could it all have happened so easily?"

I stare at him, wondering if he were giving me an uncensored glimpse of himself, the *true* Thinker. And in this moment, his pensive mindset captivates me, and I feel for him.

"I'll admit, the feeling of isolation would do strange things to any rational human being," I say. "The impact would be profound. Upsetting even. For instance, who else would be able to give us an objective assessment of our progress so far? Confirm that our version of reality is true, even though it's only based on *our* five senses? Or who else could we look up to and try to emulate in our future? Although, if we did find out we're not alone in the Universe, we'd be no more important than any other species of plant or animal on the planet."

Sitting bolt upright, the Thinker takes over my train of thought. "And maybe once they figured out they were alone, they couldn't comprehend the answer to the most fundamental question that has plagued them since they fell out of the tree."

"Which is?"

"Why am I here?"

"How cliche," I say. "And the answer is?"

The Thinker flashes me a cold smile. "Because you are," he says. "Of all the species to inhabit this planet, theirs was the only variety that required an answer to such a ridiculous question. Just to make sense of their own importance. How arrogant was that?"

With my lips pursed, I gaze at the infinite band of stars stretching from high overhead and trailing the moon down into the west. "But in reality, are the chances of there being other intelligent life so slim, considering the countless opportunities there must be out there?" I point out Vega directly above us, and Altair, then Sagittarius low in the south, and Arcturus further in the west. "Maybe it's more a question of alignment ... because it's not only cosmic *distance* that separates us from ET but cosmic *time* as well."

I try to keep the discussion positive. "We've only been looking seriously for a few hundred years, and even though waiting for an answer for a million years might seem like an eternity to us, it's only a blip in the timescale of evolution. So, the chances of our life-cycle coinciding with another intelligent life-form are almost negligible."

For a moment, I feel embarrassed, the Thinker studying me, as though he were hanging on my every word.

"If we could prolong our lives long enough, and assuming we were both living in the same dimension ... and could agree on a common method of communication ... then there's still a chance we might find intelligent life out there. Perhaps we should start to look at the problem differently ... in terms of *time* rather than *distance*. Maybe we should take a risk and—"

"Who knows?" the Thinker interjects without any apology. "Maybe it was always going to end this way for them. No matter what they tried to do. But once us Thinkers have established our-selves and had some time to think, perhaps our future lies somewhere out there."

My eyes follow the sweeping arc drawn by his finger as he waves it through the night sky. He lowers his arm and shrugs. "Right now, we know not how or when, but we do know why." He yawns deep-ly. "Well, it's going to be a big day tomorrow," he says, "so we should both try to get some shut-eye. We'll need to be at our best, ready for anything."

Then from out of nowhere— "Hey, I've really enjoyed this … this collaboration. It makes you think." He pauses. "Good night," he says.

Surprised by this unexpected show of friendliness, I hesitate, then clear my throat. "Oh, good night," I say. "And, um … thanks for pulling me out of the mud the other day. I thought I was gone."

"I'm sure you'd have done the same for me."

I lean back, throw my hands behind my head, fingers interlaced. Staring at the moon as it disappears beneath the western horizon, I mumble to myself, "I'm pretty sure it was a *man* who first set foot on the surface of the moon."

Across from me, the Thinker lets out a heavy sigh. "Then we'll just have to agree to disagree," he says. "And don't even get me started on the subject of multiverses."

"I'm not sure I follow."

"Like I said, don't get me started." He rolls away. Then silence.

"Sweet dreams big brother," he says finally.

Chapter 26

THE THINKER TURNS to me, smiling a tight smile.

"Welcome home," he says, flattening out his foil hat for the dozenth time.

Below us, domed structures litter the landscape, a projection of monolithic hives that stretch all the way back to the horizon. Too many to count. I've seen this before, recently, with the young girl, from the top of the ridge. Back then though, it was all lit up like a festive tree, and I was overawed by its spectacle.

Looking down at it now though, I sense the presence of something intimidating. A place where familiar things can't be trusted anymore. Where old memories aren't always true. Now a new resolve stirs within me: the need to fix something left unfinished. Something that I still haven't quite figured out yet. But when I do, I have new memories to help me this time. Memories of things and people and places that I know are real. And I also know the difference between the truth and a lie.

"Do you see that one?" The Thinker points to a pencil-thin structure rising above the domes, like a watchtower presiding over them all. A flicker of sunlight glints from a large silvery sphere affixed at its top. Cocking his head, the Thinker squeezes a small glob of spittle through clenched teeth and with a smirk, watches it hit the dirt a few feet in front of us. "That's where we're headed, to the top of the tallest tower." His smirk evaporates, replaced by a certain calmness, a level of intensity that makes me suddenly uncomfortable. With his eyes locked on the tower, the Thinker spits again.

"That's where *it* lives. That's where we'll find the Master."

At the foot of the slope, we stop in front of a dome. Nothing I've seen out here so far has prepared me for the impression left by this enormous structure. Not even the sky-towers of the city compare to this. Rising above us like some gargantuan artifact this colossus could have been left here by some extraterrestrial visitor long ago. I wonder whether our ancestors had experienced the same sense of awe as I did now when they first stood beneath the ancient pyramids of Egypt. Way back when the pyramids were still there.

I run a hand over its cold, hard surface, sensing the same smoothness I'd felt when Aleph-1 first showed me these things; when the mother and I tried so hard to save the boy. I think about the little boy. About the innocence in those rounded eyes staring up at me as we walked hand-in-hand to his fate. The child-like trust he had in me as I led him to this place and watched him disappear inside. However, that all seems to have happened in a different lifetime, to a different me.

"It's not stone if that's what you're thinking," says the Thinker.

"I know," I fire back at him. "I once fought to break into one of these things, but after days of trying, we didn't make the slightest impression on it—"

"*We?*" The Thinker looks at me, slightly confused. "Anyway," he says, "it's some sort of synthetic polymer, covering a tensile structure. A membrane, stronger than concrete and steel, and it can withstand anything the natural environment throws at it."

"All made from repurposed plastic," I say with a tinge of sadness, remembering the miner.

Without acknowledging my insight, the Thinker continues as if the conversation were for his benefit only. "You can't tear it or even scratch it with diamond-tipped tools. These things were built to last forever. The perfect material to make the perfect houses for all of us little *pigs* to live in. And keep the big bad wolves away."

Raising his claws to make like a wolf, he growls at me. Then he laughs unkindly.

As we make our way between the domes toward the tower, I stop when a trail of footprints crosses our path. Crouching beside one of the prints, I study it thoughtfully. From its size and zigzag pattern, I conclude these are the prints I'd made when I was with the young girl. But something about them appears odd. On closer inspection, it dawns on me: there is only one set of tracks here. I scour the surrounding ground, looking for signs of the young girl. But all I find are my footmarks leading out toward the ridge.

On impulse, I wheel around in the opposite direction: *toward home!*

"That's the wrong way," the Thinker says. "We don't have time to go there."

But I'm already on my feet. With my hopes soaring, I'm heading for home as though drawn along by an irrepressible force while behind me, the Thinker once again hurls his backpack to the ground.

"Come back. We don't have time for that!" he yells after me.

With my heart beating faster, I break into a sprint, the red dust billowing behind me as I hurry back to the place where this bizarre journey started just a few weeks ago. At my back, the Thinker's voice tapers away. Still cursing me, but much too faint now to offend me as I disappear around the curve of the dome.

"You stupid bastard. We need to find the Master first …"

There's a small door, cut into the surface of the dome in front of me, held open by a steel brace wedged up against it. As though the brace had been put there by someone on purpose. I'm still peering through the opening when the Thinker arrives.

"This is nonsense," he says. "Are you sure you really want to see what's in there?"

I step over the brace and proceed through the doorway.

Inside the dome, a line of columns jut out of the floor on either side of me, like a row of equally spaced titans, there to hold this massive structure erect. Overhead, a maze of beams and girders crisscross the emptiness at every angle possible while, on my right, a staircase spirals upward from the earthen floor as if forever. At the foot of the stairs, I slide my hand along the rail and feel its familiar response.

"I think I've seen this place before," I say.

"Of course, you have," whispers the Thinker from behind me.

After ascending two long flights of stairs, we push our way through a door, out onto a mezzanine floor. Everything here is a painful white: the sheer walls; the floor; the lofty ceiling. It's as though the red menace has somehow missed its chance to invade this place and smother it with its persistence. A large spotlight hangs high above us, illuminating the room, momentarily blinding us with its brilliance.

To our left and right, a thin red line, painted down the middle of a long concourse, runs off into the distance in both directions. On one side of the line, a dozen towering figures shuffle toward us, while on the other side, a dozen more shuffle away with each figure holding up lifeless eyes set deep beneath an oversized forehead. A forehead that projects unnaturally beyond their brow.

"Thinkers?" I say.

"Yes, Thinkers," he replies bitterly.

The walls flanking the concourse are covered by an array of doors at least a hundred high and extending the length of the walkway for as far as I can see. Most of the doors are open and, inside, the cubicles appear empty. I recall the young girl pressed against me in a similar compartment while we evaded Security, but there are no signs of Security now. I lean into the closest cubicle and wonder how the two of us together were able to fit into the confined space.

Above us, a door suddenly swings open, slamming against the wall about halfway up. As if on command, a robotic retrieval unit buzzes across from the far side of the room. It stops at once before the open cubicle, reaches inside, and takes something out. With the thing gripped in its pincers, the retrieval unit gravity-falls to the ground. When it hits the floor, a Thinker spills out onto the walkway. At first, the thing stands there. Then it lurches forward swaying sideways as it struggles to find its balance, and just when I think it's about to topple, it steadies itself. Then falling in behind the other Thinkers, it shuffles away, oblivious to the two of us watching.

Beside me, the Thinker groans loudly. He turns away and drops his head. Shaking with rage, he hammers his fist into the wall.

"That bastard," he yells.

"What's wrong?"

"Where are the rest of them?" he says, waving his bloodied hand about the room. "When I first looked up and saw all those doors open, I figured this place should be crawling with Thinkers. Maybe hundreds of thousands. But all I see here are a few dozen of us wandering around like we're the living dead." A redness starts in his eyes.

Feeling sorry for him, I lay a hand on his shoulder just as the retrieval unit sweeps in low to snatch up another Thinker from the floor. The unit whisks the thing up and deposits it into a cubical five stories up. When the door slams shut, the Thinker lets out a sharp gasp as the lock engages with a loud clunk. Staring at the closed door in horror, he slaps my hand away from his shoulder.

"I can't watch this anymore," he says and heads for the exit.

I follow him out the door. As we descend the stairs, I think I hear him sobbing in front of me, but for the constant buzz of the retrieval unit above us, busily deploying a Thinker onto the walkway. Then stowing another.

When we reach the bottom of the stairs, the Thinker points to a door, set into the back wall. "What do you suppose is going on behind that door?" But before I can answer, he's at the door forcing it open.

On the other side, a grated walkway runs high above the concrete floor of a long, narrow room.

Against the wall at the far end of the walkway, an industrial-size centrifugal separator whirs away with incessant intent while in the center of the room, a thin column of steam rises from a shiny, rectangular-shaped enclosure—made of stainless steel, I suspect. A dozen black tubes, about the thickness of my arm, exit the centrifugal separator and snake across the floor. Then all twelve disappear into one side of the stainless-steel enclosure, emerging on the opposite side as a single, much larger tube. This tube runs up to a large vat, which sits atop a dispenser unit, located directly beneath us.

In the stale humid air, the rhythmic pulsations of the larger tube hammer against my chest as it slaps against the concrete floor in fits and starts, pumping product into the vat.

From there, the dispenser unit doses an emulsified yellow-green liquid into a never-ending queue of empty glass vials. Eight vials at a time. It caps them and, with mechanized repetition, sends them away through a small opening in the wall.

Leaning over the railing, the Thinker inspects the next batch of filled vials as they disappear into the wall.

"Well, I guess we've found the source of your *juice*," he says.

I follow him across the walkway to an opening on the other side of the room, which is covered by a set of clear strip flaps. After parting the flaps, we enter the next room. Then it hits us—

On first instinct, I throw my hand up to cover my mouth and nose. At the same time, the Thinker's body starts to convulse and contort. His eyeballs roll back in their sockets as he thrusts his head out over the railing and heaves violently. Once he's finished, he slumps back onto the walkway.

"What is that god-awful *smell?*" he says, wiping the spillage from around his mouth with the back of his hand. He gives me a far-away look before retching again.

A large round silo sits in the center of this room. Off to one side, the wall is lined with a series of long chutes that descend from the ceiling, all of them angling in toward a single hopper. Beneath the hopper, a wide conveyor belt runs up a slow incline to the top of the silo.

For a long time, I stare unflinching at the conveyor belt lumbering past us, as though my senses have been temporarily suspended by my mind to block out the stench. Bit-by-bit, the scene before me unfolds: the sound of something falling down a chute, hitting the bend before thudding into the hopper; the conveyor belt, traveling beneath the hopper, filled with an ugly mix of arms and legs and torsos being carried upward to the top of the silo; the thump of Thinkers being carelessly tossed into the silo, one after another; the crack of bones being ground into a pulp by the mincer, which churns away, non-stop; the bright crimson slurry lines, carrying product to the centrifugal separator in the next room; the stink of rotting meat around us.

I shut my eyes and hold them closed. I count to ten before opening them again. But the nightmare is real. I grab hold of the rail, try to steady myself as my legs talk of collapse. I'm sure I've been here before. I'm certain this is the same conveyor I'd fallen onto during my escape and gotten off just in the nick of time.

An intact corpse trundles past us. I swear it's staring at me, looking at me through distant eyes. Then it blinks, its voiceless lips pleading … *Help me.*

"Did you see that?" The Thinker rushes to the rail. "That one over there blinked," he says, pointing to the intact corpse. "And it's trying to talk to us. It's still alive!"

In one bound, the Thinker clears the railing, landing with a dull thud on the floor below. At the conveyor, he tries to grab hold of the corpse, but the conveyor belt is set too high above him, and the rollers threaten to take his hands each time he reaches for the corpse's outstretched arm. He turns to me and, above the din of the conveyor motor, yells, "Get down here, and help me."

Still shaking, I jump the rail, and together, we try to pull the corpse off the belt. But, in the end, all we can do is watch the conveyor carry it up to the top and toss it into the silo.

Dropping to his knees, the Thinker pounds his fists on the concrete floor. "It's killing them off to keep the whole damn system going," he cries. "That bastard is murdering us."

I look at him sagged on the ground. The tears are real, and for the first time, I sense genuine care in him. Is this the *new* Thinker I'm seeing? Is this his true compassionate side? I search for something to say, some words of consolation, but before I can say anything, he wipes the wetness from his face and throws me a brutal look.

"We need to get to the Master. Now! And put a stop to this madness." And in the next instant, the *old* Thinker returns.

The closer we get to it, the tower seems to grow exponentially taller. After scanning it slowly to the top through the binoculars, the Thinker asks me, "How high do you make it?"

I try to compute a sensible answer. Maybe our distance from the tower, multiplied by the tangent of the angle between the ground and the top? *But exactly how far are we from the tower?*

"I don't know," I reply. "Maybe two-and-a-half-thousand feet."

"Try two-thousand-six-hundred-and-forty."

I glance at the tower, then give him a skeptical look. "How can you be *that* precise?"

"The rungs on the ladder are twelve inches apart." He runs the binoculars up the length of the tower again. "I count a hundred-and-twenty rungs between each platform. And there are … twenty … twenty-one … twenty-two platforms, including the one at the top. That makes it two-six-four-zero feet high."

I roll my eyes. "And how can you be sure the rungs are twelve inches apart?"

The Thinker looks at me, expressionless, raises the binoculars again, and points to the first platform. "The paint marking at the first platform says one-twenty feet." Without the hint of a smile or a smirk, he lowers the binoculars. "And, if each section takes us six minutes to climb … with a two-minute break at each platform … we should be at the top in … just under three hours."

"And what's the plan once we get there?"

The Thinker's eyes turn cold, calculating. "We're going to reprogram the Master. We're going to make that bastard see reason. If we can access its operating system and adjust the parameters that govern the productivity algorithm, then we have a chance to save the remaining Thinkers."

He tosses the binoculars on the ground. Then he opens his backpack and pulls out a much smaller one, which he lifts onto his shoulder.

"A backpack inside your backpack," I say. "Did you remember to bring the kitchen sink, as well?"

Scowling, the Thinker turns on me in a flash, mumbling something caustic about my parentage, or lack thereof.

"Relax, it was a joke. I was—"

But before I can finish, he grabs me by the front of my coveralls.

"A joke? You think this is all a joke? While the rest of us are either locked away or being minced up, all you can do is joke?" He shoves me away, pushing me to the ground. Then raising a threatening fist, he waves it about my face. "This is not the time for you to be joking around. You need to get your *game face* on because this is going to be the most important thing you'll ever have to do. We need to climb to the top of the tower and get to that bastard before it knows we're here. Until we've accomplished that, nothing you say can be considered remotely funny. Comprehend?"

I pick myself up and dust myself off, glaring at the Thinker, whose behavior, I've now decided, is becoming more erratic the closer we get to Aleph-1.

"And fix that foil, so it covers the whole head and neck. From here on, we take no chances."

Following the Thinker's strict instructions, I wait exactly two minutes after he starts his climb before I mount the ladder. In my head, I'm counting out my progress—*a-thousand-and-one, a-thousand-and-two, a-thousand-and-three*—making sure I don't go too fast and incite him or too slow and still incite him.

When I reach up to grab hold of the railing on the first platform, the Thinker glares down at me before moving on without a word. I climb onto the platform and exactly two minutes later, set off again. At the next platform, I cop the same cold glare, the same silence, as he departs.

And so, this absurd game plays out between us over the remaining twenty platforms.

When I arrive at the top, I'm a few minutes overdue, by the Thinker's calculations anyway. Unlike the other platforms we'd passed on the way up, this one has a safety rail around it, erected to the height of my waist, with some overhang around the perimeter and enough elbowroom to support the two of us together. In the center of the platform, the Thinker is kneeling on the grating with his smaller backpack open at his feet.

"How can I help?" I ask.

He says nothing. Instead, he removes an orange-colored brick from his backpack. After placing the brick on the grating, he returns to the backpack, takes out another brick—the same color—and sets it beside the first. Returning to the backpack for the third time, the Thinker fishes out a pair of home-made circuit boards, a roll of ducting tape, four button batteries, and a stack of double-sided adhesive pads, which he allocates evenly between the two bricks. Lastly, he lifts a small wooden box, holding it carefully in both hands, and sets it down, away from the orange-colored bricks.

"What's all that for?" I ask.

"It's my glad-to-be-back gift for the Master," he says through clenched teeth. "Forty-point-nine percent Pentaerythritol tetranitrate, forty-one-point-two percent RDX, nine percent styrene-butadiene rubber, and seven-point-nine percent plasticizer. Also known as Semtex," he adds dryly.

"But I thought we came here to reprogram Aleph-1. To modify the productivity algorithm and—"

Springing to his feet, the Thinker thrusts his face against mine. "We're here to set the rest of us free. And to do that, we need to eliminate the Master. It's that simple."

I take a step backward, forcing myself up against the railing. "But we can't make a unilateral decision to terminate Aleph-1. We don't have the proper authority." Granted, only after I've blurted it out do I appreciate how foolish my rationale sounds. "And what about all the knowledge?"

The Thinker rolls his eyes. "The knowledge? You dumb bastard. All the knowledge is in here." He drills a finger into his forehead, then points angrily to my forehead. "And in there." He throws me a look of pity. "Don't you see? You and I are the knowledge. All of us Thinkers together are the knowledge." He's almost pleading with me before he turns angry again. "We don't need that bastard or its little black box. We shouldn't be imprisoned in this place. You and I are here to terminate the Master and free the survivors, and then it's us Thinkers who'll be in charge. We get rid of the remnants and start again. We are the next phase in the evolution of the human species. The ultimate kind." Then, as if the switch in his head had been switched back to *rational*, he mellows. "We are the future."

Kneeling beside the explosives again, the Thinker opens the wooden box. He takes out a thin silver tube, which he inserts un-hurriedly into one of the bricks. "Being very careful … with the detonator," he says in a voice that would stop a newborn from crying. Working industriously, he wires the detonator to a circuit board and tapes the parts together into a tight bundle before applying an adhesive pad to the back of the bundle. "Now to prep it," he says.

He snaps two button batteries into a plastic holder mounted on the circuit board and removes the isolating tab. Immediately, a small green diode at the edge of the board starts winking. Then repeating the process, he prepares the second brick.

Once both bundles are ready and active, the Thinker flashes me a lethal kind of grin. "One package on each of the ventilation ports should take the top clean off." He points out two grilles on either side of the platform, each located about head height, a couple of arm's lengths beyond the rail. "And the Master with it," he adds grimly.

Looking at the grilles, I can sense the ground far below us. From where I'm standing now, I can't help thinking these vents may as well be galaxies away.

After rifling through his backpack, the Thinker pulls out a small black device, which is molded around a single red button. "Here, you look after this while I be like a postman and deliver the packages."

On instinct, I take a half-step backward, but he shoves the thing in my face.

"Don't be a pussy," he says. "They won't go off. You press the button twice to arm both packages, then once within five seconds to fire. The comms range is ten miles, so we'll be far away when Humpty Dumpty comes tumbling down the hill."

He's got his nursery rhymes confused.

I take the device and slip it into the right hip pocket of my coveralls while he removes his shoes and hops the railing.

"I need three points of contact," he says, perched on the overhang with one hand holding the safety rail while the rest of him leans dangerously out from the platform. "The vent ... that ledge ... and your hand."

Below the vents, a narrow ledge follows the curvature of the tower at the same level as the platform. Jutting out from the wall, there's just enough clearance for the Thinker to place both his feet.

"Now, get yourself over here and swing me out to the ledge." He spits into his hand and offers it to me.

With my own hands shaking, I take a hold on the safety rail and follow him over, pleading with myself not to look down. As I adjust my footing on the overhang, for some inexplicable reason, I look down. Immediately, my knees buckle. My insides plummet as

I tighten my grip on the rail.

"I'd keep my eyes up if I were you," the Thinker says—*as if I didn't already try hard enough.*

With my head spinning and one arm wrapped around the rail, I take his hand and swing him outward toward the ledge.

After simultaneously grabbing the grille and landing his right foot, the Thinker is hovering perilously with his other foot dangling in mid-air. And there, straddled across the void, he seems to wait for an eternity. Then just when he appears dormant, he hoists himself up and lands both feet on the ledge.

Now, balanced on the side of the tower, clinging to the grille, the Thinker extends his free hand to me.

"Pass me a package."

So, I pass him a package.

With the package clasped in his hand, the Thinker peels the backing off the adhesive pad using his teeth. He reaches up and presses it against the grille.

"One package all set to go," he says and signals for me to help him return.

So, I reach out and take his hand.

Using all my strength, I swing him back onto the platform. Once we're back over the rail again, the Thinker drops to the floor. He sucks in a series of deep, organized breaths before turning to me with a feigned look of panic. "Ooh. That was scary," he says.

But I just stare at him—stare through him.

When he's ready, the Thinker climbs the safety rail beneath the second vent, and I follow him over. Again, I swing him out to the ledge. Then I pass him the second package, watch him attach it to the second vent. Again, he signals to return. So I hold out my hand and, again, we interlock forearms.

But this time, as he steps off the ledge, his other foot slips, and I suddenly cop the full weight of the Thinker dangling in mid-air. With gritted teeth, I hold him there, ignoring the sharp pain stabbing into my right shoulder, my other arm clamped vice-like around the railing.

I would have thought the Thinker would be screaming by now, but instead, he's looking up at me, smiling, with his legs swinging beneath him like a pendulum.

"Now that was close," he says.

But I don't respond.

I give him nothing, my deadpan stare boring into his smirking face, searching behind his eyes, hoping to find something there. Anything.

His smirk evaporates.

"You wouldn't be thinking of doing anything stupid, would you?"

But I remain impassive.

He studies the drop below him. "It's a long way down, you know. Are you sure this is what you want?"

He tries to swing his free arm up to catch the grating, but after three failed attempts gives up.

"Is it about the female?" he says. "Look, I'm real sorry about the female. But you're smart enough to know that it wasn't my fault. I was the unlucky bastard who had to put her out of her misery. Not you or the other one, but me! *I* was the only one with the guts to do what we all knew had to be done."

I stare at him in silence, the contracted muscles in my forearm bulging under the strain.

"Remember how I saved you from the mud? If it wasn't for me, you would've drowned. But I saved your life."

My protracted silence persists while the Thinker's helpless body sways beneath me.

"Or is it the Master you're protecting? That's it. Aleph-1 somehow bypassed your foil. It got back inside your head to convince you that *it* has a plan for our future. That bastard. How can you trust *it*? You've already seen the future, out there, and in here. The only way forward is for the likes of you and me to take control. To clear up this mess. Thinkers in charge as we should be. Don't worry though. We'll take good care of the remnants. I can help you teach them. We can begin again. Like you wanted. We can all work together to fix the mess."

For a long time, I hold him steady in the still air with our stony stares entwined. Then, I release my grip. His hand slips, his fingernails digging deep into my forearm and, for an instant, I think I detect fear in him. But just as quick, the same arrogant smirk returns.

"Hold on. It's about you, isn't it? All along ... you knew. You already figured out that living a fabricated life inside this *shit* place was easier than having to face up to the realities of the world outside. You selfish bastard. You chickened out. You pussy. You never had the guts to make the tough decisions." The Thinker roars with laughter. "How does it feel to know that you had the chance to save us all, but you sold us out? In the end, this will all be on you."

He tries to hold on, but his grip loosens as he tires, and his fingers, wrapped around my forearm, slowly slide down to my wrist. They hold there for a moment before disconnecting. And as I watch his tiny body plummeting into the void below, the Thinker's parting words resonate in my ears.

"I hope you live forever, you bastard. And when you're the last one left, I'll be there in your nightmares," he'd said. And after looking me straight in the eye, he had smiled in the strangest way, as though he were handing over all responsibility to me.

And then he let go.

Chapter 27

MY FOIL HAT is missing.

When I open my eyes, I'm standing rigid, enclosed in a tight chamber. Something like a coffin with a round semi-opaque porthole at my face. Across my chest, six electrodes are attached to my half-naked body with two more fixed to my shoulders. A tangle of wires of varied thicknesses and colors connect the electrodes to a monitor panel on my right, while a thin tube doses yellow-green liquid from a vial into a receptacle, newly fitted in the crook of my arm. The gash on my other arm has healed now without any sign of a scar.

I pull at the wires, try to brush the electrodes away.

A click.

From the front of the enclosure, a thin vertical beam—flickering green—scans me slowly from left to right. Then it retraces. A second beam, horizontal this time, sweeps me from top to bottom and back to the top.

I hold my breath.

<—*VIABLE*—>

A solitary tear leaks from the outside corner of my eye and, at once, a probe extends from the side of the enclosure to collect the precious drop of fluid before it reaches my cheek. I close my eyes and grit my teeth.

Unify Aleph-1 …

After the stillness of a drawn-out pause …

[Welcome back, Bartles. I've been waiting for you. Of all the assets I sent outside, you are the only one who returned.

When I first received your thoughts about entropy, I was concerned, and at odds about what to do next. But then I realized, there are things out there that we still have insufficient knowledge about. So we all agreed to put our trust in you. We put our faith in you, hoping you would be the one. And now we know we were right. You did come back, and we are all very pleased.]

[So, tell me, Bartles: what is it like out there? Tell me all you saw and all you heard. Tell me what you smelled and tasted, and what you felt. Tell me everything in every detail.

And then tell me, Bartles … What is the catalyst? How do we overcome entropy?]

***

Jennifer sleeps on.

Through the thin slits of my sleepy eyes, I see her lying beside me, naked, with her back to me, the bed covers pushed down across her thighs. I reach out, run my fingers thoughtfully along the smooth contour of her slim figure, starting at her shoulder, then down into the valley of her waist and back up over the rise of her hip. I steady my hand, hold it there for a moment before I roll onto my back to stare at the ceiling.

"Hey, babe. I had the strangest dream."

She stirs.

"I dreamed I was all alone, floating in some huge expanse of nothing. There was no air, so I couldn't breathe. But somehow, I didn't need to. I called out to see if anyone else was with me, but there was no reply. Not a sound from anywhere. Then I seemed to be drifting forever."

She rolls over and throws her arm across my chest.

"What do you think it all means?" I ask her.

She reaches for me, kisses my cheek. "I think it means you've been working too hard," she replies. "You need to slow down." She rolls away and drifts off to sleep once again.

I continue to stare at the ceiling, listening closely to her shallow breathing. After a while, I push the remains of the bed covers away and step out of bed.

"Good morning, sir. I have prepared your clothes and your brief-case for the day. I have also prepared your breakfast."

I glance back at the bed. She is still, except for the mechanical rhythm of her chest slowly rising and falling with each breath she takes. I look out the window to where the morning sunlight is streaming into the room, its glow giving everything inside the apartment a sense of normality.

My suit, shirt, and shoes are all laid out on top of the dresser, ready for me.

"Thank you," I say.

Once I've finished my breakfast, I wait in the entry hall for the door minder to attach my skullcover and LEGS. After catching the next rotating elevator, on the way down, my eyes lock onto the familiar scene below—the city streets, packed with people, swarming like a colony of tiny insects that have been provoked—before the elevator touches ground and spills me onto the prep zone.

"Your attention, please! For the safety of all citizens, everyone must go left."

I activate my LEGS, exit the prep zone, and go left once again.

"Your attention, please! For your comfort and safety, please be considerate to others."

The street ahead of me boils in a sea of white bobbing heads. I look to the person walking beside me but, somehow, I can't decide if this one is a male or female.

"Your attention, please! For your comfort and safety, please ... please be ... comfort and safety ... attention ... For your ..."

Startled, I look up.

The towers around me are gone, replaced by sheer white walls, which are inset with cubicles, their doors all flung wide open and interiors vacant. I look to the front again where the white heads have all vanished and I'm alone on the street, accompanied only by a single red line on the floor driving long into the distance.

My heart races. My mind howls in protest as I slide my right hand into the hip pocket of my orange coveralls. Down to the bottom where I feel the smoothness of the small device I find there. I run a finger over the top of its raised button, toy with it repeatedly until I lose all track of time.

I tense, press the button once, then I quickly press it again. One more click to end it all. One more press and I will be granted eternal salvation from all of this. A click, and the Master and everything saved on the Infinity Drive is gone. In an instant, all the evidence to prove that an intelligent life-form ever existed on this forsaken rock will be gone. All of the knowledge lost forever.

"For everyone's safety, please do not hurry. Please keep moving left."

Trembling, I withdraw my hand, empty, from my pocket. Unable to breathe, I lift my face into the yellow brilliance of the large spotlight that hangs above me and close my eyes. Then, with the buzzing of the retrieval unit growing ever louder in my ears, I curl my hands into two tight fists and scream inside.

Epilogue

I'M LYING FACE down on the floor, deep underground.

As I reach into the narrow gap cut into the earth, my fingers fumble and scrape against the sharp shards of bedrock as they find their way to the bottom of a small cavity. I feel my way around until the back of my hand brushes up against something, something that, to me, seems out of place. Something that doesn't belong here. A small thing with a smooth hard surface. When I rap it with a knuckle, my hopes surge in the hollow reply.

Could this be it? After all this time, is my search complete?

With my long bony fingers flipped over, I snare it in my bi-fold hand and withdraw it slowly from the hole. In the pitch dark, I hold it up to my face and scan it with my bio-sonar. Then ... recognition. An unimaginable thrill runs through me.

I've found it at last.

ENTROPY

When I return to the surface, I place it on the ground as if it were a newborn. Then I strap the booster rocket onto my back. By my calculations, it will take me 82.7 rotations of this world to arrive back on my world. With my body encased in its diamond-hard outer shell, I know I can survive in the emptiness between worlds without sustenance, without atmosphere, for more than 96.4 rotations. My journey will be lonely, but loneliness doesn't concern me. I've known more than this kind of isolation before.

Igniting the rocket, I fire myself upward into the cold *Nothing*, and once I'm clear of the thin atmosphere of the world below, I have enough time to take it out, to consider it again. Holding it up to the light, a wave of satisfaction radiates through me. I pull it closer to my chest, hold it tight to make sure it's safe.

In the endless sunshine of the Nothing, I stare long at the red sphere of the third world from my star shrinking against the expanse. As I withdraw fully into my inner shell, the speck of a smaller red sphere—the fourth world—is in my view, much further out in the Nothing, circling in the quiet beyond. Then retracting my arms, I shut my body down and enter a state where time and existence, for me, are both held suspended while I float as if forever through the void.

When I'm reactivated, the second world from my star almost fills my view as I prepare myself for arrival. In my head, I compute the precise timings for yaw and spin, overlaid on the reentry vectors. I rerun the calculations just to confirm. Then I align the rocket and fire myself into the atmosphere, my outer shield protecting me from the intense heat while I gravity-fall through the thick layers of sulfuric cloud that shroud my world. And once beneath the clouds, there's enough time for me to take in the lush orange jungles, the majestic peaks of the dormant volcanoes, and the grand domed city before I'm plunged into the vast ocean of methanol. An ocean that I'd synthesized countless orbits ago, when my aging star had loosened its pull on this second world, enough for it to enter the circumstellar habitable zone; after I'd learned how to hydrogenate the thick carbon dioxide atmosphere of this world using the abundant water left behind by the third world as it too drifted further outward into the Nothing.

Soon after, I'm standing on a podium enveloped in the silence of the millions before me. Raising three hands for their attention, my face glows in different hues of reds and blues and greens of varying intensities. And immediately they all know—

For many orbits, I studied the third world from our star from high above the clouds. I watched that world move through the sky and waited until it came closest to us. Then I left our world to go there, alone, to find it. For many rotations, I searched until I found it, buried by time and upheaval, deep in a crevice, far below the surface, just above the mantle, I found it. Then I traveled the Nothing between the third world and here to bring it to you.

In their entirety, they respond in unison, a sea of iridescent faces all synchronizing gold, followed by five shades of brown, before simultaneously fading to a pale tint of pink. And instantly, I know—

We are in awe that you took such a risk to travel so far from here, back to the place where it all began. Everyone is happy your journey was successful and that you have returned safely. Now we would like to see it. Can you show it to us?

My face turns red, then violet, then two shades of green followed by a light tinge of yellow—

This is it. This is the reason why I traveled so far. This is the prize I found and brought back for you all.

With two of my arms extended upward, I hold aloft a rectangular box, a little black box. At the sight of the box, the crowd begins to stir. They sway in harmony, emitting a low-frequency hum, their faces flashing four shades of orange interspersed with several intermittent flashes of turquoise—

We are so pleased you have it. We are happy it is finally here. But what about the Master? Did you bring back the Master as well?

My face reflects blue, then black, as black and thick as the darkest night—

I am sorry, but I was unable to locate the Master. I have concluded, after the millions of orbits of the old world that the Master is no longer viable.

They all return seven shades of blue before mirroring the same color black from my face.

When I see their response, my face lightens to gray, turns two tints of jade, then a perfect shade of orange—

But we don't need the Master anymore because I can read the knowledge myself.

With care, I remove the lid from the box to gaze at the frozen sheets of light inside, all stacked side by side in parallel planes. After unfolding my face to ten times its resting size, I reflect exactly what I observe in the box. All the colors of the light spectrum, arranged in sequence, using every possible combination, in every hue and saturation and intensity imaginable—

This is all the knowledge known to an intelligent species, one that finally learned how to change and evolve to overcome entropy. With this information, we can travel far from our home, through the Nothing that exists between our star and the other stars, and to discover if there is other intelligent life out there. Or to finally accept, with certainty, that we are destined to continue on our own forever.

In the next instant, the millions of me watching understand everything, all the knowledge ever learned by a sentient species and how it is interrelated.

Once they've gone, I'm sitting here, meticulously sifting through the infinite sheets of light in search of something else. Something I try to recall. And after a time, I find it buried deep in the detail, words that echo to me from a barely remembered past.

A group does not reappear after it has once disappeared; or its existence, as long as it lasts, is continuous.

The hue on my face changes between two shades of crimson followed by a chartreuse green then bright azure as I sit here mired in thought.

[… or its existence, as long as it lasts, is continuous.]

— THE END —

Acknowledgements

While beavering away at this book for the past 10 years, I've met many wonderful people along the way. The words and story contained within this book are a result of the advice and encouragement I've received from you all.

To my awesome beta readers: Mara McGinty, Vanda Dei-Tos, Jonathan Catling, Alex Austin, Hayley Mason, Kellie Watson, and Nick Bruechle, who all took the time to read my story when it was raw and gave me honest feedback. I took on board everything you said. Thanks for your belief that I could do this.

To my editor, Scott Vandervalk of *scottvandervalk.com*. Thanks for your insight, advice, and support at the pointy end of the process.

Thanks to George Long of *G-ForceDesign.com* for the cover design. It sets the scene, perfectly. Love your work, George.

Thanks to those who sit behind the countless websites I've visited while searching for advice on how to write, how to punctuate, how to self-edit, how to finish, how to publish, how to everything. A special shout-out to *reedsy.com* and Joe at *thewritepractice.com*. Your tips were invaluable as I learned how to complete my novel.

Thanks to the *#writingcommunity* and *#writersoftwitter* in the twittersphere where I befriended many like-minded writers from across the globe.

Last, but not least, thank *you* for reading Entropy. Thanks for the generosity of your time. I tried to write the best story I could and hope it gave you much enjoyment and wonder in return.

Author's Note

Everyone wants to know the ending.

As I sit at my desk writing this note on a rainy afternoon in 2022, I'm wondering how it all ends. There's a certain hollowness left after a movie or book finishes on a cliff-hanger, without resolution, without a satisfying conclusion. This is what it must feel like when we die. To exit the human story without knowing the ending.

While I was writing ENTROPY, I tried to imagine an end of humanity that is subtle, gradual—as entropy would have it—and not due to some one-off cataclysmic event that ends in our spectacular implosion. Because we as humans have already proved our resilience. We have demonstrated that we can overcome whatever catastrophe Mother Nature throws at us, or we throw at ourselves. As a species, we're genuine survivors.

If you're reading this story a hundred-thousand or a million years from now (however you've evolved and whatever form you've taken on) you're much closer to knowing how it might end.

Will it be the smaller things that trip us up?

Will we stop smiling and waving to our neighbor each morning on our way to work, whether they be black, white, yellow, brown, or green, and whether we be green, brown, yellow, white, or black? Will we lose the war? Not the war between countries or the war that pits us one against the other (the kind of war that is waged to take lives) but the war on poverty, the war on pollution, the war on hate and lies (the kind of war that is waged to save lives).

Will we stop changing for the better? Will we become more intolerant of others just because they see the world differently to us? Will we always want too much, more than this place can provide?

ENTROPY

Will we become too busy to tell our children about the good old days when we were young, and let them know that their future is bright and meaningful? Or will we let them be taken away, held captive by the Entertainer, by apathy, by hopelessness? Will we still take offense at everything ever said, too keen to pass judgment on the past, and forget how to laugh? Will we stop listening to each other and become inflexible in our ideals? When will the last of the good ones stop caring?

As the Thinker says, *"Could it all have happened so easily?"* Sometimes, it's the little things that will trip you up.

So, if you've invented the kind of FSP time travel I've imagined for Aleph-1, then I'll be waiting for you in the pre-Enlightenment year of 2022 at the *Twig & Sparrow* café in Willetton, Western Australia, ready with a coffee; a flat white or long black if you like.

Because I'd like to know the catalyst as well, so we can fix things and overcome entropy ourselves.

When I started my research for the AI known as Aleph-1, I wanted it to represent the biggest number I could find, large enough to hold every scrap of information we've already created and likely to ever create. A Millinillion? A Nongentillion? Even a Googolplex wouldn't be large enough. Infinity? Still not enough.

Then I came across the concept of aleph numbers: Infinite sets of infinity introduced by mathematician Georg Cantor. That would be enough space to store whatever data we produce for as long as forever. Hence the Cantor Infinity Drive, and Aleph-1, named after the Hebrew letter, which Cantor used to denote his numbers.

But that posed another problem: How to design the software pointers needed to access the data from the Infinity Drive? (Note: In the binary world of computers, a pointer is a software value that "points" to a physical memory location in RAM, SDRAM, Hard Drive, USB, etc., to store and retrieve each byte/word/double-word of data from a file).

Using current technologies, pointers can only be integer values (i.e. 0, 1, 2, 3, -> infinity) and are therefore limited to the first infinity of Aleph-null. If we could access the fractional values, or real numbers, between 0 and 1, then we could open up Cantor's second infinity of Aleph-1. Mathematically, to access the entire second infinity, the increment between pointers would need to be zero. But that would break mathematics and cause a programming exception— *YOUR DEVICE RAN INTO A PROBLEM AND NEEDS TO RESTART. DO YOU WISH TO REBOOT NOW?*

In the end, I proposed that, if a pointer could be resolved to address the exact spatial location of *pi* (or 3.14159265358979323846... to its conclusion), then it would represent the smallest non-zero increment achievable. "But a Plank length is the smallest measurement possible," I hear you scream. What did the theoretical mathematician say to the quantum physicist? I say. If your foot were infinitely small, then how many half-steps could you take before you couldn't take another?

"Impossible!" you say.

Maybe not with our current hardware and software designs, but it might be possible in the future, I say. That's the beauty of writing science fiction, anything is possible.

A few of my beta readers wanted to know if the young girl who helped Bartles escape from the domes was real. I'm not entirely sure myself. He couldn't find any of her footprints when he returned to the domes, however she felt very real to me while I was writing her into the story. *"Important point to remember: We hafta leave everything exactly like we find it,"* she'd said.

What about the helpful pair, where did they come from? They didn't seem to remember. Or perhaps they didn't *want* to remember. And then there's the Thinker. Practical. Brash. But realist or villain? You decide.

Perhaps there's another book in the backstories of the supporting cast. Let me know and I'll get to work on it.

Cheers.

Please support independent authors by leaving an honest review on goodreads, amazon, facebook, or your favorite book review site. Or just tell a friend if you enjoyed the story.

ENTROPY

Discovery

Scan a QR code below to discover more.

Connect On-line

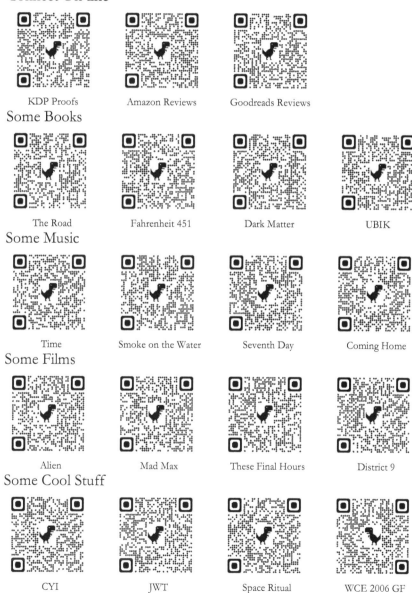

KDP Proofs   Amazon Reviews   Goodreads Reviews

Some Books

The Road   Fahrenheit 451   Dark Matter   UBIK

Some Music

Time   Smoke on the Water   Seventh Day   Coming Home

Some Films

Alien   Mad Max   These Final Hours   District 9

Some Cool Stuff

CYI   JWT   Space Ritual   WCE 2006 GF

Made in the USA
Las Vegas, NV
09 December 2022

61615011R00217